P9-DGY-810

AMERICAN
⋆ SAVIOR ⋆

A NOVEL OF DIVINE POLITICS

by Roland Merullo

ALGONQUIN BOOKS OF CHAPEL HILL   2008

Published by
ALGONQUIN BOOKS OF CHAPEL HILL
Post Office Box 2225
Chapel Hill, North Carolina 27515-2225

a division of
WORKMAN PUBLISHING
225 Varick Street
New York, New York 10014

Library of Congress Cataloging-in-Publication Data
Merullo, Roland.
  American savior : a novel of divine politics / by Roland Merullo. — 1st ed.
    p. cm.
  ISBN 978-1-56512-607-7 (alk. paper)
    1. Miracle workers — Fiction.   2. Presidential candidates — United States —
  Fiction.   3. Presidents — United States — Election — Fiction.   4. Religion and
  politics — United States — Fiction.   5. Political fiction.   6. Satire.   I. Title.
  PS3563.E748A8 2008
  813'.54 — dc22   2008021004

10 9 8 7 6 5 4 3 2 1
First Edition

FOR

Marly Rusoff
Michael Radulescu
Chuck Adams
and
Ina Stern

I have dealt with great things that I do not understand.

—BOOK OF JOB 42:3

★★★ ONE ★★★

When Jesus decided to run for president of the United States he began his campaign, sensibly enough, with a miracle. Two miracles, in fact. So I should probably start this story with a line like, *In the beginning were the miracles,* but the truth is, at the time, most media people — me included — did not believe in miracles, certainly not where a run for the White House was concerned. At first I was skeptical, and then, after I met the man who called himself Jesus, a little less skeptical. And then my whole way of looking at life was turned upside down.

So let me start the story this way: In the beginning it was a perfect New England afternoon, May in western Massachusetts. The sky was clear, the air full of the smell of blossoming trees and drying mud, and my producer and boss, Paterson Wales, was standing at his office window looking down on the troubled city of West Zenith, which we reported on every night at six and ten. We made an odd team, Wales and I. He was jaded and sad from thirty years in the TV business, and I was up-and-coming, a smooth-talking, locally famous beat reporter with nice hair and aspirations for an anchor spot in a top-ten market. Wales summoned me to his office, kept his back turned, took out of his mouth the illegal Cuban cigar he would salivate on till it rotted but would never set a match to, and said tenderly, "Got something for ya."

I remember looking at his back and realizing that the suit he was wearing — luxurious blue wool — probably cost more than I made in a month. I said, "Shooting in Hunter Town?"

"Nah."

"Cops with guns and bags of dope on a table at the station?"

"Nope."

"Leak at the sewage plant on Westover Road?"

"You're gonna like this, it's weird. Same as you."

"I'm not weird, I'm all-American."

"Right, I'm Mahatma Gandhi. Listen to me now." And then, to my astonishment, Wales—who was not known for strong eye contact—turned around and drilled his baby blues into me, letting the hand with the cigar drop to his side. "Last night in Fultonville a little boy fell off a fire escape," he said in his staccato fashion. "Three stories up. . . . Died."

"That's sad," I said. In those days—the days before Jesus is the way I think of them—I was jaded myself, having reported on a hundred drug busts and a dozen killings in the seven years I'd been at WZIZ. Gang shootouts. Domestic arguments gone sour. Schoolkids calling in bomb threats—things we've become used to and that had stopped hitting me in the gut the way they did in the early years. Kids falling off fire escapes was not on that list, however. Though I did not yet have children of my own, I wanted five or six of them someday, and I couldn't sleep after doing reports in which a child had been hurt. Wales knew that about me, so I was surprised he was sending me out on the story.

But then, after a silence, he added, "Died, then came back to life," and watched me closely as he said it.

"Good," I said, "that happens. Especially with little ones. They can survive a fall like that. Wind gets knocked out of them pretty bad, they seem to be dead, but they can bounce back. It's like people who drown in very cold—"

"It was Fultonville," Wales said, and he said it so forcefully it seemed for a second he was about to cry. Which was something that simply did not happen around ZIZ.

"Right, Boss. You said that."

Fultonville was the poor section of West Zenith. Or, I should say, *one* of the poor sections. The second-worst and second-saddest of them as far as I was concerned, after a neighborhood called Hunter Town. Ten square blocks of cheap apartments, a bleak little park, rat-infested brick townhouses, the place was populated by an equal opportunity mix of whites, blacks, and Latinos, and displayed the usual characteristics of poverty: a lot of unemployed people, a lot of single moms, a lot of drugs, fights, sometimes shootings. Fultonville was the kind of place you didn't go anywhere near unless you took a wrong turn off the highway, or lived there, or were intent on buying a class D substance.

"Shut up for once, will you?" Wales said. "I'm giving you two minutes fifty tonight, top of the hour, so save it for that, okay?"

"A large chunk," I said.

"Zip it."

He turned his back again, took a pretend puff from the Habana. "It happened different than that. If you believe the word on the street, the mother and her boyfriend were having a picnic out on the fire escape. . . . A little booze, maybe something else. The kid's two or three years old. Falls asleep. Rolls over when they're not looking. One of the bars is loose or something. He drops. It was grass and dirt he hit, but hard. The mother screams. She races down the fire escape, jumps off the last step, almost breaks both ankles. She finds the kid not breathing. A minute goes by, she's hysterical. Two minutes. Eight minutes. Neighbors come running. Sirens in the air."

"I can picture it," I said.

He paused. Even with his back turned, I could tell I'd really ticked him off, so I closed my mouth.

"Then, according to the reports, some weirdo comes walking through the gathering crowd. Street person or something. Guy no one's ever seen. Maybe Hispanic, maybe not. Longish hair. Tattoo of a flower on his left forearm. This guy reaches down and touches the kid on his shoulder. Walks away. Disappears down the street. Kid goes from being dead to crying. A minute later when the ambulance and police get there the kid is fine as fine can be."

I couldn't hold my silence. "Want my opinion?"

"No."

"My opinion is this: the mother knows she's facing a child endangerment

rap, so once she realizes her baby is okay, she makes the rest of it up. A
little positive TV time. The miracle baby. The good mother visited by an
angel. She gets off."

Wales was shaking his head. "Witnesses back her up."

"Drug clients," I suggested. "Neighbors afraid her boyfriend would
beat the bejesus out of them if they didn't corroborate her version of
things. It's something along those lines. To my nose, the story smells."

"Maybe. We'll see. Go down to Fultonville and check it out. I'll give
you two fifty at six and a follow-up at ten if it's any good. Woman's name
is Ada Montpelier, like the capital of Vermont. Try not to make me have
to repeat it."

"The French university town. I'll remember it that way."

"877 Ediston Street."

"877 were the last three digits of my ex-mother-in-law's phone number."

"Who cares?"

"The heart of darkness," I said.

"What?"

"Her."

"Right. Go."

So THAT WAS THE BEGINNING. The tattooed guy with the
magic touch was Jesus Christ come back to earth. At least that's what
I now believe. I don't necessarily expect everyone to agree, of course: a
USA Today survey, based on twelve hundred Americans, and taken shortly
after the end of the story I will recount here, said that only about half of
us think he was actually something other than an interesting human being. But let me tell the whole tale before you make your own judgment. I
reported on some strange things in my days at ZIZ, and didn't usually get
them wrong. And the Jesus I'm going to describe here might turn out to
be nothing like the Jesus the newspapers and TV showed during the campaign, and nothing like the Jesus you always had in your imagination.

✶✶✶ TWO ✶✶✶

Eight minutes after my interview with Wales, I got into my new convertible and drove to Fultonville—through what was once a pretty downtown, through a neighborhood of nice Victorians from West Zenith's glory days, and then across the river and into the sorrowful world of American poverty.

My theory about American poverty is that it is invisible. Or, at least, invisible to the people who have the power to change it. After the catastrophe of Katrina, for a brief while, we got a glimpse of the real American poor: the story was too large to ignore. But even those people—many of whom are still suffering, I would bet—soon slipped back into invisibility, and the great, comfortable mass of the rest of us, busy with our own troubles and plans, seem content to pretend they aren't there.

In any case, I found a parking spot on a busy street where the car was less likely to be broken into, checked to see that I hadn't left anything valuable on the seats, got out, locked the doors, checked to make sure I'd locked the doors, and then found my way to 877 Ediston.

A lot of things that are carried on indoors in other places are carried on outdoors in Fultonville, at least in the warmish weather, so it wasn't a surprise to find Ada Montpelier sitting on her stoop surrounded by a knot of friends and neighbors, her ankles wrapped in ace bandages and her eyes puffy from crying. There was a newspaper reporter there from the *West Zenith Sun*. Randall Zillins was his name, a familiar name now, I know, but in those days he was a strictly provincial, low wattage type of guy. R.Z. we called him, and to some people those initials stood for "Re-ally Zero." R.Z. was one of those media types who is tormented by the attention other people get. I was in his office a few times and I noticed he'd tacked up on the wall stories he'd written—about the mayor, a lo-cal hockey star, a grandmother who'd gone back to school and become a chef. On every story R.Z. had highlighted his own byline in yellow.

In any case, people looked up when I approached, and everybody rec-ognized me. "It's the Channel 23 guy," someone said. "It's what's-his-name."

Ada was holding her hefty three-year-old in her lap as if he were an infant and they were still forty feet off the ground. The kid—who went by the name of Dukey Junior—was asleep and uninspiring, though after I introduced myself, I made a point of saying how strong and healthy he looked. Ada herself was not exactly the strong and healthy type. In fact, she was as thin as a stick, with electric hair and brown eyes surrounded by swollen flesh.

She told me about the boy's fall and the sudden appearance of the stranger, and then made the sign of the cross when she finished—which was fine by me. I'm more or less religious myself, though a tad mixed up about it since my mother is Catholic and my father Jewish. When I was a boy, they used to have these tremendous fights on the subject of reli-gion, often after my mother made the sign of the cross, in fact, or said, "God bless you," when one of us sneezed. My father, good Jew that he is, insisted the Messiah is still on his way and that God's name shouldn't be tossed around for something as casual as a sneeze. And my mom, good Catholic that she is, insisted there had only ever been one Messiah, his initials were J.C., end of story. I grew up plowing neutral turf as far as that question was concerned. But, if nothing else, my mixed heritage left me with the idea that God couldn't possibly love my father and hate my mother, or vice versa; that God was bigger than our ideas about him, and greater than any name we might call him. (Jesus, by the way, agrees.)

Anyway, I have to admit that, when I first heard it, Ada Montpelier's story had the feeling of many stories I encountered in the course of my working week, as if it had been told so many times that all the juice had been squeezed out of it. You couldn't hear the so-called ring of truth, if you catch my drift. Repetition does that. I don't care how great a meal is, if you eat that same thing again and again for a month it loses its zip.

But I digress. The point is that, to my well-trained ear, Ms. Montpelier's story sounded stale. Stale, maybe a little embellished, self-conscious in the way the TV news has made us. I looked up and could see the broken bar on the fire escape, so that part of the tale seemed true, though I wouldn't have put it past the boyfriend (nowhere to be seen) to have broken it *ex post facto*. Excuse me for being apolitically correct, but, for certain people in Fultonville, filing lawsuits for this or that disability or grievance was practically considered a profession. So this would be my report to Wales: Ada Montpelier's story was stale, tainted by self-interest, maybe or maybe not true, but it was the kind of thing people loved to see in a newscast otherwise devoted to sports, weather, and the awfulness of the human animal. I was warmed by it myself, although a few seconds after Ada finished telling it, one of her associates hissed out, "He don't believe you!" and pointed a wretched finger at me. She looked like she'd been on her way home from her daily run to the liquor store when she came upon the blessed ground.

"Sure I do," I said.

"You made this thing with your mouth," the woman hissed, twisting her mouth down on one side. "You don't believe any of it! We're all liars to you, all of us down here in F-ville. I seen you on TV, plenty of times. You always have a little wise look when you do a story about people like us. Right? Don't he?"

She made a half circle with her eyes but there were no takers in the group.

"What's your name?" I asked the hissing friend.

"None of your business."

"Well, I believe the story. Maybe it's you who doesn't believe it."

"Eat me," she said.

"Fine." I turned my attention to the mother of the saved child. "Ms. Montpelier, listen, we'd like to have you on the evening news, lead story. Would you mind if I called the camera truck down here? And would you mind holding Dukey Junior while you tell the story to us on camera, just like you told it to me now? I'm glad he's all right, by the way."

Ada didn't mind. She seemed dazed, preoccupied, maybe in shock—normal reactions, as far as I was concerned, after you've seen your kid, or anyone else's kid for that matter, fall three stories. While we waited for the camera truck, she smoked one unfiltered cigarette after another, waving the smoke away from her little boy's face as if she'd heard somewhere that it might not be good for him. More friends stopped by to touch the child and hug the mother and listen to the remarkable tale. On camera, she proved to be relaxed and genuine, and even provided an excellent description of the baby's savior—tattoo of a flower on his left forearm, torn jeans, shaggy black hair. (Still eagerly standing by, Randy Zillins was jotting all this down with a smirk on his face.) The real story, of course, was that no one knew who the tattooed miracle worker was. As I noted in my concluding remarks, "The mystery man had never been seen around Fultonville before he came up and touched young Dukey Junior on the shoulder. And he has not been seen since. This is Russ Thomas, reporting live. . . ."

We aired the story at the top of the six o'clock show. Thirty seconds after the report concluded, the station started receiving calls from viewers who claimed to know the man, or claimed that similar things had happened to them but they'd been afraid to go public with their experience. The usual, in other words.

Next morning, Randy Zillins called and asked if I thought the story was real. I told him, off the record, that it smelled. "Probably," I said, "the kid fell, but probably not that far. Had the wind knocked out of him. This other guy, passing through, came up and looked at him, maybe even got down and checked him out, as if he was going to do CPR or something. And then the kid came around, the guy took off, and the rumor started."

"I agree," R.Z. said, as if I cared whether he agreed or not. "But that wasn't the way you made it seem on the show last night."

"We usually hype things up a little, you know how it works, R.Z. TV news would be pretty flat otherwise. We don't have the integrity of you newspaper guys."

"But why would all these people make it up? Mass psychology, right? That's the real story. That's what *I'm* working on."

"They didn't make it up, they exaggerated. They were upset to begin with, the mother was ecstatic that her son was okay. It just swelled into something, that's all."

"Yeah, maybe," he said.

And that seemed to be the end of it.

★ ★ ★ THREE ★ ★ ★

But then — we were into the first part of June — Wales summoned me to his office for the second odd assignment. Standing at the window in another finely made suit he pronounced this memorable nugget of observation: "Since the miracle story we've been getting a lot of calls."

"BS, all of them," I said. "We checked them out. I talked to my sources in the police, even Chief Bastatutta. False reports, as they say."

"Right. I agree. But now we have one from Wells River. Now, as in today. This morning. Seems like it could be, maybe, you know. . . ."

"Real thing?"

"Could be. Who knows? What else are you doing?"

"Not much. The football player in Homersville who's putting together a ham supper at the church for his grandparents who just got back from the Peace Corps."

"Right. Go up there."

"Wells River?"

He turned around again. "No, Mars. Of course Wells River. The hospital there, whatever the name of the place is now. Guy about the same description as the other guy, in Fultonville. Walked down a corridor of the hospital, looked in on this little girl who had . . . I don't know, something bad . . . and a lot of people who used to be dying aren't anymore. Including the girl."

"Mercy."

"Right. Third floor. Where the bad cases are."

WELLS RIVER WAS ABOUT as opposite from Fultonville as a place could be. A clean downtown with fancy shops selling four-hundred-dollar dresses, an art theater, and a dozen or so cafes where nicely dressed thirtysomethings with one child asleep in an expensive Italian stroller sat around fondling designer sunglasses and talking fair trade. A women's college where the yearly tuition was alarmingly close to my annual income. Old Victorians near old mills that young couples originally from New York were fixing up, or having fixed up, so they would be able to live within walking distance of their pottery studios.

Forgive me if I sound sarcastic. Wells River was a perfectly nice place. Every place should be so nice. It's just that every place isn't, and when you spend Monday in one of West Zenith's poor neighborhoods interviewing some mother who's just buried her only daughter who was killed in a drive-by, and on Tuesday you get sent up to Wells to talk with, I don't know, some famous writer who's teaching his two young sons how to play tennis so they can take their rackets on vacation to Barcelona . . . well, I digress.

They have a decent hospital in Wells River, I can testify to that. My girlfriend Zelda's cousin had her twins there, in a hot tub or something, and when we went to visit her afterward it seemed clean and fresh smelling. Mercy Hospital, it was now called, though the joke was that when you got the bill for your colonoscopy or whatever, the name suddenly changed to No Mercy. Anyway, I went up there, parked in the Mercy lot, and didn't worry about what I left on the seat of the car. As I approached the building, who did I see coming out the front door but Randy Zillins. Zillins was shaking his head and studying his notes and almost tripped over the curb.

"R.Z., what's it look like in there?"

"They sent somebody up from the *Boston Herald* a while ago. Guy just left. Man, they're sharp."

"The big time. You'll get there some day."

"Nah," he said in a voice that showed how bad he wanted to. During those rare moments when I was in a negative mood, I had thoughts along the lines of: R.Z. and I aren't so different. We both dream of the big time, and we're both caught in the small time. It caused a particular kind of pain in me.

"These religious people are a bunch of phonies, man," he said. "I'm tellin' ya."

"You're a nonbeliever, I take it."

"An anti-believer," he said. "Like anybody with half a brain. When you die, you're dead. Get it while you can."

INSIDE MERCY, ON the third floor, I learned that the head nurse, one Alba Seunier, was the person to see. I'd met Alba years before, in a different part of the hospital, under not very pleasant circumstances. She was fiftyish, weighed all of a hundred pounds, and you'd want her on your rugby team. She took me off to one side so we'd be away from the bustle and phones.

"Amazing stuff," I suggested, to get a conversation going. This kind of semi-neutral offering is one of the tricks they teach you in journalism school.

Alba took the bait. She said, "Your lack of belief is written all over your face, mister."

"All right. I'm skeptical. It's professionally required, like you having clean hands."

"I was skeptical, too," she admitted. "I've worked in this hospital twenty-nine years, and I've seen plenty of strange things, including things people refer to as miracles, though I don't like that word. I've never seen this. The newspaper people who were here clearly didn't believe me, but I'm telling you, it's true."

"Give me the details, if you would."

She didn't ever seem to smile. Small tight lips, small blue eyes, small nose, but somehow all of that added up to large.

"We have fourteen beds on this part of the third floor," she said. "Terminal illness, for the most part. Many of them are children. At present, nine of the beds are occupied. Various cancers. A rare blood disorder. A patient who is allergic to everything—all foods. And we have one little girl, Amelia Simmelton, who has chronic lung disease and struggles for breath. The struggle puts a strain on her heart so we take her vitals hourly. Like many patients here, she's in and out of ICU. This morning Amelia had a visitor. The man claimed to be a relative of some sort and had flowers and knew enough about the girl—her date of birth, her middle name, her mother's name—so we believed him. But, as it turned out, he wasn't a relative at all. We were fooled and don't you dare put that in your report."

"Agreed."

She looked at me like my word wasn't worth much. "He stayed all of five minutes, and Amelia isn't struggling for breath now, and hasn't been, apparently, since the moment he left her room. After this man's visit, three other patients on the floor showed what I would term extremely unlikely improvement in their conditions, though that improvement is starting to erode in one of them. Amelia's isn't eroding. Her parents—the foundation people, Norman and Nadine Simmelton—have been here most of the day and just stepped out for something to eat. They're guardedly ecstatic."

"Simmelton Foundation," I said. "Big money."

"Enormous money. And enormously nice."

"I can talk to the girl, I hope."

"You may, yes. The Simmeltons said they'd allow it as long as there was no camera. Five minutes only."

"Fine. How old?"

"Nine and a half. Until today I would have given her about another three weeks to live. Now I won't say, and you won't say anything about that either."

"Of course not. I'm not an animal."

She narrowed her eyes. "I've seen you here before, haven't I?"

"No," I lied.

"Well, I see you on the news once in a while. You look shady, if you want to know my honest opinion. You look like someone I wouldn't want my daughter going out with."

"You look shady yourself," I tossed right back, though it wasn't remotely the case. "I wouldn't want my father going out with you."

She was marching away by then, toward Amelia's room. At that point I should have kept my mouth shut—after all, she could easily have told me to get lost, or wait until the parents came back so they could tell me to get lost—but keeping my mouth shut has always been hard for me, and, truthfully, it might have been one of the impediments to my climb up the television news ladder. Plus, I didn't appreciate being called shady. So, as we walked down the hall in a kind of fast, two-person parade, me a couple of steps behind, I called out, "All right, all right. I'll give you *two* of my autographed pictures then, if it means that much to you. But I want the box of Viagra samples in return. That was the deal."

Which wasn't, as Zelda would have said, appropriate.

Hospital rooms are not my favorite places, and it's much worse, of course, when the patient is so young. But there was Amelia, coal black skin and corn-rowed hair, perched on the edge of her bed and looking happily past a vase of flowers and out the window. Nurse Alba was kind enough—given our recent past—to leave me alone with her.

"Hey, kid!" I started out, and I gave her the smile.

She turned her big, dark eyes up to me. For a few seconds I pictured myself as her dad, standing next to the bed, knowing that she had a few weeks to live and that all the money in the world couldn't save her. Even imagining it I felt like my heart was being ripped out of my chest.

"Hi, TV guy."

"So you know me, huh?"

"Everybody knows you. 'And this is Russ Thomas reporting for the Wizard, WZIZ, in West Zenith.'"

"Tell me, do I seem, you know, like a straight shooter?"

"Mom says she likes your hair."

"And Dad?"

"Dad thinks you're too hyper sometimes."

"I actually resent that."

"I'm with Mom."

"Good. I bet you can guess why I showed up."

"Because you heard the third floor has the best food in Wells River?"

Just like that, she said it. Little sweet spark in her face, and I thought:

imagine what this kid has been through in her nine and a half years. And she sits there with the IV in her arm, making jokes with a stranger.

"All right, I admit it," I said. "I made the drive for one reason and one reason only: Mercy's world-famous chicken à la king."

She smiled and pointed to the chair, the IV tube swinging with her arm. "You can sit, if you want. I'm kind of tired of telling the same story, but I'll tell it one more time if you want."

I sat. I studied her round face, the intricately braided hair, the sad, pretty, adult-seeming eyes. I asked myself—who could help asking—what God had in mind when he decided to give a kid like this a disease like that. "All right," I said, "I'll spare you. R.Z. can give me the—"

"Who?"

"Mr. Zillins, the newspaper reporter. I saw him outside. He can give me the details. But tell me, this guy who stopped by, how did he seem to you? I mean, kids have a radar for good guys and bad guys. What was he like? A freak or what?"

She sank into thought for a moment, but didn't take her eyes off me. "His face was nice," she said at last. "He had a pretty big nose that was crooked, and the way he talked was very . . . gentle. He talked to me for a while and then he touched my leg, here." She pointed to the outside of her left knee. "And then he said he'd see me later, that we had important work to do, and he went out. I thought he was just a nice guy the hospital sends around to talk with sick kids and bring them flowers, but as soon as he left, the nurse came in and checked my vitals and they were different and I feel a lot better. I'm not using oxygen, for one thing. I almost always use oxygen."

"And you're sure you weren't feeling better before he came by?"

"I've never felt this better. It's like I have another body or something. They're coming back in a few minutes to do some PFTs."

"Which stands for what? Pretty fine tomatoes?"

"Pulmonary function test."

"How do you know these things? I mean, 'vitals,' 'pulmonary function?'"

"Long story, Russ," she said.

At that point, Alba made her presence known to me. She was standing in the corridor holding up one finger. I nodded.

"Last question, Amelia," I said. "What did he say to you, this nice man?"

"That's a secret."

"Even for the TV guy?"

The look she gave me then seemed to have something in it . . . *pity* is the word I'd use, I guess, though it doesn't make me happy to admit that. I've never forgotten that look, or the sense that this nine-year-old saw through me and down into something I kept telling myself was not there. "He asked me to keep it a secret until he tells everybody, and I will," she said with conviction.

"All right," I told her cheerfully. "They're taking me away now. I'm sorry to have made you tell the story again, and I'm happy you're feeling better, really I am."

I hoped she might ask for my autograph or something, but she'd met a lot of celebrities in her life, I guess. She just nodded and looked out the window again, as if my visit didn't mean that much to her either way.

I tried, of course, to get Amelia and her parents on camera, but it was no sale. They were nice people, shy people actually, who gave millions to various inner city and environmental causes. You could see that they were hoping against hope their daughter wouldn't slip back into the iron grasp of her illness, and that they were not into having their faces on the TV for any reason. Nonetheless, I cobbled together a nice piece about the Good Visitor (Wales's idea, nobody else liked the name), trying to sound neutral, maybe slightly skeptical but definitely not cynical. Maybe like I thought it might be partly true, and even if it wasn't, it was a feel-good tale that balanced off the usual nightly misery.

✦✦✦ FOUR ✦✦✦

After my visit to Mercy Hospital I started making notes about the Good Visitor story. I had been a compulsive diary-keeper my whole life (growing up in an odd family will do that to you), so it was more or less natural to jot down the news of the day. The first entry looks like this:

June 3

W. River yesterday. Mercy. Alba S and the miracle girl. Parents say no to camera. Is there a chance all this is not b.s.? Later. Date with Z. Stewardess. Closet. Talk.

The last part of it means that, on the night of my visit to Wells River, I had a "date" with Zelda. Date is what we called it when I went over to her place for the night or she came over to mine. When we went to a restaurant or a movie, it was "going out," but we didn't do that very often because we would inevitably attract the attention of some guy with a belly the size of three watermelons, and he'd come up and slap me on the shoulder like we were former shipmates, tell me I was looking good, and then remind me I'd made a slip of the tongue a few nights earlier, saying something like "Channel 23 Nude" instead of "Channel 23 News." A guy like that can take the shine off a night out pretty fast.

A night at Zelda's carried no such risks. Her idea of a date was, for example, just what happened that evening: she met me at the door of her condo dressed up like a flight attendant: the tight skirt, the tied-back hair, the wings pinned to her white blouse (she spent a lot of time in vintage clothing stores). She had a martini in hand, and made me sit in the armchair and served me, then came back every few minutes as I sipped, and asked, in a certain tone of voice, if there was anything else she could do for me. And so on. You get the idea. Great imagination, that woman, and a pretty fair actress, too. We ended up in the closet, pretending it was the lavatory and we were thirty thousand feet above Arizona, ripping off each other's clothes. Stewardess one night, policewoman another, dental hygienist, call girl, librarian. And then, a few times a month, just a pretty woman memorializing the missionaries. She had a constantly expanding repertoire of roles and enjoyed it as much as I did, which was a great deal. Plus, there were other sides of her I liked, and other sides of me she seemed to like, amazing as that may be.

Afterward, I'd want to sleep and she'd want to talk. My listening to her talking was part of the deal, as it were, and that seemed fair enough to me, though after a day at the station or on the streets, I preferred quiet. After a day of listening to clients, she, naturally enough, wanted to talk. That night, after our exhausting flight across the country, we lay in bed, and just as I was sinking down into that heaven of postcoital rest, Zelda said, "Why didn't you show pictures of that little girl on the report tonight?"

"Not allowed."

"By who?"

"Head nurse. Girl's parents. The nurse probably shouldn't have even let me in the girl's room but the parents were away and she did."

"How old is this nurse?"

"Twice as old as you and a tenth as nice. Did you think the story was kind of flat without the visuals?"

"As flat as the front of the hospital," Zelda said. One of the things I liked about her was that she could be perfectly frank without giving offense or trying to flatter. She was lying next to me, on her back, very close, and she took my hand and squeezed my fingers. "Don't fall asleep yet, Russ."

"Okay."

"I think there's something special about this story."

"Lots of people do. You should see the calls we — "

"No. I mean it. It gave me a feeling tonight."

"That was me. In the closet. I gave you that feeling."

"Stop joking."

"Okay."

"It was as if I knew this would happen, or something. I was watching you and listening, and it was as if I'd seen the broadcast before."

"*Danger view,* is what the French call it."

"Stronger than that."

"Danger view with no ice. Straight up."

"You can be an ass."

"I've been hearing that a lot lately, in varying forms."

"You wouldn't know a great thing if it sat in your lap. . . . Plus, if you get a better job in some other city, what's supposed to happen to me, to us?"

This was, it seemed to me in my exhausted state, the actual heart of the discussion. I wanted to tell Zelda that there were days I knew I couldn't live without her, but the dust storm of my past hadn't settled enough for me to see my life clear yet, and I wasn't ready for another marriage. She was one of those women who had happiness written all over her future, and deservedly so. It's just that I was one of those men who had sadness written all over my past, and I was thirty then, ambitious as hell, and not ready. So I told a tiny lie. I said, "If a job someplace else comes through I have a plan, okay? Let's not talk about it until then, so we don't jinx anything."

From years of listening to troubled souls, Zelda had an instinct for the convenient untruth. She didn't answer. I heard the whisper of the sheets as she rolled away from me, and I felt the nice warmth disappear. And then I was alone with the person I'd turned out to be.

★ ★ ★ FIVE ★ ★ ★

You would think that the occurrence of two apparent miracles in the same neck of the woods would make a splash in the media world. But it didn't. The Wells River/Mercy Hospital/Good Visitor story evaporated from the collective consciousness like moisture off a sidewalk in a blast of summer sun. In the first place, most educated people don't believe in miracles. And in the second place, very few stories have a lifespan of more than a day or two. The American news-watching public is promiscuous and impatient in its appetites, a fact well understood by the media conglomerates.

In spite of that, for a couple of weeks I made calls to the hospital—without telling anybody, as a private project—and checked in with Nurse Seunier to see how things stood. (I kept notes about it in my journal, too. I had a weird intuition that it would turn into something big.) I was pleased to learn that Amelia Simmelton was doing well, and then continuing to do well, and then going home she was doing so well. From the sound of Nurse Seunier's voice, I could tell the story had not evaporated from her consciousness. "This is so unusual in my experience that you should come up and talk to me about it again at some point," she suggested, in our last conversation. "You people should do another story on it." I thought her invitation was nice, but I had so many other things going then that I never went back to see the nurse. Wales didn't mention the story again either, so there was, as we say, no professional impetus.

But then, one ordinary night after we'd finished the six o'clock report, and I'd gone across the street to Patsanzakis's for my usual steak-and-cheese, a beer, and two pieces of baklava (I work out like a maniac to keep the weight off; the health club membership is tax deductible), and had come back to the office and was kind of lounging around, checking to see what I might have on the docket for the next day, my private line rang. I picked up, hoping it would be Zelda pretending to be Beyoncé and wanting to party after the late broadcast, but it wasn't. The voice, masculine and unfamiliar, pronounced my name with a certain authority. "Russell Thomas?"

"Speaking."

"Meet me at Pete's Cafe in Wells River at 2:25 tomorrow."

"Sure, happy to. Who's this supposed to be?"

"The Good Visitor."

"Right. You and sixty-five other people who've called the station in the past few weeks. How did you get this number, anyway?"

"I touched Amelia Simmelton on her left knee," the guy said, and then hung up.

This fell outside even the usual bizarre territory of my anonymous phone messages. And that's saying something, because those messages ran the gamut from weird to pathological. Once, when I'd been on the job only a few years and was still green, I had a call from someone claiming to have inside information on a professional football drug scandal that was much in the news at the time. I thought it might be my ticket to a bigger market, because this was a big-market story. So, ambitious, young, pumping iron, feeling brave, I agreed to meet this someone on a not-very-nice street in a not-very-reputable section of the city at an unwise hour. The intrepid reporter. Also, the intrepid reporter who wasn't smart enough to tell anyone where he was going.

And there on that disreputable street, I stood on a dark sidewalk in front of a bar and waited. At last, a Cadillac drove up, the passenger window slid down, I was motioned in. And in I went. I was driven a few blocks to the unlit parking lot of an out-of-business candy factory and "rolled" as we used to say; that is, I was banged over the head from behind by a friend of my "source," then roughed up and pushed out of the car after being relieved of my wallet and other assorted valuables — a nice watch, a dependable cell phone, tickets to the Bob Dylan concert in Wells River the following week. I woke up in a puddle with a bloody, broken nose, a very sore head and neck, and scratches on my face, hands, and knees.

For a while, Wales and I thought about doing it as a story: brave reporter mugged by unscrupulous thugs. But, in the end, we decided against it on the grounds that it might give a disturbed segment of our viewing audience the idea that roving reporters existed to fulfill the darker aspects of their fantasy lives. I took two weeks off with pay. The police went to the Dylan concert and found the two geniuses sitting in my seats; they did eighteen months in Winford State Prison and have not been in contact with me since. After the initial emergency room visit in West Zenith, I went up to Wells River to have my nose straightened and my head X-rayed again, at Mercy, where they have a facial reconstruction specialist and a brain guy. (Nurse Seunier remembered me from that short stay, not my finest hour.)

It ended up working out well, though, because it was during that week, after my hospital visit, that I met Zelda. It was at Pete's, in fact, a cute vegetarian cafe/coffee shop a block off Wells River's main street. Zelda, I might have neglected to mention, is a therapist. At the time, in addition to her thriving private practice, she was teaching a course in counseling at the expensive women's college in Wells River, and was reading some student papers over a mochaccino with a shot of vanilla syrup and buttered wheat toast.

"There's something *jai no say qua* about a woman who eats buttered wheat toast," I offered, a terrible line, I admit, but I blame it on the pain medication. Plus, I had momentarily forgotten that my face was all scratched up, the nose bandaged, and one eye still black. So I was not looking my best.

Without even lifting her eyes she said, "Yes, and there's something *je ne sais quoi* about jerks like you."

I didn't respond but kept looking at her. And that made her glance up. And when she glanced up, she took in the awful spectacle of my battered visage. I thought, for a second, that she'd either apologize out of pity or run screaming from the place. But she didn't do either. She just appraised me, taking in the raw scratches, the dark purple swatch under my left eye, and the bandage/splint type of thing they were using to hold my nose in place.

"A sight for sore eyes, aren't I?" I said, trying again.

"The hair looks good at least."

I thanked her. We laughed. The conversation sputtered and backfired for a while before we stumbled onto one of my passions—the American political scene, which, in those years, was fitting material for a comedy show. It turned out that, in the most recent election, we'd both voted for a candidate for senator who claimed to have a secret invention, not yet patented, that would fuel cars with vanilla extract. He was from East Zenith. I'd done a story on him. Zelda hadn't seen the story (she watched our competitors) but had voted for the guy because the incumbent senator, who we both liked, had no chance of losing, and because she had a soft spot for offbeat, harmless types. Which somehow led to her giving me her "contact information," as she called it. To wit, an e-mail address. I fired off an amusing note that afternoon. She answered it two weeks later. The rest is history.

So, I suppose it was because of my pleasant associations with Pete's that I decided I'd run up to Wells River and check this guy out. There would be no midnight rides in Cadillacs this time. I knew that. The news day was pretty slow. And Wales—who I wasn't even going to tell at first—surprised me by tossing an "Okay, no problem" over his shoulder as he stared out at the city.

And that was how I came to have a personal relationship with Jesus.

✱ ✱ ✱ SIX ✱ ✱ ✱

The meeting with the Good Visitor would be the start of a new kind of life for me, but I did not know that then, and I did not feel any particular trepidation or excitement as I made the drive to Wells River. If anything, I was annoyed at myself for having agreed to the foolish errand.

It was a few days before school let out. The sky was giving forth a steady, cold rain (our weatherman, a bald bodybuilder named William Fiskawilly, referred to around the station as Willy-Willy, lived for bad weather, so he was happy). After searching for fifteen minutes, I found a parking spot half a mile out of town, and walked to Pete's with my umbrella flapping around, and an expensive pair of shoes getting ruined.

The only good side of all this was that, by the time I came within sight of Pete's Cafe, I had worked up a healthy appetite and was ready for a serving of their excellent vegetarian lasagna. Plus, walking into the place always made me think of Zelda. Pete's was full of people with small shopping bags and pricey raincoats, everyone holding coffee cups with two hands and casting annoyed glances out the plate-glass window. I had no idea what the self-described Good Visitor looked like and, honestly, at that point, I was hoping he wouldn't show.

Pete's had a small main room and, at the back, a narrow verandah with floor-to-ceiling windows that could be taken down to screens when the weather was good. It was always quieter back there, and fewer people would stare at me or ask for autographs, so I made a zigzag run between chairs and grabbed a table at one end of the verandah, keeping my back to the room. In less than a minute someone came and stood opposite me. Tall, broad-shouldered, with dark hair swept back from a high forehead and a rectangular, handsome face that showed a hint of South American Indian, this fellow might have been a typical Wells River architect or software entrepreneur, up from Universidad de los Andes, with a daughter-of-an-obstetrician wife and two beautiful kids back in their million-dollar contemporary. But he wasn't. How I knew he wasn't, I'm not sure. After a while, you develop a feeling for these things. The worst of my Wells River acquaintances (and I should say that I also had some good friends there) wore a self-congratulatory air, as if they had managed to tame this messy business we call life and saw no reason to let their awareness of that grand achievement lapse while they were in public.

I'm sorry. I'm being mean. I have my reasons. The reasons have to do with my first marriage, which ended badly and involved a young professional type, a Tai Chi master from Wells River. The point is that this guy opposite me did not seem perfectly at home in Wells River. There was a ribbon of roughness to him, just a touch around the eyes, as if life hadn't always been easy for him. The hair was black, the eyes a deep coffee-with-a-little-cream brown, the nose a sort of beak, the mouth wide and straight with the potential for a smile on it. Instead of a raincoat—uniform of the day—he was wearing a brown wool sport coat Wales would have been proud to be seen in, a tailored white shirt, and jeans—all perfectly dry. Most likely he'd left his umbrella at the door.

"Do not get up," he said, when I made a move to. He held out his hand and gave me a firm shake. "Jesus," he said, pronouncing it the way I was used to and then adding, "Hay-Zeus, to my Spanish-speaking friends."

"Russ Thomas."

Jesus sat down. Before we could say anything else, the waitress came by, smiling as if she recognized me but was too cool to say so. "Veggie lasagna and a small salad," I said. "Ranch on the side. Large cappuccino."

Jesus said, "Same."

When she left us, he clasped his hands together on the table in front of him and leaned forward. He had a presence, I have to admit, and I

noticed, or felt, this presence right from the first minute we were together, even though I was not exactly predisposed to liking him. There
were no golden flashing eyes or shimmering facial bones, just a calm,
confident-but-humble way about him, as if he had set self-consciousness
aside and was at peace with the person he presented to the world. You
don't see that in people anymore. We've been fed so much information—what we should and shouldn't eat, should and shouldn't say,
should and shouldn't think, the multifarious ways we should be feeling
guilty about our lives in comparison with this or that suffering soul
elsewhere on earth—that it's rare to come across someone who seems
fully comfortable and unself-conscious in his or her daily life. I think in
my parents' generation it was more common. Even now, my father can
chow down a cold-cut sandwich and pinch my mother's rear end in the
kitchen without once thinking about bad cholesterol, trans fats, or the
objectification of women. Even my brother Stab's situation—I'll get
into that later—hadn't moved them toward any particularly philosophi-
cal consideration of the nature of existence.

Anyway, Jesus leaned toward me and said, "I won't waste your time,
Russell."

"Russ."

"Fine. Here is the situation. I need you to quit your job, and get Zelda
to quit hers. As soon as possible."

So I understood from the get-go that the guy was, as we used to say,
"soft." But I didn't want to leave without having my lasagna, and the
weather was lousy, so, without missing a beat, and without giving much
thought to how he knew about Zelda (anybody who can get your private
phone number can find out the name of your girlfriend), I said, "I'm
drafting my letter of resignation even as we speak."

His frown was not a pleasant thing to consider. "You have an unfortunate attraction to sarcasm," he said. "It is a way of keeping people at a
distance—you know that, of course."

"Oh, my apologies." I took a sip of the cappuccino and wiped my upper lip. "Look, you call me on my private line with some half-ass story,

get me up here on a day like this, then tell me to quit my job, and get my girlfriend to quit hers. And I'm supposed to say what? Thank you?"

"Sorry," he said, but it sounded nothing like an apology. "I thought you would have understood by now."

"Well, compared to people like you, I guess I'm a little slow."

The man who called himself Jesus sat back in his chair and gave me a smile of genuine amusement. "You are somewhat cynical," he said. "Which is a manifestation of fear."

"Is that so?"

"Yes, it is so. And cynical is the persona you give off on the screen. Yet you never connect it to the fact that you are still a roving reporter after eight years, while a lot of the others who finished school in your class have moved on to the anchor desk in various parts of the country."

"I'm doing fine, thanks," I lied, but I could tell he wasn't buying it.

The waitress came and put our plates in front of us. Jesus looked her in the eyes when he said "Thank you," which is something my father taught me to do a long time ago, "a sign that you have class," he liked to say.

"Not to worry, though. I can use a cynical, scared, ambitious person in my operation."

"You're off your meds," I said, reaching for my fork. "Why don't you go and find someone else to insult. I'll pick up the tab here, and we can just agree we're not good lunch companions."

"You shall be well taken care of. As will Zelda."

"Why don't we back up a step?" I suggested, after the first bite of salad, though I had pretty much stopped caring what he said by then. I wanted to finish my meal and leave, and if the guy trailed me I was going to have him arrested for stalking and not lose any sleep over it either. "Who the hell are you?"

"Jesus Christ."

"And what do you do?"

"It is widely known what I do, and have done. You have reported on a couple of my doings in the past month."

I considered this, chewed, swallowed, looked at him. One thing about the business I'm in, a thing that's equal parts bothersome and intriguing, is that you come face to face with the limitless manifestations of the human animal. You get to meet people like Alba Seunier, devoting their lives to comforting sick kids, and people like Ada Montpelier's boyfriend, breaking fire escapes in the hope it will win him a legal settlement so he'll never have to work again. And then there were people like my new pal, Hay-Zeus, who inhabited a level of insanity most people found frightening to contemplate. The whole thing seemed clear to me at the time: he had watched my reports on the Ada Montpelier scamola, and the Amelia Simmelton recovery, and had come to the delusional conclusion that he was the man I was talking about, the mythical savior and healer. The Messiah.

Having grown up in the circumstances I'd grown up in (tough neighborhood, middleweight boxer for a dad), and having made a bad marriage at an early age into a family of the mentally disturbed, I was not intimidated by sociopaths. Whatever my other flaws and failings, I have a measure of physical courage. As I ate, there on the sparsely inhabited verandah of Pete's Cafe in Wells River, with a hard June rain streaming down the windows, I came to the belated understanding that my lunch companion was claiming to be Jesus Christ, who many people—my mother, for one—consider to be God. A large number of my fans and friends would find it unlikely that God would choose me as a lunch companion and be sitting there in a cute cafe, telling me to quit my job.

I said, "Sure it's widely known what you do. You scam people. You want attention. You're another nut, bringing trouble into the lives of those who want nothing to do with you."

Jesus laughed. It was, I had to admit, a good-hearted laugh, and completely sane-sounding. He had nice teeth. He had not touched his food—which, my mother would have said, instantly disqualified him from being God. God would not waste a good lasagna. I was halfway through my lunch and counting the minutes, when he reached across the table and touched my forearm in a particular way. It is hard to describe that touch. There was no weirdness in it. It was, at once, a sort of apology for any inconvenience he might be causing me and a quiet insistence on his sanity and goodness, a reassurance, an understanding that I might have to maintain a defensive posture in public encounters and that I might not, after all, be as happy with my, well, with my station in life as I pretended to be. The gesture caused me to look at him, really look at him for the first time, and to really listen when he said, in a quiet voice, "I brought little Dukey Junior back to life for a reason. And I cured Amelia Simmelton for a reason, as well."

I want to go on record here as saying that my doubts did not suddenly vanish at the sound of those words. But *something* happened. My arm buzzed where he had touched me. "You don't exactly fit the God description," I managed to say, but some of the wind had been knocked out of me.

He seemed pleased. "I chose you for a reason, too."

"Well, that immediately undercuts your credentials."

"You do not think very much of yourself, I take it."

"I'm okay. Not the best, not the worst."

"Deep down, you feel a disappointment in the way your life has turned out."

"Listen," I said, "my girlfriend is a therapist, so I get more than enough of this kind of stuff from her, thank you." But behind the smoke screen of those words, I felt like I was about to start weeping—which would have been about the second time in my adult life that I'd actually shed tears. The first time was at the dog track, now defunct, up in Pownal, Vermont, when I missed a ten-thousand-dollar Superfecta by a nose. Which gives you an idea how sentimental I am.

"You feel like you were meant to be doing something else," Jesus went on. "Something grander, something that has more impact on the world."

"Who doesn't? Ninety percent of the people I talk to feel that way. The guys I golf with secretly think they'd be as good as Tiger Woods, if only they'd started playing when they were four, and had the right sports psychologist. Lots of the women I know believe they should be married to Brad Pitt or Denzel Washington, but by bad luck they somehow got stuck with their plain old husband."

"I am not talking about the guys you play golf with, I am talking about you."

"All right. Yeah, I feel that way sometimes."

"I am here to tell you what the something else is that you should be doing."

"You mean Hollywood is finally going to call?"

He smiled a sad smile, and for an instant I let my guard down and started to think that, God or no, he was kind of a good guy and I was being kind of a jerk.

"I'm going to do things differently this time," he said, in that same quiet tone.

"Really."

He nodded, picked up his fork. "Last time I wasn't entirely happy with the way it worked out. To be frank, it took hundreds of years for what I did to have much impact on the world, and by then things were so muddled. . . . Well, you people have never really recovered. Look at the Middle East."

"So this time you're going on *American Idol*."

A shake of the head. "This time I am going to run for president of the United States."

This knocked me silent, but only for a second. "Smart," I said. "Good move. A lot of Holy Ones do that."

"I came to ask for your help. You, Zelda, a few other good-hearted people who were born in this place and time for this reason. But I can sense that you do not yet feel yourself worthy of being called, and I can see that you're not going to believe me at first, despite the two events."

"Events?"

"The two miracles."

"So-called," I said.

"You don't have faith, then?"

"A small amount," I said. "But it's doing battle right now with a big amount of professional objectivity."

"I understand that battle all too well," he said, finally taking a bite of his food and nodding as if he approved of it. "There is always a war going on between intellect and faith, that's nothing new."

"Which side do you fight on?" I asked him.

"Neither. Evil has been done by people on both sides of the equation."

"Well, okay," I said. His last remark had softened me up. Plus, I'm usually in a better mood after I have some coffee. "You seem like a decent guy. I'm sure you mean well. But you have to realize that going around calling yourself Jesus Christ will raise eyebrows. So will the claim that you'll be running for president. And also the tendency you seem to have to ask people to quit their jobs. I'm just offering that as free advice."

He gave me the brilliant smile, pushed his plate an inch away from him. "Why don't we leave it at this," he said. "I shall try to persuade you in a different way. And if you remain skeptical, then I shall stop pestering you and find a decent replacement."

"Sounds good," I said. I had my wallet out, was paying in cash, anxious to be on my way. "You know, send it to me in a dream or something. That's the way they did it in the old days." A pretty good exit line, I thought, but when I stood up and glanced at him one last time he was giving me a look of such profound disappointment that it actually shook me. I worried I had hurt his feelings, and while you don't want to be taken in by every huckster on every street corner, at the same time, you don't want to harden your heart to the point where you feel nothing for anyone but yourself, and maybe those closest to you. For a second I worried that I'd stepped over the line.

But then, after a firm handshake, I was out in the rain again and, may God forgive me, already more or less forgetting about Hay-Zeus heading back to the comfort and relative sanity of my co-workers, my routine, my hopes, my various appetites and assumptions, and so on.

✶✶✶ SEVEN ✶✶✶

And I would have been comfortable in those assumptions for the rest of my life, probably, if I hadn't awakened, next morning, to the sound of weeping. I'd spent the night alone, in my nice eighth-floor, five-room condo overlooking the city of West Zenith. For a second or two, when I heard the weeping, I thought it must be a dream. I closed my eyes and was trying to sink back into sleep when I felt someone sit on the edge of the mattress. I blinked my eyes open and saw Zelda there, all dressed for work in a sexy green pantsuit, crying to beat the band.

My first thought, naturally, was that she'd come to tell me she was pregnant. Why else would she let herself into my apartment at nine in the morning and be crying like that? And, even in my sleepy state, I was okay with the idea. I put my hand on her arm, and I said, "It's okay. It's fine." She was shaking her head and weeping, wet black strands of hair caught in one corner of her mouth.

I pulled her down beside me and we lay there like that for a while, Zelda messing up her work suit and me dreaming of playing catch with Russell Jr. on a weedless lawn in the Boston or New York suburbs.

But after a few minutes she sat up and said, "Jesus came to me in a dream."

"Huh?"

"He did. You have to believe me, Russ. Please believe me."

"Okay, I believe you. What's not to believe?"

"He said I'd been chosen for something, to help him with something. It wasn't like any dream I've ever had. It was much much much more real. I'm a psychologist, I deal in dreams all the time. It wasn't even a dream, really, it was a vision. You have to believe me!"

"Okay, calm down, I believe you."

"No you don't!"

"All right, I don't exactly. I mean, I believe you had the dream, but I'm not sure it was that different than any of the other dreams—"

She started hitting me, which was a first, banging a soft fist against my shoulder in a way that surprised me but didn't hurt. I took hold of her hand and said, "Okay, I'm sorry."

"I knew this would happen," she said, and there was so much disappointment in her voice that it frightened me. I'd been getting a lot of that kind of thing lately, people telling me I came across as shady or cynical or too ambitious, or one thing or another. At that moment something changed in me, I could feel it. One line of defense broke apart.

I sat up against the headboard and said, "All right, confession time."

"I knew it!" Zelda yelled. "You've been cheating. I knew it. I knew it was a mistake to get involved with a celebrity, even a minor league celebrity."

"Thanks for the minor league part," I said. "But I haven't been cheating. I did have lunch with a guy in Wells River yesterday. He—"

"A *guy?* You're cheating on me with another guy? You never told me this. I mean, it's not as bad, it doesn't hurt as much, but it's the type of thing you are supposed to share."

"Zel, listen. You're upset. Just keep quiet a minute and let me finish. I met with a guy who claims he is the miracle worker. The Good Visitor. Jesus, he said his name is. You know, as in the Bible. He said he wanted me and you to quit our jobs, that he's going to run for president of the United States. I didn't believe him, naturally, another state hospital escapee watching too many news reports. But he said he'd send the message to me in a dream."

"And he sent it to me instead!" Zelda yelled.

"All right. Calm down."

"But that's what happened, can't you see?"

"I'm thinking about it."

"Thinking about it? What's wrong with you?"

"Wrong with me? What's wrong with you? You're a therapist, a scientist of the mind. You don't think there might be something perfectly explainable going on here?"

"No, I don't. I've never had a dream like that, not once in my entire life. And you've never done stories about a stranger healing children, or saving a child who fell three stories. Tell me you have."

"I haven't."

"Then why are you being so resistant?"

"I don't know."

"Come on, why?"

"Don't therapize me, Zel."

"Answer the question. Just honestly spit it out, no holding back."

"Honestly?"

"No holding back, Russ."

"Honestly, I think it's because I want to be God. Deep down inside, I'm another Randy Zillins type, another egotistical, insecure guy who's jealous of the heroes he reports on. There it is. I want to be the special one, as special as Jesus is supposed to be, to you and to everybody else. Healing kids, having a fuss made. A lot of us want to be top of the heap, king of the food chain. Anchorman on the nightly world news. All right? Now I said it. Your boyfriend is the biggest egotist of all time."

I waited, shocked at myself, assessing the damage. There is a downside to one's defenses falling apart. Zelda was watching me as if I were some kind of orangutan that had escaped from the zoo. I suddenly had the sickening feeling she was going to walk out the door and never come back. So I shocked myself again. I said, "And how about this, as long as we're being honest: I want you to marry me. I want to get married. Will you marry me?"

"Are you serious?"

"Dead serious."

"I thought you said that, after Esther, you'd never get married again."

"I changed my mind."

"When?"

"Just now. What's your answer? Don't keep me hanging. Don't pull a Mitchell's girlfriend on me."

"I won't," she said.

"You won't. Okay. Fine. That settles that. I don't blame you, to tell you the truth. This morning I don't blame you at all. I'm in such a mood I wouldn't marry me either."

"I meant I won't pull a Mitchell's girlfriend. The answer is yes, yes I will. I'll marry you."

Her answer made me glad, naturally. Though I have to say I was still shocked at myself and half asleep, and naked. Zelda was unbuttoning and then taking off her nice green work suit, in a frenzied way, and as she climbed in beside me and wrapped her warm arms around me, I could not keep myself, momentarily, from thinking about Mitchell Honorais, a former anchorman at ZIZ. Mitch had proposed to his girlfriend on the air on New Year's Eve. She'd said no, or at least failed very obviously to say yes, and from that moment Mitch had gone into a slide, personally and professionally, and ended up losing his self-confidence, his job, his house, what was left of his relationship with the girlfriend, and then taking refuge in methamphetamines.

"We'll quit our jobs and go to work for Jesus," I told Zelda, resolutely, and that seemed to please her very much.

★ ★ ★ EIGHT ★ ★ ★

So we made love, Zelda and I, but something was different about it that morning, as if the marriage proposal had caused some fundamental change between us. Afterward we rested against each other for a while, and then she suddenly sat up straight and looked at the radio. "Oh my God, I have a ten o'clock!" she yelled. It was 9:41. If there weren't any gas line explosions or shootings along the route, it took her twelve minutes to go from my condo to her office, park her car, and sprint up the stairs, and she was positively obsessive about never keeping a client waiting. "They'll think I don't care about them," she told me, more than once. "It will revive their childhood feelings of abandonment."

"Maybe if that happened it would be an opportunity for healing," I said, because I knew the lingo by then. I'd even done a little therapy myself, after the divorce. I believed in the healing potential of talking to a professional, of course, but that wasn't the kind of thing top-ten-market news-anchor candidates liked to make public.

Anyway, Zelda kissed me passionately, ran out the door, buttoning her blouse as she went, and, for some reason, crying.

I sat in bed for an hour staring at the wall. What had just happened? My brilliant and down-to-earth girlfriend had seen Jesus in a dream. I'd asked her to marry me. It seemed I'd agreed to quit my job, though I couldn't be sure about that part. The whole thing terrified me. For a while I thought I should go into therapy again. But at that moment I couldn't move, couldn't get out of bed, couldn't think straight. The phone rang.

"Hello," I said, in a dazed voice.

"What are you doing?"

"Who's this?"

"Jesus."

"Great."

"What are you doing right now?"

"Sitting in bed with a bulging bladder, worrying."

"Worry drains the spirit."

"Easy for you to say. I didn't just appear to *your* girlfriend in a dream."

"You have nothing to fear as long as I am with you."

"Sure, okay. You going to pay my car insurance, which is due tomorrow? And after that the condo fee? Golf club dues for next year? Pay for the ring, the wedding, the honeymoon, the diapers, the tennis lessons, the braces, the college tuition? And so on?"

"Yes, I am. Indirectly, perhaps, but your work with me will pay for all those things."

I sat there a minute and didn't say anything.

"You are cherishing a doubt," Jesus said.

"Exactly."

"In spite of the dream I sent Zelda."

"It seems a bit hocus-pocusy to me, that dream stuff. It's a few hundred miles outside the realm of ordinary screwiness I deal with every day of my life."

"Zelda, on the other hand, has no doubts whatsoever, have you noticed that?"

"Sure, I—"

"Are you smarter than she is?"

"No way."

"Wiser?"

"Not on your life."

"Is she especially gullible?"

"Not at all. Gullible's the last thing she is."

"Then how do you explain the difference between your response to me and hers? Have you thought about that?"

"No, honestly, I haven't, until just now."

Jesus was quiet for a few seconds, and I thought he had hung up. But then he said, "When you make love, Zelda likes you to take hold of her right earlobe between your thumb and second finger and squeeze it gently."

I sat there staring at the wall. In the name of full disclosure I should admit at this point that, hearing those words, and traumatized as I was by past marital troubles, it occurred to me that Zelda might have been cheating on me with this Hay-Zeus character, and the rest of it was just an elaborate cover-up. Her way of getting me to finally pop the question, maybe. Her own childhood abandonment trauma being played out.

But then, in the calmest of voices, Jesus went on: "When you were fifteen you were coming out of a baseball game with some friends in North Salem, all of you happy, raucous. In your boyish joy, you ran out into the street and came very close to being hit and killed by a man driving a red Chevrolet Impala."

"You've been talking to my mother."

"You masturbated for the first time in the bathroom of your parents' home when you were thirteen."

"Okay, you haven't been talking to my mother," I said, but he was scaring me.

"When you shave you always start to the right of your Adam's apple and take an upward stroke. Esther used to criticize you for preferring to use only a particular kind of spoon when you ate oatmeal. Sometimes, as you are about to take your backswing on the golf course you think about an old girlfriend who dumped you. Her name was—"

"Stop," I said, quietly and calmly. "You can stop now."

"Or I could go on and on," he said.

"You're not just a particularly talented psychic, are you?

"You don't need me to answer that."

"Right, okay. Next question then: why me?"

"Again with the self-hatred."

"Nothing to do with self-hatred. You'll excuse me, I'm just surprised that, of the six billion people on earth, you pick Russell Thomas to come down to."

"The fishermen were surprised, too. Mary was surprised. Joseph. Lazarus. Magdalene. The whole gang of them, surprise everywhere. What would it say about somebody if they *weren't* surprised?"

I thought about it. It felt like some kind of compliment. I said, "All right. Okay." And then I had to force the next words out because I thought I knew what the answer was going to be. "What do you want me to do next, then. I mean—"

"Go to the station and give your notice."

"Today?"

"Yes. This morning."

"How much notice?"

"Two days."

"Two *days?* You've got to be kidding. I've been there almost eight years. I'm supposed to go in and tell them I'm leaving in two days!"

"You are not that hard to replace," Jesus said.

"Thanks. Appreciate it."

"Courage is the main thing in this life. And it comes in various forms. Give your notice and we'll talk," he said. "You won't regret it."

✷ ✷ ✷ NINE ✷ ✷ ✷

I got up and used the toilet and shaved, starting off, as always, to the right of my Adam's apple. There were, it seemed to me, two choices: I could write the guy off as a complete crank who happened to have psychic abilities, start screening my calls, and refuse to have lunch meetings ever again with anyone who referred to himself as Jesus Christ. I would keep my job, that was the good part. The bad part was that Zelda would lose all respect for me, probably break up with me, and if it turned out that Jesus was actually who he said he was, I'd be up the creek for eternity.

The other option was not much more pleasant: I could drive over to WZIZ, walk into Wales's office and tell him I was leaving in two days. Boom, career gone. I'd never get another job in the industry after a stunt like that because if there is one quality you have to have if you work in TV news it is dependability. I had some savings. I could probably get by for a few months, maybe even half a year, without losing the condo and the car. And then I would be starting from scratch in some other line of work.

It occurred to me, as I took a shower, got dressed, made my way downstairs into the garage and drove to the station, that it was perfectly easy to go through life saying you believed in God as long as there was no price to pay. You believed in God, you didn't believe in God — maybe it would make a difference after you died, but saying one thing or saying the other didn't make much difference in terms of actual, immediate consequences in your ordinary walking-around life. And then something like this happened, and you were forced to put your money where your mouth was, as it were. Walk the walk, so to speak. I'd grown up with stories about people who had to pay a price for their faith. My dad was always telling me about his relatives in Poland (our real name had been Tzomascevic before the people at Ellis Island Americanized it), who'd never tried to hide the fact that they were Jewish and had been tortured and killed for it. And my mom was big on the early Christian martyrs, who could have avoided being burned at the stake or eaten by lions, just by saying, "Nope, not me. I don't believe in the guy," but hadn't done that.

I don't mean to compare myself with those people, but for once in my life I believed I could relate to them. And even though I could understand that there was an important difference between being eaten by a lion or sent to the camps and losing my job, still, the point was I would be paying a price for saying I believed in something. And, usually, in this blessed nation at least, you can go a whole lifetime without having to do that.

At the office I went to my desk and procrastinated. Shuffled papers. Listened to phone messages. Checked e-mails. At last, I got up and went into the men's room, stood at the sink and looked at myself in the mirror. And then I pronounced, pretty quietly, these strange words: "Nice face. Trustworthy face." And then, two seconds later, "But what good is it going to do you?" And then I unlocked the door and walked out, still in a kind of trance, toward my boss's office.

★ ★ ★ TEN ★ ★ ★

After making it past Enrica Dominique, Wales's martial-artist secretary, I knocked, opened the door to the corner office, and saw that my boss was standing next to his gracious wife, Esmeralda van Antibes, and the two of them were hard at work taking things from his shelves and drawers and placing them into cardboard boxes.

"Hi, Boss. Hey, Ezzie," I said, cool as could be. I closed the door quietly on Enrica Dominique's not very subtle snooping. "Let me guess," I said. "You got promoted to general manager and you're moving to the big office upstairs."

Wales did not look at me. Struggling clumsily with a sheet of bubble wrap, he was packing his lone golf trophy—eighth place, net, at the local muni. His wife of only a year or so, a mostly blonde, bejeweled, braceleted creature I liked quite a lot, said, "He quit."

"Quit what?"

"You're as much of a moron as you ever were," Wales said, but I had learned, over the years, that he spoke that way only to people he admired.

"He resigned this morning," Esmeralda said calmly.

"You can't quit, Boss, and you can't resign either. *I'm* the one who's quitting."

They did not seem to hear me, or to care. They went on wrapping and boxing, as if intent on clearing out twenty-one years of memories in half an hour.

"I'm giving my notice."

I waited. No response.

"Two days."

Nothing.

"I've been hired to work on a presidential campaign."

Still nothing. Wales finished with the bubble wrap and then sat in his chair with a kind of tired-of-you sigh, at a desk that was now as empty as it had been the day he moved in. He picked up an unlit cigar he'd set down on one of the boxes, and then, at last, looked at me. Esmeralda, ten years younger and in possession of more energy, went on working.

"Sit," Wales said, pointing the Habana at the chair opposite him. When I was seated he put his elbows on the desk and leaned forward so that his face was only a few feet from mine. You could see the signs of age, the jowls forming at the sides of his mouth, the wrinkles around his eyes. Rumor had it that Wales had considered a life in the clergy as a young man, but for those of us who met him in later years that seemed preposterous. Well into middle-age he'd been the quintessential vodka-and-party-loving guy who enjoyed deep-sea fishing, sports on TV, and the company of women. And then, a month after we threw him a surprise fiftieth birthday party, he announced he was marrying the very well-off Esmeralda van Antibes, with whom he'd been keeping company for a year or so. Ezzie had so much money we assumed Wales would retire and fish and golf and watch the NBA. When I saw him packing, naturally enough I assumed that time had come.

"He'll be here in five minutes," Wales said.

"Who?"

He blinked. Without releasing me from his hard gaze, he brought the cigar up to his mouth, took a pretend puff, and lowered it again. "How does it feel," he asked me in the most sincere of tones, "to be stupid?" He paused, as if waiting for an answer, though I knew he wasn't. "You could have had a nice career in this business. The face, the voice, the man-of-the-people attitude. But," he tapped his graying head, "not enough upstairs. Low octane. Short weight. Small thread count. You grasp my general meaning?"

"Everything I know I learned from you," I said, and Esmeralda half turned her head toward me and bent her pretty mouth into an approving smile.

"Jesus," Wales said.

I misunderstood. I thought he was being critical of me for my decision to quit and was, as my mother would have said, taking the Lord's name in vain. So I defended myself with a line I'd been rehearsing during the drive to the station. "At some point in a man's life he has to make the tough choices and stick by them. I know it seems nuts. But this opportunity came up and it felt like the right career move at the—"

"Jesus will be here in three or four minutes," Wales said, still skewering me with the baby blues.

"We spoke," I said, too surprised to be thinking. "Just recently. An hour ago or less."

"And you decided, on the basis of that conversation, to torpedo your career and work on his so-called campaign, am I right?"

"Yeah, sure, but 'torpedo,' you know, that's a bit strong."

"I know."

"Good."

"Know why I know?"

I shook my head. Esmeralda turned to look at me. I was suddenly uncomfortable.

Wales said, "Because I'm doing it, too."

"Doing what?"

He kept looking at me in what appeared to be disbelief. Slowly, relentlessly, an understanding was coming over me. It would be years before Wales would reveal, after several martinis at my daughter's first birthday party, that he'd had what he called "a visitation" shortly after the miracle in Fultonville. He'd been taking a lunchtime walk in a city park and Jesus had come to him as "more or less a ghost," as he put it. That was why he'd steered me in the direction of the Amelia Simmelton story when producers at the other two stations in town had chosen to ignore it.

Wales turned to his wife. "Can't be sure," he said to her, "but if I had to guess, I'd say there's a light coming on in there. A small light, but a light all the same."

"You're joking about quitting, correct?" I said, but just then we heard a knock on the door. Two sharp raps. I thought it must be Enrica Dominique, making sure I was not overstaying my welcome. She was the daughter of a Roller Derby queen. She ran a Thai kickboxing school at night, and she guarded Wales's privacy as if it were the crown jewels.

Wales yelled, "Come on in," but before that he jabbed his eyes back into me and said, "We're on the campaign, too, Einstein. Ezzie and I."

Which was, and let me not hyperbolize this, the astonishment of my life.

★ ★ ★ ELEVEN ★ ★ ★

It had been a day of shocking news, and I was still wobbling from that latest blow, when who should walk into the room but my friend from Pete's Cafe. He was dressed—and these were the kinds of things I noticed—in a stunning gray suit and red power tie against a white shirt. Diamond-shined black tassel loafers on his feet. Cufflinks. An elegant gold and sapphire ring on his left hand. His hair had been slicked straight back, and it looked like he'd just shaved, or had just come from the makeup room. For one awful, awful second, I was revisited by the stray, buzzing, nasty thought that the man was moving in on my territory: he'd tricked me into quitting so he could take my spot at ZIZ, plus he was after Zelda. He'd done his research, played his hand perfectly, and here he was, pushing me out the door.

I stood up, and saw that Wales was on his feet, too.

"Cease with the formalities," Jesus said. "Let us get to work." He sat in the high-backed leather chair in the corner, the chair nobody but Wales ever sat in. Wales not only failed to object to this, he brought a chair over closer to Jesus, carried one over for Esmeralda, and, scowling, motioned for me to scoot over, as well. We formed a little half circle around the man who, after my brief flirtation with true faith and potential martyrdom, I was starting to doubt again. Maybe it was because of the image I'd held in my inner eye all those years. This particular Jesus simply did not fill the bill. He looked more like the character they always found to play the leg breaker in mob movies, though trimmer, classier, better dressed.

I have to admit he brought a certain something into the room with him. Same thing I'd noticed at lunch. A presence. I glanced at Wales and was shocked to see him looking at the Good Visitor with reverence painted all over his sagging face. Esmeralda looked like she was, as Zelda liked to say, about to have a tremble.

"We announce next week," Jesus announced. "Wednesday." He pointed at Wales, "campaign manager"; at Esmeralda, "fundraising and etcetera"; then turned his eyes to me and paused before pointing at my chest and saying, "And you of little faith . . . security."

"What? You? I thought—" I was hurt at first. I'd hoped for bigger things.

"You were hoping for bigger things," Jesus said, and he winked at me with the eye that Wales and Ezzie couldn't see.

"Yes, frankly."

"You'll do an excellent job," Jesus said. "I'm thinking of making Zelda my press liaison. What's your opinion on that? You know her better than anyone here."

I sensed some kind of trick. I did battle with a wave of jealousy.

"Good thought," I managed.

He nodded. "And I want your parents on the team."

"You have to be kidding."

"Not kidding in the slightest. I want them on the team."

"My father's a Jew."

"We have that in common. My dad was also a Jew." He smiled. Wales and Ezzie were smiling, too.

"The Jew part isn't that important," I said. "The important part is that he's a nut. My mother's even nuttier. And the two of them know as much about running a political campaign as they know how to, I don't know. . . ."

"I want them. And I want your brother, Stab, too."

"Stab's, you know. Different."

Jesus looked at me for a few seconds, then turned his eyes to Wales. "Everything you said about him is true," he said.

"What did he say about me?"

My question was ignored. I was beginning to harbor the suspicion that this whole thing was an exercise in ego destruction, and that my ego was exhibit A.

Jesus said, "We will announce one week from today. Here, in West Zenith. Banfield Plaza. Noon. Get everything set up."

"Banfield Plaza?" I said. "There were two shootings there last month. Even the news guys are afraid to go there. Even in daytime. Even Randy Zillins, who'd go anywhere for a story, and who hangs out at Pinkie's Shooting Range with some of the wildest guys on—"

"Zillins is not to be considered part of our operation," Jesus said firmly.

"Well, I'm glad we're particular, at least."

Jesus ignored me again and turned to Ezzie. "The Simmeltons are on board?"

"They are," Ezzie replied. "I saw Nadine today at the club. She said they'll make an initial contribution of two million."

"All right. That's a start. No one else knows about this, I hope I'm right in assuming? No leaks?"

We all shook our heads.

Jesus got to his feet and motioned for us to stay seated. "Think about Enrica Dominique for your team," he said to me as he headed toward the door. "I could barely get past her."

"But—"

"Noon, Wednesday. Banfield Plaza. Get a few dozen banners printed up that say "Jesus for America." Use the Rodriquez Brothers for the printing. They're friends. Go in peace, the meeting is ended."

When he had closed the door, we sat there, not moving. "One question," I said to my boss after a minute had passed. "Why does he ask if there have been any leaks? I mean, if he is who he says he is, he already knows if there have been any leaks, correct? Is there something I'm missing?"

"Always," Wales said. "He's trying to act human. He tries to limit himself, same as last time."

"So he's God and he isn't, simultaneously. Right?"

"Probably," Esmeralda said to me—she was a good, kind, attractive woman, too sweet for Wales, many of us thought—"probably we shouldn't expect to understand those types of things. Just take them on faith."

"Yeah," Wales agreed, "especially for those of us with small brains. You follow?"

"What do I know about security?" I said. "That's what worries me."

"Use your creativity. Talk to your vaunted 'police sources.' Learn as you go."

"Right, okay. You're the campaign manager. I'm just in charge of—"

"Keeping God alive," said Esmeralda sweetly.

★ ★ ★ TWELVE ★ ★ ★

Zelda always kept the hour between one and two open. At one o'clock I was in the hallway outside her office, and when she opened the door she hurried over, wrapped me in a tight hug, and held on. "I'm afraid," she whispered in my ear. She seemed to be shaking.

I said, "I know, I know. Don't worry. It's going to be fine. We'll work it out, don't worry." We stepped into her office and sat on the couch, close to each other.

"I went to the station this morning and resigned," I said, thinking that might ease her fears.

She put a hand on my thigh and squeezed hard. "I love you, I love you, I love you."

I looked at her: the wide-set, dark eyes, the turned-up nose, the pretty mouth that could bloom into a smile as bright and lovely as sunlight pouring down into a mineshaft where you'd been stuck for a month. The intelligence, the goodness, the compassion shining there. It was not a small thing, given my history, to have a woman like that saying she loved me. Not a small thing.

"Jesus showed up," I said. "Or Hay-Zeus, or whatever he calls himself."

"He *did!*"

I nodded. "He came into Wales's office when we were all in there — me, Walesy, Esmeralda. He called me the man of little faith."

"Really?"

"He said we're kicking off the campaign a week from today. You're the press liaison."

"Press liaison? I don't know the first thing about dealing with the press."

"Right, but he thought you'd be great at it. I'm in charge of security, if that makes you feel any more secure."

"Not much, honestly."

"Well, how about this, then: He wants my parents to be involved. My brother Stab, too. Wales. Ezzie. Maybe even Enrica Dominique. We've raised a couple million dollars already."

"Then it's serious now. It's real."

I felt a zipper of chill go running up my arms.

"What's wrong, Russell?"

"Nothing."

She took hold of my chin in one hand and turned my face to her, lovingly, gently. But the eye contact was intense. "Full honesty."

I looked away, looked back. "You haven't met him," I said.

"I know. I can't wait."

"Right. But I have met him. Twice now. And, well, you know, there are certain aspects of this that don't exactly inspire confidence."

"For example."

"For example, he doesn't fit the description."

"What description?"

"He's saying he's *Jesus*, Zel. Jesus. The Big Guy, you know, *God* for a lot of people."

"And?"

"And he doesn't fit the description. I mean, don't get me wrong, he seems to know things about people that I'm surprised he knows. And when he comes into the room you can definitely feel a sort of, I don't know, a power or something. But, look, I feel that when the Patriots' quarterback comes into the room, for God's sake. I've felt it with nurses on kids' wards, with—"

"Your friend, what's-her-name, for example."

"Yes, my friend what's-her-name, who you also haven't met. And stop being jealous, that's my territory. Listen, he's an impressive guy, but look at what we're doing. I'm quitting my job. We're about to go public in support of this guy, saying he's Jesus, I mean, *the* Jesus. What does that do for my reputation, and for your reputation if we're wrong? If it's some kind of scam? Have you considered that?"

She looked at me. She sat back on the sofa and just looked. It was a look that made you feel like you were three and a half and had knocked over your bowl of cereal for the second time. "You're wavering," she said, after a few bad seconds.

"Probably."

"Do you have any idea how much wavering I see in this room?"

I shook my head.

"Husbands who say they want to love someone forever, and then they waver. Mothers who decide to have children and bring them up in a loving home, and then they waver. Men and women who promise this, and promise that, and they keep to the promise for a month or a year or ten years and then something happens, life happens, and they wobble, they waver, they crack and crumble. You know what that does to the people in their lives?"

"I was divorced, you know that. It happens. It's called a mistake, bad judgment, youth. It doesn't mean—"

"I'm not talking about breaking up with a crazy or abusive spouse, or when a marriage is unhealthy. I'm talking about faith. Constancy. You're worried about your reputation. Do you know what Gandhi said?"

I shook my head.

"He said, 'A man of courage can do without a reputation.'"

"That sexist bastard," I said. "And all these years I thought he was a cool guy."

She almost smiled. Almost. After a second or two she said, "You asked me to marry you this morning. Are you going to waver on that, too, Russ?"

"Never."

"Maybe I don't fit the description."

"It's a different situation. You're not claiming to be God. You didn't ask me to quit my job and help you run for president. You've got a nicer body than he does—"

"Be serious, please."

"All right."

"What, exactly, would he have to do in order for you to believe he is who he says he is? Think about it, Russ, two miracles and a dream sent to me—that isn't enough?"

"It should be. I mean, it would be, and he seems like he knows my whole history . . . but, in person, I don't know, maybe I've met too many con artists in this business. Maybe it's what I said this morning: I'm too egotistical to want anybody else to have all that attention. Or maybe it's the opposite: I mean, really, if God came to earth, would he come to *me*? Would he come to West Zenith, of all places?"

"West Zenith is *exactly* the type of place he'd come to. And maybe you're more special than you give yourself credit for. Maybe we all are. Maybe that's the whole point—that we're all, you know, we're all *worthy* of something like this happening to us even though we don't believe it. We're caught up in our failings, our bad stuff. We walk around feeling we should be better all the time because the society is constantly sending us that message. Not thin enough, not young enough, not nice-looking or rich enough. . . . I see it in this room every day, every hour."

"That argument has a certain appeal," I said.

"You can't take anything seriously, can you."

"Sure I can. When the kid fell off the fire escape, when I heard about that, I took it seriously."

"Because you were able, for those few seconds, to relate to your own damaged inner child. The only compassion you can have for yourself is via someone else's story."

"Stop please."

"Don't you see what's happening?" she said. "God comes to you, in the flesh, and you reject him. And why? Because of your profound but subtle lack of esteem for yourself. You're placing limits on yourself that aren't there. It has to do with your childhood trauma and, before that, your parents' childhood trauma."

"Zel. Stop. Please."

"All right. But I'll say one more thing: You don't have a lot of time to decide. You have a week to get ready for what's essentially going to be a mob scene."

"And to go see my parents. Which is more daunting, actually."

"Take me with you," she said. "They're my future in-laws, I should meet them. Or are you wavering on that, too?"

I was shaking my head.

"Not wavering? Or not taking me to see them?"

"Not wavering. I love you. You can take that to the bank and make a deposit and get the interest on it for a hundred years. I love you, I want to marry you, and have kids with you, and live with you until I die. Okay?"

The smile had come out. The mineshaft was lit up again, and you could see your way up and out of it and into full daylight.

"And the other part? Jesus?"

"I need another hour or so," I said.

I hugged and kissed her and went out of her office and down to the street, and I walked around for a while, aimlessly, which is what I do when I'm upset, just looking at the world going by, people hurrying here and there, cars, trucks, buses, skateboards. I went into American Soldier's Memorial Park and sat on a bench, with a handful of street people scattered around on the lawn, and the leaves on the trees shimmering in the sun. I wasn't thinking, exactly. It was more that my mind was twirling and coasting, flitting this way and that, a tiny fish caught in a tidal pool. After a time, I don't know how long, a guy came and sat down not far from me on the bench. Dreadlocks, rotten old sneakers, stained pants, a flannel shirt on in the June warmth. He asked for some change, and I reached into my pocket and handed him a ten-dollar bill. I could see the surprise on his face for an instant, and then he covered it over as if he didn't want to appear too grateful, or thought he didn't deserve anything more than a couple of quarters. And then he hurried off to buy whatever it was he was going to buy with it—a hamburger, a hit, a bottle.

So did it all boil down to what Zelda had said? Were these guys out here, and these women walking the streets at night in their short shorts and halter tops, these kids shooting each other in Fultonville and Hunter Town—was it all an elaborate dramatization of the fact that they had no "esteem" for themselves, as she put it? Did the drunks drink, and the whores go out on the sidewalk, and the high school girls smoke another chunk of crack just to prove to themselves—or to their parents—how worthless they were? And the people who understood they weren't worthless—the Amelia Simmeltons and Alba Seuniers and Steven "Stab" Thomases of the world— how did they get that way?

I did not know. I did not know. I did not know.

✴ ✴ ✴ THIRTEEN ✴ ✴ ✴

On days when I knew I would be driving down to North Salem to see my mom and dad, I always awoke with a mix of feelings, as if anticipation, love, and anxiety had been blended together into a lotion, overnight, and some mysterious spirit of the dream had applied it to my skin from hairline to toenails. And that was before an ordinary visit. Imagine what it felt like to add an engagement announcement to that (they had never met Zelda). And then, of course, on top of everything else, there was what I thought of as the Jesus Stuff.

Adding to the fun was the fact that Dukey McIntyre, Ada Montpelier's boyfriend and the reputed father of her child, had been assigned to my security crew by Jesus himself, had called to introduce himself, and was already making me crazy. Thrilled by his new responsibilities, he'd taken to phoning the condo every ninety minutes with progress reports. He had friends in the Panthers, a local motorcycle "club" (supposedly enlightened, we'd done a story on them; they had refreshing rules like Members Are Not Allowed to Punch or Kick Their Girlfriends; Members Are Not Allowed to Sell Drugs to Kids in Grade School), and they'd agreed to park their bikes in a ring around the center of Banfield Plaza, with openings for "VIPs" to come in and out. An hour and a half later he called with more news: The guys at Dermott's, a rough bar on Versifal Street, had chipped in time and money to build a stage for Jesus to stand on when he spoke, and they would be "taking up positions" on all sides to make sure no "punks" gave our candidate any trouble. And so on.

Though she had not yet met Jesus, Zelda told her clients she'd be taking an indefinite leave of absence. This was traumatic for her, naturally:
she'd built up a successful practice over the years, and felt almost a parental responsibility to the people she counseled. Later that day, she'd met
with Wales and, on his instructions, started contacting press outlets. Zel
told me that the major newspapers, TV and radio stations, and national
magazines were being appropriately cautious. No stories would be printed
or aired for another day or so, until they'd had a chance to check out the
accounts of the miracles, get corroborating witnesses. They knew that
once this particular cat was let out of the bag it would instantly mutate
into a thousand prowling tigers, and no one, no trainer with a whip and a
piece of steak, was going to be able to get them back in. During my years
in the business I'd developed a kind of sixth sense about these things, and
now it was as if I could hear a million voices whispering to each other in
a circle that kept expanding outward from Banfield Plaza.

Zelda and I did not say much about it, but something was different
between us, expectation tinged with fear. I liked it, when the fear part
wasn't too strong. I think she liked it, too. We had new meaning to our
lives, not to mention the engagement, of course (no ring yet, but I'd given
her a pair of sapphire earrings to make her feel better about suspending
her practice, and she loved them).

But it wasn't all joy and fun. Getting dressed on Saturday morning
before heading out to see my parents, I found that my hands were shaking as I buttoned the collar of my shirt. There was a war going on inside
me. By that point I had made my commitment to Jesus, really I had,
and to Zelda and Wales and Ezzie, and even, in a certain way, to Dukey
McIntyre, too. I felt part of a community of impossible hope. It was like
being a Red Sox fan prior to 2004. But, even though I was officially out
of the TV business, I was still living the story as it swelled and rolled,
still doubting it, checking it, wondering what the twist might be. Because
the journalist in me said there had to be a twist. If this Jesus was really
perfect, that part of me reasoned, he would have stayed up in heaven and
left us to our swagger and sleaze.

Dressed and ready, wrestling with my doubts, thinking about the day ahead, I went down to my convertible with all that in my mind, and waited for the other shoe to drop, as it were.

The shoe dropped as I drove up to Zelda's apartment building. She was standing on the sidewalk in her best dress, and Jesus was standing close beside her. It was 7:45 in the morning, and so, naturally, my first thought was that they had spent the night together. I understand that this might seem like a weird first thought to have. We were, after all, dealing with Jesus and not some local Romeo; with my engaged and faithful girlfriend, not some cheap, to use my father's word, *slattern*. But the unfortunate truth is that Esther Gilbanda, my ex, had engaged in some extracurricular activity after we'd been married for three or four months. Not surprisingly, that activity had led to our divorce. And not surprisingly either, it had left a deep bruise on my psyche. I had been so sure of Esther's faithfulness, so sure she was happy in the marriage, so stunned when I found out she was cheating, that I wondered sometimes if I would ever really get over it. I mean, how did you trust your judgment after that? How did you know it wouldn't happen again? You had to go on faith, and do the best you could. In that way, I guess, getting married was like believing in God, or in some Great Spirit, or even just believing the world ultimately revolved around goodness. Unless you came upon your spouse *in flagrante delicto*, as they say, it was hard to be a hundred percent sure one way or the other. And unless God gave you absolutely undeniable proof of His existence, well, you were always left with a nagging doubt.

Anyway, I'm making excuses for being jealous, but I think they're good excuses. So when I came driving up West Broadway toward Zel's condo and saw her standing out on the curb with a handsome miracle worker right next to her, at quarter to eight in the morning, when he hadn't been part of our day's plan . . . it wasn't a stretch for me to wonder if maybe something not that beautiful was going on.

But I didn't say anything, naturally. Accusing Jesus of sleeping with your fiancée is not the suavest thing you can do, especially not in front of said fiancée. So I kissed Zelda when she got into the car, and I reached back between the seats to shake Jesus's hand as if I'd been expecting all along that he would introduce himself to Zelda early in the morning and then join us for our trip to North Salem.

"Are you sure you don't want to sit in front, Lord?" Zelda asked, turning around to look at him and moving a lock of hair off her face in a way that I—and I think many other men—found particularly sexy. "Your legs are so much longer than mine."

I felt a twinge of something bad.

"Enough with the 'Lord' stuff," Jesus said. "And I am fine right here."

"What should we call you then?" I asked. "You have a nickname or anything? How about Jeez? Or Jeepers Cripes?"

Unfortunately, that is what happens to me when I get upset about something—jealous, nervous, anxious about seeing my family. I get "wise," as we used to say where I grew up, though *unwise* would probably be a better word. I get fresh-mouthed, as Zelda calls it.

Zelda reached across and punched me on the shoulder. It did not escape my notice that, until Jesus had come into the picture, she had not been the hitting type, and now twice in the last few days I'd gotten a whack.

"What? It's a reasonable question."

"It's disrespectful."

I noticed, in the rearview, that Jesus was looking out the window as if he was studying the sorry spectacle of West Broadway—its chain doughnut shops and pawn shops and signs saying you could sell your gold and jewelry there, or cash your checks there; its boarded-up storefronts and litter and men wrapped in blankets sitting with their backs against a building in the sun.

"Just Jesus is fine," he said.

"I thought it was Hay-Zeus."

"For Spanish speakers, it is."

I stole another glance, thinking he might be making some kind of joke, but it was hard to tell. His handsome face gave away nothing.

"What about the Italian-American vote?" I asked, since my mother was of that blood. "Shouldn't we say *Gesu Christo* when we're in certain neighborhoods?"

There was a patch of uncomfortable silence.

"Is he always so much trouble?" Jesus asked Zelda, after a minute.

By that point, she had turned away from me in disgust. But to her credit she said, "No, not always." And then, "Only when he's going to see his family."

"Some residue of stress there, I take it," Jesus said. "I will help you with that if you want."

"Okay. Thanks. And sorry about the wiseass stuff. It's a little hard for me that you don't want to be called Lord or God or anything. I don't think it's going to help the campaign, either, to tell you the truth. I mean, if you perform miracles and call yourself Jesus, people are going to expect you to be a cut above the ordinary Bob Dole or Mike Dukakis."

"I am aware of that."

"All right. Just advising. If you want me to stick to security issues, I will."

By this point we had gotten our toll ticket and were climbing the ramp that led to the interstate. I knew from hundreds of other trips along this road that there would be a stretch of sorrow before we got out into the countryside: abandoned factories ringed West Zenith like the ruins of old fortifications, their brick walls alive with a garish graffiti of red and blue paint, gang tags, comic book faces, political slogans, or phrases expressing a kind of modern American angst. BRING MY JOB BACK HOME! was a typical one. The rooftop water tanks were rusty; the windows had more broken panes than whole ones; the parking lots had become vast tar plains littered with shards of glass and old tires. Once, something good and solid had been made inside; now it was all broken bricks and scraps of crap. I wondered what he thought of it. The Big Man, I mean.

"No," Jesus said. "I don't want you to stick to security. And, Zelda, I don't want you to stick to press relations. You are two of my chief advisors. As a matter of fact, I decided to travel with you today in order to talk strategy. I value your opinions."

We were silent, both of us warmed by the remark. Jesus could do that,

I was starting to see, could shed his all-business personality in an instant and make you feel like he'd known you all your life. I stole another glance in the mirror, and it seemed to me that his features had softened. The high cheekbones and slightly bent nose, the high forehead beneath the shock of black, swept-back hair, the large crooked mouth—they had taken on, by some otherworldly magic, a glint of mellowness. In full realization that I am driving onto thin ice with a forty-ton tank here, risking the perpetual ire of the *appropriatists*, as Wales calls them, I will suggest that Jesus was able to move from a traditionally masculine roughness to a traditionally feminine kindness, though, of course, those terms are outdated, offensive, and possibly useless. Still, that's what I thought. He seemed like a man's man sometimes, the way he talked, carried himself, the things he said. He might have had a hockey helmet on and been sitting in the penalty box, spitting between the gap where his front teeth used to be. And then, in the course of a single sentence, all that changed and he was, well, almost motherly . . . in the best sense.

"If you like advice, you've come to the right couple," I said, and I could feel Zelda look at me when I used that word. "Because we're two of the most opinionated people we know."

"And two of the smartest," Jesus added.

"Not exactly. Zel here is no bright bulb, as you've probably already realized. Yours truly, on the other hand—" I got that far before she whacked me again, harder this time, though in a loving way.

"I want your take on where the campaign stands," Jesus said.

"But you know all that already, Lor—" Zelda caught herself before pronouncing the whole title. She had swung around in her seat again so she could look at him. "You know everything, don't you?"

"I let there be gaps," Jesus said, still gazing out the window, where the scenery had changed now to thick hardwood forest and hills. It's a beautiful part of the world, western Massachusetts, very different from the eastern part of the state, geologically and politically. Driving from the woodsy west to the energetic east, where I'd been raised, always made me slightly anxious, as if the world around me was moving faster and faster and I had to work harder just to keep up.

"We don't understand that part," I said. "The gaps, I mean."

"On one level, I know everything, yes, of course. On another, while I am here, I limit myself. Purposely. I have detached myself from the Great Spirit, the Father and Mother Spirit, and taken this form, which, I have to tell you, is not my favorite of the physical shapes—"

"But you're *wonderful*-looking," Zelda broke in.

Another bad twinge. I tried to tell myself it was because she'd never known her real father.

Jesus went on as if he hadn't heard. "What you might not understand is that the rules of this planet are fixed. Just as water freezes at thirty-two degrees Fahrenheit, for example, or earth makes its rotation in approximately twenty-four hours, there are certain spiritual laws here, set in place even before the physical creation of the sphere that houses and nourishes you. To a certain extent, I can bend those laws whenever I want to—perform a miracle, for example. But if I eliminate them altogether for my own purposes, then everything is upended and my taking human form is purposeless. I have to operate within the confines of your understanding, your thought system, even, for the most part, your physical limitations."

"But why the 'have to'?" I couldn't keep myself from asking. "That's the tough part, for me at least. It seems to me you could do anything you damn well please."

"My mother has so ordained," he said.

"Your mother?" Zelda sounded excited. "In the Bible you're always speaking of the father. 'My father in heaven,' and so on."

"Same thing. Mother, father, me. Same thing."

"The holy trinity," I suggested.

"Sure," Jesus said, "if you like that model. The whole point of the teachings I gave in those days was to try to break you people out of your insistence on identifying with the physical body. All suffering comes from that identification, that should be obvious enough. They have been altered, unfortunately, but the original meaning of my words had to do mostly with that." He paused for a moment. I saw him staring out the window, and it did seem to me that he was communing in some way with the trees and stones there. *This is my body. That is my body. I am not my body.* I had a little stretch of wishing I'd paid more attention in Sunday school.

"Listen," Jesus said. He leaned forward so his head was closer to us. "I do not want to get too far into this right now. Later, if you like, we can take a walk in the desert or something and have a private tutorial. I would be happy to do that. But right now, we have a couple of hours together on the road, and it might be our last quiet time for a while, so I want you to fill me in, to the extent possible, on the situation I am getting into."

Zelda and I looked at each other. "You first," we both said at the same moment.

"Okay," I said. "I'll do the Republicans and you do the Democrats, deal?"

She nodded. "You first."

"Okay. But I want to preface my remarks by saying that these are crude approximations."

"Fine, it is the big picture I want. And be blunt."

"That's never a problem for him," Zelda noted.

"The big picture," I said, "is that, at this point, less than five months before the actual election, you are way behind the eight ball. Everyone else has had at least a year's head start, raised a lot of money, been through a series of tough primaries, contentious debates. You're going to be seen as a Jesus-Come-Lately, if you want the harsh truth."

"I do."

"All right, then. The good news is that the two main people you'll be up against are not exactly. . . ."

"Divine," Zel put in when I hesitated.

"Right, divine. On the Republican side, you have Marjorie M. Maplewith, hardass senator from Idaho. Her husband, the Reverend Aldridge Maplewith, is pastor of a megachurch in Boise, famous TV preacher, multimillionaire, proud Christian conservative. Marjorie inherited a fortune from two family-owned businesses—ski resorts and aluminum mining—and when she married Aldridge it was like two empires coming together. She calls herself the 'Proactive Protector' of American values and territory. Wants to double the size of the armed forces. Got a bill passed in Congress that increases penalties for any crime that harms a child, and people admire her for that. Molesters go to jail and never get out. Parents who hurt their kids in any serious way go behind bars for a decade, automatic loss of parental rights, that type of thing. She talks about privatizing government services, the post office, for example, so big business likes her. She picked Adam Clarence, congressman from West Virginia, for her running mate—he's basically a nobody, and people wonder if there is something behind the scenes, a favor owed or something. She's raised lots of money from a relatively small number of wealthy donors and conservative PACs, and she flies around the country to these carefully screened rallies that her staff puts together and then films in a way that makes them look larger than they really are. Well-oiled campaign. Ruthless in what she'll say about her opponent. Abortion is murder, period. Homosexuality is a sin against God and should be outlawed. She would also outlaw X-rated movies, shut down X-rated Internet sites—though nobody has been able to pin her down as to how she'd actually accomplish that. She believes there should be no public money for birth control education in this country or abroad. The government should get out of people's lives . . . except if it wants to eavesdrop on them for national security reasons. That enough, or you want more detail?"

"Fine for now," Jesus said.

"Your turn, Zel."

"Well," Zelda touched her new earrings in a contemplative way and then said, "in a nice twist, the Dems have put up a military man this year. Dennis Alowich. His grandfather emigrated from Lithuania, and the name was formerly Alowicious. There might be some Jewish blood there, we're not sure, but you can bet it's being looked into. Not the biggest military man, only a colonel, but a war hero who retired, invented a kind of insecticide called GreenBiscuit that kills bugs without harming people, made a fortune selling that, served as governor of Washington State for a term, secretary of veterans affairs for a term, then retired a few years ago to get his campaign together. Chose Senator John-John Maileah from Hawaii, because Maileah has been a party stalwart for thirty years and they owed him something. Not as much money as Marjorie Maplewith, a more pleasing personality by most estimates, but not as good a campaigner, and not as bright. He tends to hedge on the social issues when he's speaking to certain audiences, though he's generally progressive. Talks tough on national defense. His big issue is raising teachers' salaries, making schools safe, college affordable, etcetera. Plus, his wife is the famous soap opera star Lenda Elliot. She draws some big crowds and people like her."

"Fine," Jesus said.

"They have both bases covered pretty well," I said. "The right loves Maplewith; the left likes Alowich. What I'm wondering is, where do you fit in?"

"The middle," Jesus said.

"Everybody wants the middle. The closer you get to the middle, the more votes you get. Poli-Sci 101."

"I'm running on the beatitudes."

There was a stunned silence in the front seat. After a minute, I said, "You mean blessed are the meek and so on? Those beatitudes?"

"Exactly."

"They'll hammer you on national defense," Zelda said, voicing my thoughts. "They'll say, 'What do you propose if the U.S. is attacked again, turn the other cheek?' People will mock you."

"It would not be the first time."

"But would you say that, really? Turn the other cheek, I mean?"

"I said it before, didn't I?"

"But, if you're head of a nation and you do that, you'll . . . you'll go the way of Tibet. The enemy, whoever it is, will come in, torture people, kill millions, take over the country in a week. You have to get fifty or sixty million votes to be elected president. Say something like that and you won't get two million. It would be like saying, 'I want to take from the rich and give to the poor.' Nice idea. But a presidential candidate says that and he might as well run off to, I don't know, Venezuela or something. You'd be finished."

"Let me handle it," Jesus said. "I think I can say it in a way that makes sense to people. We're not going to hand the country over to the bad guys. I am not naive."

"I'm glad to hear you say there *are* bad guys."

"Of course there are."

"Why?" Zelda said.

"What do you mean, why?"

"Why are there bad guys? Why did you make them, or why did your mother and father make them? It's a personal question; it has nothing to do with strategy. I've always wondered. Every day I deal with people who've been raped, or abused, or abandoned by their spouse, or something like that. And I've always wanted to ask you why you let that happen?"

"The laws of earth," he answered. "It's not that way everywhere. Once you get off this troubled blue sphere, there is not so much pain. This is the sphere of suffering. It is something you all, individually, have to figure your way out of. A life here, in the eyes of most of the rest of creation, even the great blessing of a human life here, is not considered a day at the beach. You work harder than souls in most of the incarnations. You suffer more pain, and more different types of pain. You worry much more — especially in the industrialized societies, where true peace of mind is rare. A lifetime on earth is the equivalent of a difficult childhood. Eventually you grow out of it. What scars and lessons you carry forward from this childhood, that's completely up to you."

"But why do you allow it to be this way?"

"It is the law."

"But why can't the law have no pain in it? Why can't we all be happy to start out with? Why was there original sin or whatever it was? Adam and Eve and the apple, and so on?"

"Like this universe, you are engaged in a constant expansion of yourselves," Jesus went on. "That expansion takes effort. Pain is involved in that effort. I could go into more detail, but now is not the time."

"Why not? She's asking an important question."

"Too complicated for you."

"Even for me?" I said.

"Especially for you."

I looked in the mirror, and I was glad to see a smile at the corners of his mouth. So God had a sense of humor after all—all my golfing friends thought so.

"How about a hint, at least?"

"All right. When you have a dream, you feel it is absolutely real, correct?"

"Sure, sometimes."

"And then you wake up and you realize it was not absolutely real."

"Okay," I said. "So this is the dream."

"I have come, as I did last time, to show you how to awake from the dream."

"Into paradise," Zelda suggested.

"Yes, though even paradise is not static."

"It's like my work," she said. "Not to compare your work and my work, but my job is to help people move beyond the memories and bad thoughts that haunt them."

"A perfect analogy," Jesus said. "You cannot snap your fingers and bring them peace. They themselves must do the work, though you and others can help them. Similarly, the saints and angels are helping you. . . . I shall tell you more in future conversations."

"Why not now," I said.

"Because at the moment I am interested in things political. The rally on Wednesday, for one thing. How are security preparations going?"

I told him things were going well, which was more or less the truth, but Zelda gave me a funny look, as if I had just lied to God, and then an awkward silence fell over us for a few miles. We pulled into a rest area because Jesus said he had to use the facilities.

We made a bathroom visit, then rendezvoused out in the eating area. That same awkwardness sloshed around among us, as if we'd grown close there in the car, and it had made us—Zelda and me at least—self-conscious. I bought three cups of coffee (Jesus likes it black, with two sugars), and we were standing out in the fresh air when I said to him, "You should prepare yourself for the spiritual shock of meeting the Thomas clan. We're a bit . . . well, let me put it this way, I'm the most normal one of the bunch."

"I will not be meeting them today," Jesus said. He drank his coffee in gulps. "I am heading back to West Zenith now."

"Now? But we're going the other way."

"I shall hitch a ride."

"It's not safe," Zelda said.

"And I'm in charge of security. I won't let you."

That remark produced the first full smile I'd seen from him on that odd day. It was a phenomenal smile. His lips spread wide, revealing the perfect set of teeth. It made you happy to see that smile, made you hope for better things, and I began to think that maybe, just maybe, in spite of the beatitudes, he might do okay on the campaign trail.

"I will be fine," he said. "Remember, I would like to start out from Zenith on the day following the kickoff rally. Ask your father to set up a schedule, Russell. He is our transportation guru, our logistics man."

"Okay," I said, though what I wanted to do was take him by the lapels of his sport jacket and shout, "The transportation guy? My dad? He's lucky he can find his way home from work! Are you nuts!"

Jesus tossed his coffee cup in a trash barrel and put his hand on my right shoulder. I felt a tremor go through my body. Now, I should say that I had minimal experience with drugs, a few experimental moments in my college years, no inhaling, and so on. Lucky for me, I suppose, those experiments never resulted in any great thrill. But I had some experience with prescription painkillers, and I had used alcohol on a number of occasions to alter my mental state, so I was not unaware of the possibilities of chemical joy. His touch gave me a clearer sense of all that. It made me happy in a way I can't describe. Happy, optimistic, confident. It lasted maybe half a minute after he took his hand away.

"Everything is fine exactly as it is," Jesus said, before he walked away. For a few minutes after he touched me, I found that easy to believe.

We watched him cross three lanes of high-speed traffic, the median, and then three more lanes, as casually as if he were crossing a side street in a country town at six a.m. When he was safely on the other side, we got into my car and drove east.

✭ ✭ ✭ FOURTEEN ✭ ✭ ✭

It was only about twenty-five miles from the interstate rest area to the humble city of North Salem, where I had been born and raised and where my parents, Arnold and Maria Thomas, still lived. Given the city traffic, however, twenty-five miles translated into about forty minutes, plenty of time for Zelda and me to have one of the worst fights in our history.

Not fifteen seconds after we'd said our good-byes to Jesus and told him to be careful, she started in on me. "You are utterly, utterly disrespectful to him," she said, pushing herself to the far side of the front seat.

"I'm respectful in my own way. You're like a teenage girl with him. Lord this and Lord that. You're so *wonderful*-looking, Lord."

"Well, he is."

"Flattery is not what he wants. He said so himself."

"You're jealous."

"If so, I'm jealous of Jesus, and you're jealous of fifty-year-old nurses. And, anyway, what's there to be jealous about? He's Jesus. He's God. He's celibate and so on. I'm not that jealous of celibate type guys."

"He is not celibate."

"How do you know?" I asked, and at that moment I thought she was going to tell me they had spent the night together, and if she had said that, I was going to pull the car over to the side of the highway and hand her the keys and I was going to be done with all of it—Zelda and the engagement, Jesus and the campaign. I was going to take my savings out of the bank and go to Bermuda or Belize or Saskatchewan for a long vacation and then figure out a new existence for myself. A career as an atheist. A life on the streets. I was going to start my own hedge fund. That's how deep the old bruises were.

"I can feel that kind of thing in a man. Celibate is the last thing he is."

"Did he come on to you?" I asked, before I could stop myself. "Did you sleep with him or something?"

"You are disgusting. You really are."

"I'm just asking. And you're just not answering."

"Some questions are not worthy of being answered."

"And maybe some men are not worthy of being engaged to."

"I didn't say that. You have no faith in anybody, even yourself. It's like you're going through the motions with him. Did you really do the security stuff he asked you to?"

"Talk about questions that aren't worth being answered."

"Did you?"

"Of course I did. It's all set. Chief Bastatutta himself told me everything is in place. Did you do the press stuff?"

She nodded, arms crossed, eyebrows and mouth squeezed into unhappy lines. "I wish you'd let go and trust for once in your life," she said, in a less belligerent tone. "I've never given you one reason to doubt my faithfulness, not one, and you know it. He's performed miracles, and chosen you for the most important work of your life. And you're wavering inside."

"I quit my job, Zelda. That's not exactly a sign of wavering."

"You quit your job for me. You were afraid you'd lose me if you didn't believe in him."

"Would I have?"

"I don't know."

"Honest, at least."

"And I quit my *practice*. Do you have any idea what it feels like to leave forty-three people hanging, people who depended on you? Some of whom can barely get through a day without thinking of ending their lives?"

She started to cry. We went along for a few miles that way. The tall buildings at the center of the city came into view. The traffic thickened. I paid the toll and, after worming my way through the cars and trucks for another few miles, took the ramp that led to the bridge that crossed the river that separated North Salem from the sophisticated world, the world of atheists and journalists, the world of doubt, complications, moral relativity.

"Do you believe I love you?" Zelda asked, as we were in the middle of the span.

"Most of the time, yes."

"Do you believe it's possible for me to love you and worship him at the same time?"

"Sure, in principle. In reality, he's so damn human-seeming that it's hard for me. He's handsome. Dresses well. The guy would make a great anchorman."

"Can you let go of that anchorman obsession? Please! Do you think my dream in life is to be married to an anchorman?"

"No. It's my dream in life. Some of them are pretty cute. Nice bodies. Plus—"

"Stop it."

"I'm nervous. The family, you know."

"*I'm* the one who should be nervous, Russell. And you're changing the subject."

"I need a drink," I said.

"Changing the subject again."

"My dad makes a decent martini."

"And again. You can't give yourself totally to him. God comes to earth, you hold back. Is that what it's going to be like to be married to you? Are you going to be one of these husbands who lives behind his armor? Out with the guys all the time? Talking sports all the time? Sex at night and silence in the morning?"

"Am I like that now?"

"No, but the way you are with Jesus worries me."

"The way *you* are with Jesus worries *me*. And here we are at the street where my parents live, and we're right back to square one again. Perfect."

"Your fault," she said.

"And you're the one who knows. The therapist. The one who sits in judgment as people parade their troubles before you. As if you don't have any of your own."

Which was a terrible thing to say, a stupid thing. But I am not the finest human being in the world, and I'm not going to make myself out to be for the convenience of this story. In fact, after worrying over it, I have decided to include this personal material precisely because it demonstrates my, our, humanity. For me, for all of us, being around Jesus didn't suddenly turn us into perfect lovers and perfectly happy saints-on-earth. He came down into the grit and dust and nastiness of ordinary life, and, while it hardly seemed to touch him, the reverse was true also: his divinity did not wash off on us. We still had our own expanding to take care of, our own bad dreams to wake up from.

I found a parking space a block from my parents' house, locked the car, and we walked toward the front steps with a good three feet of air between us, Zelda smoothing out the front of her dress and me chewing the inside of my cheek and remembering I hadn't brought anything for a here-we-are gift. Which, in my family, was a kind of sin.

★ ★ ★ FIFTEEN ★ ★ ★

My parents live in a triple-decker. For those who don't know, a triple-decker is three boxy, one-story apartments stacked on top of each other, usually with three porches front or back and a flat roof. In the old days in North Salem, it was mostly recent immigrants who lived in triple-deckers: the Irish and Italians and Jews, the big families from Nova Scotia or Russia who didn't have much money and weren't quiet. My parents belonged to that basic demographic — Mom from a clan of dark-headed Neapolitans, and Dad's people from the no-man's-land that has been Poland and Ukraine at various times in history. He was a typical Jew: big, athletic, terrible with money. And she was a typical Italian Catholic: blue-eyed, and a lousy cook. Despite their own weirdnesses, they had been good parents to me, and excellent parents to my brother Steven Anthony Bernie Thomas, or Stab for short. Stab had been born with particular challenges and still lived with our parents in the triple-decker, which they now owned. They occupied the top floor and rented out the two lower apartments.

As we started up the wooden front steps I turned to Zelda and said, "My hair look okay?"

"Who cares?" was the answer.

"Thanks. You nervous, too?"

"Of course."

"They'll love you."

I was trying to patch things up, but when Zelda got mad she thawed at the rate of snow melting on a December day in Nome. Up the two flights of stairs we went in painful silence. The smells—old wood, brick dust, paint thinner, the tenants' cooking—swirled through my mind, stirring a million memories. On the small landing at the top, Zel moved aside so I could stand at the door, and I gave my signature knock—three quick taps, a pause, then two more.

I heard feet hitting the kitchen floor in a familiar fast rhythm, and my mother's voice, "Stab! Walk! Please!" and then the door was flung open and my twenty-seven-year-old baby brother had his arms wrapped around me and was trying to lift me off the floor while making loud grunting noises, "Unh! Unh! UNH!" He eventually let go, grabbed my hands one at a time, and kissed them with a loud smack, and his face, his misshapen face with the almond eyes and loose mouth and bad shave, was lit up like a wet street in front of a house on fire. "Ma, Russ is here! Pa, Russ is here!"

It was a greeting that restored your faith in your own lovability. It was pure Stab. I hugged him back, kissed him, and then, with one arm around his shoulders, turned so that we were facing Zelda, and I said, "Stab, I would like you to meet my fiancée, Zelda Hirsch. Zelda, my great brother, Stab."

"Mom! Dad!" Stab yelled out, and his big voice went booming back into the apartment, down the stairs we had just climbed, and out through the windows onto Shirley Street. "Russ is ENGAGED! His girlfriend is a FOXY BABE!"

Zelda reached out to shake my brother's hand, but Stab was having none of that. Almost exactly her own height, he grabbed her by the waist and pressed his lips to hers, and then put his face to one side of her neck and squeezed hard. I could hear the breath being pressed out of her lungs. The next sound was my mom's heels on linoleum. Another hug, another introduction.

"Oh, my sweetheart!" my mother said to no one in particular.

And then my father was behind her, booming out, "What's this? What's this news?" with so much relief in his voice that it made me laugh. Since the divorce, he'd been worrying that I'd gone gay. I knew it without a direct word being spoken, knew it from his anxious questions about girlfriends, about what had *really* happened between Esther and me, about what kinds of things I did when I wasn't working. I teased him mercilessly. "I go to the clubs in New York, Pa," I'd say. Or, "I'm always at the gym, getting buff." Or, "I have to hang up now, they're coming to interview me for *Out Media* magazine."

In any case, I introduced him to Zelda and could see that he appreciated her, in a manly way, and I even liked it that he almost broke my fingers with his fatherly congratulations.

"What are we doing, standing out here?" my mother squealed. "Come in, come in!"

In my family's house, you sat at the kitchen table even when you weren't eating. Stab ran and got the extra chair and held it for Zelda as she took her place there. He then stood behind her and put his hands on her shoulders. And she endeared herself to me still further, and to the rest of the Thomas family, by putting one of her hands over one of his and holding it there.

"All right already," Pa said. "I'll run down to Schwab's and get the champagne. We don't have any in the house. Ma's making blintzes."

"Lasagna," she corrected.

"Call and get Schwab's to deliver," I said. "We need to talk."

A sudden silence fell over the little kitchen, with its old porcelain sink and gas stove, its crucifix hung discreetly to the side of one cupboard, its Give Thanks for This Day calendar, on which a bright, happy saying was printed below the name of each month: EVERYTHING HAPPENS FOR A REASON AND THE REASON IS BLISS! and so on.

"What's the matter?" Mom asked.

And Stab, still proud that he'd been vouchsafed the facts of life a decade or so earlier, said, "Is she PG?"

Zelda laughed.

"No," I said. "We wanted to come and tell you about the engagement in person. You're the first ones to know. That's all."

"So I'll run down to Schwab's then," Pa said.

I put a hand on his arm. "Call, Pa."

Pa called. Mom had already assembled her weapons—the ricotta, the flat lasagna noodles, the jar of sauce—and Stab sat with us at the table and asked Zelda one hundred and five questions, the types of things my parents would have asked if they hadn't worried so much about her liking them: How had we met? What did she do for a living? How much money did she make? Had she been married before? Did she know that Russ had been married before and that "it hadn't worked out, that's all, nobody's fault, it just hadn't worked out." Did she want to have children and would she like him to tell her how they were made? And so on.

When Stab heard that Zelda's parents had died when she was young, and that she'd been raised in foster homes, he got tears in his eyes and kissed her on each ear. The nice thing about having someone like Stab in the family was that it was hard to keep secrets, and secrets are what eat families alive. Secrets, lies, the holding-back that grows larger and becomes habit as the years pass—we didn't have much of that, and so even though the family was *trays weird*, as the French say, we'd never had any major troubles, and we felt the bond when we were with each other, and I was hoping that Zelda was feeling it, too, on that sunny afternoon and that she was forgiving me for my lack of faith.

It took Mom a while to overcook the noodles and get the lasagna in the oven, and the kid from Schwab's about the same amount of time to hustle over with three bottles of good champagne. My father and I had a hand-slapping contest in the hallway as to who would pay, but I let him win, and soon we could smell the food cooking, and Stab was settling down, staring at Zelda and grinning a grin that would cheer up a dead man. In another little while we had the table set and were sitting around it with the food and Pa was raising a toast.

"To my famous son," he said, and then he caught himself and added, "to the older of my two famous sons. And to his beautiful, smart, nice bride-to-be, all the health and happiness on the earth."

"Amen," my mother said.

"And good sex!" Stab said—it was the kind of thing he said in all kinds of company, in the supermarket, in church, at funerals— and I took it as a good sign that everyone laughed.

Zelda was sitting next to me. After the toast, and after we'd made some progress on the lasagna—which wasn't half bad for a change; my mother must have rushed things, because she'd somehow avoided messing it up the way she usually did by deciding to be creative and tossing in a handful of chives, or some other original and amusing oddity she'd misheard on the Food Network—Zelda started nudging me with the side of her shoe. I thought, at first, it was a love touch, her way of making up. But after the second or third time, as each nudge became more forceful, I realized she was urging me to get the second big piece of news out onto the table.

I kept telling myself I'd raise the subject at the next pause in the conversation, or after the next bite of lasagna, or the next glass of champagne (Pa and I were both going at it a bit hard for that early hour). But I couldn't bring myself to break the happy mood by introducing the Jesus Stuff. At last, the meal was finished, my mother was at the freezer pulling out three or four cartons of ice cream, and Zelda had taken to more or less standing on my new $215 wingtips with the heel of her shoe.

I cleared my throat. "There's something else," I finally managed to say, and I could feel my father's eyes shift over to mine and lock on. My mother was doing what she always did when she got nervous: overfeeding people, bustling from cabinet to refrigerator, bringing bowls to the table, spooning out ice cream, four different flavors to a dish, without having asked what anyone liked.

"You got fired," Pa said. The dime-sized birthmark on the side of his chin twitched.

I shook my head. "I quit."

"I had a feeling. What—"

I held up a hand, looked at Zelda, told my mother to sit.

"She *is* PG!" Stab yelled.

"No, pal. She isn't. Not yet. When that day comes, I'll tell you first, okay?"

"Why did you quit?" my mother asked. "Were they giving you a hard time about your nationality?"

"He quit because we met Jesus," Zelda said.

It was her inaugural venture into Thomas family conversation, and though I know she was trying to make things easier for me, it was, let's say, a misstep.

"Oh, Christ," my father said. By now, his birthmark was jumping all over the place.

"Arnie, stop it. You know I hate that," my mother said.

"They're Jesus Freaks," my father practically shouted. Once he got started on an idea, once he formed an opinion, there was no stopping him. We'd be on vacation someplace, in a pool at some resort he couldn't afford to take us to but had taken us to anyway, and he'd start in with some other guy about nuclear power, or taxes, or unions, and he'd be off and running. He was especially opinionated on the subjects of religion and politics. The "fake Christians," he called certain groups of people. The "so-called Jews," the "nut-Muslims." "Mister Rich Republican with the Dyed Hair" was his name for our former governor. Like that.

"Pa, wait a second," I said, holding a hand up to him like a traffic cop at the intersection of Proselytize and Debate streets. "It isn't what it sounds like."

"Sure it is," he said.

"Pa, it isn't."

"Sure it is. You quit your job, you found Jesus. Plain as the nose on my face."

"Arnie. Stop. Now."

"Pa, willya?" Stab said.

"Gang up on me. Your brother and his wife are Jesus Freaks, he quits his job." He turned to me and the hairs in his ears were twitching. "How are you going to support a family, can I ask you that?"

I sat back and looked at him for a few seconds. I said, "Pa, Zelda doesn't know you. She'll think you're certified."

"Gang up, gang up," my father said.

Zelda put a hand on his arm, and he looked at her, startled. No one ever touched him when he got into these moods. "Mr. Thomas," she said.

"Arnie."

"Arnie. It came out wrong, what I said. Let Russ explain. Please."

He grumbled and muttered and gnashed his crowns. "All right. Sorry. Go ahead."

"Nice impression you make on your son's fiancée," my mother couldn't resist saying at that moment.

"Ma," I said, and though I said it kindly it brought tears to her eyes. Stab hugged her, my Dad downed the rest of his champagne and poured another glass. I was ready to storm out the door. In short, it was the usual family scene at 98 Shirley Street. I took a breath and squeezed Zelda's hand under the table. "Pa," I tried again. "Ma, listen."

"What about me?"

"Stab, my pal, I figured you were already listening. We have something funny to tell you. Not funny exactly, but different, okay?"

"Okay," Stab said, and then, "Pa thinks you're gay. So is Zelda really a man?"

"No, but thanks. Zelda's not a man."

"What's the Jesus crap?" my father said. "Spit it out."

"Arnie!"

"Don't go crying on me now!"

"STOP!" I yelled, so loud that even Zelda was startled. And then, more quietly, "Stop. All right? Listen, just listen. After I finish talking, if you think I'm a nut, that Zelda and I are nuts, say so. Say, 'You're a nut,' but for Pete's sake at least give me a chance to say what I have to say."

"Notice that he used the term, for *Pete's* sake," my mother remarked pointedly, to my father. "There are ways for smart people to express themselfs without taking the Lord's name."

"Start in on me," Pa said.

"STOP!" I reached out and refilled Zelda's champagne glass, and then mine. She drained hers. "What Zelda said is true, sort of."

"What do you mean, sort of?" she said.

I held up another hand to her. "A month or so ago a three-year-old kid fell off a fire escape in West Z, and everyone thought he was dead until some guy stepped out of the crowd and apparently brought him back to life. I covered the story. I was skeptical. Very skeptical. But then, a couple weeks later, a girl who was dying in the hospital up in Wells River was cured, and the same guy was at the center of the story. So I'm skeptical again, but maybe a little less. The rumors were flying, okay? A couple of the big media outlets mentioned it, but they were careful not to make a big deal of it, not to make it sound like it was real. Then this guy, the guy who apparently was doing the saving and the curing, he calls me on my private line. We had a sort of secret meeting. He was impressive, but I still wasn't sure about him until he sent a dream to Zelda, and told me in advance that he was going to send it."

"So?" my father said, when I paused for a breath. "This makes you quit your job?"

"He calls himself Jesus, Pa. He cured one kid and brought another kid back to life."

"A trick. He's a doctor with a complex. Big deal."

"I thought so, too, but now I don't think so anymore. I think he might be the real thing." Zelda kicked me under the table. "I think he *is* the real thing. I'm sure he is."

"You don't sound sure."

"He's running for public office and he asked me to quit my job and work on the campaign, so I did. Zelda left her practice, and now she's working on the campaign, too."

A stunned silence. They were all staring at me, though Stab's eyes would occasionally flicker over to Zelda and then back again. "You met God?" he asked, in a voice filled with awe.

"I think so. Yes. Or at least some kind of holy man. I did. We did. You can meet him, too."

My father leaned in. "Of all the things you ever did, Russ. All the stupid things—don't let me make a list in front of Zelda here—and I include the marrying of what's-her-name—"

"Esther!" Stab put in happily. My mother shushed him.

"This takes the absolute cake, okay? I think you might be a screwball, okay? A nut. Maybe it's a good thing for your fiancée to find that out now rather than later. Save everybody some pain. Sorry. Just what I think. I'm being up front about it."

My mother kept silent, looking at my father when he spoke, then at me, at Zelda, squeezing Stab's hand. Her pretty blue eyes made the rounds of the table and then settled on my father and caught fire. "You atheist," she said, icily.

He did not look at her. "I'm a Jew," he said.

"We're half Jewish," Stab explained to Zelda.

"You're not even a Jew," my mother said. "You're an atheist. An agnostic."

"Thanks for the 'not even,'" Pa said, still not looking at her. He seemed sad now. The spirit of celebration had drained out of him in the course of a few minutes.

"The first time, I could see," my mother went on, still burning him up with the eyes. "You people had your traditions. You interpreted it a different way. He was just a rabbi, a great teacher, nothing else. The first time, forgivable. . . . But now, if you do it again, Arnie. . . ."

"What, I'll go to hell?"

"Don't be so sure you won't."

"And what about you? You married a Jew, where does that leave you as far as your Jesus is concerned? He's going to make you the next pope? Oh, I forgot, sorry, no women allowed, right?"

My mother made the sign of the cross. It was the word *pope* that had done it. There were pictures of several popes in her bedroom, a fact that drove my father absolutely crazy. He had confided to me once that the papal pictures sometimes affected his ability to "perform," as he put it, and early on in their marriage he'd convinced my mother to turn them to the wall before the lovemaking got started.

"I raised my children Catholic," she said.

"Mistake number two."

Zelda cleared her throat. I could feel what I thought of as her therapist's personality rising into her face. It was a kind of calm detachment, almost as if she were stepping out of herself. Most of the time I liked it. But it could drive you nuts if you were fighting with her and she went into this detached zone. "Mr. Thomas," she said, "Arnie. May I say something?"

"Of course, dear," my mother said.

"Does Jesus have a big penis?" Stab inquired innocently. The thought had simply occurred to him, and he had spoken it; that was what he did.

My mother shushed him. My father almost smiled.

"I know you think Russ is a little weird," Zelda began. "I think so, too, sometimes."

"Thanks," I said.

"But this time, if anything, he's being too cautious. I've met this man we call Jesus, and I am not in the least a religious type of person. I don't pray. I don't go to church, or synagogue. I try to be a good person, but I'm not much on the idea of a God who runs the universe. But when I had that dream it completely changed me. Completely. And it was the last thing I expected or wanted."

"I'm not buying," my dad said. He wasn't looking at her, which is what he tended to do when he got angry at people, or lost respect for them.

"I'm not asking you to buy, really," Zel went on calmly. "What I'm asking you to do, and I realize that you've just met me and don't know me, and I'm not even officially part of the family yet—"

"Yes you *are*," Stab insisted.

"Thanks, Stab. I want to be."

"Then you're nuts just for that," Pa said, but he was looking at her again, and there was a small note of affection in the words. Zelda had turned so that she was facing him full on, and the top of her low-cut dress had somehow traveled another half inch down her chest, and she was pushing the hair out of her eyes in a certain way, and I could see that she had my father's full attention.

"I want to be," Zelda repeated. "I love your son. And I admire him for having the courage to put his beliefs above financial security. All I'm asking is that you come and meet Jesus and decide for yourself. If you believe he's a charlatan, I'll understand that, but I'd ask you, with all respect, you and Mrs. Thomas—"

"Call me Mudgie."

"You and Mudgie, to come and meet him in person. He's giving a public talk next Wednesday in West Zenith, and we'd like to invite all three of you to come and listen."

"Never happen," my father said, but in his voice I heard what I'm sure Zelda didn't, which was the slightest weakening of his position, the smallest note of surrender. This was my dad all over: He'd put up this big bluster, he'd yell and say things that hurt, and he'd storm out of the house and say he was never coming back, he wasn't buying, didn't want to be part of this crazy family anymore. . . . And then he'd come home an hour later with flowers and ice cream.

"Because he's an atheist," my mother said. "He wouldn't know God if God came down and ironed his underwear."

We had reached that point where the flames had burned hot for a while, and then Zelda had come in with the hose and started to put them out. But little fires were still burning all over the room, giving off smoke she couldn't know about. Poisonous gases. I was embarrassed, too, who wouldn't have been? I wanted only to do what I had done as a boy, go into my room, shut the door, curl up on the bed and pretend I was from outer space and had ended up at 98 Shirley Street by accident, and soon my funny-looking friends from the planet Quelaty would come and take me away. But I had nothing to lose at that point, and I was frustrated, and disgusted, and maybe even ashamed because my father's reaction had awakened the doubt inside me. So to make up for that I finally blurted out, "Jesus is not just running for public office, he's running for president of the United States."

My father looked up and met my eyes. He thought maybe I was making a joke. That the whole thing had been some kind of grand prank TV newscasters played on their parents when they announced their engagements.

"No joke," I said, and it was as if I had punched him. "And he wants you and Mom and Stab to work on his campaign with me and Zelda."

A long silence, and then, "You're kidding, right?"

I shook my head.

"You're not kidding."

"No. Not kidding. Not fooling around. Not a joke."

"Only an atheist would ask," Mom said.

"Then you're a nut. And your pretty girlfriend—excuse me, I like you, but I'm a man who tells the truth—is a nut, too. First of all, goddammit, too much fuss was made about Jesus the first time, if you ask me."

My mother was strangling a dishtowel. She mouthed, "No one asked you."

"I'm not saying he was bad, all right? And for me, coming from the people I come from—people who were chased into a corner or burned alive or shot by people who loved Jesus—you ever hear the stories of the Jewish shuttle?"

"*Shtetl,* Pa," I said, but he was in fourth gear by then, roaring along, and wouldn't have heard me if I'd had a megaphone. It was a point of pride for him to mispronounce certain words. No matter how many times we showed him the dictionary, he insisted that his pronunciation was correct, or also correct: asprim, Lou Gehrigs, shuttle, Vaddicun, Madeline Monroe, etcetera.

"Coming from those people even, I can say he was a good man. Did good things, helped people, meant well."

"God forgive him," my mother mouthed.

"But too much fuss was made, I'm telling you. Too much! Look at these so-called Christians now, what they're doing! Would you look? They're starting all over again. Every other word out of their mouth is *Jesus.* It makes you sick. He wins football games for them now, they really believe that! Next thing, another few years, they're going to be coming to the door with a gun and asking if you believe in Jesus, if you have a personal relationship with Jesus, if you've accepted Jesus into your heart. You say no, they'll slice your tongue out before they shoot you. I've lived with this crap my whole life, okay? So how am I supposed to feel when my oldest son comes home and tells me he met Jesus and quit his job? Tell me, really, I'm asking you: how am I supposed to feel?"

"Give it a chance," I said. "Half a chance. You're a good judge of people.

Come meet the guy. Come listen to him talk. If he's a phony, you'll know in a second. He's announcing his candidacy next Wednesday. Come up, you can stay with me or I'll put you up in a nice hotel. Listen to him talk, and *then* let me know how you feel."

"Never," my dad said. "Never happen. And I'm, for the record, worried about you, and I think it's lousy that a happy event like getting married, a happy thing like telling us you're getting married, had to get spoiled with this, with this — "

There was a knock on the front door, and a second later we heard the squeaking hinges. After our argument over who should pay for the champagne, we must have left the door ajar, which was a mistake, because the second-floor tenant, one Mrs. Wu, had been born in a part of China where, we had always suspected, a neighbor's open door was an invitation. She was tremendously lonely, Mrs. Wu, and her loneliness expressed itself in her habit of inviting herself into other people's homes, often at mealtime, and her ability to talk for an hour or more without pausing for breath. You said hi to Mrs. Wu on the front porch and you'd be there for sixty minutes listening to stories about her childhood in the Ying Yang Valley. You could pass high school geography without ever opening the book. You could go all the way through puberty standing there on the front porch between that first, "Hi, Mrs. Wu," and the time your mother started calling you in for supper.

She shuffled in, but before she could get beyond her opening line, before she could really get deeply into the rhythm of her nonstop talking, before we could go from the fact that it was my fiancée Zelda sitting at the table, not Esther, and from there to the taste of fish caught in the Ying Yang River and grilled over an open fire whenever there was a wedding, and how the little girls were taught to cook the rice that went with it, and how even the eyeballs of the fish were eaten in those days, and how awful the river smelled at certain times of the year because of the factory upstream, and how she and Mr. Wu had sneaked across the border into Nepal . . . my father stood up. "Too much," he said. "Mudgie, if you and Stab want to go, you go. Go ahead. But this is too much for me. I'm going up to Lincoln Park to hit golf balls. You hit the ball, it goes in the woods or it doesn't, it makes sense, it's simple. Mrs. Wu, here, sit here. Zelda, Russ, I'm sorry, it's too much for me today. I'm happy for you."

And he was gone. And, after Zelda had been forced, along with the rest of us, to listen to Mrs. Wu for an hour and fifteen minutes, we said we had to get to the hotel and check in, and we kissed my mother, who looked like all the plants in her garden had died, and we hugged Stab, who looked confused, and we said that, if they wanted, we could pick them up the next morning and take them to West Zenith, so they could listen to Jesus give his big speech.

"WELCOME," I SAID QUIETLY to Zelda as we walked down the creaking steps, "to the Thomas family."

★★★ SIXTEEN ★★★

The next morning there were no takers for the ride west. Zelda and I made the drive back home more or less in peace.

My mother had told us she and Stab would wait two days and come up on the train—I think Ma wanted to have that time to see if my father would change his mind—and during those two days Zelda and I worked overtime, trying to get things in place for the big announcement at Banfield Plaza. What troubled us, troubled me at least, was the fact that Jesus had gone incommunicado. At some point on Friday, we realized that we had no way of reaching him. No one—not me, Zel, Wales, Ezzie, no one—had been given a phone number. Zelda did receive a letter with a substantial money order in it and a handwritten note saying the funds were to be used to rent one of the vacant storefronts on Main Street and turn it into campaign headquarters, to hire a car and driver for the Wednesday event, to cover incidental expenses (nothing about my rent was mentioned). But there was no return address on the envelope and no way to trace the money order. While waiting for the headquarters lease to be signed, the rented furniture to be brought in, the placards and posters to be printed up, we did our work out of the house that Wales and Ezzie owned, in Shetland Village, a development of oversized new homes in the rolling countryside fifteen miles west of Zenith proper.

We sat in their living room with boxes of pizza and trays of sushi (Ezzie's idea), and we talked and planned and made phone calls, expecting Jesus to show. But he did not show. I started to get nervous. I started to feel, though I was afraid to mention it to Zelda, that my father might have been correct: we were victims of some elaborately staged dupery. We were going to show up at Banfield Plaza on Wednesday at noon, and thousands of other people were going to show up, and there would be no sign of the man who called himself Jesus.

To make things more nerve-wracking, on Monday, two days before the big event, the press seeds that Zelda had planted started to sprout. In a major way. Whether or not they believed this guy was the actual item, the fact that someone was going around calling himself Jesus Christ was interesting enough to attract the attention of at least the regional media. And the idea that he was running for president, in a climate where the newspapers and TV were already heavily geared up to cover the race, had the potential to be a giant story. National and international. Those of us who've been on the inside know that the media has a herd mentality. After the first two or three cautious days, when the big outlets were trying to make sure we weren't just a bunch of crazies led by a lunatic, they all seemed to decide, simultaneously, that the story had appeal. And then they swarmed.

The trouble was, they didn't know where to swarm *to*. There was no headquarters as of yet. The candidate wasn't there for them to interview. Zelda had given them the Waleses' home number, but there was only one phone line, and so they swarmed around the Simmeltons, already public figures despite their reclusive nature (wisely, the Simmeltons decided it was a good time to take that long-planned trip to Costa Rica) and around Ada Montpelier, who, while not the most eloquent spokesperson, seemed to be enjoying the attention; and around her boyfriend, Dukey McIntyre, who'd taken to wearing combat fatigues and boots, even though he had never served in the military, and to telling reporters that he was CEO of Scorched Earth Protective Services, a company that specialized in security arrangements, bodyguards for hire, armored limousines, and transportation of large sums of money. (Against great odds, Dukey would go on, after the campaign was over, to make a small fortune running this business.)

My mother and Stab were supposed to arrive via Amtrak on Tuesday afternoon, but at the last minute Ma called and said there had been a delay—she'd explain when she saw me—and that they'd be arriving on Wednesday morning, on the 8:30 train. She hoped that wouldn't be a problem.

By Wednesday morning, Zelda and I were already exhausted and the campaign hadn't even officially begun. We'd been at Wales and Ezzie's until three a.m. for four straight nights, answering calls from everywhere: How did people get press credentials? Would there be face time with the candidate? Did we have empirical proof that this man was actually *the* Jesus? Were there any more details on the miracles? How could one obtain a press release? Position papers?

And we'd been driving all over the city, from Banfield Plaza to police headquarters, to the printer, the balloon supplier, the outfit that handled the PA system, the company (called Poop Safe) that provided portable toilets. Some local clergyman had organized a protest and arranged for members of his church to stand on street corners with signs that said, THOU SHALT NOT HAVE FALSE GODS BEFORE YOU! And we'd had word that hotels, motels, and campgrounds within a fifty-mile radius were filled up. The streets of downtown West Zenith, usually half deserted, were crowded with the curious, the faithful, the skeptical, the legitimate and illegitimate press. Restaurants were doing the kind of business they usually did only in the week before Christmas, when a few hundred brave souls came for the traditional lighting of the lanterns at the West Zenith Public Library—a happy event at which two people had been stabbed a few years earlier.

Zel and I had not eaten a decent meal, not made love, and not had a conversation of any substance in almost a week. A volcano of doubt was shaking and bubbling inside me, and, though I knew she could sense it, I did not say one doubting word to her until we were on the way to the train station, in atypically heavy traffic, to meet my mom and brother. "What if he doesn't show?" I asked, innocently, through the haze of exhaustion that hung in the front seat of my car.

"He'll show."

"But what if he doesn't?"

I could feel her turn to look at me. "If he doesn't, that would mean he was lying to us. He doesn't lie."

"You say that like you know him," I said. "Intimately."

There was no response.

"What if he's been assassinated? Or kidnapped by some evangelical mental patient who doesn't want him moving in on lucrative preaching territory?"

No response to that either.

"You're going to say I don't have much faith."

"Exactly."

"I have plenty of faith. I just need the tiniest bit of evidence now and then to support it. It's like you know a woman loves you, you believe it, you have faith in it, but a kiss on the cheek every couple of days sort of helps fortify your confidence. The occasional 'I love you,' or 'honey,' or 'sweetheart,' the occasional card with 'To the Sexiest Man Alive' on the front. Something along those lines."

Nothing. She seemed to be off in another dimension, which was not like her. To use a term I dislike, Zelda was one of the most *present* people I know. She looked at you when she talked. She really listened, despite the fact that her entire workday was composed of listening. "Where are you?" I asked, after another few bad quiet seconds.

"I'm worried."

"Yeah, me, too. I was saying—"

"Not about that. I'm worried we aren't prepared. I don't mean for the campaign, I mean for today."

"We ordered ten potties from Poop Safe."

"I'm starting to think we should have ordered a hundred."

"Nah. A hundred. That's crazy."

"I just have a feeling. The traffic is so heavy. I've never seen traffic like this in West Zenith."

We were at the train station by that point. I found a parking spot without too much broken glass in it, and we locked the car and climbed the old stone steps that led to the platform. We were talking at least, Zel and I.

"Do you think your father will come?"

"Not at first."

"I really liked him."

"Well, if you could like him after that display, after he showed you his worst side, then we're all set."

"He reminds me of you. A lot."

I wasn't sure how to take that remark, so I just held the swinging door open for her, and we went and stood on the platform and watched for the westbound 8:37.

The westbound arrived on time—the first of what I hoped would be several small miracles. It chugged into the station, brakes squealing, porters hopping out and setting the safety steps in place below the doorways. And then all hell broke loose. As always, there were six passenger cars, and on an average day you might see ten or twelve people getting off. On that morning, a stream of passengers poured out of each door. Some of them were actually normal. But a lot of them were in what might charitably be considered Halloween costumes: men with plastic crowns on their heads, or circular crowns handmade of twigs; women wearing sheets that were supposed to be robes. One couple—they were kids, really, late teens—was carrying a huge wooden cross that they'd gotten onto the train in two pieces and were assembling there on the edge of the platform. More silver, gold, and plastic crucifixes than you could count. Picnic baskets with fish heads and baguettes sticking out of them. Cameras around necks. Bibles, pictures of the pope. JESUS FOR PRESIDENT placards, most of them handmade, in every imaginable shape and color. I'D DIE FOR YOU! one of them said. SAVE US! TURN AMERICA INTO HEAVEN! BANISH THE HEATHENS!

You name it, we saw it.

What we didn't see was my mother or Stab. We backed up against the wall, watching in a kind of horrified excitement as the mob hurried past. "My God, you were right," I said to Zel at one point. "And this is just people coming on the train. What about—"

And then my mother and Stab appeared, at the tail end of the crowd. We hugged and kissed. I noticed that my mother was carrying a picture of the pope, who was Pope Benjamin IV at that time. Stab had a picture, too, but in his nervousness he had rolled it up and was busy trying to flatten it out again. In my nervousness, instead of keeping my mouth shut, I greeted them with, "I'm not really sure about the pope pictures, Ma."

"What do you mean?"

Zelda was shooting me a look. We were going down the stairs to the street and the moment had the feeling of a baseball or football game about it, all those happy, excited people headed toward a great communal rite. You expected to see some kid walk by, yelling, "Hey, popcorn here!"

"I mean, it's Jesus, but I'm not necessarily sure he's Catholic. You know. . . . There are going to be Protestants here, too, and the pope doesn't do that much for them."

"Why not?" Stab asked. By then Zelda had let go of my hand.

"The pope's Catholic, Stab."

"So is Jesus."

"Not really."

"What do you mean, Russ? What does he mean, Ma?"

"Nothing, honey. Your brother says stupid things sometimes, that's all. It's in the genes on your father's side. You were lucky not to have gotten any of it."

"It's crowded, huh, Russ?"

"Sure, pal. Wait till we get there if you think this is bad."

"Do we have front seats because you and Zelda are God's friends?"

"We'll be right up on the stage, pal. You'll see."

"Russell has been asked to introduce him," Zelda said when we were all in the car and clicking our seatbelts.

I looked at her.

"You're introducing Jesus," she repeated.

"Says who?"

"Jesus."

"When?"

"Yesterday. Late last night, actually. He called and told me, but he made me promise not to tell you until," she looked at her watch, "after nine o'clock this morning. I decided to have mercy on you and tell you five minutes early."

"You're joking, right?"

"Nope. Let's go. We need to get to Padsen's for the car. You might want to call Chief Bastatutta and tell him to keep Wilson Street open so we can get through."

I had the key in the ignition but I did not turn it. Zelda could not quite meet my eyes. "Anything else I should know?"

"Nothing."

"Are you and your wife fighting already, Russ?"

"A little bit, pal."

I still hadn't started the car. "Has he been in touch with you?"

"I just told you."

"Have you seen him?"

She shook her head.

"This was the only phone call?"

"Last night at one a.m. I couldn't call and tell you then, could I?"

"You could have told me this morning."

"He said he wanted you to be spontaneous. He said you were great at thinking on your feet in front of a microphone and he didn't want to spoil that by having you stay up all night worrying over the right thing to say. He said you should just get up there and say it the way it comes to you, no notes, no thinking ahead."

"As the Holy Spirit moves you," my mother chirped from the back-seat.

"Yeah, Russ."

I started the car and pulled out into traffic. The train station was a little over two miles from Banfield Plaza, Padsen's Livery Service about halfway between, and with each block more people were crowding the sidewalks. We drove slower and slower, and soon we came to a complete stop. I got on the phone to Bastatutta's cell.

"Where are you?" the chief yelled. I could tell from the sounds — sirens, truck engines — that he was outdoors.

"Coming from the Amtrak station. I just picked up my mother and —"

"Have you seen the plaza?"

"No, how could I? I just—"

"I'll tell you what, you better make some calls. More toilets, for one thing. More buses to get people out of here when this is over. I'll tell you what, Thomas, you got something on your hands here that you didn't expect, that you didn't warn me about. I've been talking to the mayor. He's not happy."

"Not happy? First of all, whaddaya mean *I've* got something on my hands here that *I* didn't expect. You're the damn chief of police."

"Be polite, honey," Mom said from the backseat. "He's an important man."

"And second of all, the mayor should be happy as a clam in salty mud. His city is on the map for something other than a high unemployment rate. We'll be famous."

"Famous for what, is the question," Bastatutta said. "What if the guy don't show?"

"He'll show."

"You sure?"

"Of course, I'm sure. I'm going to pick him up right now."

"Yeah? Where?"

"Where? I don't know. First I have to go to Padsen's."

"Padsen's!" Bastatutta yelled into the phone. "Jesus is renting a car from Padsen!"

"He picked Padsen's, not me. He wants us to show up in a limo, so things seem professional. We need you to keep Wilson Street open so we can get him to the stage."

"A little late for that," Bastatutta said. "Wilson Street looks like Times Square on New Year's. You'll have to find another way to get him here. To hell with Padsen. Rent a damn helicopter or something. I've got three-quarters of the force down here already, and it's all we can do to keep people off the stage. Your moron friend Dukey—a convicted felon, I might add—is actually helping."

"Just give me a lane down the middle of Wilson Street, and I'll take care of the rest," I said, and then I hung up, and the car moved forward at walking pace.

"If you know where he is you should tell me," I said to Zelda, and I said it quietly and calmly.

"I do not know where he is."

"Excellent. I'm going to introduce an invisible man."

"He said he'd show up. I trust him."

"I do, too," said my mother.

I felt the doubt twisting and scampering inside me like a lizard in a box. "You okay back there, Stab? Enough leg room?"

"Sure, Russ. Will we be on TV?"

"Definitely. We might be on TV all over the world." And then I turned to Zelda. "Who can you call to get another two dozen portable toilets? More buses, too. What else?" and she was on her cell, and we were, finally, pulling into the gated lot of Padsen's . . . where a black Hummer limo was waiting for us.

The fenced-in lot was an oasis of relative peace. Outside the fence the crowds flowed toward Banfield Plaza as if walking toward a parade or an amusement park or an Olympic event. More signs (I HAVE COME TO DESTROY THE TEMPLE. AN EYE FOR AN EYE. HE WHOM LISTENETH TO ME SHALL LIVE!), people singing hymns. Four guys holding up a banner that read JEWS FOR JESUS.

"Pa should see this," I said.

"That's why we took the later train," my mother said, but she did not seem inclined to explain the remark in front of Zelda.

Jocko Padsen, the owner of the car rental operation, emerged from the little white shed with a stogie in his mouth. He was, as we said around West Zenith, "connected," which meant that he had friends who, for a price, would do you bodily harm, so he was not someone to be trifled with despite his bottom-of-the-class IQ.

"Jocko," I said. He squeezed my hand as if it were a walnut and his fingers were nutcrackers. "Who asked for a Hummer?"

"Your people aksed. Whattaya mean, who aksed?"

"It's a little, you know, inappropriate."

"Huh?"

"Environmentally, and so on."

He shrugged. "Hey. We got a call for it, you gut it, and it ain't free, let me put it that way, even though your buddy's inside and he's, ya know, a piece a work. Nice suit, too."

"Who? Wales?"

"Wales is a jerk. God's inside. Ya know. Jeesum."

"Jeesum?"

"I don't say it in vain no more."

"Really. Since when is this?"

"Since when? Since now. Go see him. Guy's readin' a book. I made him coffee. I din't have no notice to do nothin' about the calendars. So it goes."

With some trepidation, Zelda and I, along with my mother and Stab, walked around the black Hummer and headed toward the twelve-foot-square shed where Jocko accepted bets on football games and sold pornographic magazines, wholesale. I opened the door. There, inside, seated on a cheap gray metal chair that probably had been stolen from some government office, surrounded by walls on which hung calendars featuring naked women in provocative poses, and perusing, with a frown on his face, a well-thumbed copy of *The Da Vinci Code*, was Hay-Zeus himself. He was wearing a magnificent suit, somewhere between gray and silver in color, with thin lines of scarlet running through it, a white shirt, and a gold and red tie. Clean-shaven, his black hair brushed straight back, his nails perfectly manicured, and his black loafers brilliantly shined, he looked like he'd bathed an hour earlier in preparation for his wedding. When we came through the door he raised his eyes to us and said, "At last. My flock."

My mother was looking at him with some suspicion, I noticed, but Stab was already down on both knees in the little office and he was crying. Jesus tossed the paperback aside and stood up.

"Jesus," I said, "this is my mother, Maria, but everyone calls her Mudgie. And this is my brother, Steven, who everyone refers to as Stab."

Jesus came over and kissed my mother on both cheeks, in the European fashion, hands on her shoulders. She shivered and I knew that she'd felt the same current I'd felt when Jesus had touched me. Whatever suspicions might have been hovering behind the flesh of her face flew out the barred window. Jesus then reached down, lifted Stab to his feet and embraced him. "My number one guy," he said. "Good of you to come all the way here. They gave you time off from the sandwich shop?"

Stab was positively weeping by that point, tears dripping from his chin onto the collar of his shirt, and from there onto the rolled-up picture of the pope. He nodded.

"Who told him about the sandwich shop?" I said, and when my mother heard me she made the sign of the cross three times. For some reason she chose that moment to hold out the picture of the pope to Jesus, as if she wanted him to autograph it. Jesus looked at the picture and smiled in a way that was completely ambiguous. In a voice that was gentler than anything I'd heard from him up to that point, he told Stab, "We have a lot of work to do today, you and I, so dry up the faucet please."

"Yes, God," he said, and Jesus did not correct him.

My mother was saying a prayer under her breath. Her eyes were fixed on the man in the suit. The man in the suit winked at her.

"It's a madhouse out there," I told him.

He nodded. "We will make some waves today."

At that point Jocko came through the door in a cloud of stogie smoke.

"Why don't we settle up?" he said, looking at me. "I'm prepared to give this here guy a discount. For bein' a good guy. Ya know, special."

"*Capo di tutti capi*," I said, but Jocko apparently did not see the humor in this, and he did not smile.

"Let's say ten percent discount. The Hummer limo is usually a grand a day. Let's make it nine, even."

"You should give it to him free," Zelda told him. She had been standing quietly off to the side, but she pronounced this sentence with a force that was all too familiar to me. "This is Jesus Christ," she went on. "As in Jesus Christ sent from heaven. You're going to charge him for a car?"

"Huh?"

"What if he's president of the United States by next year," I said, taking up the refrain. "Do you want to be known as the person who charged him for your services?"

"Hey, I run a business here," Jocko said. He looked from Zelda to me to my mother and back, as if everyone but him got the joke. Jesus seemed not to be paying attention.

"This is God!" Stab said loudly. "Are you crazy? Are you a bad man? Do you want to go to hell forever?"

I put a hand on my brother's shoulder to quiet him, but I have to say I liked seeing Jocko squirm there behind his smokescreen, shifting his weight from one foot to the other, taking the cigar out of his mouth and working his thick lips. If nothing else, it gave him a taste of the same medicine he'd been forcing down his debtors' throats for years. After a few seconds of indecision he said, "Twenty percent then. Best I can do. Comes wit a driver, ya know."

The driver was a short fellow of indeterminate ethnicity named Oscar Oswald. He sat behind the wheel, silent as a stone, and turned the Hummer limo out into the crowds. For a few blocks we went along unmolested. But then, even though the windows were tinted, the word must have gotten around that Jesus was inside, because people began pressing against the glass and fenders.

"Russ, it's scary," Stab said. He was sitting beside Jesus, his back facing the direction we were going, and he had a hand on the candidate's knee.

"Can you move faster?" I asked Oscar.

"And what, mahn, kill some dude?"

"Without killing someone, could you move a little faster?"

"They crawlin' on the hood, dude."

It was true. At least two people were on the hood and a dozen others pressed their faces against the windows on either side. Jesus was sitting calmly in the seat facing us, Stab clutching his knee, with the crumpled picture of the pope in his other hand. As the security chief, I felt that my first big assignment was not starting off well. For one thing, I did not like the look on some of the faces we could see. The people crawling up the hood, now onto the windshield (Oscar had the bright idea to turn on the wipers and spray them with wiper fluid, which momentarily made them stay still but after that it made them angry, and they started banging on the glass with the palms of their hands), were especially disconcerting—two middle-aged men with stubble and jean jackets. Another second and one of them took out a gun. Oscar leaned on the horn in panic, but the man raised the gun and fired twice into the air, and suddenly you could feel the release of the weight that had been pressing against the sides of the car. The second man peered in through the windshield, saw me, and gave a thumbs-up. He shouted something I could not hear. He shouted it again, louder. "Dukey's guys!" And then, "Scorched Earth, man."

"Everything under control?" Jesus asked calmly, without turning around to look at them. Stab still had a hand on his knee. My mother was saying the rosary under her breath. Zelda was looking out the window and sitting so that there was space between her thigh and mine.

"No problem."

"That's a Glock, dude," Oscar said, with some admiration.

"He works for us," I said. "Plow on."

With the two Scorched Earth employees riding on the hood and threatening those who pressed too closely against the car, we made it to Wilson Street, where the first uniformed person I saw was Chief Bastatutta. He was thrusting one arm this way and that and shouting orders through a bullhorn. Wilson Street was, if not clear of people, at least thinly enough populated that it seemed we could make it to the stage. As we went past, I rolled down the window and said, "Excellent work, Chief." He turned to the side and spit.

There, near the stage, as Dukey had promised, was a ring of Harley Davidsons, chrome pipes gleaming, owners standing with their huge arms crossed, facing the crowd. And what a crowd it was! As we stepped out of the black Hummer I became aware of the thundering noise. The term *sea of faces* came to mind, as did the term *Poop Safe*. I held my mother in one arm and Zelda in the other. Jesus and Stab were in front of us. As we approached the ring of bikes, Dukey himself appeared from behind one of his employees, and, with an expression as somber as a funeral attendant opening a car door for a new widow, he moved one of the bikes aside to make a narrow alley. Jesus and Stab passed through and we followed. On the way I patted Dukey hard on the flak jacket and said, "Excellent work."

"Yes, sir. Thank you, sir," he said.

In another few steps we were up on the stage that the guys from Dermott's had put together the night before. I recognized the podium — it had been "borrowed" from Anderson's Restaurant, where the monthly Rotary Club meetings were held. Some smart soul had thought to cover over Anderson's logo with a purple cloth on which these words had been stitched: JESUS FOR AMERICA.

I went up to the podium. The crowd filled the huge square completely; all the side streets leading into it were full of people as well. Men, women, and children were leaning out of open windows everywhere, some even standing on the rooftops. A noisy helicopter circled overhead. Police lights flashed on all sides. The press were corralled in their roped-off section, pointing cameras at us. The Poop Safe truck was trying to work its way from the outskirts into the center, a supply of new potties wobbling precariously on the back. Oscar was sitting on the roof of the Hummer with his arms crossed over the top of his knees, and here and there one of Dukey's biker pals was shoving somebody away from the stage. Zelda had an enormous smile on her face. For the first time in what seemed like a year, she put her arm through mine and squeezed. "I know you'll be great," she shouted into my ear . . . at which point I remembered that I was doing the introduction. And then I was at the podium, holding up my hands to try and bring some measure of quiet to the throng. In front of me stood twenty or thirty microphones.

"Hi," I said. "Good morning." The rumble and roar quieted a decibel or two. I held up my hands trying to quiet it further. No luck. People were yelling out things, cheering, weeping. Finally, I just pointed to Jesus with both hands and the crowd went berserk. Here and there I could see skeptics standing alone or in small groups. They were watching, not

cheering, not applauding, not standing up on their tiptoes to get a better glimpse, not wearing crowns of thorns or waving crosses or carrying
placards with biblical quotations on them. For a moment I felt a guilty
kinship with them.

In response to this new wave of cheering, Jesus did an odd thing. He
took a step forward and held up one finger, like an athlete making the
claim that his team was at the top of the national rankings. When I
turned to look, I thought I could see a glow around him, a subtle shimmering in the air. After letting the cheers and screams go on for a minute
or so, he raised both hands, palms forward, and the place quieted immediately.

"We are tired," I heard myself saying, without having prepared to say
it. The words went echoing around the plaza. "We are tired of politics
as usual!"

There was a huge roar. I held up my hands, waited, leaned into the
mikes, absolutely winging it. "We are tired of war and greed and lies
and unfairness, of our great country being divided up into competing
factions. As some of you know, I've spent eight years reporting the news
here, and in those years I've met with thousands of ordinary people, and
the message I've gotten from those people has always been the same:
what happened?"

This was true, actually, and I thought it was a decent line, but the
crowd didn't go wild for it the way I'd hoped they would—a few tenta-
tive cheers, that was all. For a moment I did not know what else to say,
an unusual situation for me in front of a microphone. I closed my eyes,
opened them, looked out at the ocean of faces.

"What happened to my city?" I went on. "What happened to my country? What happened to the sense of decency and compassion we used to
know? . . . Well, the Great Spirit I'm about to introduce"—huge cheer
here, and it went on and on until Jesus finally held up his hands and
silenced them. "The Great Being who is about to speak to you and make
what is probably the most important announcement in American political history, . . . he has come to give us our city back, our country back, our
way of life back!" More of the tremendously loud cheering, and a sense

of excited impatience rippled through the crowd and across the stage. "So without making you wait any longer, I give you the next president of these united United States, Jesus Christ!"

I stepped reverently away from the podium, and I can tell you that never before or since have I ever heard anything like the sound that greeted Jesus as he took my place. Utterly deafening. A weird symphony of screams, thousands of voices, whistles, chants, all of it echoing around shabby old Banfield Plaza with its crappy metal-grated storefronts and weedy, now trampled, patches of grass. Stab ran over and hugged me. Zelda gave me a big wet kiss. My mother, tears again running down her cheeks, could not stop nodding, at me, at Jesus, at the crowd. I noticed that Wales and Esmeralda had come up onto the stage. She gave me a lovely smile, and he nodded twice in my direction — about as big a compliment as you'd ever get from the guy.

"Thank you. Thank you all for coming," Jesus was trying to say, but the thousands of people in Banfield Plaza would not let him speak. For several more minutes they went crazy, and there was a mad pushing and shoving down below us as a few idiots tried to rush the stage. One of the Harleys got knocked over. I saw at least one punch being thrown, and I hoped the ambulances could get through. I worried that Chief Bastatutta would be having a heart attack somewhere on the edges of Wilson Street, trying to keep an open corridor. In fact, I noticed that some of the most attentive listeners and enthusiastic applauders were in police uniform.

"Thank you. Thank you all." Jesus held up his hands and the crowd soon quieted. "I am going to keep this short. As my good friend Russ Thomas just told you, we are doing something here today that has never been done. I have come to you, come back to you" — another prolonged cheer — "because you are a nation in grave spiritual danger. You are in the process, well into the process, of losing your moral leadership in the world, losing your way in the modern frenzy. What I am offering is not a campaign based on gain, personal or political. There are some of you here who will not necessarily be better off under my leadership, not materially better off, at least. I cannot say I will cut your taxes and raise your salaries. What I can say is that you will have a nation based on kindness and goodness, not some mere slogan that includes those things, but actual kindness and goodness. You will have a sane, sensible foreign policy based on moral rather than strategic imperatives and founded upon the principle of considering the other as yourself; you will have a country in which children are no longer hungry, and you will live on a planet that is not being ravaged by our greed and stupidity. In the name of my father and mother, the greatest of great spirits, the ones you know in the secret depths of your souls but have been blinded to by the concerns of ordinary life; in the name of the Creator's Creator, the inventor of time, the great pulse of love that spins the universes, I have come into this humble body, in this humble place, on this troubled planet, to become its most powerful citizen. Here, today, in the city of West Zenith, I, the Son of Man, announce my candidacy for the presidency of the United States of America. And I ask you for your support."

Forget support. At that moment, the people in that square—Bastatutta later estimated the crowd at sixty thousand—would have given Jesus their lives. It was pure pandemonium. Jesus stepped back from the podium, took my brother's hand in his left hand, and Zelda's in his right, and raised them, and you couldn't have heard a cannon if it had been discharged ten feet away. Wild, it was. Near chaos. We'd arranged for a thousand balloons to be set free, and they were released at that moment, making about as big an impression as one kid blowing bubbles in the stands at Fenway Park. My brother Stab started jumping up and down, holding Jesus's hand and yelling "Jee-zus! Jee-zus! Jee-zus!" The chant caught on, and it seemed to me that the stage and the sides of the buildings were all shaking, trembling, about to crash to the ground. "Jee-zus! Jee-zus! JEE-ZUS!"

After it had gone on for I don't know how long, ten minutes I'd guess, Jesus let go of Zelda's hand and motioned me over. He put his mouth against my ear, and he said these words: "Call your dad."

★★★ SEVENTEEN ★★★

So, as Jesus walked from one side of the stage to the other, pointing at people in the cheering crowd as if he knew them, raising an index finger above his head like a quarterback after a touchdown throw, mouthing, "Thank you! Thank you!" I crouched at the back of the stage, and dialed my dad's number. He picked up on the first ring. "Pa!" I yelled, and he yelled something back. I could hear his voice but I couldn't make out the words. "Pa, you there?"

"—tching the TV!" I thought he yelled.

"Do you see us?"

"Bltng di font if sel!" it sounded like.

"He's something, isn't he?"

"Lie shoe. Shoe aw!"

"Okay. I can't hear you too good. It's crazy here. We miss you. Come up, okay? You don't have to believe or anything. Just come and be with us. All right? Pa?"

The line had gone dead. I couldn't tell if he'd hung up or if the thunderous noise of the crowd had knocked over a cell phone tower on a nearby hillside. We had a group hug then, me and Zel and my mother and Stab, as Jesus went back and forth across the stage, now lifting Wales's hand into the air, now Ezzie's, now flashing his phenomenal smile, now pushing up two fists in time to the JEE-ZUS! JEE-ZUS!" chant.

Eventually, he decided it was time to go, and looked over his shoulder at me the way the lead singer in a rock band looks at the drummer and bass player to signal the end of a song. I relayed the signal to Oscar, who crawled back into the Hummer and set himself up behind the wheel, and then to Dukey, who got his beefy leg breakers lined up in such a way that we had about a yard-wide corridor from stage to car. Even with the bikers pushing and shoving, people were reaching out to touch Jesus on the shoulder or the arm, or falling on their knees, or yelling things. As we climbed into the Hummer, two police cars backed in through the crowd, sirens going, lights flashing. With the cruisers running interference we made it out of Banfield Plaza and onto what was now a slightly less crowded, litter-paved Wilson Street.

"That went well," Jesus said, as we were running red lights behind the police cars, on our way back to Padsen's.

"A blast!" Stab said.

"What now?" I asked excitedly. "What's next? Give us our marching orders, Boss."

He looked at me and I noticed that, behind the chocolate brown eyes, there seemed to be a deep well of absolute calm. On the surface he seemed, if not excited, than at least pleased with how things had gone. Gratified. Optimistic. Those were the types of emotions you would have expected; there was something *human* about them, for lack of a better term. A few hairs had been knocked out of place. There was a thin coating of sweat on his neck and forehead—all normal. But the bright stillness in his eyes was something not of this world. My mother noticed, I was sure. In her adoration, she was almost shrinking back into the corner of the seat. The picture of the pope was gone, and she was working the rosary beads a mile a minute, and staring.

"What now?" the object of her adoration answered. "Now I am going to wander around alone for a few hours and you should all go back and get something to eat, get some rest. Tomorrow we will talk about strategy."

"Wander around?" I said, perhaps too forcefully, because Zelda swung her knee sideways against my leg. "As your security guy, I don't want you wandering around. People know you now. They'll recognize you. They'll crush you to death trying to get close. Plus, this neighborhood is not exactly known for—"

"Let me worry about that," he said. Calmly.

"It's nuts. We have to get you off someplace, some safe house or something. It's all different now. That scene we just came from, that was broadcast around the country, probably around the world."

"Let me worry about it, Russ," he said, and at the sound of my name on his lips a chill ran across the skin of my arms, a thousand tiny eight-legged creatures scurrying.

"You sure?"

He nodded. A little smile. "Maybe tomorrow Stab and I will find a bar where we can play pool."

"He knows about Stab and pool," my mother whispered.

Jesus looked at her and said, "In these two sons you should be most proud. And in your future daughter-in-law as well."

My mother, naturally, started to cry. Stab reached across to comfort her. I watched.

In a little while we were passing through the gates of Padsen's. The irony of police cars leading Jesus into such a place was not lost on me. I have to admit that another spark of doubt flew up in my mind: as Bastatutta said, why was Jesus doing business with an underworld guy?

Standing in the lot, we thanked Oscar for his good driving. Oscar asked Jesus for his autograph and held out a parking ticket, which he'd pulled from his back pocket, and which he appeared to have no intention of ever paying. Jesus obliged, scrawling his name in blue marker across the orange paper. And then all of us—my mother and Stab, Zelda and I and Jesus—crowded into Jocko's shed (Wales and Ezzie had gone to see about the headquarters rental; Ada Montpelier and her son had stayed behind at Banfield Plaza with Dukey Senior), where the calendars had been taken down and the shrink-wrapped stacks of porno mags hidden away, and where Jocko was standing next to the coffeemaker pouring an evil-smelling black brew into Styrofoam cups and setting them on the desk in a crooked line. Zelda wrote him a check for eight hundred dollars, which made him blush—probably the most shocking of all the shocking sights I'd seen that day. But his embarrassment did not keep him from folding the check in half and pushing it into the pocket of his tailored pants.

"Would you give us a moment alone?" Jesus asked him, and blushing and dipping his head in small pseudo-reverent movements, Jocko stepped out into the sunlight and closed the door.

Jesus held out the one chair, and motioned for my mother to sit in it. She hesitated, shook her head, worked her beads.

"Ma, sit," Stab told her. "He wants you to, Ma."

Jesus kept his hands on the back of the chair until she was seated, and then he stepped away and stood with his back to the door. He took off his tie, folded it neatly, and slipped it into the side pocket of his jacket. "You did well," he told us. "This is a proper beginning. I shall leave you now for a short while, but," he looked at me, "do not lose faith."

"What do we do next, Lord?" Zelda asked.

Jesus made the smallest of frowns. For some reason, he seemed not to mind when Stab and my mother called him God or Lord, but with Zelda it did not please him.

"You work it out," he said. The tone was not unkind, but it was tinged with impatience, as if we should have known, by then, everything he wanted us to know; as if we should have been experts on running a campaign, at the center of which was the most famous man in Western history. And then, more gently, he added, "I have spoken to Wales about our schedule. I understand he is going to get you all together tomorrow."

"Will you be there?" Zelda asked.

Jesus looked at her more tenderly. "Perhaps. Stab and I are playing pool later in the day. After that we should begin our travels."

At that moment, I heard what sounded like a gunshot outside in the lot. I dove across the room and knocked Jesus down, covering him with my body the way I'd seen Secret Service men do on television.

"Russell!" my mother yelled.

Jesus was not happy. "Off me, get off," he said. We stood up—I made a point of keeping my body between him and the window, thinking it might have been Padsen taking a pot shot. Zelda and Stab were glaring at me as if I were a lunatic. Jesus was brushing the dust from the pant legs and sleeves of his excellent suit.

"I heard a shot," I explained. "I thought someone was shooting at you."

Jesus straightened his sleeves. "A car backfiring, Russell."

"You could have *hurt* him," Zelda said.

I started to explain to him in more detail, to say that I'd heard what sounded like gunfire—not exactly a rare sound in West Zenith in those days—but he put a hand on my shoulder, and I felt the usual zip of current. Our faces were not more than a foot apart. I could see then that he had very little facial hair, and I wondered if he had Indian blood. The strong nose was slightly bent, the skin remarkably unlined. It occurred to me that we had no idea how old he was. "We have a problem," I said. "You have to be born in America to be president."

"Not an issue."

"You have to be thirty-five."

"Also not a problem."

"Where *were* you born? The press is going to ask. They're going to start asking a million questions now, about where you stand on various issues. There have already been some blog postings that wondered about your past—and we don't have so much as a paragraph of biographical material."

"Make something up," Jesus said.

"We can't *lie*."

"You won't be lying."

"But you just said to make something up. What do you mean it won't be a lie? Of course—"

"Russell," Zelda said. "Stop."

"Fine," I said. "You do it." Maybe it was a sort of decompression after the morning's tension, but I felt a bubble of anger at Zelda working its way up into my mouth. I loved her, I admired her, but I'd pretty much had it by then with the idea that her adoration of Jesus—which I did not object to in principle—seemed to go hand in hand with her ignoring me. God knows I had been trying my best, and it wasn't easy, what with the family dynamics to think about and the introduction and everything. And all I had been getting from her were these nudges, these turned-down lips, the rare hug. I felt that I deserved better.

"She will," Jesus said. "That is part of her responsibility. You are the security man, and, for the record, I appreciate your knocking me down. It reminded me of my football-playing days in Kansas. So there, you have a bit of biographical information. Football. Kansas. I also studied ballet at a school outside of New York City, but dropped out when I pulled my oblique muscle, right side. Build on that. Do your research. We will discuss my positions on the issues once the campaign gets on the road. I love you all and shall see all of you very soon."

And with that, he went past me and out the door, closing it quietly, and leaving the air of the room filled with what I can only call an affectionate awkwardness. We were not yet used to being in his presence. None of us had ever felt that kind of straightforward, no-nonsense, divine, and immeasurably deep affection. And we were, I think, afraid, because on that morning we had realized that we were at the center of some kind of sandstorm, something massively powerful and unpredictable. I was used to the spotlight, so in that way, possibly, it was five percent easier for me than for the others. But the spotlight I was used to had been like one of those penlights people read with on a train. This was like the sun.

I could not look at Zelda, and could not think of anything to say, so I turned to my mother and offered the first thing that came into my mind. "I called Pa."

"What did he say?" Stab wanted to know, and he wanted to know it very loudly. "What did Pa say? WHAT DID PA SAY!"

"He was watching us on the TV. I couldn't understand the rest of it. I think he said he misses us."

"I miss him," Stab said. "And I'm tired, Russ. And I feel like, I feel like, I feel like. . . ." This happened to him sometimes when he was excited or upset. The record got stuck. My mother and I were used to it, we let him go on for six more *I feel likes,* and then he got it out, "I feel like I'm very fast inside. I feel like I did something wrong."

"You think Jesus would want to play pool with you if you did something wrong, Pal?"

"I don't know. I just feel bad. I think I should feel good but I feel bad." He was on the verge of crying again.

"*I* did something wrong. I tackled God. It was almost a sin. But I was trying to save him from being hurt. I'm kind of like his bodyguard, you know. That's my new job. You're his first assistant. I'm his bodyguard."

"But why would anybody want to hurt God?" my brother asked, his big pale eyes even more turned down at the corners than usual, his mouth quivering.

"They wouldn't," Zelda said. "You don't have to think about that. Nobody's going to hurt anybody. Your brother's being foolish."

It was a more or less harmless remark, I suppose, just Zel trying to make Stab feel good. But the bubble of anger came up into my mouth then, and I was biting down on it hard, and needing some space, and unable to look at her, and I knew my mother could sense that there was some trouble between me and my new fiancée—mothers have a radar for things like that—and so I said, "Listen, you guys take my car and go out to get something to eat, and then go over to Zelda's. Go over there, watch TV, and let me know what they're saying about us. I have to, you know . . . get with Wales for a while and figure out how we're going to handle things from here, schedulewise. Come over to the condo later and I'll make a big dinner for everybody. Okay, Stab?"

"Okay, Russ."

I gave him a big hug, and gave my mother a big hug, and, though Zelda was reaching toward me, I just squeezed her shoulder without making eye contact and went out the door and into the lot. Jocko was there, smoking. He started toward me, but I waved him off and went out into the street and hustled away, hoping nobody recognized me.

I know it was petty, the way I acted. I admit that. I confess—I am a petty man, prone to jealousy, easily made insecure. In the midst of the confusion and excitement and the newness and scariness of it, all I wanted was for Zelda to see that I was on unfamiliar ground and trying to keep my balance, trying to do the right thing. It was, though—I was thinking about this as I hurried along West Zenith's tattered east side—it was as if she were expecting me to suddenly become someone I was not. She seemed to have fallen immediately into a warm relationship with my mother and brother, and I was happy about that, of course. And I knew that Jesus had seen how smart and capable she was, and that he'd picked the right person for the press liaison job. I was happy about the idea that we were working on such an important project together, not even a project really, more like a crusade.

But something seemed to have changed between us since Jesus appeared in our lives. We'd had a couple of fights, the fights had left a residue, and the residue was hardening like paint on a brush. I know I shouldn't have been thinking about such things. I mean, the campaign for Jesus was so much bigger than all that, so much more important. I shouldn't have been thinking about it. But I was.

I believe, if you look in the Bible, you'll see that the same type of thing was going on then: the people Jesus chose for his disciples, they all had their petty sides, their fears and doubts, their competitive nature and need for approval. They denied him at times, ran away at key moments, were afraid and unsure. I'm not going to pretend I was any better.

★ ★ ★ EIGHTEEN ★ ★ ★

I walked the streets for an hour. During that walk, Randy Zillins reached me on my cell and said how shocked he was that I was "part of this Jesus scam."

"How much are they paying you?" he wanted to know.

I said, "Man does not live by bread alone," and told him I had a call coming in from *Good Morning America.*

Back in my condo, I watched baseball for a while and sulked. Only a little while. Not very long. All it took to snap me out of it was switching channels at the top of the hour and getting a news report. The report led off with a shot from the helicopter showing the crowd filling Banfield Plaza. The camera zoomed in and there was yours truly, looking pretty decent, saying, "And the next president of the United States. . . ."

Naturally, the national news people, being the cynics they are, had to pretend to be evenhanded and sophisticated by showing the handful of naysayers in the crowd with the he's a fake! signs, and then running an interview with some preacher from Oklahoma who was going on about how the man on the stage bore no resemblance to the biblical Jesus, and how the biblical Jesus would be a humble man, not one who cared about worldly approval—running for president, wearing an expensive suit. Where had this charlatan been born? Who were these other charlatans surrounding him on the stage? Why, they were nothing more than TV people, *local* TV people at that, and Massachusetts types—known to be out of favor with the Lord. The whole thing, including the two so-called miracles, had been staged to get ratings and to take the focus off the brilliant campaign being run by Senator Marjorie Maplewith, whose husband Aldridge was a *real* preacher and a true man of God.

It got better. After a commercial for panty liners and one for the new Ford F-150, they aired Maplewith herself, giving a noncommittal statement, saying she hadn't yet seen the video of the so-called Jesus announcing his candidacy, but it sounded to her like a desperate strategy her opponent had dreamed up because he was sinking fast in the polls and knew he couldn't win without splitting the vote of religious Americans. The "New Christian majority," was the way she referred to her backers. The "values voters." As if, I thought, everybody wasn't a values voter in some way or another.

And then the Dems had their turn, in the person of Colonel Dennis Alowich, who made the mistake—which would end up sending his campaign into a downward spiral from which it would require weeks to recover—of attempting levity. "Sounds like Ms. Maplewith should get on over to church and say a few prayers for her campaign. Ha, ha. She's been going around for the past year claiming to have God on her side, and now God has come to earth and isn't endorsing her. Ha, ha, ha."

Part of the problem here was that Alowich actually laughed like that, two or three *ha-ha*s spaced about a second apart, and his lower teeth weren't as even or as white as people would have liked them to be. American politics has descended to this, I guess: we vote for people based on what their teeth look like and how they laugh. So, courtesy of the right-wing slime machine—financed by the notorious home mortgage magnate Justin Dreaf—this clip was shown over and over for weeks in the Bible belt, with the punch line added by a deep-voiced announcer: "Do we want a president who laughs about prayer?" and the camera zooming in on the colonel's faulty lower incisors.

I was standing there, facing the TV, considering the priorities of the American voting public and worrying about how Jesus was going to make allowances, when I heard the key turn in the front door lock. The door swung open, Zelda walked in, hair tousled, eyes on fire. She closed the door, hard. "What's wrong, Russ?"

"Nothing." I gestured at the TV. "Coverage."

"What's wrong."

"Nothing's wrong. I needed a little space."

"You didn't hug me when you left. Stab noticed. Your mom noticed."

I shrugged.

"What's going on?"

"Where are they?"

"Exhausted. I got them takeout from Siam Temple. They're at my apartment, eating, watching TV. They both want to take a nap. What's going on?" She went over to the television. "Can I?"

"Sure."

She snapped it off. "Talk to me, Russ."

"Same old stuff," I said.

"You're jealous of Jesus."

"Not the right way to put it."

"I thought your introduction was brilliant. Just as he said, you can do that stand-up stuff like no one I know. I couldn't have done that in a million years."

"Thanks. It was exciting."

"You sound about as excited as a turtle."

"Thanks."

"Do you want to call off the engagement or something? You seem so, *distant*. I feel like I forced you into it against your will. You weren't fully awake, I was weepy—"

"I don't want to call it off. Do you want to call it off?"

"Of course not! Why would you even say something like that?"

"Because we haven't made love in a week. Because you barely look at me. Because all I've seen from you these past few days has been this kind of mocking smirk, or frown, or I don't know what it is, as if everything I do is stupid, or not reverent enough. The rest of the time you basically ignore me. Which is fine. Okay. It's a busy time, I know that. But I'm as busy as you are and every once in a while I at least make eye contact with you, and I don't try to make you feel dumb for falling all over the guy like you were in ninth grade and he's the senior quarterback or something. Sorry. I'm just me. This is the best I can do."

She just stood still and looked. I looked back. And then she said, "You're right. I'm sorry."

"Okay."

"We always said we wouldn't let work be first and us be second, and I have been doing that."

"Well, unusual circumstances," I said.

"You were great out there today. Really."

"Thanks. You were right about the crowds. Bastatutta thinks sixty thousand. The TV said seventy-five. It's all over the news."

"And you're right with the ninth-grader remark. I am feeling that way, I admit it."

"Don't worry about it. I'm in the eighth grade most of the time."

"I think what it is is that, after all these years of having leaders I couldn't feel good about, having a country that was going the wrong way, to think maybe that could change, maybe we could be, I don't know, a shining moral beacon in an awful world. It almost seems like a fantasy or something."

"I know. I feel the same way."

"And to be part of making that happen, I mean, my last set of foster parents used to talk about the feeling they had in the sixties, like they could actually remake the world for the better. To feel that now, and to feel like the power of God is behind it . . . It's almost too much to absorb."

"Not to mention you get to order Poop Safes and ride in Hummers."

She smiled. It was a magical smile. With the possible exception of turning away from a life of sin, there is no feeling in the world like making up with somebody you love after a fight in which you thought everything was going to fall apart. Especially after you've seen everything fall apart for real with somebody else. We stood like that for a minute, enjoying it, and then Zelda flipped the hair out of her face in a certain way, and said in a certain tone, "Actually, Captain, the reason I stopped by was to get my driver's license renewed. I know it's after hours, and I know I've had some speeding issues in the past, but I was hoping there might be some way, well, I'm embarrassed to ask for help, but do you think. . . ?"

"Let me see the license," I said. "Maybe there's something I can do."

She hiked up her dress a few inches, as if there were a pocket under there and she was looking for her wallet. I could see the smooth skin of her thigh. "I can't seem to find it," she said.

"Here, let me help," I said, and soon we were resolving the licensing issue, as it were, wrestling around on the couch like two youngsters, clothing being unbuttoned, unzipped, cast aside, sections of tender skin being given careful attention.

"Isn't there some test I'm supposed to retake," she whispered in my ear.

And the rest of what happened is private.

But the license had not quite been approved when I heard a knock on the door. We kept doing what we were doing, though more quietly, hoping it was just my next-door neighbor, the retired hydraulics engineer Emmanuel Vespa, who liked to stop by with a six-pack in the late innings of Sox games and talk about the coefficient of restitution while I pretended to listen. But we had no such luck on that day.

There was a pause, and then more insistent knocking, and then, "Russ? Hey, Russ?"

It was my dad's voice. It turned out that he'd hung up the phone and driven as fast as he could all the way from North Salem.

"Russ? Russ? You in there or what?"

★ ★ ★ NINETEEN ★ ★ ★

I am not sure whether it is more difficult for a man or a woman to pretend that they have not just been having sex when, in fact, they were just having sex. Zelda grabbed her clothes, hurried into the bathroom, and turned on the shower. I straightened myself out as best I could and called, "Coming, Pa!"

He's not a stupid man, my father. Odd and quirky at times, stubborn as the day is long, but not stupid. When I opened the door he took a look at me and said, "What's goin' on, did I wake you up?"

"Nah, watching the Sox. Come on in."

He came in, stood in the middle of the living room, and looked around. The TV wasn't on. We could hear the shower going.

"Zel's here," I said. "She'll be glad to see you."

"Oh." He looked at me, then away, then back. "Good timing, I guess."

"Don't worry about it, Pa."

"Where's your mother and Stab?"

"At Zel's place. Wiped out. They wanted a nap."

"And you guys wanted some time alone."

"Forget it, Pa. Turn on the set, I'm getting you a beer."

"No, listen. I didn't drive all the way up here at ninety miles an hour to watch the Red Sox."

"Sorry about the phone connection. It was so loud I couldn't hear what you were saying."

"I watched it on TV." He paused. He made a three-step half circle, which was a habit of his—he'd lived most of his life in small rooms. "First off, I was proud of you. You did good up there in front of all those people. You looked relaxed. In charge. I was proud."

"Thanks, Pa."

"And second of all." Another pause, more glancing around. It was almost as if he had a toothache and was looking for the cabinet where I kept the Ambusol. "Second of all, I want to say . . . well, he seems like a good egg."

"He is."

"Don't get me wrong. I haven't changed my mind about it. I've had it up to here with the Jesus worship, believe me. Between your mother, customers trying to convert me over the years, the stupid things people say to us—'I *love* lox and bagels, Arnie, really I do'— it was not that easy being a Jew in this country, you know. It still isn't, on certain days. And I am who I am. I'm not about to abandon my religion at my age."

"Nobody's asking you to," I said.

"I know, I know. You wouldn't. I know that. What I'm saying is, you know how I am. I'm a family guy. I fight like hell with your mother, but I couldn't live without her for a week. Not to mention Stab. What I'm saying, I guess, is that I have nothing else to do these days. What do I do all day? I listen to Mrs. Wu, I play a little golf, do stuff around the house, play cards with my pals. So . . . I came to see if I could help you out with the campaign without, you know—"

"Without converting."

"Yeah."

"Absolutely," I said. "I don't get the feeling he's into converting people. I don't think that's what his campaign is about."

"I didn't either," my father said, and I could hear the relief in his voice. It was true what he'd said about not being able to live without my mother. That had always been a mystery to me, the way they could fight about every little thing and then kiss and make out in the kitchen the next day. Having Stab had brought them closer, I know that was part of it; both of them had told me so in different words. But there was something else. "A good physical relationship," my mother had said once, in an unguarded moment. "An attraction."

Just then, Zelda came out of the bathroom looking radiant and wet. She had a big smile for my father and went up and hugged him, and I could see that he was on the verge of apologizing, when he decided he didn't know her well enough yet. After a few awkward seconds he said, "I saw you all on the TV. I had to come up. That was something."

"I'm still in a state of excitement," Zelda said innocently.

And that made my father look out the window.

I was on my way to get all of us a much-needed drink when there was another knock on the door. Long before Jesus came into my life, I'd gone to great pains to be as anonymous as possible. This was one of the things they advised you to do when you got a one like the job I'd had at ZIZ: try to keep a private life for yourself. So I'd actually rented the apartment under another name, and put another name on the mailbox downstairs. My phone number was unlisted. I'd bought this condo, in part, because it had an underground garage, and you could go from the garage into the elevator or vice versa without anybody seeing you on the street. So it was surprising to have two knocks on the door in one afternoon. I hoped against hope it wasn't Manny Vespa, and when I opened the door it wasn't. There stood a man in a UPS delivery uniform with a small cardboard box under one arm. Until he took off his hat, the man looked remarkably like Jesus. After he took off his hat, he looked exactly like him.

★★★ TWENTY ★★★

I shook Jesus's hand, which seemed to be his preferred method of greeting. At least with men. Zelda went up and hugged him warmly, and he hugged her warmly in return, pressing his hand against the back of her hair and squeezing her tightly against him. My father was watching. "Pa," I said, "this is Jesus." There was more handshaking, though I could see, from the way he'd lowered his head and was looking out from beneath his eyebrows, that my father was uncomfortable. Slightly suspicious. Ill at ease.

"I saw you on TV today," my father told Jesus. And then he added—and this was classic Arnie Thomas, one of the things that made me admire him so much, despite his quirks—"I have to be honest, okay? I liked what I heard. I agree with you about what America needs. I came up here to say I'll help you any way I can. Don't have much money to contribute, but I work hard, have a few minor skills. . . ." He paused and scratched the birthmark on the side of his chin, a sure sign that he was nervous. "But, I have to say this: I'm a Jew. I was born a Jew and raised a Jew, and, well, you're Jesus, *the* Jesus, I guess, or at least that's who you say you are. And, well, I can't just all of a sudden start believing you're the Messiah or somebody. I want to be straight about it. If that doesn't work for you, I understand, and I'll go my own way and not have any hard feelings, and I hope you won't either."

My dad finished with a wave of one hand, a wave that encompassed a sort of helpless but confident irony, as if history was what it was, and would continue to be that way, and all you were left with in the face of that was the ability to laugh and endure. He kept looking Jesus in the eye. Jesus seemed to be studying him the way you would study a museum piece. We heard sirens outside in the street. And then Jesus said, "Agreed."

"Good," my father said. He could go back to his friends at the Deli Hillel in North Salem and say that he'd stood his ground. Sure, they'd seen his son Russ up on the stage with the character who claimed to be Jesus, and yes he'd done a little work for the campaign. But he had done it because his family was involved, and he was working for the *campaign*, not the religious figure. There was a crucial difference.

"You are quite a character," Jesus said. He was still appraising my dad, but now there was a tiny grin at the edges of his mouth. "Like your son."

My father looked at me and we had a nice moment. "Two crazy bastards," he said.

Jesus nodded.

"But when we have a friend, we live and die for the guy."

Jesus nodded again. "Let us hope it doesn't come to that," he said, and he said it in a way that made Zelda shiver, and when I looked at her she was frowning and holding each shoulder with the opposite hand.

"Now, Arnie," Jesus went on, "I am also a Jew, as you may remember. Let's you and me take a walk and leave the soon-to-be-married couple to finish their licensing process, or whatever it was. Do you follow?"

My dad experienced a moment of confusion, then nodded.

"Two things first, though," Jesus said. "One." He turned to me and Zelda. "Tell Wales I want you to rent a commercial jet for the duration of the campaign. Something that seats twenty and comes with a pilot. Get the best deal you can, the money will be in the account."

"We'll do it, Lord," Zelda said. I think she was as traumatized as I was about the licensing remark, and I worried that we'd never make love again, or never make love again without feeling like there was a set of divine eyes upon us the whole time.

"If you call me Lord again, I'm firing you," Jesus told her. "You're causing your future father-in-law discomfort, for one thing, and I personally don't like it, for another. It's an outdated term, and it has caused nothing but trouble throughout history."

"Sorry," Zelda said.

"And forget the apologies and the guilt. Do what you tell your clients to do: let it go. You know you're a good person, and so do I and so does Russ and so does Arnie. It shines off you like sunlight off gold."

"Okay . . . Jesus."

"Better. My friends call me the Boss, if you must know. And I have about thirty other nicknames. Big Guy. The Comeback Kid. Etcetera. But 'Jesus' is fine for the purposes of the campaign. Hay-Zeus in the Hispanic precincts. And for the record, I never came to be worshipped, not the first time and not this time. I came to be *emulated*. That's what people didn't get. *Followed*, as in being an example, as in making your interior world resemble mine. Clear?"

"Not exactly, not yet," Zelda said, with her typical honesty.

"But that is your work," he went on, more animated now, with that rustle of impatience in his voice, as if he expected ordinary human beings like us to see the universe the way he saw it. "What do you do all day? You help people straighten out their interior worlds, yes?"

"Yes. I mean, I used to. I—"

"Well then, take that to the next level. You, yourself. Go past the father and mother abandonment stuff and the struggling-to-overcome-your-tough-childhood-professional-woman stuff and to the next level. You people don't realize what is in there. Your own scientists say you use less than ten percent of your brain. Well, what do you think the other ninety percent is capable of? Think, will you? All three of you." He was on a roll now. I could see he'd have no trouble sounding passionate on the stump. "I don't personally care, Arnie, if you think I am God or the Messiah or if you don't. What possible difference could that make to me? Think about it. Is it going to hurt me? Make me feel insecure? No. What I care about is that you figure out what I am trying to tell you."

"So you *are* a great teacher then," my dad said hopefully. "A rabbi. I mean, that's what you were the first time."

"Sure, if that makes you feel good. Use whatever word you want. Just don't say that's *all* I was. And forget about me and start focusing on yourself, your potential, your *inner* potential. Okay? If I lose this election, do you really think I am going to be in pain, disappointed in myself, unhappy? I am not doing it for me this time, and I was not doing it for me the last time. Clear?"

"Clear," we all three said at once, to be polite.

"Now, as far as you two lovebirds go, don't worry. From this day forth I turn off that part of my celestial vision and give you privacy. Enjoy your intimacy, that's what it was invented for. Those who are judgmental about sex tend to be judgmental about everything. Hard-hearted. Stingy. Overprotected. I would not choose anyone like that to work with me. Hear me?"

"We hear," Zelda and I both said, with some enthusiasm.

"Lovemaking is one of the Wonderful Mysteries."

"Okay."

"Plus one more thing," Jesus said, and he went over to my father, put both hands on his gray head, then touched the birthmark on the side of my father's jaw. The birthmark disappeared. We could see that happen, my dad couldn't. Zel gasped, my dad looked at her—and then Jesus put his arm around my father's shoulders, and the two of them walked out the door without saying good-bye.

The package was left lying on the table, unopened. For a few minutes Zelda and I walked around uncomfortably, not saying anything, not making physical contact, avoiding each other's eyes. She got a towel from the bathroom and finished drying her hair. I had half a mind to turn on the ball game, or flip through the channels to find out what else they were saying about Jesus and the campaign, but instead I went over and checked the address on the cardboard box: RUSSELL THOMAS AND ZELDA HIRSCH. It was very light. I used a kitchen knife to cut the tape, and then lifted open the flaps, and by the time I was taking the bubble wrap out, Zelda had walked over to me and was standing at my shoulder. Inside was an envelope, nothing more. And inside the envelope was a note. "Back to what you were doing!" the note said, and there was what appeared to be a smiley face at the bottom, and a bank check for ten thousand dollars.

Inside the card, otherwise blank, was written this mysterious line, "Her name shall be Delahi. This is for the college fund."

Standing side by side, we shook our heads and puzzled over it for a minute or so. And then there was nothing else to do, really. The day had been tremendously weird, Zel and I were shaken in about three different ways, and we had seven million details to attend to. So, naturally, we took the classic medicine, and sought comfort in each other's body, and had fun doing it.

As a footnote, I should mention that it would not be until some years later that a child would be born unto us. We would name her Delahi. Which, we have come to learn, means "the licensed one," in ancient Cyramaisaic, one of the dialects spoken in Bethlehem about the time of Jesus's birth.

TWENTY-ONE

We rented the plane, as Jesus had told us to, a BizzAire 527, with a small kitchen, two bathrooms, a bar, and comfortable seating for twenty. Jesus informed Wales that our first stop would be Topeka, Kansas. We would fly there in our new jet, then rent two cars and spend a week driving the back roads of Kansas and Nebraska and talking to people. This struck both Wales and me as a terrible idea.

"Kansas is one of the cornerstones of Marjorie Maplewith's base," Wales complained, when I went over to discuss security arrangements with him before we left. Ezzie was at the tennis club pursuing fundraising possibilities, so the house was empty. He was sitting at the granite-topped counter in his kitchen and fondling a fishing lure in such a way that I thought he'd put the hook through a fingertip. "There isn't a chance in ten million that anybody but Maplewith carries the state."

"Plus it's dangerous," I said. "Those fanatical so-called Christians can be nasty, and the plains are crawling with them."

"Tell me about it," Wales said.

It seemed to me, from the way he turned his eyes away and gazed out the kitchen windows, that Walesy was still scarred by the repercussions of a story ZIZ had done a year or so earlier about an evangelical church—House of the Holy Loud Voice—in West Zenith. The preacher there, the Reverend Jonathan "Buck" Scythe, had raised the impressive sum of $3.4 million, supposedly for a new building, or, as he put it, "a grand tribute to the joyful face of Christ." Then he absconded with the money, accompanied by a dark-haired college sophomore with nice legs. He was apprehended, after a fun month on the island of Eleuthera, and brought back to Massachusetts to face charges, and Wales had put together what I thought was an inventive story on him, interspersing shots of the arrest and arraignment with glowingly positive reports from members of his lunatic cult.

Somehow, this one news story, which lasted all of two minutes on a sleepy weeknight, came to the attention of an online group — headquartered in Kansas, as it happened — called Defenders of the Earliest American Faith, which made it their business to rush to the defense of any "Christian" preachers who ran into unfavorable publicity. DEAF had a membership of a couple hundred thousand, and the ability to stimulate them to fits of e-mail fury at the tapping of a few keys. So for the next week or so the spineless types who own the station had to field all this phone and e-mail traffic. It was unpleasant. All they knew to do with the unpleasantness was to make Wales miserable — memos, staff meetings, empty threats about job cuts.

We recovered, of course. In the end, Preacher Buck went off to jail for three years and six months, the college sophomore got a generous book contract, and the station returned to business as usual, more or less, though the bosses forced us to stay clear of religious stories for a while.

Wales had never forgotten it. As he was looking out the kitchen window I made the small mistake of saying, "What if Topeka is filled with Preacher Buck types? What if DEAF sends hecklers to the rallies?"

He shrugged, maintaining the lack of eye contact for which he was famous. "Let's cross that river when we get to it. I'm more worried about getting some sense of where our candidate stands on the issues. We've been getting requests for position papers. Zelda's been hit hard with questions. I've been trying to get him to speak to that, but he keeps putting me off."

"Careful you don't put that hook through your finger," I said by way of a response, but I was as worried as he was.

A DAY LATER, still without knowing where Jesus stood on the major questions of the day, we all climbed onto the plane—Jesus, Wales, Ezzie, me, Zelda, my mom and dad and Stab, Dukey McIntyre with Ada Montpelier and Dukey Junior, and the Simmeltons, just back from Costa Rica.

The flight was smooth—Pa mixed the martinis and Stab dictated a tape-recorded letter to his girlfriend—but once we landed, things went sour pretty much right away. No sooner had our motley crew disembarked at the Topeka airport, Forbes Field, and moved into two white limos (non-Hummers, this time) than we were confronted by the righteous "Christian" anger that was spreading like a virus through parts of the country in those days. On that particular morning, this anger took the shape of a coterie of locals, standing at the gates, blocking our path. There were sixty or seventy of them, ranging in age from kids in strollers to grandparents with canes. There was a predictable assortment of signs saying things like BLASFIMY! and SATAN COMES IN A THIN DISGIZE! and the holders of these signs were chanting "FAKE! FAKE! FAKE! FAKE! YOU MOCK THE ONE TRUE LORD!" and pushing toward the car in what could be interpreted only as a threatening way.

Zelda and I and Wales and Ezzie were in the seat together, facing Jesus, who liked to sit beside Stab, who liked to ride facing backward. My parents were in the second car with Dukey and Ada and their son and the Simmelton family. Stab was making "pup, pup, pup, pup" sounds with his lips, which is what he does when he's afraid, and, seeing that, I started to get angry.

"Calm yourself, Russell," Jesus told me, calmly.

"I'll calm myself. As head of security I'll get out and start calmly throwing punches."

"Pup . . . pup . . . pup . . . Don't, Russ," Stab said.

But I didn't have to worry. It was Dukey McIntyre who got out and seemed ready to start throwing punches. His very short, rust red hair seemed to be standing up straight on his head, and his arms were held out away from his body as if he were squeezing stale loaves of bread in each armpit on the way home from the Piggly Wiggly. Combat boots.

Flak jacket. The whole nine yards. He must have drunk eight Red Bulls on the flight west. He was striding toward the protesters with a menacing expression on his face and the Scorched Earth logo (our pretty blue planet engulfed in flames) on his shirt. I reached for the door hoping to stop him before he killed someone and had to spend the rest of his life in Leavenworth, but Jesus rested a hand on my arm. He put a finger on the button and rolled the window down.

"Dukey," he said. "It's all right."

"All right?" Dukey screamed above the chanting. His face was almost purple, veins standing out on his forehead and neck. "I'm going to bust some head! I'm going to take one of those signs and start busting some redneck head!"

"But you *are* a redneck," Esmeralda said, in a voice Dukey could not hear.

"Let me take care of it," Jesus told him evenly.

Dukey hesitated, glanced at me, his nominal boss. Not knowing what else to do, I nodded. When Jesus got out, I followed bravely and resolutely, though sweat was already running down the insides of my arms. I waved for Stab and Zelda to stay in the car.

Jesus—whose wardrobe was unpredictable—had dressed that day in jeans, work boots, and a striped short-sleeved shirt. He had the powerful shoulders and strong hands of a day laborer, and, with his coppery skin, he looked as if he'd been out in the fields for most of that spring. As he stepped out of the car and walked toward them, the protesters seemed, very quickly, to run out of gas. I don't believe any kind of divine power was used; it was his presence, an extraordinary presence, but fully human all the same. He walked toward them as calmly as if he were strolling over to buy a glass of lemonade from a kindergartener at a sidewalk stand, and then he stopped a few yards short, put his hands on his hips, and looked at them. One or two people in the back were still yelling, but everyone I could see—and Dukey and I were only a few feet behind Jesus—was quietly watching him. The children seemed especially moved, as if some combination of Barney, an Action-Figure, and the lead singer from the Wiggles had stepped out of the TV set and was about to give them a present. I noticed a camera crew getting out of a satellite truck and running over. They took up their position at the left side of the crowd, close against the gate, and started filming. "You're not real, are you?" one brave soul in the front row managed to say, but his voice had a tremor of doubt in it.

"Quite real," Jesus answered. "Perfectly real."

"But you're not the Risen Christ," a woman ventured, more forcefully.

"It is possible that I am not," Jesus said, looking straight at her. "But it is possible that I am. And if I am, and if you see me as I am and do not believe, what becomes of you?"

The woman fainted, just lost her legs and dropped. Her husband started to minister to her. The camera swung over to them. A tall, thin young man with a red shirt on pushed hard from the back of the crowd to the front and began thrusting his finger at Jesus and spraying spit. "Fake! Fake! Fake!" he shouted, but the crowd was not taking up the chant any longer. The camera turned to the young man. He stopped yelling and glared.

"I am Jesus, the Christ," Jesus said, tenderly but surely. "I offer you my blessing and I ask for your vote."

At this, at the tone of his voice more than the words, I think, three or four protestors in the front row dropped their signs and went down on their knees. About a quarter of the people behind them did the same. The woman who had fainted got up onto all fours and then fainted again and fell flat on her face on the tarmac. I could hear the reporter talking into his microphone, "We're here at Forbes Field in Topeka, where the man calling himself Jesus has. . . ."

"Let us pass now, if you would," Jesus went on quietly. "We have a rally today in Veterans' Park, and we'd like to get to the hotel and prepare. I invite all of you to come to the rally and hear what I have to say about rescuing America."

One of the elderly women at the edge of the crowd suddenly threw her cane across the metal barrier and shouted, "I'm cured!" Someone else pushed one of the sections of fence aside, and for a moment I thought there was going to be a wholesale stampede. They were pressing forward, or about three-quarters of them were. There was still a fair-sized minority of nonbelievers hanging back. They had not knelt. They'd lowered their signs and stopped chanting, but the expressions on their faces were thick with disdain. Dukey and I circled around in front of Jesus and held out our arms, hoping he'd hurry back into the limo. Instead, he came forward between us, waded right into the crowd, and started touching people on the shoulder or the top of the head. Some were shivering. At least one of them started speaking in tongues. Jesus crouched down and put his hands on the shoulders of a boy who could not have been more than three, and instead of crying at the sudden attention of this dark-haired stranger, the boy flashed a toothy smile. Naturally, at that point, the reporter pushed his way through, with the cameraman right behind him, thrust the microphone in Jesus's face and said, "What is your stance on the question of abortion?"

"I have no stance on it," Jesus said after a moment, looking up from his crouch.

"But is it right or wrong?"

"Right and wrong," Jesus said calmly.

"But would you appoint justices who'd outlaw the taking of human life in the womb or wouldn't you?" the reporter pressed.

I could feel myself cringing. I could feel the mood of the crowd swinging back toward where it had been before Jesus had first approached them. The answer to this question, it seemed to me, was going to send the campaign careening in one direction or another, toward the red states or toward the blue, or, possibly, toward a premature end. On this issue, more than any other in American politics, there was no compromise.

"There is God's law, and the law of the nation," Jesus said.

I cringed again. I moved toward him, looking for a way to get him safely back into the limo and get us out of there.

"What you're saying is 'render unto Caesar,'" a man in the crowd called, taking up the questioning before the reporter could get his next word out. "But what if Caesar allows people to slaughter the unborn?"

"I have come to bring the two laws together," Jesus said.

"To make murder illegal then," a woman said hopefully.

"To make unkindness unacceptable," Jesus said to her. "Anger and hatred and unkindness and greed and selfish behavior of all kinds." And then, patting the boy's head a final time, he stood up and turned, and in another minute we were back in the limo with the doors locked and an awful silence floating in the air among us. The driver took us slowly forward through the crowd, which was neatly divided now into those who were waving and smiling and those who were standing still with scowls on their faces. I turned my head as we went through the gates, and I could see the reporter speaking animatedly into the camera, and small arguments already beginning to break out. What did he mean? What kind of political doublespeak was this? He wasn't a liberal, was he?

After we'd been cruising toward the hotel for a few minutes, Wales, God bless him, had the courage to break apart the terrible quiet that had settled over us. "It's a question that's going to haunt you all through the campaign, you know," he said carefully.

"What is?" Jesus asked him. "The inclination toward universal compassion?"

"You know what I mean. The abortion question. Pro-choice. Pro-life. It's not a fence you can sit on. Not here especially. But not anywhere really."

"I've been wondering what you wanted me to say to the press about it," Zelda said. "We've all been talking about it."

"Tell them I will answer any question they ask."

"But this is the American media," Wales said. "They don't want parables, and they don't want cryptic sayings. They're going to try to pin you down."

It was not the finest choice of words. For a second or two, Jesus almost seemed to grin, and then he turned to my brother and said, "Stab, we're glad you're here, do you know that?"

My brother smiled his tremendous smile, a smile without any defense in it, any sophistication, any cynicism, any armor. "I'm happy I'm here, too, God," he said.

"But if you hadn't been born when you were, to your mom and dad, with this joker here as your brother, your spirit would have found another way to come to us. Do you understand?"

"Sure I do," Stab said. "But nobody else would love me like this mom and dad, right? And this brother?"

"Nobody."

"I knew that was right," Stab said. "And I know how they made me, too."

Jesus patted him kindly on the knee. I could feel myself almost leaning toward him, could feel the words climbing up my throat toward my lips. "But say it plain," I wanted to yell out. "Let us know what you think about it!"

Jesus turned to Zelda. "Let me take care of that answer for now," he told her, and she was nodding her head in rapid beats.

"But we want to know," I blurted out. "Is it murder, or is it okay? Or are we going to get into situational ethics? As president, what would you do?"

Wales and Ezzie were murmuring their agreement, so at least I wasn't left out there hanging.

"I shall teach," Jesus said. "I shall teach kindness and compassion. That's what I've always done. And it has always made certain people angry and violent."

"But you're avoiding the question," I said. Zelda was nudging me with her leg. I knew I was pushing things, but I could not stop myself.

Jesus looked across the space at me until I became uncomfortable, but I kept my eyes on his eyes.

"You have ultimate freedom in how you behave," he said at last. "You were given an unlimited freedom to determine your fate. None of you seems to understand that yet."

"Even so —" I started.

"I understand it," Stab said, which was the kind of thing he always did, picking up a few words of a complicated conversation and responding with some kind of semi *non sequitur*.

"Your brother here understands it," Jesus said, boring his eyes into mine. It wasn't a look of coldness; it was the definition of direct, though his words had a soft lining to them. "You, on the other hand, are a bit slow."

"I've been telling him that for years," Wales said, and everyone laughed.

I joined in the laughter, content to let the subject fade away for the time being, but it felt false to me. I had been cast back into the zone of uncertainty again, and I knew Jesus could feel it, and Zelda, too, and I was glad my parents hadn't been in the car to hear the conversation.

As we were checking into the Topeka Sheraton, Wales waited until no one was near us and said, "That's going to kill us, that kind of answer. You know that, don't you?"

I said that I knew it, and then I went upstairs with my good wife-to-be, and we showered and changed clothes and got ready for the rally without saying a word to each other.

✶✶✶ TWENTY-TWO ✶✶✶

Among the crowd in Veterans' Park, a number of people were holding up placards with photos of dead fetuses on them, and I was worried that Jesus was going to try to smooth over the abortion issue by talking about something else, or that he would give the kind of evasive answers he'd more or less gotten away with at the airport. I introduced him again. It was easier this time, though I felt the crowd was less sympathetic. It wasn't only the people with the fetus pictures, and the fruit-heads yelling, "Thank God for the war!" (meaning, we found out later, that they believed God had put America in what was looking more and more like a thirty-year war, as punishment for our tolerance of homosexuals). It wasn't only the EVOLUTION IS THE DEVILS DOCTRINE! ADAM AND EVE WERE MADE IN THE FIRST DAY! crowd (grammatically challenged, as so many of the loudest mouths seemed to be) either, although, as my mother noted, even if you read the Bible literally, Adam and Eve weren't made until later than that. It wasn't that the people were unfriendly. In fact, everyone we'd met, from the hotel bellhops to the limo driver to the police officials with whom I'd arranged for security, was friendly and nice. It was just a general sense I had — my own prejudices maybe — standing up in front of the microphones and five or six thousand souls, that this new flat world we were in was less than welcoming to the Jesus candidacy.

So I kept the introduction short and to the point, and then yielded the stage to Jesus. He began more or less the same way he'd begun in West

Zenith, saying America was in grave danger of losing its soul, and that
he'd come to spread love and good will again, and so on. But then—perhaps sensing a growing restlessness in the crowd—he surprised me, surprised us all.

"Now I know that the campaign is new," he said in the same gentle,
even-toned way he said almost everything, "and that there are many unanswered questions. As I have said before, I am going to answer every
question I am asked, although the answer will not always make everyone
comfortable. At the airport today—and I want to thank the good people
who were there for making us feel excited about being in Topeka—at the
airport today I was asked about abortion."

He paused and even the fruit-heads fell silent. You could hear crows
flying overhead, making their harsh laughing sounds. You could hear
skateboard wheels on the nearby sidewalk. Jesus drew the silence out,
stood there not saying anything else for ten or fifteen seconds, just looking at the crowd. I was aware, naturally, of all the cameras focused on
him, all the dead air time.

He took a breath and started up again. "I understand that it is an issue
that divides this great nation, divides brother from sister, father from
son, mother from daughter, friend from friend. I understand that. I am
aware of that and deeply saddened by it. What is at the heart of this issue?
What can we say is the truth at its center?"

"That abortion kills!" someone yelled out.

Jesus ignored him. "The truth is that some people, good people, believe
human life begins at conception, and anything that interferes with the
growth of the fertilized egg to maturity is the equivalent of murder."

"It *is* murder," the same guy yelled. "It's not the *equivalent* of murder.
It *is!* It *is!*"

I saw Dukey moving through the crowd toward this loudmouth, pushing people aside roughly as he went.

"And other people, good people also, believe that life begins at birth.
Or at some point between conception and birth. Or that certain circumstances make abortion the lesser of two difficulties. Or that it is a quint-
essentially private matter. I understand this. I see all this. . . . What I

see even more clearly is the hatred that has grown around this important issue. People have actually been killed in the name of not killing!"

"So what are you going to do about it?" the same guy yelled. Just as he got the last word out, Dukey reached him. There was a scuffle, a little knot of people blocking my view of what happened next, and I was wondering, not for the first time, if Dukey McIntyre would prove to be a net gain or a net loss for the campaign.

Jesus did not seem to notice. Or, if he did notice, he went on without reacting. "And so, with full respect for the complexity of this matter, as president, within the first two months of my first term, I will convene a national conference on the issue of abortion. Held here in Kansas, the heart of the nation, televised nationally. It will not be a debate. Hate speeches will not be allowed. It will be a conference, with speakers representing each position given equal time. This will not satisfy everyone, I realize that. I think of it as a first step only, a small but important first step. The reality is, if abortion is made illegal, people will continue to have abortions by the millions—there is ample proof of that from this and other societies. And the reality is, if abortion remains legal, people will continue to have abortions by the millions, and the hatred and anger surrounding this issue will not cease. So let us come together as a nation, with good people on either side of this question, and see if we cannot find one small foothold of national reconciliation, an intelligent and compassionate way of *reducing* the number of abortions, at least. Surely we can all agree on that."

As soon as Jesus had delivered himself of this mild, sensible idea, people started throwing things. Someone about twenty feet from the stage was the first: he or she sent a tomato flying toward the podium. The tomato splattered against the floor and onto my mother's shoes, looking like a splotch of blood. For a second or two I thought she had been hurt. Taking this as an example of proper behavior, someone farther back threw a stone. He had, thankfully, not been quarterback for the KU Jayhawks: the stone did not reach the stage but fell into the front of the crowd. More objects were thrown—hot dogs, corn dogs, cans of soda, sticks, stones, small briefcases; I even thought I saw a Bible go flying through the air. Then there was a backlash against the throwers, and soon a dozen skirmishes had broken out in the crowd, and the police were wading in, and what we had there in the heartland, instead of peace and national reconciliation, was a melee. My mother and Zelda and Ezzie and the three Simmeltons huddled around Jesus as if he needed protection. And my father and Wales and Stab and I huddled around them, moving like some bottom-of-the-sea, twenty-two-legged organism toward the relative safety of the limousines.

"THAT WENT WELL," Wales remarked dryly, when we were all seated, straightening our clothes and hair, checking for injuries, and looking worriedly out the windows, where the police seemed to be gaining the upper hand.

"Actually, it did," Jesus told him.

And in a way he was right. As we started our five-hundred-mile tour of the plains states, he repeated his call, at every stop, for a national conference on abortion. Listening to him, I wondered if he was crazy, or naive. But, if nothing else, it garnered lots of attention. Within two days some in the media had started calling us the Divinity Party, and though I think they meant it ironically, it caught on, and then, as the video clips were replayed on the Internet and the TV talk shows, it was the fruitheads throwing briefcases and tomatoes who looked foolish.

The biggest news of all—and this reached us four days later in Kearney, Nebraska, a pretty college town where we had a rally that attracted some thirty thousand folks, and where the reception had been quite a bit warmer—was that two of the loudest voices from opposite sides of the abortion question, Milly Osterville of the National Confederation of Women, and Edie Vin of Americans for Life and Liberty, said they would be willing to take part in such a conference. That, as you might guess, was front-page news in every newspaper in America, top-of-the-hour story on every big news show, liberal and conservative. Zelda came running into the dining room of the hotel where we were having a late lunch and she was waving three newspapers and smiling exuberantly.

The two major-party candidates did not fail to notice this shift in tectonic plates, of course. Even after the wild rally in West Zenith, they had been more or less able to ignore Jesus and hope he'd go away. But with his mostly successful foray into the heartland, and all the publicity his abortion conference idea generated, they went into panic mode. And faith in our candidate's divine savvy—if not in the goodness of humanity—was restored.

★★★ TWENTY-THREE ★★★

A few polls had been taken immediately after Jesus's announcement in West Zenith, but no one put much faith in them. He was still a novelty item at that point, amusing news. For the real polls, we had to wait a couple of weeks. By then, we had completed our tour of Kansas and Nebraska, spending time mainly in small and medium sized towns there, and had flown to Denver and made another limo loop: Greeley, Aspen, Salida, Colorado Springs, and Pueblo. One thing that surprised me was the variety of individual responses Jesus received, everything from the well-dressed couple in Aspen who walked up without saying a word and handed Wales a large check, to the diner waitress in Salida who refused to serve us. Some people looked Jesus up and down very carefully, as if they were purchasing an expensive golf bag; some people just wanted to touch him, or have him lay a hand on their child; some people seemed not to care very much about his divinity or lack of it, and they took the opportunity to engage him in a thoughtful give-and-take about the war, immigration, terrorism, taxes, or health care.

By and large, though, we had the feeling that he was seen as a welcome breeze in a campaign that, for months, had been full of bitterness and stale rhetoric. On route to New Mexico and another busy day of appearances and interviews, we stopped over in a rustic roadside motel in Trinidad—the Wagon Wheel Inn, it was called; I'll never forget it—and were watching the news there when CNN flashed the prestigious Yansman-Carver poll up on the screen. It looked like this:

MARJORIE MAPLEWITH (R)	36%
DENNIS ALOWICH (D)	26%
JESUS CHRIST (I)	32%
UNDECIDED/OTHER	6%

We were having what passed for one of our strategy meetings at the time—thirteen of us sitting around in a motel room with take-out food (decent Mexican, in this case). There were four or five seconds of stunned silence, and then, well . . . all hell broke loose. Everyone but Jesus was standing and yelling at top volume. It was, for me at least, the moment when our campaign went from being a David vs. Goliath enterprise, a quaint road trip with nice people for a good cause—to an actual run for the White House.

Only Jesus stayed seated. He was sitting there with a paper plate on his lap and a glass of cheap red wine in one hand. I turned to look at him, in midcelebration, and saw the sharp-cut, handsome face wrinkle from the smallest wash of pleasure and then fall back again into the expression of preternatural calm he seemed to wear at all times. Stab did what I wanted to do but was afraid to—he went over and clapped Jesus on both shoulders and hugged him. Wine sloshed onto the already ratty rug (next morning, as we were checking out, Jesus quietly instructed me to leave the motel owners money enough for a new one). Jesus laughed quietly at the spilled wine, looked up at my brother, and said, "Good news, isn't it, my friend?"

"Yeah, it sure is, sure is, sure is!" Stab told him, and then, "What is it, Russ? What . . . what . . . what . . . what. . . . What happened?"

"Jesus is doing great in the polls, pal."

"Super duper! What are the polls?"

"It's a thing where people go around asking other people who they think they're going to vote for. And a lot of people said they're going to vote for Jesus."

"Why aren't they *all* going to vote for him, Russ?"

"Because they all don't know him yet. That's why we have to drive around like this and fly in the plane and everything."

"Okay, great then. Great, Ma, huh? Pa, isn't it great?"

In a while, Amelia Simmelton and the little McIntyre-Montpelier boy were in their beds in other rooms, and Ada Montpelier, tired out by her three-year-old and still nursing sore ankles, had gone to lie down, too. We had watched the news reports and the analysis, full, as always, of war imagery: "Well, it's early, of course, but it would certainly seem that the campaign of the man who calls himself Jesus has gotten traction and is going into the trenches with the better-knowns." "Yes, but traction where, is the question." "Right, and, of course, what we're seeing is mainly the novelty factor. The other candidates have been out there pressing the flesh for eighteen months. They've survived the primary battles, taken some blows, licked some wounds. People are weary of them." "The fatigue factor, yes." "We've seen third parties come and go over the years, haven't we." "And it's a stretch to call this a party." And so on.

We had gone through two six-packs of Busch Lite (alas, Dukey was the beer buyer for the group and considered local ales and foreign lagers to be unpatriotic), and a bushel of burritos, tortilla chips, a nice spicy salsa, and four gallons of ice cream. With the possible exception of Jesus, who took short naps when we flew but otherwise never seemed to tire, we were all, I think, weary from the travel, from the strain of the rallies. We were starting to understand that we were too small a crew to be carrying on something like this. We couldn't even begin to field all the phone calls that were coming in on the half-dozen new cell phones we'd registered. Zelda was up late every night trying to deal with requests for interviews. Wales and Nadine Simmelton had set up a Web site, and there were contributions and offers from volunteers pouring in, and a small paid staff in the headquarters back in West Zenith; still we couldn't come close to doing what had to be done. Yet Jesus insisted that he did not want to hire a big staff, that he wanted to go along the way we were going, generating publicity "the old-fashioned way," as he called it—i.e., working ourselves to the bone. If people wanted to set up their own local chapters of the campaign, he said, they were free to do so. We had even gotten two feelers from high-priced political operatives, guys who'd worked on presidential campaigns in the past, one on either side of the aisle. Jesus had instructed Wales to respond with polite no-thank-yous.

So there we were in the Wagon Wheel Inn's only largish room—Jesus, Stab, Ma and Pa, Wales and Ezzie, Dukey, the Simmeltons, Zelda and yours truly—reveling in the news that, after being on the road for only a couple of weeks, we were in contention. It was exciting, I have to tell you. Exciting like nothing else I had ever known. Scary, too. Especially when, after downing the last sip of his wine, Jesus said, "Now they are going to come after us."

"Who and how?" Ezzie asked him. The woman was as sharp as a sewing needle, and unfailingly gracious. Over the past few weeks, Zelda and I had come to adore her, and to have, I must say, a greater admiration for Wales.

"Listen," Jesus said, as if we weren't already doing that. "Put yourselves in the places of the people who work for our fellow candidates. If their candidate gets in, they will have a good job for four years—secretary of state or head of Parks and Forestry or some such thing. Not to mention Alowich and Maplewith themselves, and their running mates, all of whom claim they are in this to help the country, but are, in fact, absolutely bursting with ambition and eager to be the center of international attention. They're in a hotel room just as we are, somewhere on the American road, looking at those same numbers. What do you think they're feeling?"

"A desperate panic," Zelda suggested.

"Exactly. And what do people do when they panic?"

Dukey, who could rarely contain himself in any situation, and who seemed, not without reason, perpetually flattered to be invited to participate in these discussions, burst out, "They shit their pants, is what they do."

"My thought exactly," Jesus said, which plastered a big smile onto Dukey's face. "And then what?"

"Then—" Dukey pursed his lips as if he'd eaten something sour. He plucked at one red sideburn.

"Then they go vicious on us," Wales said. "Then they go vicious."

TWENTY-FOUR

Walesy was correct, and it did not take long for the viciousness to erupt, like a burst of swamp-gas from stepped-on marshy muck. Within twenty-four hours, some of the right-wing blogs had posted a photograph of Jesus and my brother Stab. They were embracing, and from the angle of the picture it looked like they might be kissing. In the photo, you couldn't see that Stab had a face and head built in a different way than we consider normal. The photo quickly made the Internet rounds. The *Washington Times* ran it on their front page with this caption: SO-CALLED JESUS CANDIDATE REVEALED TO BE GAY. FORMER HOMOSEXUAL LOVER ADMITS TO FIVE-MONTH AFFAIR.

Zelda, whose responsibility it was to keep tabs on press coverage of the campaign, saw the story first and showed it to me in private. My initial response was a personal one: fury. Stab had preserved a lovable innocence into his midtwenties, and I hated to see that tampered with. I hated the thought of having to break the news that there were people in the world who told lies at the expense of others. People so convinced they had the approval of God that anything they did was justifiable.

Soon we started getting phone calls from the press, asking for verification or denial. In her best don't-mess-with-me voice, Zelda told them that the young man in the photograph was her fiancé's brother, who had Down syndrome and a special attachment to Jesus. But in the course of talking with those representatives of the press, she learned that the bloggers had used Stab's photo only as illustration. The character who claimed to have had this relationship with Jesus was from Vermont, had already been booked on one of the right-side radio talk shows, and was being invited onto all the major TV networks, both conservative and liberal. Johnston V. Paege Jr. was his name.

We were in northern New Mexico at this point, at a motel that made the Wagon Wheel look like a Hyatt (all the decent accommodations in the area were booked by the time we called; a big rodeo was going on), and about to start another day of appearances, and I knew the question was going to be thrown at us from the first moment. "Seen this?" I said, showing Wales the computer screen version of the *Washington Times* story.

He looked at it for about two seconds, then turned his eyes away. "Nice," he said, bitterly. He was facing out the motel window. "They used to do that to me before I got married. Reminds you of ninth grade. I'll talk to him about it."

"Brings up a larger question, Boss."

"That he's got no past," Wales said.

"Exactly. Zelda's been getting a ton of requests for biographical information, and we have nothing to give the vultures, no résumé, no place of birth, no known relatives."

"I'll talk to him."

"We're due at the West Edfort Rodeo in two hours. Press is going to be there."

"See if you can find a way to keep your brother otherwise occupied, just for today."

"Right," I said. "Thanks."

"For what?"

"Nothing. Forget I said it."

Norman Simmelton and his wife Nadine were big horse people, and Amelia had ridden, too, before she'd fallen ill. And my dad had ridden at a Jewish camp in the Poconos as a boy. Stab had been in the saddle a few times over the years and liked it, so I made a couple of calls and arranged for the five of them to do an easy half-day trail ride up into the foothills. "Sooner or later we'll have to tell him what's going on," I said to my father, "but if we can put most of the fire out by the time you get back, it might be something we can ignore."

My father was combusting. When he got angry, he had a habit of squeezing things in his bricklayer's hands—beer cans, baseballs, sheets of paper, articles of clothing—and, as he looked through the blogs, he was compressing a paper coffee cup down to the size of a pea. "It's the damn Christians doing this," he said, between his teeth. "The *goyim*. You see what I've been up against all these years, Russ?"

"Arnie, calm yourself," my mother said.

"Easy for you to say."

"Pa, I don't think it's a Christian-Jewish issue this time. They're just afraid of Jesus's surge in the polls and are trying to swiftboat him. You know, a knockout punch. Dean's scream, Dukakis on the tank, Muskie getting teary-eyed, Kerry claiming to be in Vietnam getting shot at when he was actually in college going to parties and skipping his ROTC meetings—that type of thing."

"It's that Carl Jove," my dad said. "The *goyim*."

"Pa, our candidate is the original *goy*."

"Says who? He told me he was a Jew."

"Says the Bible," my mother said.

"Your half of the Bible, Mudgie, not mine."

"There's only one Bible. There's only one God."

They started in along the usual lines, but after a few minutes of squeezing various objects down to the size of single molecules, my dad started to back off, his anger worn down by my mother's certainties. Mudgie might not be as forceful, but she could go on, and on, and on, and on, saying the same thing in the same tone of voice until you'd do anything to get her to stop. It's in the Bible. There's only one God. It's in the Bible. There's only one God. It's in the Bible. . . . So Arnie soon surrendered, stopped talking entirely, and went off with my brother and the Simmeltons to trot and canter.

Meanwhile, Zelda and I, along with Dukey and Ada, were trying to keep ourselves busy in the adjoining room, waiting for Wales and Jesus to emerge. A couple of things were going on. First, like Wales, Zelda and I worried about the lack of a past. We knew it would have to be straightened out soon—Jesus would have to tell how he'd been born in a stable in Kentucky, or a penthouse in Manhattan, or a log cabin in Alaska, something, anything, and fill us in on how he'd gotten from there to here. We'd tried to talk to him about it on several occasions, and he'd given us only the bits about playing football in Kansas and studying dance for awhile. Now it worried us. What *had* he been up to all these years? It was, Wales quipped in an unguarded moment, the greatest story never told.

Second problem: Dukey McIntyre seemed to be taking the charges personally.

"They're saying he's a *fag?*" he yelled, pacing rapidly back and forth across the room and glancing in what he thought was a surreptitious way at Ada. "That I'm working for a *fag?* That the guy who saved my little boy's life is a *faggot?* That God's a freaking *queer!*"

"Dukey, relax," I said. "And the word you are using, believe it or not, would be offensive to some people who might vote for us."

"What word?"

"Look, they're going to say all kinds of things about Jesus. This is only the beginning."

Dukey seemed profoundly puzzled. In his own rough way he was almost as innocent as my brother. "Where I come from we mess people up, big-time, for saying stuff like that."

"I know. Where you come from is where I come from. But we have to handle this professionally."

"I'll handle it professionally," he said, glancing at the mother of his child. "I'll find them and I'll mess them up like a professional. Big-time."

At this happy moment, my cell phone buzzed and rang. I dug it out of my pocket and flipped it open, only to have the moment made even happier by the sound of Randy Zillins's squealy voice in my ear.

"Russ, how goes it?"

"You've seen the polls. It's going good."

"Sure, sure. But I'm calling about this other thing."

"What other thing?"

"You know, the gay thing."

"You didn't call me when Yansman-Carver came out."

"Yeah, I know. Been super busy. But what about this one? It looks bad, I'll tell ya. Can you give me a quote, a little inside info or something?"

"We'll be making a statement, later today."

"I know, right. But can't you give me nothin, buddy?"

"Nothing official, Randy. Nothing for the record."

"But off the record. Looks bad, don't it?"

"Off the record," I said, "a piece of advice. One journalist to another."

"What?" he asked excitedly.

"Consider the lilies of the field," I said, and I hung up.

I'm not sure what, exactly, I meant by that. It was one of the few biblical lines I remembered from my Sunday school days, and I was nervous then, and anxious to get him off the phone. Randy wasn't sure what I meant either: I found out later that the conversation convinced him I would turn out to be some kind of Deep Throat, the inside source that was going to provide his big scoop, his ticket into the farther orbits of journalistic renown. Months later, I would learn that he'd made notes after our conversation, and written: *Some kind of code? Lily=gay sex term?* in his reporter's notebook.

As I pocketed the phone, Wales came out of the inner room looking like he'd just seen someone die in a car accident. He slouched in one of the armchairs, and all of us except Dukey sat in a rough circle around him on the two couches and other chairs. Dukey paced. "He won't deny it," Wales said.

"What!" Dukey yelled. "What the hell!"

At that moment I wouldn't have put it past him to grab Ada by the hand, hoist Dukey Junior onto his shoulders, and walk through the door and out of the campaign forever.

"Calm down," Wales said to him, "or I'll send you home."

"Send *me* home?" Dukey yelled. "I don't work for you. I work for *him!*" He pointed at me.

"I'll send you home, too," I said. "Let him finish."

Dukey fumed and spat air for a moment and paced near the windows, but he kept quiet.

"He won't deny the report," Wales repeated. "It isn't true. He told me himself it wasn't true. He's never heard of Johnston V. Paege Jr., but he won't issue a public denial."

"Why not?"

"He won't dignify the remark."

"We're sunk then," I said. "When's the last time America elected a male homosexual to its highest office."

"Or a female homosexual, for that matter," Zelda said. "Or anybody besides a white Anglo-Saxon Protestant male."

"John Fitzgerald Kennedy," my mother chipped in.

"The larger issue is his lack of a past," Ezzie told her husband.

Wales was nodding, looking at his hands. "We covered that."

"And?"

"And he's planning to give a full accounting of his past at the rally today. After the rodeo. All he said was, 'They asked, and they shall receive.' I didn't want to push him."

"A lot of people in Fultonville said he looked familiar," Ada put in meekly.

"A lot of people everywhere have said that," Wales reminded her. "Thousands, probably tens of thousands of people, think he looks like someone they know. To my eye, for example, he looks like the young Jackson Browne, a shade or two darker."

"Who?" Dukey shouted. We ignored him.

"But no one has claimed to have had an affair with him before this," I said.

"Not true," Wales fiddled with the pocket flap of his expensive sportcoat. "We have four different women from four different cities in California. We could trot them out if need be. One is an exotic dancer, and actually—"

"Oh, please," said Ezzie.

Zelda nodded.

"What's happening," I said, "is what he said would happen: we're being thrown down into the dirt."

"The public loves dirt," Zelda said. "We've been *National Enquirer*–ized."

Ada started to say something, then thought better of it and called Dukey Junior over so she could sniff his pants and see if he needed what she referred to, for some reason, as "an oil change."

"Speaking of which," Wales said, and he was about to let us in on the latest from the "tabloid shit-sheets," as he called them, when Jesus came out of the inner room. He was brushing his hair back, and I noticed that he was now wearing a small diamond stud in his left ear lobe.

"How are my disciples on this day?" he asked in what I had come to think of as his happy voice. There were times when he seemed distracted—as if he were tending to business in some far-flung galaxy—and many times when he seemed disappointed in us, or impatient with us. But once or twice a day he'd appear to forget the weight of his responsibilities and just be a lot like an upbeat guy with a good career, a solid love life, a car he liked, a normal family, admiring friends, a low golf handicap, a thousand shares of Google from ten years ago, and a body that had not yet started to give him any trouble.

"We're in turmoil," Ezzie had the courage to tell him.

He stopped in midroom and set the brush down on one end of the glass-topped coffee table. "Let me guess," he said happily, smiling around the room at his motley crew, "too many unanswered questions."

"Exactly," I said. Wales shot me a look.

"My position on combating terrorism," Jesus went on. "My position on climate change, taxes, providing birth control to minors, needle exchanges, the war, the war on drugs, the war on poverty, the immigration question. My ideas about a running mate, most especially."

"Not to mention your past," I added, because I was in one of those moods where I could not keep my mouth closed.

"My past is an open book," he said.

"Cool," I said. "Problem is, most of the American public hasn't read it yet. Us included."

"What would you like to know?" he asked.

And Dukey, who also could not keep quiet, burst out, "If you're a homo or not, number one."

"Since it means so much to you," Jesus looked at him in what might charitably be described as a tolerant way, "I am omnisexual and asexual."

"Huh?"

"It means he don't do it," Ada said across the room to him.

"Huh? Why not?"

"Because he's God," she hissed. "Everybody ain't an animal for it like you."

Dukey smiled, then quickly forced the smile down with the muscles around his mouth. His masculinity, if not the Lord's, having been safely established, he felt emboldened. "But what about this here Vermont guy? Is that where you're from, or anything?"

"I was born in Texas," Jesus told him.

"Just what we need," Dukey said. "Another one." But he was grinning broadly now. Judging, at least, by his state of origin, Jesus did not seem to be gay; all was right with the world.

"I was born to a Navajo mother in a clapboard shack on the plains of West Texas. My mostly Caucasian father died on a Gulf of Mexico oil rig while she was pregnant with me. She's from a famous Indian family—my dad was an older man and basically stole her off the reservation in New Mexico, though her parents liked him. After his death she returned. She homeschooled me, except for two years when we lived in Kansas because she had fallen in love with a man from the reservation who'd moved there hoping to find work. That man was killed in a meat-packing factory accident, and we moved back to the reservation, where we led a quiet existence filled with prayer and tribal ritual.

I did not go to college, but left home when I was seventeen, went to study dance in New York, yoga and meditation in Tibet and Nepal, then roamed the world meeting people, helping people, living in various disguises. In adult life, my roles have varied. I was the heart surgeon, the friendly waiter, the fellow who leapt out of his car to save a child who had fallen into the street, and on and on. The kidney donor who never wanted any attention, the philanthropist who remained anonymous. I surfaced in Fultonville, Massachusetts, at the ordained moment, as the Scriptures had indicated I would, and decided it was time to come out." After that unfortunate choice of words he looked around at each of us and said, "Anything else?"

"What Scriptures?" I wanted to ask, "Which Scriptures were those?" But like everyone else in the room I could not get a word out just then. I think we were all ashamed. As soon as our opponents turned vicious, we had all traveled back to adolescence, when the wrong accusation at the wrong time would render us an outcast. I looked at Jesus then, looked at the earring, and I thought I was beginning to have an understanding. He was holding a mirror up to us so that we could see ourselves in all our dishonesty and fear and pettiness. He was planning on doing that for the whole nation, I suspected, as president, and I did not see how a candidate with an agenda like that had the remotest chance of winning the election. And at that moment, I was very sad.

"Where's my pal, Stab?" Jesus asked mischievously.

"Out on a trail ride. We sent him away. We didn't want him to have to face, you know, the accusations."

"Which accusations are those? That he's an affectionate soul? Which ones, exactly?"

"That he's, that he might be a queer," Dukey blurted out.

Jesus looked at him for a long moment. It wasn't the nicest of motels, as I mentioned, nor the cleanest. In fact, there was a fine layer of dust or desert sand on the coffee table where the Son of Man had set his hairbrush. Without saying anything else, Jesus squatted down and began writing something in the dust with one finger. Dukey watched for a second like the rest of us, and then abruptly said, "I'll get coffee for the whole gang," and hurried out of the room. Jesus stopped writing, scuffed the letters away with one hand and said, "Everybody ready for the rodeo?"

★★★ TWENTY-FIVE ★★★

My mother told me, as we sat together in a quiet part of our rented bus on the way to the rodeo, that in the Bible there was a scene in which a group of men wanted to stone a woman for being an adulteress.

"That much I remember," I told her.

"Good," she said. "The Sunday school classes weren't wasted. Do you remember what Jesus did?"

"He told them not to stone her. After that it's a blur. I think he went on about it in his blog for a couple of weeks."

She made a face. "He squatted down and started writing with his finger in the dust."

"In some language no one understood, I bet."

"Don't be fresh. People understood, all right. He was writing down their sins, their secret sins. When they saw that he knew everything bad they had done and was getting ready to tell everybody, they all walked away."

"To get coffee for the whole gang," I suggested, but she did not catch the reference, and made a *tsk* with her tongue and teeth and looked sadly at her hands as if something had gone wrong along the way, and her son, after leaving the sane atmosphere of her home, failing at marriage, and abandoning the church . . . had become blasphemous. Successful and nice, a good boy, but irreverent to the point of blasphemy all the same.

I wanted to tell her it wasn't blasphemy at all. I wanted to tell her that humor was a kind of prayer for me, and that growing up Catholic with a Jewish father had been a great education, a twenty-year tutorial in the art of tolerance, in the value of appreciating the ancient wisdom, in looking for something beyond the everyday, something that didn't die with the body. It was becoming clear to me that what Jesus wanted from us was not pious obedience to a narrow set of rules, but a smart, limitless open-mindedness that allowed us—in real life, in actual day-to-day, modern American life—to treat the other person the way we would want to be treated. Gay people, Jewish people, dumb people, rich people, poor people, women, men, right-wingers, liberals, soldiers, and antiwar protestors, maybe even animals—we were supposed to see through the disguise they were wearing, all the way down to the I AM in them. That was it. That was the big commandment, I was almost sure.

But I wasn't sure how to say that to my mother, how to pick the right parable, the right symbol, the right phrase. So I wrapped an arm around her for a minute, and I said, "I've started to reread the Good Book, Ma. Because of you."

Which made her happy, and cost me nothing.

THE WEST EDFORT RODEO turned out to be a huge affair, five thousand people probably, Native Americans, Mexicans, and New Mexicans, a lot of beef being barbecued and tortillas being fried, tobacco being chewed, and people wandering around in cowboy hats and decoratively stitched boots, their faces sun-darkened and dry. We hadn't been able to rent the usual two limos anywhere in the vicinity, so we drove to the event in one of those half-sized school buses, a plain white banner with JESUS FOR AMERICA printed in red letters on the side. My mother had wanted to put a cross next to the letters, but Jesus would not allow it.

Maybe it was the poll numbers, or maybe the rumor of gayness had gotten around very quickly, because more than the usual number of reporters were waiting to meet us as we got off the bus. Standing on the top step, Jesus gave a brief statement saying he would be happy to answer everyone's questions a bit later . . . but first he wanted to ride a bull. All of us—staff and press alike—smiled at this. Ride a bull. It was the type of cute remark any candidate might come up with, something about liking maple syrup in New Hampshire or potatoes in Idaho, or being a big Crimson Tide fan in Alabama, a line intended to make the locals feel proud of whatever it was they had a reputation for being proud of. A nice line . . . except, as we soon learned, Jesus wasn't joking.

From the edge of the crowd of reporters a real cowboy stepped forward, the boots, the hat, the sun-cooked skin. "I'm Jake," he said. "Jake Best." He reached out and gave Jesus a hearty clap on the back. It appeared, from this warm greeting, either that Jesus and Jake had known each other in a previous lifetime, or that Jesus had made arrangements on his own without telling us. "You ready, Boss? Got some duds for you to change into."

And before any of us could stop him, our candidate was striding off in the direction of the corral, talking animatedly with Jake Best about things we could only guess at. There was nothing for us to do but follow. Nothing for the press to do, either. Like a swarm of ground hornets going after a bare ankle they buzzed excitedly toward the enclosure and took up positions around the fence and in the small grandstand. I had a seat there myself, squeezed between Wales and my mother. Zelda was handing out a short bio she'd printed up at the motel office: Jesus the West Texan, world traveler, yoga student, heart surgeon in disguise, anonymous organ donor. I felt like it had the potential to explode in our faces. What if he'd just made it all up? But, at that point there were no other options.

We watched a young Native American on a vicious black bull, his spine and neck whipped this way and that as the animal tried to buck him off its back. The young guy held on for the count of six and then went flying off the animal and landed with an audible thump in the dust, breaking, it seemed, his left wrist.

"Let's have a hand for Austin Pine Needle," the announcer was saying, as Austin hobbled off cradling the wrecked wrist with his good hand. We were all still clapping for him, and the mounted assistants were using their horses to nudge the black bull toward a gate . . . and there was Jesus, fitted out in jeans and a western shirt, leather gloves, boots, chaps, no helmet. He was in the fenced waiting area with one hand on the wooden slat and the other hand gripping the strap that held him to the bull. Cameras were flashing, reporters scribbling. None of us could take our eyes off the man.

"This," Wales said out of the side of his mouth, "is pure genius."

"Either that or we end up doing a press conference from the orthopedic wing of the nearest hospital."

"Watch. I have a good feeling."

The bell sounded, the gate burst open, and out came Jesus on his bull. If Austin Pine Needle's animal had been vicious, then this bull was a four-footed demon, a behemoth of muscle and horns that seemed to take it very personally that some human type had decided to perch on its spine. His hind legs kicked up higher than a basketball forward's sweat-band. He spun like a car out of control on an icy road, kicked and bucked and twisted. And Jesus hung on, one arm whipping in circles, his ear-ring flashing in the sun. He stayed up for an eight count that seemed like thirty, and then, letting out a happy whoop, allowed himself to be shucked off the bull's back like so much loose skin. He went flying up in the air, arms flailing, and somehow managed to land on the soles of his boots. He trotted toward the gate as cool as any starting quarterback coming off the field with a big lead, and ducked between the slats of the fence where a trio of other cowboys slapped his shoulders and nodded their approval.

"Unbelievable," Wales said.

Within seconds, the press was all over him. In fact, on that day, Jesus never was able to give the speech he had planned to give. His past re-mained clouded. The gay issue floated off into the northern distance, because all the major networks had headlines like the one in the *Amarillo Chronicle:* CANDIDATE CHRIST TAKES BULL BY HORNS.

It was occurring to me that Jesus knew more about manipulating the American press machine than any of us did. That night, and on the Sun-day morning political talk shows, the image that was shown again and again, until it etched itself into the national consciousness, was Jesus as Cowboy—which went a long way toward making the whole West Texas/Native American story believable and winning him votes in the

Southwest. Overnight he had become a man's man. A stud. Men liked it. Republican women liked it. Gay men and gay women liked the fact that he had not rushed to distance himself from them by denying the earlier story. Conservatives swelled out their chests at the thought of a real cowboy, not another fake one, in the Oval Office. Liberals smiled indulgently and wondered aloud why anyone would risk breaking bones for the thrill of eight seconds on a bull. Jesus's popularity soared in rural America, to the point where a week later the famous country music singer Andy Ray Pressbine came out with a song titled "Our American Savior, the Bull-Ridin' Redneck." It immediately went to the top of the charts. Pressbine volunteered to play for free at Jesus for America rallies throughout the south, and we were more than happy to accept his generous support.

Within a few days, thanks to diligent reporting by the *Minneapolis Star,* Johnston V. Paege Jr. was revealed to have been convicted, twice, of passing bad checks, and he soon was persona non grata on all but Harry "Hurry" Linneament's radio show, which aired coast to coast on the ED Network. I liked to listen to that show in short bursts, though it always made me angry after a while—which probably was Linneament's intention. I liked his voice and admired his authoritative tone. In any case, Hurry kept giving CPR to the story long after it was obviously dead, kept saying how he did not, simply did not understand how America could let something like this go so easily! When a Republican senator had been caught in an airport men's room taking a wide stance and picking pieces of toilet paper up off the tiles, Hurry had argued the opposite point: watch the Democrats drag this out. Now he was the one doing the dragging.

Adding to our big week was a Newsweek/CBS poll taken two days after the rodeo that showed Jesus pulling ahead of Marjorie Maplewith by four points, one point over their margin of error.

However, once the cloud of sweet publicity began to fade like dust in the bull ring in West Edfort, there were tough questions to face. At our next big appearance, at the Organic Spas of the Southwest festival in Santa Fe, Jesus told us to schedule a press conference before his speech, and the questions came fast and hard.

Why hadn't he chosen a running mate yet?

He would introduce her in exactly one hour, at the rally. (This was, I must say, a shock to all of us on his campaign. The word "her" in and of itself made news.)

Was he, himself, really part Hispanic?

Well, as a West Texas boy, there was the distinct possibility that some Mexican *sangre* had gotten mixed in somewhere, and, if so, he was proud of it. He spoke Spanish fluently, had even been nicknamed Hay-Zeus when he played wide receiver for the Nessland, Kansas, Fighting Meadowlarks in high school. Anybody could get ahold of the old yearbook and see that for themselves.

What did he plan to do about what everyone now called the Endless War in South America?

He would end it.

Just like that?

Just like that. He'd bring the young men and women home and station them along the borders of their own country, train them to help with the inspection of inbound shipments to make sure nothing dangerous or illegal slipped into our great nation.

What about the threat of terrorism?

It was a real threat, he said. Anyone who thought that all the human inhabitants of this world were decent, polite, and friendly, was living in a dream. The question facing America now was the same question that had faced humanity since the first violent act had been committed: how to respond? In protecting yourself against evil, did you allow yourself to be turned into an evil society? Allow the national mood to be dominated by fear? By hatred? Allow your natural prejudices to be inflamed? No, he said, we'd been doing it wrong. Unless the terrorists took over a nation-state and controlled its army and its weaponry, the war on terror was, by and large, a police action, police and special forces (I cringed at this, because, some years earlier, that had been John Kerry's line, and I knew how far it had gotten him), and he would divert half of the vast amount of money now being spent on the war to those areas; the other half would fund his domestic programs, including veterans' health care.

He would immediately appoint a group of the country's best scientists
to found a lab dedicated to ending America's reliance on oil. They would
be fully funded by the U.S. government, on the proviso that income from
private companies purchasing patents for these inventions would be used
to repay that public investment, no interest. Other scientists would be
given the task of finding a way to erase the long-term effects of a nuclear
weapon, should such an awful thing happen on our soil or anywhere else.
This technology, the products spawned from these labs, would be sold to
the rest of the world and would reinvigorate the American economy with
"products invented by our people and made by our workers," as he put it.
There would be an increase in aid to poorer countries, but this aid would
end the very day those countries were found to have sponsored violence
anywhere in the world, including in their own prisons. We would no
longer fund dictatorships, period. There would be no torture of any kind,
and no technical arguments about how to define it. He would make a
concerted effort to rid the earth of nuclear weaponry.

What about gun control?

He had no plans to restrict guns used for hunting. Hunting was a
natural thing, as long as the hunters ate what they killed, or gave or sold
it to others who ate it. As for automatic assault weapons and easy-to-buy
handguns, he hoped Congress would outlaw them. (This remark set off
another firestorm. Within an hour of hearing the news, Brenda Battley,
the first female head of the NRA, endorsed Marjorie Maplewith and
began raising significant sums of money from gun owners to be used in
anti-Jesus commercials. Political analysts would later estimate that the
remark had cost Jesus between four and six percent of the final vote; he
did not seem to care.)

"Have you ever been married?" a reporter asked.

"Not yet. I'm looking. If you know anyone who wants to live in a nice
white house and be surrounded by Secret Service agents night and day,
let me know."

"Are you, or have you ever been, gay?"

"Next question."

"Have you had homosexual encounters?"

"Next question."

"Have you used mind-altering drugs of any kind?"

"Next question."

"Can you name three of your closest friends so that we can approach them for more detailed biographical information?"

Jesus named eight people—five Americans, two Nepalese yoga masters, and a farmer in Argentina. It would turn out that the Americans were easy to find: a banker in Montgomery, Alabama, a cardiac nurse in Saint Louis, a musician in Tampa, a coal miner in eastern Kentucky, and Anna Songsparrow Endish, his vice presidential choice, who would be on the stage with him in ten minutes, and who, he added, "happens to be my mother in this lifetime."

Hearing this astonishing piece of news, reporters began shouting questions from all directions, most of them about Anna Songsparrow: What were her qualifications? How old was she? Why hadn't we heard of her before? Would she participate in the vice presidential debate? Jesus waved one arm to his right, "Yes to everyone on that side," and one to his left, "and no, never, not under any circumstances to everyone on that side," and left the podium to a hundred smiles.

An hour later, when we arrived on the stage after sampling various treatments at various booths promoting various organic spas (Ezzie convinced Wales to have his ears irrigated with distilled water and sea salt) we noticed a small woman standing there with her hands folded in front of her. She wore traditional Indian dress—mocassins, skins, beads—and turned out to be Anna Songsparrow Endish, a Navajo who had been born and raised outside of Flagstaff, Arizona, moved to New Mexico to live on the reservation, and came, we were told, from a long line of famous Navajo mystics. Her father had served in the United States Army in Europe during World War II. Her grandfather had been Chief Prancing Stallion, one of the most revered Native American leaders at the turn of the century. There was an obvious resemblance to the candidate.

Jesus wrapped his mother in a big hug, and held her hand aloft with his. He referred to her as "this great woman," and "one of the real spiritual queens of our era," and she took this in with a tiny Buddha-like smile on her pinched brown features. He asked her to say a few words, and she addressed the assembled in English, then Spanish, and then briefly in her native Navajo, saying, among other things, "I am honored to have been chosen for this important work. Respect for one's mother is a central tenet of Native American life, and it pleases me deeply that my son has remembered this, even as he stands at the center of the biggest American stage. Much hard work lies ahead of us. Our country is in desperate need of spiritual guidance, a guidance that is based on the principle of inclusion, not exclusion." And so on. It was a solid, if not particularly exciting performance, in keeping with that famous first rule for vice presidential nominees: don't outshine your running mate.

The rally went well—cheers, signs, no troublemakers of any kind. Afterward, Anna joined us on the jet, and proved to be a likable, if extremely quiet, member of the team. She and Jesus would sometimes touch each other when they passed in the aisle; once in a while he'd get up and bring her a glass of water, or lean down and whisper something in her ear. But they rarely seemed to feel the need for long conversation, and, as I noted in the journal I was keeping: "If you looked at it without knowing him, or who he was, you'd think Jesus had a love relationship with every woman on the staff, as well as every woman in the audience at the rallies. He reminds me of a rock star in that weird way—he's not flirting, but there is a real body-to-body energy there, something different in the way he looks at women and the way they look at him. You never got a sense of this from the Bible."

In any case, Anna was a welcome addition to the group, and her name on the ticket only increased Jesus's popularity. By the time we finished our broiling hot July tour through New Mexico, Arizona, and southern Utah, and landed in Palm Springs, California, we were, in spite of the NRA and Hurry Linneament, five or six points ahead of Maplewith, and ten or eleven ahead of Alowich, in all the polls that mattered.

✯✯✯ TWENTY-SIX ✯✯✯

I have to say that, on a personal level, I found Jesus to be peculiar and somehat unpredictable. This troubled me. It also made me think about how we had all come to form an image of him in our minds. If we'd been exposed to the Bible, it was usually only to *pieces* of the Bible, a few parables, a few key quotes. Added to those pieces were scraps of things we'd heard, paintings by people who had never seen him, and scenes from films. And added to that, I guess, were elements of our own psychology: we wanted Jesus to be a certain way—a savior, a martyr, a pacifist, a radical political figure, a quiet and gentle man of peace, a drinker of wine, a good friend, a guy who could be comfortable around women—because those things made us feel good about him and maybe about ourselves.

But in real life he defied any kind of label. Sitting up there on the bull, he had looked like nothing more than a good ole boy Texan, shoulder muscles bulging, a steely glint in his eye. At other times, he'd move gracefully down the aisle of the jet like a ballet star, or step out of his hotel room in a suit so stylishly tailored that even Wales's wardrobe paled in comparison. Talking to a university crowd he'd use words like *segue* and *ramification*, and then, out in the country someplace, he'd be having biscuits and gravy at a diner, looking like the kind of guy who'd tell an off-color joke at the VFW bar or come over the hill riding an ATV and howling the rebel yell.

In another politician, this would have felt like phoniness. In Jesus, somehow it all seemed part of one parcel. The press kept trying to squeeze him into a box: he'd talk about prohibiting assault rifles or sentencing nonviolent drug offenders to counseling instead of jail, and they'd brand him a bleeding-heart liberal who would probably raise taxes; the next week he'd be going on about real threats to American security in the coming years, and the necessity of people doing things for themselves rather than looking for handouts, and all of a sudden he was a right-wing, hard-hearted, so-and-so. What was particularly interesting was that, the more the political analysts tried to push him into one corner or another, the more ordinary voters, the ones who counted, seemed to appreciate that he actually spoke from his heart, without any calculation.

He could be gruff, but most of the time what you saw was a bed-rock kindness. This came out most obviously in the way he talked to my brother — as if Stab's mental capabilities were the equal of any Einstein on earth — but also in the way he'd sometimes pick up little Dukey when the kid was throwing a tantrum and his mother looked like she was at her wit's end. Jesus would lift him up and whirl him around in circles. He'd play chess with Amelia Simmelton, a quiet, brilliant girl who Zelda and I believed was actually a grown woman in disguise. When there were children in the crowds at our rallies, they would inevitably try to touch him. Lots of politicians make a fuss over kids, it's not a new idea in the I-want-your-mommy-and-daddy's-vote category, but Jesus did it with such obvious joy that he seemed almost like a child himself. He had a sweet tooth and was always asking the bus or limo driver to pull over "for just a second" when we drove past doughnut shops. He had an incredible physical vitality and would go out for a jog in the early-morning darkness, or do difficult yoga poses on the back lawn of the motel, facts which made his late-sleeping security chief very uncomfortable. He did not pay attention to money (we were all well paid, however, automatic deposit, every two weeks), to what people wore, or to whether they were handsome or ugly. I would realize, as the campaign went on, that he slept only an hour or two at night, and woke in the early morning hours to sit in meditation for long stretches. Despite our crazy schedule, he found ways to have alone time with each of us, going for a walk with Ada when she was particularly stressed, shooting pool with Stab or Dukey, meeting with Wales and Ezzie and Zelda to go over the day's events, chatting with the Simmeltons — avid readers — about the great books. When time allowed, he'd call me into his room to watch the local news with him, and he liked it when I pointed out tricks that reporters use — moving their heads to keep the image from being too static, pronouncing words at different volume and pace.

What was strange, to me at least, and I know to Zelda also, was that Jesus never went anywhere near the subject of religion. We expected more miracles. We expected him to talk to church groups, to court key religious figures, or to toss words like *faith, God,* and *morality* into his speeches. The press wondered about this, too. Along with their exhaustive — and futile — attempts to find evidence that would discount the two big early miracles, they wondered in column after column, talk show after talk show, why he didn't do more magic. I mean, if he really was Jesus, why didn't he, say, go to the rescue of some western Pennsylvania coal miners who were trapped by an explosion and eventually declared lost? Or tour a military hospital and vacuum the trauma out of the brains of soldiers who had fought in the Endless War?

Jesus refused to talk about these things, with us and in public.

But once we'd settled into our Palm Springs lodging, a ritzy golf resort (this was another of his tricks: he'd instruct us to stay in moldy fleabag no-tell motels some nights, and then set us up in the lap of luxury on others), he passed word that we were to be on the bus at ten the next morning for what he called "an unofficial side trip."

By midmorning in early August it's scorching hot in Palm Springs. We had been working hard in similarly hot places, for weeks, and would have preferred to lounge by the pool for a couple of hours before his appearance that evening, or to lie in the air-conditioned rooms and read a good book, or watch Rachael Ray on the tube.

But, faithful workers that we were, at ten a.m. we went out and climbed onto the bus. Anna Songsparrow did not join us: my mother said she had seen her wandering away in the direction of the nearest mountains. It was strange, she said; no one seemed to recognize her, and none of the press people followed her.

When Jesus appeared, he was all turned out in a pair of shorts, sandals, and a collared jersey with PALM SPRINGS INN AND CLUB stitched on the arm.

Twenty or thirty print journalists and photographers pressed toward him as he walked out of the hotel. The bus door was open and I could hear them calling out, "Jesus, Jesus!" and "Lord, Lord!" and "Candidate Christ!" "People are wondering why you won't participate in the last big debate?" "What is your position on the strikes in Argentina?" "Can we get a bio on Ms. Endish?" "Have you seen the latest polls?" "What do you think of Dreaf's He's Not *My* God ads?"

Jesus smiled and nodded and answered none of the questions. At the door of the bus he stopped and turned toward the reporters, sweating and pushing, photographers jockeying for the best shot. "I would like to ask a favor of you," he said in his calm way. "My staff and I are going into the countryside for a strategy session, and I would appreciate it if none of you follow us. If we can have this privacy, I promise that when I get back we will have a thoroughgoing, informal press conference up in my suite. A separate half hour for the Spanish-language press, as well. Why don't we say three to five thirty, cameras allowed. Anyone who follows us will not be allowed into the conference. Agreed?"

Sure, they all said, absolutely. "You'll let us into heaven this afternoon if we don't sin this morning, right?" one of them joked, and it got a hearty laugh from the group.

But, once we were on the road, despite their promises, a few of them jumped into their cars and followed at a discreet distance. We headed out into the desert on State Highway 94, a two-lane asphalt road running between oceans of sand. I went to the back of the bus and watched, but soon most of the cheaters decided it was too obvious, what they were doing. They didn't want to risk their two hours of full access at the press conference. Most of them dropped away, but one group—tabloid photographers and reporters, I think they were—stayed with us. I could see their tan SUV turn when we turned, and speed up when we speeded up. We were really out in the desert by then, heat shimmering off the sand,

and the gray mountains standing in the distance like a mirage. A plume of steam rose suddenly from the SUV, as if a hose had burst. I thought: there are some people you should not lie to.

Jesus was sitting up front with my brother. As if he knew where he was heading, he told the driver to turn here, turn there, guiding us, it seemed to me, deeper and deeper into the wilderness. I hoped we'd started with a full tank of gas.

And then, at last, ninety minutes after we'd set out, Jesus had the driver pull off the road into a sort of picnic area. It was run by a conservation group, the sign said. One by one, we piled out of the air-conditioned bus into the terrible heat. The driver unloaded a few coolers with cold drinks and sandwiches in them. Jesus asked us to take something to eat and drink and then seat ourselves at the tables, but he drank nothing and paced back and forth in the blistering sun with his hands behind his back. After he'd given us a moment to arrange ourselves he stopped pacing and turned to face us.

"I wanted," he said and then paused and looked up into the white-hot sky as if he were asking his divine father and mother for inspiration. "I wanted to change the surroundings, get us out of hotel rooms and into the good fresh air." He paused again, and it almost seemed he was expecting us to voice complaints about the heat, or about the interruption of our promised half day of rest. No one said a word. "I myself have always liked hot weather, for one thing. And, for another, I wanted to ask your opinion, in private, as it were, on why we are doing so poorly."

There were stunned seconds of silence, and then Wales said, "Poorly? We're up eight points in today's poll. Given the big head start the other two had, the money gap, the bigger staffs, I think we should all be pleased as can be."

Jesus looked at him as if he'd just said north was south. He was standing with his sandaled feet apart, hands in the pockets of his shorts, his eyes slightly hooded against the brightness (unlike the other adults, he never wore sunglasses). "Everybody should be voting for me," he said. "Stab thinks so, and I agree."

My brother pushed out his lower jaw and smiled.

But Wales looked worried. "Everybody? Nobody gets everybody's vote. Except in Uruguay or someplace. Uzbekistan."

"I am not an ordinary candidate."

"Agreed, of course," Wales said. He had taken off his sunglasses now to show that, for once, he was making eye contact. He seemed to me, as the campaign manager, more than a little defensive.

"Have I done something wrong?" Jesus asked him.

"No. A couple of strategic missteps. The remark about assault weapons didn't play well in Wyoming, that type of thing."

"Then why isn't everybody for me?"

"Some of them are Jewish," my dad piped up. I think he meant this as a joke, but at times his sense of humor was lost on everyone but himself. This was one of those times. Jesus didn't smile. My father's chuckle drooped like a sunflower at midnight. "I mean, I guess I mean that some people are not predispositioned to accepting you. Your name is kind of . . . loaded. It divides people."

My mother jabbed him with an elbow.

"They expect you to do miracles," I said, partly, I think, because I was feeling bad for my father. "More miracles, I mean."

"I am not going to."

"Why not?" Ada Montpelier asked. "You did a big one for us. Why don't you do the same thing for somebody else?" She was a nice woman, really. Not the sharpest mind in the world, but she doted on Dukey Junior and treated Dukey Senior with more kindness than some of us believed he merited, and she was always the first to get to work when it came time to clean up the pizza boxes and used chopsticks.

"I'll second that," the normally reserved Norman Simmelton said.

"It would be too easy," Jesus told them. "People would vote for me because of the miracles, just as, in the old days, some of them believed in me only because of the miracles. I want them to vote for me because of my *ideas*, because of my mother's *experience* — as a mother, a woman, a household leader — don't those things count for anything anymore?" He looked at all of us but did not seem to expect an answer. "I want them to vote for me because I would make the best president, not because I can cure a blind woman in a Montana church or something."

"Then there's going to be doubt," my dad said.

"You are speaking for yourself, Arnie."

"Yeah, I guess so. I admit it. You know how I feel about you, I just draw the line at the God stuff. Look, people are made different. Two people can go to the same movie and one likes it and one doesn't. That's why we have Republicans and Democrats, Jews and Christians."

"Wrong and right," my mother added, with a note of sarcasm that was unusual for her. It seemed clear to me that working on the campaign had increased the stress in their marriage.

"Part of the problem is you haven't appeared on any of the big interview shows," Zelda said, trying to diffuse things.

"For example?" Jesus asked her.

"Popopoffolous."

Jesus put his hands up near his head as if he were making fun of Roger Popopoffolous's hair, which tended to look like he'd climbed out of bed three minutes before his show started.

"Or Spritzer," Zel suggested.

"Spritzer is a character," Jesus blurted out. "Loves drama."

"What about *Meet the Media*?" Ezzie asked.

"Bobby Biggs? Biggs, I would do, if you think it would make a difference."

"I think you should do them all," Zelda said. "I've been saying that right along. All of the above plus NPR, public television, Fox, Linneament."

"Dukey," Jesus turned to our resident tough guy, "Do you wish to weigh in?"

"I don't know any of these dudes," Dukey admitted, with a sheepish glance at his wife. "Nobody I know watches them. What about *Survivor*, is that still on?"

"What about *Ultimate Fighting*," I could not stop myself from saying, though I was glad, after a few seconds, that no one seemed to have heard.

"I shall go on Bobby Biggs's show," Jesus said. "Anna Songsparrow will do Popopoffolous. Walesy will go on Spritzer."

"Lenny Queen?" Dukey suddenly burst out. "He does presidents, don't he?"

"You do Queen," Jesus said, pointing at him.

"Me?"

"You'll be great," Ezzie told him. "Just be yourself."

I thought we were quickly approaching the point where we were being too nice.

"Mr. and Mrs. Thomas will go on Linneament, the divisive one, the anger monger."

"What about me?" Stab said. "What do I go on?"

Jesus did not seem to hear. "I am a perfectionist, I admit it," he said. "I am not pleased with an eight-point lead. Eight points does not suffice with me."

"We'll work harder then," Wales said, and the rest of them chimed in with nods and yes-sounding noises. Everyone but me. And pretty much everyone but me and Stab and Zelda and the reclusive Simmeltons, I noticed, had been singled out to do an interview. And I had more media experience than all of them combined. It hurt, I have to admit that.

But then Jesus said, "You are all free to head back on the bus and relax and rest up until the rally at five. I can handle the press on my own, don't worry about it. . . . Russ, let's you and me take a walk."

"But the bus," I said.

"We will hitchhike back. Do not fear."

"What about me?" Stab said.

This time Jesus heard him, and I was glad. "I have something special in mind for you, my best friend. Special information. For now, go back with the others and make sure everyone gets home safe. You are acting director of security until your brother gets back."

"Yes, God."

ZELDA KISSED ME as if I had done, or was about to do, something special for the campaign or for the world. Mom chipped in with a warm hug, and my father came over and shook my hand hard, with the other hand on my shoulder and a lot of eye contact. Between all that and the way the others were looking at me before they turned to climb the steps of the bus, well, I might have been saying good-bye before heading off to Parris Island for Marine boot camp. The bus rumbled off, leaving us in the middle of the desert without any wheels. Jesus and I studied its progress until it was a spot on the horizon, and then he put an arm around my shoulders and we walked into the wilderness.

"I assume you have a plan for getting us back to the resort," I was dumb enough to say.

"O Russ of little faith."

We walked. I sweated and watched the ground for snakes, but he was lost in thought again. We went along another few dozen steps without speaking. "You seem agitated," I said. "It's not like you."

"It's nothing. Just that, the last time I went out into the desert, some bad character gave me trouble. This time I wanted my chief of security along."

"So there is a devil then. I mean. . . ."

"Ignorance," he said. "Ignorance. Arrogance. Egotism."

"Not an actual evil spirit, though?"

"Not with any power that worries me, particularly."

"But you just said—"

"I was joking. I am untouchable, unhurtable. So are you."

"Why doesn't it feel that way, then? And why do you even need a security chief?"

"Because, as I once told you, we are locked in a dream."

I thought about that for a minute. "Let me guess," I said. "You have the key, and I don't."

He smiled. "We both have it. I know how to use it, you do not . . . not yet, anyway. At the instant of death, if your mind is pure, still, calm, if you have been kind to others, if you have been selfless enough, then you step free of the dream forever, and, in doing so, step free of pain and fear, and you move into a much more pleasant realm of existence."

"Heaven," I suggested.

"A sort of heaven, yes."

"Good to hear. What about hell, then?"

"You make your own hell. You, not the devil."

"But who would want to?"

He laughed; it was not a happy sound. "You are a strange and masochistic race. I can provide examples, if you'd like. Let's see, which chapter in the history book should we begin with?"

"All right. I'm just trying to, you know, slip out of the grasp of ideas I was brought up with."

"Good. That is the whole point and purpose of your existence. Old ideas, bad memories, regret, doubt, fear . . . imagine all that as the devil in the desert, tempting you. Your job is to cast him away."

"We used to wonder why he tempted you. I mean you, of all people. Seems like a losing proposition."

"There was no 'him.' It was metaphorical. I allowed myself to be human. You people do not escape pain, you do not escape death, or temptation . . . I wanted to experience it all."

"Thirst, at the end," I said, "if I remember right."

"Are you hinting?"

"A glass of water would be nice right about now."

He squeezed me against him, then let go. It felt like a gesture a loving father might make with a son who was struggling to figure his way through adolescence. "I imagine you noticed I did not assign you any TV or radio duties."

"I noticed."

"Hurt your feelings?"

"A little."

"You speak the hard truths," he said. "You have your father's strength of character."

I almost said, "You, too," but managed to hold my tongue. By that point I had sweat dripping into my eyes, and I was glancing this way and that hoping to see a shady spot where we might take a break. Nothing. Cactus, dry gray stones, mountains in the distance; the rest was sand and sky and rattlesnake nests.

We walked on in silence until Jesus said, "I had the feeling you wanted to say something to me back there in the picnic area, but you were holding back."

"Well, I'm not the press person. And I'm not the campaign director."

"No matter. I want your advice."

"Well, I think putting Dukey on the *Lenny Queen Show* is a risk."

"What is the worst that could happen?"

"The worst that could happen? Queen could slip and say something Dukey finds offensive and Dukey could flip out on national television. I can see the headlines: ADVISOR TO JESUS JAILED ON FELONY ASSAULT CHARGES."

Jesus smiled. Though he had what might be described as a sunny and upbeat personality, he was not an easy guy to make laugh, but I could see I'd almost managed it.

"When you are free of the dream and united with God," he said, after a moment, and I was surprised to hear him use the word, "you have to be a master of balance. Gentle and firm, hard and soft, masculine and feminine, ferocious and forgiving."

"Ying and Yong," I said, because I knew something about the Eastern stuff.

"Exactly. Whatever else his failings might be, Dukey is a man of deep loyalties, and I appreciate that."

"All right."

"What we do not want is to look like everybody else, Russ. I came down the first time because humankind had gotten set in its ways. All those ritual sacrifices, all that stoning, all the rules. I was trying to break you people out of that, out of the dream. And I am trying to do the same thing here. The political talk shows—the campaigns themselves, really—they're infected with polished spin doctors. I mean, in actual fact, what does one's ability to perform well in sixteen debates have to do with the act of governing? It's just verbiage, positioning, jousting. People listen to that for a while, and then they stop paying attention. I am trying to shake them up, get a real, true dialogue going again, get people to think in a fresh spirit, and care about something other than their own supposed security."

"So far, so good, in the shaking people up area," I told him. "Though I have to say there's a good chance Hurry Linneament is going to chew my mom and dad up and spit them out."

"You'll be surprised," he said, "but I did not get you out here to talk strategy."

"You got me out here to sweat off twenty pounds," I said, and then he did laugh, a gentle, happy laugh that made me feel good.

"No, I got you out here to tell you how everything works."

When he said those words I felt a shiver go across my skin, a desert spider running up my backbone.

"Do not be afraid," he said.

Another big shiver. I tell you, they were the two worst things anyone has ever said to me.

"Okay," I managed to squeak out, and then I cleared my throat for a few seconds while I was trying to get up the courage to speak again. "Okay . . . but . . . and I say this with all respect, you know, for your judgment, and so on. But, if you were going to share the secrets of the universe with someone, well, I mean. . . ."

"You feel you are not worthy."

"Lord, I am not worthy," I said, an old line from the days when I used to go to church. And for once, the "L" word didn't seem to upset him. "I mean, I appreciate it. I don't want you to think I'm ungrateful. It's just that, well, Zelda, my mom, even my dad in his own way, Stab, Ezzie, Ada, the Simmeltons—I'm the smartass of the bunch, the doubter, the cynic. And they're all, well . . . *good.*"

"Let me worry about whom I give the secrets of the universe to."

"Right. Sorry. Absolutely."

"I will keep it simple: There is an energy that runs through all the vastness of creation. On earth, for human beings, this energy takes the form of a stream of consciousness. What you call thought."

"I'm with you so far."

"Thought is composed of words."

"Right. 'In the beginning was the Word.'"

"Exactly. For some people the force of that stream is overwhelming. These are immature souls, new to the human realm. They are the ones who cause most of the trouble. To make the stream of consciousness, the force of thought, bearable, they feel, mistakenly, that they must narrow it down. They want to take an enormous river and build one small side channel into which they hope to divert it. But, of course, the force of the great river only increases the more you squeeze it into a narrow enclosure. For immature souls, this usually results in terrible violence. Hitler is a superlative example. He came up with his racist and nationalist theories because the complexity of creation was too much for him. That there were good Jews, that there were bad Aryans—too much. Instead of flowing freely through him, the enormous force of the universe was squeezed into his narrow theories. The result was . . . well, you know what the result was."

"Okay, but what happens to somebody like that, I mean, punishment-wise."

"If I were to tell you in a parable, I would say: he lives for six million more lives, suffering in all of them, until he gets the message."

"Some people would claim you're going too easy on him."

Jesus did not seem to hear me. "At the opposite end of the spectrum is love, the complete ability to see the other as the self. I do not mean merely sexual love, infatuation, attraction, loving someone because of what they can do for you. I mean full-scale, selfless, pure love. The love of a good parent, for one of many examples, or of a selfless mentor. Where there is that kind of love, the power of the thought-energy is flowing directly through the person, and the person is unafraid of life's complexities, does not need every other soul on earth to be exactly like him or her."

"Nine eleven."

"Meaning what?"

"The people who attacked us on nine eleven wanted everybody to be like them."

"Precisely. Of course, there are millions of places on the spectrum between perfect love and pure hatred, between the saint and the serial killer. Some people manage the thought-energy in partial fashion, in certain compartments and not others. These would be, say, a great composer who is unkind to his or her spouse. A charismatic politician who rises to the heights of power and then misuses it, in a stupid, but not a murderous way."

"A husband who loves his wife only fairly well."

"Good. You understand, then. The fact is that you live many lives, you know that, of course. It is in the Bible."

"No, actually, I don't believe it is. My mom knows the Bible inside and out and she never once mentioned anything about multiple incarnations."

"Someone must have edited harshly then," he said, and I could not tell if he was joking. "In any case, ultimately, after many lives—or many years in purgatory, if you prefer, which is the same idea expressed in different imagery—you learn the full management of this thought-force. You come to master it the way a piano player masters his instrument after decades of arduous practice. At that point, to go back to the water imagery, your life on earth is the equivalent of swimming in a river, or perhaps surfing on a wave. You surf the thought-energy, you are part of the great force of life. The only trustworthy measurement of this is one's capacity to love—not how often you attend religious services, not how often you smile and say nice things, not your ability to perform miracles or read minds, and certainly not your degree of worldly success. The only measure of that capacity is the ability to inhabit the psychic space of another soul, to fully understand him or her or them—which always results in kindness. A wise, not a foolish kindness."

"And that's what you came to earth to teach us? This time, I mean? That's what you're going to do as president, make the country more . . . tolerant, for lack of a better word? Kinder and gentler?"

"The important thing is to push down the barriers at the borders of your thought patterns, to go beyond labels. I have come to help you—all of you—do that."

"Thank you," I said, without intending to.

At that point we came over a rise, and where I was sure there would be nothing but desert, we saw a small town, a paved highway, a water tower. We kept walking toward it without breaking stride. I was hoping for a cold Coke, or something stronger, but I was caught up in thinking about what he'd told me, and I did not want to say anything as ordinary as, "How about a drink?"

"For the time being," Jesus said kindly, "we have reached the limits of your understanding."

"And so soon."

"I want you to remember all this when things play out as they will. Remember this conversation. You might want to make notes about it in your journal, if I can presume to ask you to do that."

The shiver again. "I don't like the sound of that," I said. "The *when things play out as they will* part."

He squeezed me against him again and said, "One of my chosen people, even if he doesn't know it; maybe especially because he doesn't know it." And then he let me go, and I could tell it would be useless to ask him anything else, and I probably couldn't have in any case because he'd sent that electric current through me again. I felt like my bones were buzzing.

The other thing I felt during that walk, and this might sound odd, is that I had a true friend. Before I joined the campaign, my work had been sociable work. I had never lacked for people to invite over for a birthday party celebration or to watch the Ryder Cup. I'd always had this dream, though, I think a lot of people do, of finding one person with whom I shared some kind of soul-deep understanding. I don't mean a girlfriend or wife or family member, I mean a friend. The feeling I had with Jesus on that day was something like what I'd always dreamed of. It must have been what Zelda felt in his company, too—who knows, maybe he made everyone feel that way—and it helped me to understand her better, and helped me let go of my idiotic jealousy.

Without anything else being said, Jesus and I walked to the town, a hamlet really, one gas station, a general store, a dusty bar with wooden railings outside, and places to tie up your horse. Strictly a Wild West movie set. Inside the bar it was cool and dim. They had a decent local ale on tap called Oasis Amber. Jesus and I each ordered a glass and drank it standing there with our elbows on the bar and one foot on the rail, not talking to or looking at each other, like cowboys after a long trail ride . . . except that he was dressed in shorts and sandals and had his earring on again. It seemed to me after a time that he was flirting with the waitress, a middle-aged and, to my eye at least, wholly unappealing woman. He was asking about her life, how she liked it here, what her dreams were. Little by little, she opened up to him. She said that all she'd ever dreamed about was being a cosmetologist and starting her own shop, cutting hair, doing nails, makeup, eyebrows. That would be enough of a life for her. Jesus listened to this as if she were telling him she intended to find a cure for cancer. There was no judgment in his face or voice, no snobbery, no mockery, and sentence by sentence you could see the woman's expression change. Half an hour into the conversation she was almost pretty.

"I have a brother with a pickup truck," she said, when she heard we'd been stranded out there, reasons unspecified. "Let me give him a call."

When the brother arrived, it turned out that he worked at the Palm Springs Inn and Club—I don't know why I should have been surprised—and that he was just heading in for second shift. He'd be happy to give us a ride back if we wanted. We listened to a Willie Nelson tape on the way. Jesus seemed to like the music very much.

★ ★ ★ TWENTY-SEVEN ★ ★ ★

Shortly before the start of the two-hour bilingual press-feast in the Palm Springs Inn and Club, Jesus gave Zelda a scrap of notebook paper on which were printed, in his neat hand, the names of those reporters and photographers who had tried to follow us into the desert. They were excluded from the press conference without apology. At first, the sinners complained loudly to Zelda, maintaining their innocence, but in the end they gave up and tried to cut deals with those who had been admitted to the event, asking them to carry a small tape recorder, to show them their notes, and so on. It made me glad I was out of that business. And it made me see again that Jesus had a stern side.

During the press conference, Jesus sat in one of the soft chairs in the oversized suite, hands folded in his lap. The reporters packed in around him, flashbulbs popping, tape recorders whirring, keys on laptops tapping. The second or third question was asked by a woman from the *Wall Street Journal:* "Jesus," she began, and it sounded like she was making an effort to sound reverent and respectful, "half an hour ago, Marjorie Maplewith's husband, the Reverend Aldridge Maplewith, who, as you know, presides over a megachurch in Idaho and a TV empire with several million viewers . . . half an hour ago he demanded, in his weekly TV sermon, that you prove you are who you say you are or drop out of the race."

Jesus appraised the woman with what I would call a pleasant curiosity, as if admiring her haircut. "Meaning what?"

The reporter hesitated for a moment. You could see the little balloon of confidence that surrounded her start to deflate. But then she pumped it back up again. "He demanded you prove you are God."

"God?" Jesus said with an amused lifting of his eyebrows. "Have I spoken that word?"

My father was sitting in the corner, and I turned and looked between the bodies of two photographers and saw him scratching the place where his birthmark had been.

"Well, aren't you?" the reporter had a smile at the corners of her mouth now; she knew she was about to make news.

"You say I am," Jesus said. "The most I have ever called myself in this campaign is the Son of Man, and even that—"

"But you use the name that most people in this country use to refer to God," the reporter pressed.

Jesus waited an interminably long time, probably a full twenty seconds, before speaking again. You could hear the *plock . . . plock* from the tennis courts next door. "Tell the good Reverend Maplewith that if he allows me to use his pulpit for one Sunday sermon between now and the election, I will give him the answer he requires."

It was another smart chess move, and everyone in the room was scribbling or typing or snapping pictures in a mad frenzy. The Reverend Maplewith would not do it, of course, because it would mean millions of dollars worth of free publicity for one of his wife's opponents.

Still, there was an impression left that Jesus was not directly answering the question on most people's minds, and it was to cast a shadow over the campaign as the weeks wore on.

The middle part of the press conference was predictable enough except for the thirty minutes where the candidate answered questions in Spanish. This seemed effortless for him, and allowed the non-Spanish-speaking reporters time to take a bathroom break. Nadine Simmelton sat beside me at the back of the room and translated everything she thought I'd want to know. On immigration, Jesus came down on the side of fairness: legal was fine, illegal was not. On foreign aid, he reiterated his statement that dictators would receive nothing from his administration, and that it was important to the nation's well-being that the gap between rich and poor be narrowed. Neither of these stances was particularly original or shocking. The question about the war on drugs put him on thinner ice: Jesus placed most of the blame not on the Colombians, the Afghanis, or the street corner dealers, but on the users here at home. Moral responsibility for any pain associated with the drug trade lay squarely on their shoulders. He did not believe that dealers or users should automatically be sent to jail unless they resorted to violence or thievery. Sometimes punitive measures were appropriate, yes, but he would promote an elaborate system of education, fines, extensive treatment, and community service instead of filling up the prisons with nonviolent addicts. Scribble, scribble went the reporters. (It would be another blip in the campaign, another small target for Maplewith and Alowich: Jesus, they'd say, was soft on crime.)

Jesus had already stated his positions on the key issues of the day—he was vehemently opposed to capital punishment, for instance—and did not seem to like to repeat himself, even when the questions were again asked in English. Four or five times he said, "I have spoken to that already, go back and check your notes," and, "I have nothing new to say on that subject." Since announcing his choice of his own mother as running mate, there had been a flurry of investigations into Anna Songsparrow's past, but all of them had come to the same conclusion: her past was that of a simple Indian woman, raising an unusual child, a single mother who worked in the reservation food market while her son was growing up. Every inhabitant of the reservation who was interviewed said the same thing: that she was a good woman, wise and intelligent, hardworking, very quiet, the daughter of a famous chief, a remarkable though unambitious woman who had chosen to live a life out of the local spotlight. She was known for being generous, for keeping up on world events with a shortwave radio to which she listened every night. With the exception of one fairly brief relationship that had taken her to Kansas, she'd had no other men in her life once Jesus's father had passed on. She did not drink or smoke, and made periodic trips into the desert for a few days to be alone—a vision quest, some thought, though no one could say for sure.

Often, when there was a conflict on the reservation, the parties came to her and she usually managed to mediate it to a peaceful resolution; other than that, she stayed in the background.

So the press-feast was basically uneventful—until the final disaster . . . or what seemed, at the time, to be a disaster. Near the end of the two hours, a reporter from the *Salt Lake City Star* asked a question no one had posed before. "Jesus," he said, "could you tell us in one simple sentence what sets you apart from the other two major candidates?"

Jesus smiled at him. Reporters stayed up all night thinking of questions like that, new angles into old territory, something that might get the candidate to make an incautious detour from practiced remarks. The slipup would be news, and the reporter would get a promotion. But there was something close to compassion in Jesus's smile, as if he knew the game, knew it was an essential and messy aspect of democracy, knew what the question was intended to do, and knew, in advance, the kind of reaction his answer would bring. After a brief pause and without ever breaking eye contact with the reporter, he said, "I have more woman in me."

There was a stir in the room. Reporters' hands shot up. The guy from Salt Lake City was trying to shout above the noise that he wanted a follow-up. He'd asked for a single sentence, and now he wanted a follow-up. I was sinking down in my seat and couldn't meet my dad's eyes across the room. For tough-guys like him, this was not an attractive answer. *More woman in me.* That one line, I worried, would spread faster than videos of Howard Dean's Vermont rebel yell. Jesus would be judged a wimp, a sissy, a mama's boy who wouldn't fight; no doubt the sexual preference question would be revisited.

The candidate seemed unaffected by the stir in the room, unworried by the sentence he had just spoken. He grinned broadly and stood up. He had changed into jeans and a sport coat for the occasion, and he buttoned one coat button across his flat stomach, nodded his thanks and left the room. Like a herd of mad roosters, the press corps ran off to file their stories.

I went into the room I shared with Zelda and lay on the bed, waiting for her to come in. I imagined the next day's headlines: MASCULINE ENOUGH TO BE PRESIDENT? WAS IT CODE FOR JESUS' ADMISSION OF HOMOSEXUALITY? IS JESUS TRANSGENDERED? Others would wonder if it had been a vicious slap at Marjorie Maplewith, whose . . . how should I put this . . . whose womanliness had never been the strong suit of her own candidacy.

I sank into a depression. I had given up my job for the guy, and he was going to blow the whole deal with a few ill-considered words. I did not want to speak to Wales. The phone rang; I was sure it was my father. I did not pick up. I did not want to get on the plane the next morning and head to San Diego for a rally we'd planned with a supportive movie star. I felt as if Jesus and everyone on the campaign were lying out in the desert, wounded, and the vultures were flying in. Another day, another few hours, and they were going to be sitting on our chests and pecking at our eyeballs, making cries that sounded like *more woman in me, more woman in me.*

And then I heard the door lock click and Zel come into the room. "Wasn't it wonderful?" was the first thing she said.

★ ★ ★ TWENTY-EIGHT ★ ★ ★

Zelda might have thought it was wonderful, and no doubt millions of other women in the country heard the remark as a compliment or, at least, a sign of Jesus's appreciation of their gender. It's possible that it even took some of the female vote away from Marjorie Maplewith, who was not shy about playing what the press called "the gender card" when it suited her: rolling her eyes and offering a casual aside about how little her husband did to help around the house, and so on (though the fact was, the Maplewiths were millionaires many times over, and neither of them had washed a dish or raked a leaf since the Kennedy assassination). But, as I'd feared, the big media outlets (all of them controlled by men with very little inclination to admit they themselves had some woman in them) jumped on Jesus's remark like lions on a crippled zebra. For the next week you couldn't turn on the TV, listen to the radio, or pick up a newspaper without seeing or hearing some commentator suggesting (delicately; they did not want to offend those women who thought a bit of womanliness in a man was a good thing, or thought their own womanliness was a good thing, for that matter) that Jesus was not man enough to lead the nation in a time of Endless War.

"What kind of man," Hurry Linneament blustered, "I ask you, what kind of American man says a thing like that when our enemies are looking for any sign of weakness and waiting for the opportunity to strike?"

And Dr. Michael Wild, the outrageous late-night radio king, noted that Jesus had a meeting scheduled in San Francisco later in the month, and "we all know what San Francisco symbolizes in the modern American consciousness." He was able to say this without stating that he himself had moved to San Francisco from New York twenty years earlier.

And Bull O'Malley, who had recently wriggled out of an extremely embarrassing sex scandal, settling in court for an undisclosed fee after having sworn up and down that he would "fight to clear my name," kept on crudely intimating that Jesus "might have had the operation already" and wasn't telling anybody.

NPR did a piece on the etymology of the word *woman*.

Pundits on the evening news with Jim Wearer discussed Jesus's remark with one liberal and one conservative, both of whom probed deeply and at length into whether or not the terms "man" and "woman" really meant anything anymore.

Fox's tickertape read, CANDIDATE CHRIST ADMITS TO "WOMANLINESS," the inaccuracy of which did not keep them from running it for several days.

Bobby Biggs ignored the remark completely, maybe because he knew he'd landed the exclusive interview with Jesus and didn't want to risk cancellation by offending the campaign.

But on his Sunday show, Popopoffolous and his guests spent the whole hour on it, with charming smiles on their faces (except for George Bill, who did not smile), pondering aloud whether or not it was a slip, or the latest in a series of stunningly clever political strategies coming out of the Jesus campaign. "Who is the mastermind here," Slam Davidson concluded the discussion by asking, "and how will it play out?"

After my initial pessimism, I tried my best to ride the wave, as Jesus had suggested. There was plenty to do. Immediately after the press conference in the desert, we broke into two camps. Jesus sent Anna Songsparrow off to make a tour of the Deep South, beginning in the Florida panhandle and traveling across Alabama, Mississippi, and into still-recovering-at-a-snail's-pace-after-all-this-time New Orleans. Songsparrow liked her son's idea, but suggested they make this tour about half as fast as he'd planned, riding Greyhound buses from one small town to the next along the route he'd outlined. Jesus agreed. He sent the Simmeltons and Esmeralda van Antibes to keep her company and coordinate logistics. Dukey McIntyre was to go with them for the first few days, or as long as it took to recruit a dozen like-minded machos to protect her. The rest of us—Zel and I, my mom and dad, Stab, Wales, Ada and son, and the candidate himself—took the jet over the mountains to San Diego.

It was during that short flight that something changed inside me; I could feel it physically, the way you feel, I don't know . . . the way you feel it when you wake up one day after having been in bed with the flu for a week and realize you can stand up and have tea and toast for breakfast. Something changed in Zelda, too, and in Wales and Ezzie and my mother and father. I would not find out until months later that, during our short stay in Palm Springs, Jesus had managed to have private conversations with all of them. I was the last. In the hot picnic area in the desert I'd been on the receiving end of all that congratulatory hugging, kissing, and shoulder-squeezing because they'd already had their hour alone with him, their glimpse into the true workings of the world, that experience of pure friendship. It's a measure of my conceit, I guess, that I thought he had reserved that specially for me. But that's not the point. The point is, I think, that all of us moved closer to where Stab had been all along.

Don't get me wrong here. I had been around more Down syndrome people, more mentally handicapped kids and adults, than almost anyone I knew, and that tends to strip you of any sentimental notions you might have about people like that being better or holier or kinder than anyone else. It isn't so. Some of them are wonderful and some of them not so wonderful, the same as in any other group, including reporters, therapists, conservatives, liberals, whites, blacks, Native Americans, rich people, poor people, and New England Patriots fans. But Stab was one of the wonderful ones. I remembered, as we flew across the mountains between the California desert and the coast, that, the first instant he'd seen Jesus, my brother had fallen down on his knees. There was no doubt in him, no cynicism; he didn't need to see miracles or talk over his feelings with a friend. He didn't need to be convinced. It was as if he saw something in Jesus that I had been blinded to. Physically *saw* it, I mean.

Even Zelda, who'd accepted Jesus much more readily than I had; even Wales, who'd quit a job that paid more; even my mom, with her Catholic certainties and rosary beads—not one of them had fallen on their knees at the first glimpse of him, the way Stab had. It was easier for the Simmeltons and for Ada and Dukey, maybe: they'd seen their children brought back to life by the guy with the flower tattoo on his forearm. The rest of us had been offered smaller miracles (my dad's birthmark, all the mind-reading stuff), and they came later in our acquaintance. The rest of us had to go on faith.

Somehow, by the time we landed in San Diego and headed off to the hotel in our white limousines, that faith had been given to us in full measure. Being around Jesus did not feel the way it had in the previous weeks. In the limousine, for instance, I found that I could not easily meet his eyes. I wanted to be there with him, of course, but another part of me wanted to run away and hide. *Lord, I am not worthy.* It was like being in the presence of an actual giant or something. It was as terrifying as falling in love. Maybe, I thought, it was like having children: you'd been given a gift that was so precious, so *large,* that the idea of its being taken away from you was unbearable.

Imagine what it felt like, then, to be the guy in charge of making sure nothing bad happened to him.

IN SAN DIEGO, we checked into another elegant hotel, the La Jolla Hyatt Regency. Zelda and I had just finished unpacking our suitcases and hanging our clothes in the closet when the phone rang. It was Jesus, summoning her to his suite for a strategy meeting with Wales.

"Do you feel, I don't know, a little different?" I asked her before she left. We were standing between the bed and the door. She had taken hold of my arm and was about to kiss me good-bye. Her pretty face wrinkled up slightly when I said those words. She nodded.

"What do you think it is?"

"A wall of some kind breaking down," she said. "A line of defense falling. I see it in my clients all the time. They get to a certain point in therapy and this old fortification comes crashing apart. It's terrifying."

"What do you think happened?"

She shrugged, looked away, then back. "I was thinking about it during the ride on the plane. I think, when he said that about the woman in him, he was giving us a kind of signal. Showing us something. He knew people would attack him when he said that, but he said it anyway. He opened himself up to that in a way that was fearless. I think he was showing us we could open up that way, too."

"No way," I said. "There's no woman in me, Zel, not a drop. Zero. *Nada.* I'm a hundred percent *macho hombre,* and if you so much as hint otherwise in front of someone else, I'm telling you, I'll—"

It took her a second or two to figure out I was joking, or half joking at least. She gave me a wry upturn of one side of her mouth, kissed me full-on, and went out the door.

I HAD FALLEN into the habit, when we had downtime, of surfing the television channels to try to keep my finger on the pulse of national opinion. As press liaison, this was technically my fiancée's job, but from morning until night she was overwhelmed with calls from reporters asking for this or that special favor, or pressing her for an official comment on various issues, like the medical treatment of returning soldiers, what might be done to improve the performance of the intelligence community, details of Jesus's health care plan, or figures from his proposed budget. At night, often as we lay in bed, I'd fill her in on what I'd seen or read. It had become a kind of foreplay for us.

So on that morning, tired, worried, and afraid in this new way, I lay down on the bed, turned on the TV, and started going through the channels. Nothing much of substance at that hour. I'd been lying there for fifteen or twenty minutes when there was a knock on the door. I got up and opened it and saw my brother Stab. He had tears in his eyes. "Come on in, bro," I said. "Let's order some room service onion rings and coffee milkshakes and talk it out."

I picked up the phone and dialed room service. Stab ignored the TV, which was unusual for him. He went to the window and stood there with his wide, rounded back to me, sniffling. Every once in a while he'd brush away a tear. When I hung up I convinced him to sit with me at the side table. I turned off the tube. His misshapen face, round and red and bulging in the wrong places, was a portrait of sorrow.

"Tell me who hurt you and I'll go after 'em," I said. It was a joke, of course, though it hadn't been a joke when we were boys. Plenty of times he'd come home from school crying about something an inconsiderate moron had said to him, and I'd have to go up to the inconsiderate moron the next day and convince him, at times roughly (starting in kindergarten, my dad had given me boxing lessons every Saturday morning out behind the triple-decker), about the advisability of being kind to those who had not been blessed with his own abundant gifts.

"It's Jesus," Stab said, still teary.

"What? Because he isn't sending you out to any of the talk shows? Look, he didn't send me either. He has something bigger in mind for you, he told you that himself."

But Stab was shaking his head in the exaggerated, solemn way he favored when he knew that the person he was talking to had gotten it all wrong.

"What then? Did he say something unkind to you?"

More headshaking.

"What then?'

"They're going to kill him!"

"Nah." I reached out and put my hand on his arm, but the words had made me suddenly go cold. "Hey, listen, that was last time. That wouldn't happen again. I'm in charge of security, and before we go anyplace I always call up some big shot in the state police and tell him we're coming, and they send out dozens of guys to protect him. You've seen the cops at our rallies. Where do you think they come from, huh? And plainclothes detectives are there, too."

"He told me."

"Who told you?'

"Jesus. God."

"Told you what?"

"I told you."

"Tell me again, pal."

"They're going to kill him!"

"Jesus told you that?"

He nodded. A tear dropped from his right eye onto the tabletop and made a small star there.

"Are you sure? When did this happen?"

"A-a-a-a-a-a-a . . . a while ago. In his room. He told me. He said bad people were going to kill him again, but that it was all right, he'd see me in heaven. I wasn't suppose to be sad about it, Russ, and I wasn't suppose to tell anybody, so I smiled and I hugged him and when I left I came right to see you and I started crying in the hall and I can't stop, Russ."

There was a polite knock on the door. A black-haired young woman in a pink uniform brought in the tray and set it on the table between us: a covered plate of onion rings, and two metal shakers with coffee milkshakes. She poured part of each milkshake into the tall glasses. She smiled at Stab and told him, in careful, Arabic-accented English, that she liked onion rings, too. He held one out to her. She politely refused. He grew sadder, kept pushing the onion ring toward her, and finally she had to accept, and she smiled at me as if she'd done something wrong, and did not look at the bill I pressed into her hand to see if it was a one or a five or a twenty.

My brother had a tremendous appetite and the belly to prove it. Like most people I know, his mood was always improved by eating. We munched and sipped for a while. I reminded him to wipe his upper lip with the napkin and he did so and then started crying again.

"You're sure he said that, pal?"

"Sure, sure, sure."

"He wasn't making a joke or talking about the last time?"

"Sure, sure, sure."

"And he didn't want you to tell me?"

"Sure, sure, sure."

I had chills running over the skin of my arms and back but, for Stab's sake, pretended that what he'd told me was no big deal. "We'll take care of it," I said. "Dukey and I will make sure no bad guys get anywhere near him."

"But Dukey's gone away."

"Only for a week."

"But what if it happens before he gets back?"

"Then I'll take care of it."

"But when God says something is going to happen, doesn't it have to happen?"

"Usually, but maybe there's some wiggle room this time. How did he say they were going to kill him, do you remember?"

"He said 'shoot.' He said they were going to shoot him two times but that he would see me in heaven and I wasn't suppose to be sad about it. But I am."

"Did he say when or where?"

More headshaking. Droplets flying off left and right.

"Don't worry, pal. I'm telling you. It's gonna be okay."

"Really, Russ?"

"Sure," I told him. "Absolutely. Next time you see him, ask him not to let it happen. Tell him it would make you too sad, and that you're his best pal, and that it isn't right to make your best pal unhappy. Try that, okay? And don't tell anybody else about this, all right?"

"Okay, Russ. Brother secret?"

"There you go," I told him. "Brother secret."

It was something we'd been saying to each other for twenty years. He'd break a piece of my mother's china while stomp-dancing in the kitchen, or I'd sneak a girlfriend up to my room when our parents were out at a New Year's party, and we'd make it into a brother secret, a mutual protection pact. It had always helped us feel we had a special bond. This time, though, to me at least, it felt almost like I was lying to him, making him believe we did not really live in a dimension of life where the worst of us could kill the best of us. For another hour or so, Stab and I hung out in the room watching Emeril make gumbo on the Food Network, as if the world was nothing but neatly sliced onions and simmering stews.

★ ★ ★ TWENTY-NINE ★ ★ ★

As much as I loved and admired my brother, I wasn't convinced he'd gotten the story right. He tended to mishear or misunderstand things people said to him, and to jump off one emotional cliff or another several times a day. Did it heighten my already high state of anxiety about someone taking a pot shot at our candidate? Sure it did. But I was already doing everything I thought humanly possible, with enormous help from the boys and girls in blue. And it wasn't like I really believed that Jesus knew he'd be killed and had chosen to reveal this information only to Stab Thomas and not do anything else about it.

In any case, no one shot at Jesus in San Diego. It would not have been difficult to shoot at him there, because he spent a good part of the visit standing on a surfboard near a crowded beach. The part-Indian, maybe part-Mexican kid from West Texas, it turned out, was as capable on a short board as he was on a bull. I don't know why we should have been surprised at that. He cooked, he sewed, he sang in a voice that sounded like Johnny Cash, he removed splinters from Amelia Simmelton's fingers with a pair of tweezers and a steady hand, he spoke knowledgeably with her parents about investment strategies. We had a renaissance man on our hands this time around.

Anyway, at noon on that day, Richard Sprockett hosted a Jesus for America rally up on the hill in La Jolla. Sprockett, for the three or four of you who have been living with an Amish family in a cabin in the Alaskan wilderness for the past decade, was *People* magazine's sexiest man alive for three years running, a thirtyish movie idol who got paid forty million dollars to star in films that involved him getting into bed with one or another of the world's most glamorous young women. For the first few years of his success, he'd done the usual stuff: jetting around from Saint-Tropez to Bora-Bora with one leggy beauty after another, diving off yachts into the Adriatic, getting arrested for possession of this or that, punching paparazzi, taking off his shirt for magazine covers. Lately, though, he'd had a conversion of sorts. He still made the films, still took off his shirt, still had the yacht and the nice-looking female companions, but he also spent millions of his own money to rebuild houses on the Mississippi coast, where he'd been raised, and to start youth centers so kids in the poorest sections of rural America would have something to do besides watching the cows burp on a Saturday night.

Andy Ray Pressbine, the aforementioned country singer, was a friend of Sprockett's—a couple of southern boys who'd grown up on grits and NASCAR, and gone on to make it big. It was through Pressbine that Sprockett had gotten interested in Jesus's campaign, and it was because the movie idol offered to host the rally that we'd ended up in San Diego (where the yacht was parked that season, I suppose).

The rally itself, while well attended, wasn't anything special. A lot of young and middle-aged California girls who'd come to see Richard Sprockett in the flesh; a bunch of well-heeled couples who stood around not clapping and who seemed to have nothing better to do on that morning. Sprockett gave a personable and gracious introduction, saying, "Been waitin' ma whole lahf for a president we can be this proud of," then he yielded the microphone to Jesus, who thanked him and gave a speech that we on the campaign were becoming familiar with—about the America that could be, an America that cared for all its people and was revered in the world again as a beacon of fairness and decency. Near the conclusion of his remarks, Jesus mentioned that he always felt at home near the Pacific Ocean because in his youth he'd spent a couple of months "finding himself" as a surf bum a little way north of here in Santa Monica.

After his talks, he always had a brief Q&A (unlike the other candidates, who were whisked away in their limousines, kept safe from any difficult questions), and during the La Jolla Q&A some light-haired, long-haired, skinny guy in cutoffs and an old T-shirt called out, "Hey, dude, surf's up! Wanna head out?"

And Jesus called back, "Walkback, baby," which was, apparently, some kind of surfing jargon. Fifteen minutes later we were riding down to Black's Beach behind a Jeep with two colorful surfboards strapped on top and Jesus Christ sitting in the passenger seat. Richard Sprockett came along—a nice guy, I thought, though Zelda didn't like the patch of hair he had grown beneath his lower lip. Naturally enough, a crowd gathered on the shore. I was happy to see a full compliment of photographers among the curious and the tanned. From somewhere, a bathing suit was offered up. Jesus went into the concrete bathhouse to change, and then he was paddling out to sea beside the surfer dude who'd asked him the question and whose nickname turned out to be Big Worm.

For the next hour, as the press corps swelled and the TV cameras rolled, and Richard Sprockett signed autographs and posed for pictures with teenagers in bikinis, Jesus rode the waves. He'd paddle out, wait for a suitable swell, get to his feet, and you'd see him outlined against the clear sky with his arms out for balance, dancing along the board, hanging his toes over the front edge, turning around and walking back, then making a quick cut to the right and diving over sideways into the water as the wave petered out. He had the physique of a yoga master, and when he surfaced and grabbed hold of his board again, you could see the pure joy on his features. Zelda could not stop looking at him, though she was surrounded by reporters badgering her about why this intriguing nugget of biographical information had not been included in the résumé she'd handed out.

"What do you think, Boss?" I asked Wales, when we found ourselves standing together.

He took my arm and led me off down the shore. A photographer separated himself from the crowd and walked parallel to us, snapping pictures. One of these shots would be published in the next issue of *Newsweek* (Jesus on the cover) above a caption reading, "Two of Jesus's key advisors huddle on a California beach." My father clipped it and carried it around in his wallet, bringing it out at every diner and coffee shop to brag about me to his latest new acquaintance.

"I don't think we can be beaten," Wales said. He had to keep his mouth close to my ear because of the noise of the surf.

"In spite of the 'more woman in me' remark, and things of that nature? In spite of the NRA? The slurs? The unalloyed viciousness of our opponents?"

"Big word for you, 'unalloyed.'"

"Thanks."

"But you haven't gotten any brighter since being in the company of genius."

"You bragging?"

He actually smiled, then tilted his gray head in the direction of the country's most famous surfer. "Everything he does, every step he takes, is calculated to hit them where they're weak. The bull-riding shows his physical courage, his manliness. The 'woman in me' line shows his sensitivity. Hanging with Richard Sprockett shows his sex appeal. This surfing trick showcases his youth and vigor, in relation to the two fogies."

"Who are about ten years younger than you, by the way."

"Know who he reminds me of?"

"Who?"

"Muhammad Ali. He's going to outsmart them, just like Ali did. He's got all the skills, and he's smarter than the other two, smarter than us, by a long shot."

"Speak for yourself." We strolled along for a while without saying anything else. The photographer went back to more interesting subjects. I said, "When the other two figure out they're about to lose, they'll swiftboat the crap out of us in the last few weeks, and our man is not exactly invulnerable."

"Barring some major gaffe, I think we're in," Wales said, and for the first time I heard real excitement in his voice. "No more West Zenith for you and me, buddy. We'll be working the White House beat. At long last we'll be doing something that could make the world a better place, instead of reporting on what a crappy place it actually is."

"Right. We'll be able to wrangle memberships at Congressional Country Club, too, don't forget about that. Listen. I wasn't going to tell you
this, but I have some disturbing news."

"Shoot."

"Bad choice of words. A while before we came out here, my brother
knocked on my door in tears and said Jesus had told him he was going
to be shot."

"What!"

"Right. Shot and killed, but that he would see him in heaven and he
wasn't supposed to be sad."

"He say where or when?"

"Negative."

"Not good."

"It's not the kind of thing Stab would make up, though I have to tell
you from experience there's a fair chance he got the details wrong."

"No more surfing photo-ops then," Wales said. "We'll have to keep
tighter control."

"He'll never let us, you know that."

Wales needed only two seconds to see the truth in this comment.
"There's a committee that votes on who gets Secret Service protection.
As security chief, you must know that, right?"

"Sure," I said, though actually I didn't know it.

"Homeland Security boss, big shots from the Senate and House—that's
who is on the committee. Well, they got together last week and decided
Jesus rated it. We got the call in Palm Springs."

"You should have told me."

"Know why I didn't?"

"Why?"

"He refused."

"Jesus?"

Wales nodded. "'No Secret Service for me until I am officially elected
president,' he said, and he said it in a voice you don't mess with."

"I know that voice. Give it one more try on the Secret Service stuff,

will you? I'll call in our secret weapon, Enrica Dominique. We'll have to
watch the crowds better. I'll tell the others what Stab said and ask them
to keep it quiet."

"Does Zelda know?"

"Not yet."

"You two okay?"

"The truth? She's in love with him. It's a little hard for me. Tough to,
you know, compete with God."

"Tell me about it," Wales said. "Ezzie adores him, too." He clapped a
hand on my shoulder. "Lucky we're not egotistical, right?"

"Exactly. What keeps me awake at night, though, is the idea that all
the men in America aren't as enlightened as you and me. I picture some
guy out there who can't bear to see Jesus getting this attention. He's on
the plump side, this guy, thanks to a lifetime of too many beers. His looks
are gone, brain cells going. He lives someplace he doesn't want to live
and works someplace he doesn't like to work, and his daddy made fun of
him when he was little for not being able to beat up the kid next door,
and he enjoys rifles, this guy, goes out into the woods behind his house
and shoots chipmunks on Sunday morning when his wife and kids are
at church. One evening, after a lousy day at work, he comes home and
finds his wife sitting in front of a TV news story about Jesus coming to
town for a campaign stop. She has a certain look on her face. Her cheeks
are red, hands sweating, toes curled up. The Spam is going cold in the
kitchen. They haven't had sex since Y2K. Next day the guy skips work,
comes to a rally with an AK-47 hidden in the leg of his pants . . . you get
where I'm going."

"Yeah," Wales said. We were squishing along in the wet sand near the
edge of the water, ruining our good shoes. He put a hand on my arm and
turned me a hundred eighty degrees so that we were heading back toward
the crowd. "I'm old enough to remember when they took a shot at Gerry
Ford . . . who wasn't exactly—"

"Richard Sprockett in the charisma department."

"Not to mention Reagan, King, Kennedy, Lincoln, McKinley."

"Archduke Ferdinand," I chipped in. The subject was not a light one; in fact, it scared me down to my toenails. But I was doing my best not to let it drag us toward the Paxil bottles at the local CVS.

We went along for a few steps with the sound of surf, seagulls, and screaming fifteen-year-olds. "You know," Wales said. "We had a chat about this stuff."

"Who?"

"The Boss and me."

"About security?" I felt another twinge of hurt that they'd left me out of it.

"Not your kind of security," Wales said. "Security security."

"Oh *security* security. I thought you were talking about the other security."

"Moron." He spat into the surf, and then turned his head torward me again so I could hear him better. "We took a walk. Palm Springs. Early, you know, before that weird bus ride. I was telling him that, after all those years of struggling—well, I'm a little bit like that guy you described, shooting the chipmunks."

"Big belly," I said. "Your looks gone."

"No, I mean, after years of being single, not finding a woman I wanted to spend more than two nights with, not loving my job, feeling like I was doing nothing more than walking the treadmill and making the paycheck, after all that, you know, I find Ezzie, and it works out the way it has. So great. Then Jesus comes and picks me to be his campaign manager. Guy could have had anybody on earth for the job, right? Now I wake up in the morning and I look at Ezzie asleep next to me and I think about her and me and the job I have, the privilege of it, the thrill, and I worry this will all be taken away from me. Finally I have it, you know? My own little paradise—even your presence doesn't spoil it for me. And I spend part of every day thinking: what if I lose this? It's weird."

Not on the golf course, not on the job, not in Patsanazakis's over late-night beers, or in an unguarded moment at a birthday party when he'd had four martinis had Wales ever talked to me the way he talked that day on the beach. It was what Zelda had said: as if Jesus had magically shown us how to take off the armor-plated vest. I was shocked into silence. We were coming close to the screaming fans by then, the surfing safari.

"He said something I've been thinking about," Wales went on. "Can't wrap my mind around it."

"Let me figure it out for you."

"He said you have to say yes to everything. He said Job had trouble when he said no, and then once he said yes, everything worked out; that was the whole point of the story. That kind of trust."

"Sorry," I said. "All those sores and everything. Losing the condo, the car. Not for me."

"Be serious a minute, Russ." Wales turned and looked at me.

I felt, at that moment, childish and afraid. I did not like the feeling. I tried to swallow my fear, but it stuck in my throat and made my voice come out funny. "So, what then? We're supposed to let someone shoot Jesus and kill him and say yes to it? We're supposed to let, I don't know, let Zelda or Ezzie die, or leave us, and say yes to it? That's what you're saying?"

Wales kept looking at me. I could hear the waves breaking and splashing. "All those years you did the news," he said. "All those stories about kids who died in car crashes on prom night. All those guys who got shot in Fultonville and Hunter Town. Earthquakes. Floods. Cancer. Parents whose kids got kidnapped and were never heard from again. Didn't we learn anything from that?"

"I interviewed a lot of those people in person," I said. "I can tell you, 'Yes' or 'Yes, thank you, God,' was not exactly the first thing that jumped to their lips."

"Naturally," Wales said, but he was looking at me like I was missing something.

"When I found out Esther was, you know, doing the mattress tango with the Tai Chi guy, the first words out of my mouth weren't, 'Hey, thank you, God.'"

"Good example," Wales said. "Think about it for a minute." We were having more eye contact in those few seconds than we'd had in eight years.

I blundered on. "When Stab was born the way he was, my mother and dad didn't jump for joy about it."

"Good example number two."

Wales kept looking at me. I started to have an understanding of what he might be getting at. "Okay, fine," I said. "But there are things that don't work out for the best in the end. I can give you ten examples from the news reports you just mentioned. The mother and dad who—"

He held up his hand. "I know that," he said. "Norm Simmelton and I had a conversation about it. You don't go up to them and say, "Hey, it's all right, you're kid's going to die in a few weeks but everything happens for a reason." You don't say that. You can't. You shouldn't."

"But," I began.

Wales waited for me to go on, and when I didn't, he said, "But." And then. "Maybe." And then. "You don't ever really know."

And then somebody in the crowd was calling us to come over and watch Richard Sprockett, who had decided to get on a surfboard himself, first time, just to see what it felt like.

★★★ THIRTY ★★★

What Jesus was trying to do, I realized after that conversation with Wales on the beach, was to push us deep into the part of ourselves we habitually ran away from. "There is," he said, during an ad-lib speech somewhere in the brown stucco sprawl outside San Diego, "a golden alpine field within each of you, a place where you are bathed in approval, not because of anything particular you have done, but simply because of your own sacred nature. If you had a president who could show you the route to that place, what a difference it would make in your lives, and in the culture of the world!"

I imagined intellectuals and anti-intellectuals mocking him in living rooms across the country. "Golden alpine field," they'd be saying. "My own sacred nature. What kind of bullcrap is that?"

But by then I had started listening more and more closely to what Jesus said. On the one hand, our work with him was very much *exterior* work: the speeches, the logistics, the nitty-gritty of trying to convince large numbers of people to vote for him. On the other hand, in California especially, all of us felt that he had his own global warming thing going: he was trying to change the interior climate we'd been used to our whole lives, the way we thought, the kinds of assumptions we made — assumptions about ourselves, the people close to us, the country. "Enlarge your definition of possible," was something he liked to say when a member of the staff told him we couldn't do something he wanted us to do. It was almost as if he were simultaneously running for national office and conducting a private seminar in spiritual healing.

We spent a large amount of time in California, unreasonably large, both Wales and I thought. But Jesus insisted on it. "The arena of enlightenment" was his nickname for the state, though, as with many of his other remarks, we couldn't be sure how seriously we should take it.

From San Diego we worked our way northward at a tedious pace, doing sometimes as many as eight rallies a day. Instead of going by a fixed itinerary, Jesus told Wales to accept any reasonable invitation that was offered, and once that word got out, we had requests from every small-town mayor and school committee from Escondido to Santa Cruz. He went out to Twentynine Palms to talk to the U.S. Marines there (telling them that their arduous basic training had been the equivalent of a spiritual apprenticeship, a way of gaining control over their fears). Up to Fresno to address fieldworkers in Spanish (telling them that their sweat fed the nation). Back down through San Bernardino, LA, Oxnard, Ventura, Santa Barbara, Bakersfield, San Luis Obispo, and every little truck stop and hamlet in between.

The effect of these events was a kind of saturation of the local news media—which loved the fact that they had real stories to report, rather than having to use trickle down from the big news wires and national networks. From the first day of the campaign, Jesus had always shown a preference for doing things differently, partly to get publicity, and partly because that's just who he was. But in California that tendency was turned up a couple of notches. He seemed to want to talk personally with every citizen of the state.

In San Francisco he arranged a meeting with a bunch of big-money bankers and investors called the Feltonov Group, after Pavel Ivanovich Feltonov, the Russian-émigré, hedge fund billionaire. Strictly a behind-closed-doors event, this meeting was held in the San Francisco Hilton. I'd had a sit-down with the chief of police there, and with a state police captain, passed on word that there had been a specific threat to Jesus's life (though I said I had no more details than that), and they responded by giving us more protection than the Queen of England would have had.

There were plainclothes sharpshooters on the roof of the hotel, motorcycle cops on all sides of us as we drove in from the airport, bomb-sniffing dogs in the fancy lobby.

Jesus emerged from the meeting saying he'd had "substantive discussions on the future of green investing in all sectors of the American economy." And that same afternoon Feltonov himself went on record as saying Jesus was the candidate who would best serve the economic interests of the American people. It was a huge endorsement as far as America's business elite was concerned, and we saw an immediate upward bump in donations.

A few hours later, Jesus earned another big endorsement, this one from the U.S. Association of Public School Teachers. He'd attended a book group at the home of a supporter in Marin County. In advance of this, the press had joked that no teachers could afford to live in Marin County, but this proved to be inaccurate: there was at least one. Andrea Welsh's husband had made millions selling plastic fireplace inserts that looked like a real fire, but in spite of her wealth she'd kept her job as a sixth-grade teacher at Mill Valley Elementary, while raising three children and hosting a monthly book group with eleven well-connected women friends. That month they were reading *Christ Stopped at Eboli*, and someone in the group had half seriously suggested they inquire as to the possibility of Christ stopping at Marin. Zelda jumped on the idea. Jesus sipped tea, nibbled sandwiches, and spent an hour talking about the book (the first and last chapters of which he read on the ride up from San Jose), and though the title turned out to be misleading (it was an account of southern Italian poverty in the time of Mussolini; Christ made no appearance), they had a lively discussion nevertheless. Jesus suggested that, in place of No Child Left Behind, which teachers universally loathed, they develop a national program in which kids in elementary and middle school were required to spend part of every week reading to the blind, to people in nursing homes, to invalids, and so on, and then to write an essay about their experience at the end of the term. Andrea Welsh had invited the head of the USAPST, who loved this idea. So we got another big endorsement.

Maybe the highlight of the Big State Tour, as Wales named it, was a meeting with its governor, Markus Stradivarius, a moderate Republican whose support Marjorie Maplewith had been courting for a year and a half. Stradivarius, a poet and descendant of the famous violin-making family, had emigrated to the U.S. from the Balkans and come to national prominence when he was chosen out of a comely pack of six young studs on *Bachelorette's Number One,* a TV show that had been popular in the late nineties. No one understood how he had done it, but Stradivarius had parlayed his date with a Victoria's Secret model, Zindy Zathro, into a career in politics. He'd had a couple of minor setbacks—a brief groping scandal, the whiff of rumor that the bachelorette show had been rigged—but had proved to be a survivor. He liked Jesus's abortion conference idea, he said, and was intrigued (he pronounced it "intricked") by the environmental economy comments, and though he stopped short of offering an endorsement, he did allow photographers to take a picture of him shaking Jesus's hand, and he did promise to write a poem for the inauguration, should Jesus get that far.

By the time we finished our three-and-a-half-week tour of California and flew to Medford, Oregon (more white limos waiting there), national polls showed Jesus with a double-digit lead in the largest electoral state, and it was clear which campaign had momentum and which did not. I don't know if it was the "more woman" jab, or the empty challenge from her husband's pulpit, but Republican hopeful Marjorie Maplewith's campaign stops had taken on an unfortunately desperate mood. The crowds were small. Her frequent trips to California looked like a tardy attempt to counter Jesus's flanking move there. It was common knowledge that her closest advisors were making a frenzied search for the right slogan.

Colonel Alowich had figured out how to laugh in a more pleasing fashion—*unh, unh, unh,* instead of his teeth-revealing *ha! . . . ha! . . . ha!*—and that, combined with an energetic tour of the Northeast and a new proposal for improving public schools, had brought him back into a near dead heat for second. Unfortunately for him, he had hired disgraced advisors from the Dukakis and Kerry campaigns, and their advice was not always sound under pressure. In a blatant attempt to court the *Ul-*

timate Fighting vote, for instance, they sent Alowich moose hunting in Maine, even though he had not been known to have hunted since one weekend trip with his dad, in third grade. His campaign ran a spot showing him with a shotgun over his shoulder, a deep voice in the background intoning: "The *man* to keep America safe and strong!"

Maplewith's media people were not much more sophisticated.

Her officially sanctioned ("Hi, I'm Margie Maplewith and I approve this ad") effort was somewhat more decent than an unofficial ad, later attributed to her people, that showed a Jesus look-alike in drag, and played well in parts of Utah. The more widely circulated spot showed, in fast sequence, shaggy-headed antiwar protestors carrying signs that said END-LESS!, racy scenes from a *Girls Gone Wild* segment on late-night cable TV, men in turbans shouting, "Down with America!" (in English, strangely enough), all of which, she seemed to be implying, were Jesus's fault. He was shown in a still photo with his mouth open and his usually neat hair wind-blown and unruly. And then, much more slowly, and accompanied by John Philip Sousa music, the candidate herself came striding onto the stage of a small-town rally at which everyone was white and hundreds of flags were waving. The camera panned to a young girl in the front of the crowd, blonde and ecstatic, and then the announcer was heard asking: "Would you trust your children to be cared for by someone you don't know? Someone who comes suddenly on the scene claiming to be good and pure? Someone who won't commit to belonging to one party, one religion, or even to one gender? Someone who hasn't spent his life in the United States of America but has wandered around doing things that cannot be verified? Or would you put their future in the hands of someone who has built a business, stayed true to her faith, served in the halls of Congress, a woman who has raised two fine children of her own in a stable, lasting marriage, and fought for the well being of families for thirty years? Now, and on Election Day, the choice is clear: Maplewith for president!"

But everything they did had the scent of staleness to it. The American voters (and just as important, for our purposes, the American news media) had seen candidates giving speeches, shaking hands, leveling charges, talking technicalities, slinging slogans. What they had never seen before was a candidate who spent a whole precious morning hiking with three environmental engineers in the Cascades, or wielding a hammer—not for ten minutes, but for six hours—at the Warm Springs Indian Reservation in northern Oregon, where new houses were being built to replace those damaged in a mudslide. Jesus took a yoga class in Portland, went into nursing homes and gave speeches sitting in a wheelchair so he could "know what it felt like." He had an apparently unlimited store of original ideas and, on that West Coast swing, he put them out on the table for us to accept or reject. And we accepted most of them, and watched the money and the endorsements pour in.

Working on a political campaign can be tremendously seductive. When it's going well, it is a thrill like almost no other, and through the last part of that summer it went very well for us. I remember one night, after a particularly large rally, when Zelda and I lay in bed unable to sleep. "It's like people are doing a transference," she said. "They're projecting onto him an idealized version of their father, or themselves. And I feel like some of that is rubbing off on us, don't you, Russ?"

My mother had a slightly different take on the whole thing. At one point, after Jesus had gone kayaking on the Columbia River near a place called Chenoweth, she and I went for a stroll along the bank there, and she said, "Being around him makes me feel like I feel right after confession. It's like all your sins have been forgiven."

"I don't picture you having a lot of sins to forgive, Ma," I told her.

"Marrying out of the church?" she said, in a pained voice. "Being late for mass all the time, in the early days, because of your father's . . . romantic advances."

She started to go on with the list, but I saw a small opening and stopped her. "I think Jesus is trying to say that the church, you know, well, it's a big church. Big door. Anybody can walk in, and the rules aren't as important as, I don't know, loving your husband, for example."

She did not argue the point, which astonished me. I took it as a good sign.

THIRTY-ONE

We reached Seattle in late September, and we had three straightforward rallies there in two days—no surfing, no book discussions, no bull-riding or hiking or wheelchair rides—and huge police protection at all of them. The good will in California and Oregon had, I suppose, taken the edge off my paranoia. We were feeling the love, as Enrica Dominique put it, when, having taken a leave of absence from WZIZ, she joined us at the Seattle airport and saw how happy we looked. Enough time had passed since my brother's teary talk about Jesus being shot that I no longer worried about it night and day. Still, I want to go on record as saying I did not slack up on the protection of the candidate. I had tried and tried to get him to wear a bulletproof vest and to have more indoor rallies, but he steadfastly refused. He did not mind the police around him, he said, but under no circumstances would he say yes to having his own Secret Service detail until the election was over. Given those restrictions, I did everything I could.

Randy Zillins called again on our second morning in Seattle. I had not heard from him since our lilies of the field conversation. "Just want to let you know I went down to the Jesus headquarters in town and the place was mobbed," he said. "I still can't believe how many people are buying this act."

"What if it isn't an act, R.Z.? Then what?"

"Then I burn forever, man," he said, and when I hung up a few sentences later, I felt like I should take a shower, or have a stiff drink to wash the sound of him out of my soul.

The third and last of the Seattle rallies was an outdoor event held in light rain in a park in a particularly liberal suburb called Westonborough. The crowd was friendly and enthusiastic. Jesus finished his speech with a not-very-good Elvis imitation that made people smile, and then he walked around in front of the podium holding the microphone. He was getting ready to take the first question when there was a disturbance in the front of the crowd, the kind of thing we hadn't seen since Kansas. Someone there was shoving people and shouting—all I could make out was the phrase "the true lord!"—but it would turn out that this was a feint. My attention went to the shouting and shoving, as did that of the police: several officers moved toward the heckler, who slipped away.

In the midst of this planned distraction, shots were fired from the roof of a three-story building to Jesus's right.

The first bullet missed him and plowed into the wooden stage about six feet to his left. The second grazed the flesh at the back of his neck, below his right ear, missed his spinal column by an eighth of an inch, and cut through the back of his left shoulder before ricocheting off the metal stair rail and breaking the window of a police car parked forty yards away. It was, after about one second of paralysis, as if someone had pushed a pandemonium button. People screamed and stampeded toward the park exits, police pointed toward the rooftop, drawing their weapons, yelling into their radios.

It took me two seconds to react. I'd been distracted by the shouting lunatic in the crowd, and then I hestitated, not wanting to knock Jesus over again for no reason. I heard the second bullet make a strange sound—*tink!*—when it hit the railing, and I looked up and saw Jesus stagger sideways and then catch his balance and go down on one knee. A patch of blood sprouted on the back of his sport jacket. I was next to him in the time it would take you to say "goddammit." Wales and two policemen had the same instinct. Two more seconds and we had Jesus on the floor of the stage, covering him with our bodies. Somebody, possibly me, was yelling, "He's hit! He's hit!" We pulled his jacket off, which wasn't easy with the jostling and screaming. In the confusion I was pushed flat onto the stage so that my face was near his, and I saw the strangest otherworldly calm in his eyes. You would have thought he'd just awakened from an afternoon nap and was checking the bedside clock to see how much time there was before he had to be at his friend's house for cocktails. One officer was ripping open the back of his shirt, the other was pressing a hand against the neck wound — I remember that the fingers looked slippery with blood. But Jesus just gazed at me with those bottomless brown eyes and said, very quietly, "I'm fine, Russ."

"You don't look fine. You're white as a ghost."

"More votes that way," he joked, before he lost consciousness.

Six or eight state troopers had formed a sort of wall behind him, standing between his prone body and the place where the shots had come from. It started to rain harder. A doctor rushed up from the crowd. She was an Asian woman of middle age — a pediatrician, but no one cared; a doctor was a doctor at that point. She looked at both wounds and told us not to move his neck, not to press too hard on the spinal cord. And then the ambulance was pushing through the crowd and attendants were up on the stage, and drawn guns were everywhere, amidst the screaming and police radios and sirens. Only one person from the campaign was allowed to get in the ambulance with Jesus; I was that person. I had time enough for one quick look over my shoulder as I trotted beside the stretcher. Zelda and my parents were standing out in the middle of the stage, soaking wet and traumatized, trying to get my brother up off his knees. And then we were racing toward Swedish Hospital with a police escort front and back, and Jesus was either dead, unconscious, or so deep in meditation that no one could reach him. The ambulance attendant had started an IV. "He has a pulse," she told me after about sixty seconds.

I found myself praying. I could not remember the last time I had said a real prayer, and I did not know exactly who I was praying to, but I was saying, "Please let him live," under my breath. "Please let him stay alive."

At the hospital, attendants wheeled him toward the emergency room between rows of photographers, cameras flashing, reporters screaming out questions as if the first priority at that moment was to make sure they got their story. In the examination room, a nurse pulled a curtain around the bed, and two doctors went to work. I wouldn't let them kick me out,

and a few minutes later, when Stab arrived, I wouldn't let them kick him
out either. He was bubbling one prayer after the next, "Hail Mary fulled
of God, God loves you. He loves you and among all women and the fruit
of your wound."

Much later on, Jesus would tell Stab it was his prayers that had brought
him back down from heaven, and some of us would believe that, and
some of us would not.

Fourteen long minutes passed before Jesus opened his eyes. There were
all kinds of machines hooked up to him, doctors painstakingly cleaning
the wounds, checking monitors, sending things through the IV, taking
X-rays of his upper spine. At the sight of Jesus's lids raising, Stab stopped
praying and started jumping up and down. With his big belly, the medicine bottles on the table were shaking so much the doctors finally made
us get out. We retreated a short distance to an anteroom off the main
waiting area and stood there with Zelda and Mom and Dad, Wales and
Dukey and Enrica Dominique. "Why, why, why, why, why?" my mother
kept saying.

"He's going to be okay, Ma. Stab, don't worry, he's going to be all
right."

"They shot God!" he said in a furious tone. "Somebody shot a bullet
at *God!*"

The emergency room was crawling with police, the pavement outside
the door jammed with reporters, the parking lot beyond them packed
with people praying and crying. My cell phone rang. I stepped into a
small office to answer. It was the assistant chief of the Seattle Police
Department. "We caught the bastard," he said.

The doctors sewed Jesus back together with twenty-three stitches,
started him on an antibiotic to prevent the wounds from becoming infected, pumped blood into him to replace the large amount he'd lost, and
made him lie there for hours, while news flashed around the world that
someone had tried to kill him.

After a time, Zelda went out and spoke to the assembled press corps.
She gave them the facts: Jesus's condition was good; unless there was an
infection or some damage the doctors had not seen, he'd be released the

next day and, barring complications, would resume his regular campaign schedule later in the week. The shooter had fled on foot and been caught in a Starbucks men's room. He called himself a "true, living Christian," and was a member of a radical church with a few thousand members, spread out mainly across the Northwest. The Temples of the Devoted Angels of Judea it was called, and the shooter had been working in concert with the fellow who created the disturbance in front of the stage—and who had so far eluded arrest.

We stayed in the waiting area a long time, sitting around in hospital chairs drinking coffee and trying to settle ourselves. Experiencing something like that is a strange combination of the familiar and the surreal, as if part of you has already been through it or you have seen it on the screen a thousand times. Another part of you can't believe it has happened.

My father seemed particularly affected. "Maniacs," he kept saying. "Idiots." He hadn't smoked in twenty years, but I could tell from the fidgety movement of his strong hands that he wanted a cigarette then.

"They don't like him claiming to be God," I told him, my own voice jittery. "They have the monopoly on God. They know who he is, what he looks like, how he would act, how he would vote, what he would think about sex, taxes, guns, and hunting."

"They're maniacs," he repeated. "The guy never said he was God in the first place, did he?"

Stab came out to see us. I showed him a big, optimistic smile and told him, "Maybe this is what he was thinking of when he told you that, pal. He said they'd shoot him. Well, they did, and he survived."

My brother gave me the walleyed stare for which he and his tribe are famous, and then he said, "He told me they'd shoot him two times, not one time."

"Sure," I said. "Right. There were two bullets weren't there? I think we're okay now."

And I almost believed it myself.

THAT NIGHT, AFTER Jesus had been moved upstairs and had spoken with his mother by telephone, and after everyone else had gone back to the hotel, Enrica Dominque and I took up positions in the hallway outside his room. Police, plainclothes and uniformed, were posted at both ends of the hall and at the hospital entrances. Dukey and his cohorts were out on the back lawn in the rain, making sure no one got close enough to fire a rocket-propelled grenade through Jesus's window. But I had the sense that the worst was behind us. The person responsible was in jail, his co-conspirator had been tracked down in the next county, and there just aren't that many crazies out there. Even the pastor of the Temples of the Devoted Angels of Judea had issued a statement distancing the church from the event and the perpetrator. "While we do not accept this imposter as the One True Christ," the statement graciously proclaimed, "we never encourage the use of violence to achieve spiritual ends."

It was three or four o'clock in the morning, Enrica and I propping ourselves up with one cup of hospital coffee after the next, when I told her I thought we'd gotten safely through the roughest part of the ocean crossing and would be okay from there on in.

She looked at me as if I had started reciting the Koran in Russian. Deep down, Enrica was a kind woman, really. Of indeterminate sexuality and age, she had short black hair and a face like a small cement block set on the wider foundation of her body. She favored black pantsuits and giant hoop earrings, and pulled-pork sandwiches for lunch. The skin of her forearms was covered with tattoos of mythical figures wielding swords. As I might have mentioned, she was a practitioner of Thai kickboxing and had something like an eleventh-degree black belt. She had worked at the station about the same length of time I had, and we'd always gotten along. What I liked about her was her unflagging devotion to Walesy and her fondness for vulgar jokes. What I didn't always like was her tremendous prejudice against anyone she thought had not grown up in as rough an environment as she had. This was the lens through which she saw the world: there were the very rich, and then the "spit-sucking yuppies," then a small slice of working-class types that included most of her students at the Kickboxing Palace and the guy who fixed her eighteen-year-old Chevy Nova, and then there were the real human beings, like her, who had grown up in abject poverty. Only the real human beings saw the world the way it actually was. Wales told me that, between her salary at the station and the proceeds from her kickboxing empire, most of which she thoughtfully invested, Enrica Dominique could have retired to Gstaad and lived in the lap of luxury for the rest of her days. But that was not the point. The point was that she had found a comfortable identity for herself, based equally on the deprivations of her youth and the mental inflexibility of her adulthood. That was her story and she was sticking with it, like the rest of us.

"For a guy who used to report the news," she said, fixing me with her dark eyes and pausing for dramatic effect, "you are about as freaking out of touch as a professor."

"Thanks."

"You surprise me, Russ, when you say naive things like that. I mean, I thought you grew up in kind of a real family."

"Real as it gets," I told her. "My dad is a Vietnam vet, former boxing champ, and retired bricklayer. My mom made beds at the Scabies Motel for seven years."

"And you think this is the end of it? That nobody else is going to try to hurt him now? What, it's all dim sum and Bocelli from here on in?"

"Dim sum and Bocelli?"

"Yuppie crap. Nicey nice."

"I didn't say that. I just hope we're done with the target practice for a while."

She pursed her lips and appraised me. "Don't you know," she said at last, "that people get their ideas from what other people do? There's about six original people in the world. The rest of everybody else are copycats. When it comes to religion and politics, ninety percent of people do what their parents did and think they made up their minds for themselves. They watch the news to see what the latest trends are."

"Sure," I said tiredly.

"And in a significant portion of humanity, the latest trend is let's kill Jesus."

I made sure I was standing more than a leg-length away and told her I hoped she was wrong.

THIRTY-TWO

While this was going on, Anna Songsparrow Endish was in the middle of her tour of the Deep South and making headlines of her own, though they were overwhelmed, for a time, by news of the assassination attempt. In her quiet way she was an inspiring public speaker. Unlike Jesus, she didn't make jokes, do Elvis impersonations, or go for a swim in the Suwannee River. She didn't flatter local tastes by riding bulls or surfboards. She went along quietly on her bus tour, stopping in small towns the other campaigns didn't know existed and making stump speeches she had not written down and on which she continually improvised. "We are all one tribe," she'd say, according to what Esmeralda told me, "and we need to begin to act as one tribe, to care for one another, and to contribute to the whole. My grandfather was a great leader, a great wise man in our tradition, and he often said that we should try as hard as we can to understand that we are, in fact, one body. He would tell us that each day we should spend time imagining ourselves as other people in the tribe, especially if we had difficulty with a particular person."

To some ears these talks were the pinnacle of naïveté. The *New York Times* ran a sarcastic article entitled "Navajo Platitudes Play Poorly to the Poor," saying her speeches were like spoon-feeding chocolate to the starving. But, in fact, the poor, the otherwise invisible poor, seemed thrilled that she had come to speak with them, and were madly infatuated with her. Old men and women, many of whom claimed to have Indian blood, came out of the woodwork, in southern Mississippi especially, plying her with gifts of hand-carved war sticks, moccasins, ceramic pots, and pieces of jewelry. She proved to have a flair for the symbolic, too. On the way to New Orleans she purchased a rake—a simple yard rake—in one of the better-off suburbs. When she arrived in the city she got off the bus with her rake, and her small staff, and her hundred or so press followers, and walked, without uttering a word, until she came to a vacant lot that was strewn with broken glass, metal scraps, reams of paper, and other detritus. And she began to rake. She raked without speaking, the press photographers crowding around her, taking pictures from various angles. She just kept raking, not answering any of the questions that were thrown at her, until, finally, someone else had the good sense to get a rake and join in. From what Norm Simmelton (who got hold of a trash barrel himself and went to work) told me, even members of the press bent down to grab a scrap of metal or an advertising insert and toss it in the pile.

When he regained his strength, Jesus called his mother and asked her to turn north. She was to make her way along the mighty Mississippi, staying as close to the river as she could manage, stopping where she thought she should stop and saying what she felt she should say. "I like the rake idea, Mother," I heard him say. And then, "The main thing is to show people what a fine president you will make if anything should happen to me."

★★★ THIRTY-THREE ★★★

The doctors at Swedish Hospital made Jesus spend a second night there, and then a third, to be on the safe side. Being sued was one thing; being the physician who let a not-safely-recovered Jesus go back to work too soon was of larger consequence.

When he did walk out of the hospital—to throngs of cheering supporters in the parking lot—Jesus instructed the limo driver to lose the press and then take him to the local hoosegow so he could have a word with the man who'd tried to assassinate him. I thought this was a bad idea and told him so.

"A bad idea morally, or a bad idea strategically?" he asked me. We had picked him up in one of the hired limos—just me and Dukey and Enrica; the rest of the gang had stayed at the hotel and were preparing a special meal complete with a show of get-well bouquets and cards that had been sent to him by the score (including attractive arrangements from Maplewith and Alowich).

"I'm beginning to see," I said, facing him across the space between the limo's backseats, "that there is no distinction."

He smiled, but seemed distracted.

"You okay?"

"Physically, fine."

"And nonphysically?"

He shrugged his big shoulders. "It might not make sense to you, but the goings-on here on earth sometimes fill me with sadness. Everything here happens the way it is supposed to happen, I know that as well as anyone. Not so much as a single hair on your head stands outside the Law and the Great Plan. Not a breath. Not a sniffle. Nothing. But there are moments when the human state of consciousness surprises me—not in its ignorance, but in its *persistent* ignorance. Compared to the rest of creation, your attraction to violence, for example, is baffling. In certain moods I find myself wondering why that has never changed, never evolved."

"Welcome to the real world," Enrica told him.

Dukey was staring alertly out the window.

"There are moments when I lose patience," Jesus said.

"Don't do anything rash."

He smiled. "Do you know that, if, as a race, you could forgo violence for even a few days, a huge karmic weight would be lifted from you?"

"Karmic?"

"The weight of sin. Transgression. The Law. Cause and effect. Use whatever term you'd like, but even a few days and you would see a noticeable drop in what you term 'natural disasters.' Floods. Earthquakes. Mudslides."

"'Acts of God,' the insurance companies call those things," I said.

He shook his head, sadly, it seemed to me, and waved once to signal that the conversation was finished.

I was left, as usual, with at least forty-five unasked questions.

The folks at the county jail were not overjoyed to see us. It was a bland concrete building with bars on the windows and a skimpy patch of lawn out front. We got out of the car, walked up the path, went through the front door, and stood at the reception desk until someone noticed. Jesus asked for the person in charge. When the person in charge, a plump sheriff named Henrik Wegen, arrived, Jesus said he wanted to see the man who'd tried to shoot him, Alton Smith III.

"For what purpose?" Sheriff Wegen inquired. He looked as if he were being literally, physically, pinched between the force of the bureaucracy behind him, and the force of the man standing in front of him. His eyes wobbled behind his spectacles. There was sweat on the folds of his neck.

He worked the wedding ring on his finger back and forth as if it were causing him acute pain.

"For the purpose of forgiveness," Jesus said.

"Forgiveness," the sheriff repeated, pushing the glasses back against the bridge of his nose. "Forgiveness? You know he's still gonna do his time, don't you, whether you forgive him or not."

"I don't care about that," Jesus told him. "That's your business, not mine. I'm here on my business."

After a few minutes of this back and forth, we were allowed through a sliding barred door and down a hallway between cells, about half of them occupied. The occupants of those cells paid almost no attention to Jesus, and roused themselves only to hiss imaginative vulgarities at Enrica Dominique. Who hissed back. The place felt like an anteroom to hell, where every distraction and pleasure had been taken away from you, and you were left to face yourself. It would be, in many cases, like being forced to listen twenty-four hours a day to music you did not like.

We stopped in front of Alton Smith's cell. "Person here to see you," the guard said, and Smith raised his shaggy head from the book he was reading and swung his eyes in our direction. Jesus was standing to my left, a few inches separating our bodies. As the prisoner looked up, I felt a wash of heat against my left side, and I thought for one awful second that Jesus had been lying about forgiveness and was going to incinerate the man then and there. Shoot a bolt of fire between the bars and turn Alton Smith III — and the campaign — to ash. I swiveled my head. Jesus was standing absolutely still, fixing Smith in his calm, loving gaze. Nothing about him that I could see was different. But he was giving off heat. Alton Smith, however, must have seen something that I could not. His eyes went very wide. He dropped the book on the floor (red-edged pages, black leatherette cover, Holy Bible in gold), took a step toward us, and then prostrated himself on the cold concrete, facedown, arms forward, and began to weep in such a pitiful fashion that if I'd been the sheriff of King County I would have been tempted to commute his sentence to time served and let him walk. Not so, Dukey McIntyre. "Scum," he whispered harshly from Jesus's other side. Enrica was behind us. I could hear her teeth grinding. Jesus ignored them. He stood there for what seemed a long time but was probably only fifteen seconds or so, said quietly, "I forgive you," and then he turned away and we retraced our steps down the hall. Except this time, in the place of the "Hey, sweet one," and crude kissing noises, all we could hear were the wails of Alton Smith III: "No! No! No! No!"

We rode back to the hotel in silence. Jesus never mentioned the incident again, except to ask us not to say a word about it to the press. At the modest welcome-back party he seemed relaxed, happy, and fully himself again.

★ ★ ★ THIRTY-FOUR ★ ★ ★

By the time we had worked our way across Interstate 90 to Spokane, stopping for a rally at Moses Lake and a good night's sleep at Ritzville, there were only forty days left until the election. We were moving toward that worrisome week when we were supposed to hit the TV and radio shows *en masse*, as they say. From Spokane, Jesus instructed us to head over to Coeur d'Alene, Idaho, for one fast rally in the heart of Maplewith country.

It surprised me that Jesus would do something that smacked of in-your-faceness. I have a journal entry for the night before his speech that reads: "Is he worried about Maplewith?" And at the rally, in front of only about a hundred people and a hundred or so members of the press, he surprised me again by mentioning the Bible. As I've said, he had made it a point not to talk about religious issues. There were no biblical references in his speeches. It was as if he wanted to win the election on human merits, as it were, on the strength of his ideas. This seemed crazy to me because, though his ideas were good, original, sound ideas, and his personality was likable, even charismatic, it was obvious — at least to Wales, Zelda, and me — that our success to that point was based more on name recognition than any other single factor. With a tiny, unprofessional organization like ours, someone who *wasn't* named Jesus Christ would have had a snowball's chance in the Republic of the Congo of being noticed by the national media.

After the assassination attempt, Jesus himself seemed to understand this. Or maybe he'd understood it all along, and all along had planned to wait for the final weeks to play the God card. In any case, standing on the stage of a hotel conference room in Coeur d'Alene, he talked about the Bible for the first time in the campaign, and for the first time came close to attacking one of his rivals. I would realize, much later, that this was another chess move, all part of his grand plan, but at the time it surprised me.

"You know," he said, microphone in hand, walking back and forth near the front of the stage, "not that much has changed in the last two thousand years. Yes, we have computers, cars, and televisions now, we dress differently, we do different kinds of work in some cases. But the mix of good and bad, faithful and faithless, has remained consistent. In those days there were people exactly like the Reverend Maplewith, Marjorie's husband. They enjoyed a large following. They lived in grand houses. They were sure, absolutely sure, that their words were the word of God. And yet when the Son of Man came into their midst they did exactly what Reverend Maplewith did: they demanded a sign. Well, I can tell you something: I didn't give them a sign then, and I am not giving them a sign now!"

There was a fairly enthusiastic cheer from the small crowd, but I didn't think it was a particularly strong line. In another ten days Jesus would be on national TV, on Bobby Biggs's *Meet the Media*, probably the most watched and most respected of the political talk shows, and his big line was going to be, "I didn't give them a sign then and I'm not giving them one now"?

Still, as the reporters in the crowd smirked and scribbled, Jesus pressed confidently on. "What the good reverend doesn't understand, and what most of the Scribes and Pharisees didn't understand in those long-ago days, is that the issue here is not what God can do for you, it is what you can do for yourselves! Could it be that God has already given you everything you need? That the Kingdom of Heaven is, in actual fact, within you? Could it be that you are always looking outside yourselves for solutions, looking for a savior, when you yourselves are capable of making this world into a kind of paradise, of making your own lives peaceful and

productive? Even living in such a way as to make your own death free
of fear and anxiety? If any country on earth is capable of understanding
these things, it is this country, with its riches, its long history of accepting
the bold and optimistic from all corners of the earth, its great tradition of
doing what no one else in the world thought possible. That is the message
of America, that kind of limitless thinking. And it is a message, an attitude, that, with your help, I will bring back to the office of the president
of the United States. Thank you!"

For once, Jesus did not take questions. He left the stage to what seemed
to me polite and perhaps puzzled applause. With police and a couple of
Fultonville tough guys walking on either side of us, we moved him out a
side door and into a limousine, and raced back to the airport. The whole
event had a strange flavor. So much so that, in a private moment, Zelda
asked me if I thought the assassination attempt had changed him.

"Too early to tell," I said. "But that rally didn't exactly fit in with what
we've seen so far."

"A doctor at the hospital told me they thought they would lose him
there, for a few minutes. Maybe he saw the white light and got a new
perspective, or something."

"I think he always sees the white light. And I think that bullet would
have killed him, if he'd let it. We're talking about an eighth of an inch."

"I sense a change in him," she said.

"Maybe he's tired of being shot, crucified, stabbed, beaten, yelled at,
betrayed. Wouldn't you be, if you did absolutely nothing to hurt people,
ever, and they treated you like that? He's mad as hell. He's not going to
take it anymore."

"Be serious, Russ."

"I am serious. I think he has a big problem with the attitude of a lot
of so-called Christians, and I think he's been looking for a way to send
them a message ever since we went to Kansas. Maybe his whole reason
for coming here now was to make the point that they're doing certain
things — hating people, judging people — in his name, and he doesn't
want those things done in his name. He forgot about it for a while, in
California, because there aren't any so-called Christians there, and be-

cause he was having so much fun, surfing and eating doughnuts. And then one of them took a couple of shots at him, and now he's fighting back. I kind of like it, I have to say."

Zelda was pinching her eyebrows up, playing with the earring in her right ear. "There are plenty of good Christians," she said.

"I know that. Joe Lesteen is upbeat and fun to listen to. What's her name, Fryers, makes sense, too. It's not that type that gets to him, it's the hateful ones, the small-minded ones, the ones who—"

"I feel like he's always one or two steps ahead of us," she went on, as if she wasn't really listening. "I feel like this is going to trigger something, that triggers something else, that ends up where he wants it to."

I nodded thoughtfully, but it wasn't until much later, after the chess game had played itself out, that I understood how right Zelda was.

THE PLAN WAS for us to fly east and spend the week leading up to the *Meet the Media* interview on a tour of the upper Midwest—Chicago, Detroit, Madison, Minneapolis.

But once we were in the limo, Wales, who'd been as surprised as Zel and I at the biblical reference, made a casual remark. "We've had a generous new invitation," he said sarcastically. "Not on our schedule. Wanted to run it past you anyway."

"What is it?" Jesus asked him.

"Bit of a risk," Wales went on. "But it's more or less on our way, and as long as you seem to be in a combative mood. . . . Well, this guy who invited us has a church out in eastern Montana. Border with North Dakota. Medium-sized church, maybe a few hundred. Along the lines of Maplewith's place, you know, call themselves Christians. Politically active. Anti-tax. Anti-government. Anti-gay. Anti-abortion. Anti-evolution. Anti-Catholic. Anti-Jew. Anti–people of color. Pro–raking in the big money. Anyway, guy's name is Pitchens. Issued a challenge for you to come talk to his congregation tomorrow. Sunday, you know. Isn't interested in miracles or anything, just wants to let you have your say in front of his people. I'm leaning no, seems fishy to me, but wanted to—"

"We'll do it," Jesus said.

"Really? Montana's got all of three electoral votes, and we haven't spent any time in—"

"I'm not interested in electoral votes. Electoral votes mean nothing to me. The first order of business when I get elected is to move to abolish the electoral college."

"All right. We'll set it up. It means getting in late to Madison, and we have a rally there that night—"

"Set it up," Jesus said, and then, almost immediately, he seemed to fall asleep. It would turn out that this wasn't sleep at all, but a kind of trance, a meditative state he would go into frequently over the coming weeks. After it happened half a dozen times in my presence, I asked him about it, and he told me it was a practice he'd learned in Tibet. He needed to recharge periodically, he said. "In the old days, I'd walk out into the desert and people would leave me alone. But that's not possible here, so I go into the internal desert. I rest."

He "rested" in the limousine on the road south to the Boise airport, while Wales and Zel and I busied ourselves with phone calls to arrange the church event: transportation, media outlets, police. We were pros at it by that point. My brother, sitting beside Jesus as he always did when we traveled, took Jesus's hand in his and closed his own eyes in imitation. Since the assassination attempt, Stab hadn't been his usual happy self. I'd made a point, more than once, of telling him that I thought we had nothing to worry about. Jesus's premonition about being shot at, twice, had come true; he'd survived both shots, so we were all set. But I could see that Stab wasn't sure, and I wondered if he knew, or sensed, something the rest of us did not.

As Wales had suspected, the Montana church event turned out to be a setup. The day after our Boise rally we flew into Frank Miley Field near Miles City, Montana, then drove a short distance to Kinsey, where the church was located. Looking around at the slanting, empty prairie, I could not see how there could possibly be very many people at the Sunday service, but we had been reminded that this was Montana, where a six-hour drive was like going to the corner store for milk.

Sure enough, when we pulled up to the modern steel and glass Church of Christ in God, it was a mob scene. Two TV trucks were there, which should have been a tip-off. Months after the election, we would learn from various sources that the Reverend Maplewith had arranged the whole thing. It would have been too risky to have Jesus at his own church, given the fact that his wife was one of Jesus's opponents. So he declined and then secretly arranged for his good friend the Reverend Peter Pitchens to hold the event at the Church of Christ in God, to which Maplewith bussed five hundred of his most radical followers. We would come to think of it as "the ambush."

But, at the time, we were just doing what Jesus wanted us to do. We arrived at the church in our white limos and pulled up as close to the side door as we could get. We had added another limo to accommodate the beefed-up security force—a few more of Dukey's biker pals. They jumped out first and moved people aside to make a corridor for us. Wales and I, Enrica and Dukey, Stab, my mom and dad, Zelda—we followed Jesus into the church, walking through unfriendly air. There were no placards being waved—Pitchens and Maplewith must have given the word that their congregation should not look like an attack force in front of the cameras—but there was a nasty murmuring and only a fraction of the local police I'd asked for. Instead of stopping to shake hands and make small talk, as he ordinarily would have, Jesus kept his eyes forward like a man going to his executioner. He ducked into the side door of the church without saying a word to any of us.

Places had been saved in the front pew for the campaign staff. As security chief, I was allowed to stand against a side wall with Enrica, Dukey, and his boys. Without consulting us, Pastor Pitchens had asked the uniformed police to remain outside, and they did so. It occurred to me, looking around at the traditional church decor, that all of it—the crosses and stained glass, the pulpit and hymnals—was actually in honor of the man who now sat up on the stage beside Pastor Pitchens. But it didn't feel that way. Pitchens, tall, stick-thin, dressed in a dark suit, got up and read a passage from the Old Testament, and went on about it for half an hour or so while I alternately scanned the crowd for lunatics and watched my mom and dad and brother and fiancée to assess their mood.

Nervous, is the way I would put it. Jittery to the max. You can feel hatred, even when you can't see it, even when no one has said so much as one hateful word. It was a strange juxtaposition, being surrounded by the religious imagery, listening to the biblical phrases, and feeling the pulse and flutter of that hatred.

Pitchens was the setup man, and he played his role perfectly. "And now, my friends," he said (he had one of those deep, resonant voices that seemed almost to be the voice of God but was really closer to the voice of Hurry Linneament), "And now we have the great honor of hearing the words of one of the candidates for the most important political office on the face of our earth. This is nothing, of course, in comparison with the heavenly offices, but nevertheless, as we have seen over the years, our president is often called upon to do the work of our Lord on earth, the work of Christ, in some ways, in certain arenas, until the day when Christ himself shall return to separate us the good from the bad, the wheat from the chaff, and cast the sinners into the eternal flames, and bring the saved to glory with him in heaven for all eternity. And so now, let us give our full attention to one of the candidates for this great office."

I noticed, as I'm sure everyone else did, that Pitchens neglected to refer to Jesus by name. Jesus stood, shook Pitchens's hand, and walked slowly to the pulpit. The crowd stirred uneasily. I watched my brother, fear painted on his face, turn around and swing his eyes over the rows of people behind him.

Jesus put his hands on the sides of the pulpit, and offered his beautiful smile to the congregation. "Thank you for having me," he said, in his own version of the resonant God voice. "It is a real honor to have been invited to speak to you, and I would like to thank the Reverend Pitchens for his kind hospitality." He paused. Someone at the back of the crowd said one word, quite loudly, but I could not make it out, and Jesus did not respond. I nodded to Dukey, who dispatched two of his friends to go and stand near the back, in case the heckler needed a reminder about whose house he was in.

"With the reverend's permission," Jesus said, turning to look at Pitchens,

"I would like to take for today's New Testament reading a little used passage from John. Chapter 7. It is titled Feast of Booths."

Jesus cleared his throat and began, "*Jesus moved about within Galilee. He had decided not to travel in Judea because some of the Jews were looking for a chance to kill him. However, as the Jewish feast of Booths drew near. . . .*" He paused and looked up. "The Hebrew word for this feast is *Sukkoth,* as you may know. It was held roughly at this time of year, the autumn, and it commemorated the harvests and the time when, after the Exodus, the Jews wandered in the wilderness and lived in huts. Let me continue. *As the Jewish feast of Booths drew near, his brothers had this to say: 'You ought to leave here and go to Judea so that your disciples there may see the works you are performing. No one who wishes to be known publicly keeps his actions hidden. If you are going to do things like these, you may as well display yourself to the world at large.' (As a matter of fact, not even his brothers had much confidence in him.)*"

Jesus paused at that point, and looked at the pages between his hands with a curious expression, as if he were remembering something very personal. "Interesting, don't you think," he asked, looking up at the congregation and letting his eyes move across it from side to side, "that there were disciples in Judea. 'Disciples' is what it says. Not 'friends,' or 'supporters,' or 'sympathizers,' but 'disciples.' And interesting, too, that, in this translation at least, Jesus seems to have brothers. Twice that word is used." He paused again and looked down, and it seemed to me that he was remembering those brothers, perhaps that he was nostalgic for them. He shook his head with a small movement and went on. "*Jesus answered them*—I'm skipping a couple of lines here— '*Go up yourselves to the festival. I am not going up to this festival because the time is not yet ripe for me.' Having said this, he stayed on in Galilee. However, once his brothers had gone up to the festival he too went up, but as if in secret and not for all to see.*"

"*As if in secret,*" he repeated, looking up again. "What could that mean?"

He seemed to actually be waiting for an answer from the congregation. No one spoke up.

"And it goes on: *During the festival, naturally, the Jews were looking for him, asking, 'Where is that troublemaker?' Among the crowd there was much*

guarded debate about him. Some maintained, 'He is a good man,' while others
were saying, 'Not at all—he is only misleading the crowd!' No one dared talk
openly about him, however, for fear of the Jews."

Jesus looked up again. He seemed to be smiling, though what felt to
me like a murderous silence had fallen over the congregation. "Just a little
more," he said. "Bear with me. So Jesus teaches at this festival—not
the kind of thing that would happen in today's society. He teaches at a
festival, and the Jews marvel at his teaching because in those days rabbis
would always mention, as a way of giving respect, the teachers who had
instructed them, their own lineage of teachers. But Jesus did not do that.
Why?"

Again, nothing but the bristling silence.

"And then, when he was finished with his teaching . . . well, let me
read from Scripture again: *This led some of the people of Jerusalem to remark:*
'Is this not the one they want to kill? Here he is speaking in public and they
don't say a word to him! Perhaps even the authorities have decided that this is
the Messiah. Still, we know where this man is from. When the Messiah comes,
no one is supposed to know his origins.'

"*At this, Jesus, who was teaching in the temple area, cried out—*" And at
that point, Jesus closed the Bible, looked up, and spoke the rest from
memory: "*So you know me, and you know my origins? The truth is, I have*
not come of myself. I was sent by One who has the right to send, and him you
do not know."

When he finished speaking these words, Jesus paused and ran his eyes
back and forth over the crowd as he had done earlier. It was at once a
sympathetic and a challenging look. "The Jews were my people then," he
said at last, and I saw my father sit up straighter. There was, at the same
time, a scuffle or disturbance, very minor, at the back of the church, near
where the person had shouted earlier. I turned and saw someone being
escorted out the door, but could not, from that distance, see what was
going on or who was doing the escorting. It seemed nonthreatening,
though, so I stayed put. "The Jews," Jesus repeated. More people were
squirming. "Who would these Jews be?"

"We know who they are," a young man called from midway back in the congregation. "The Christ killers."

Jesus looked in the man's direction. I saw him glance at my father. He went on: "The Jews, in that time and that place, were the people of religious power, under the Romans' secular power. They were the holders of the law, the religious law, and of the ancient knowledge. They were the ones who were sure they knew what God wanted—how the Sabbath should be observed, for example. What kinds of sacrifices were appropriate. Who was condemned and who was saved." He paused again, looked down, looked back up. "It seems to me that, in our time and place, the Jews would be not the actual Jews as we now know them. If we use the Bible as our guide, we could come to the conclusion that the Jews, as the word is used in this passage, are not an ethnic or religious group, but the ones who are sure they know, the ones who are quick to judge others for not obeying God's word, the ones who tell us what God's law is."

I shifted my weight and looked around. People had begun to sense what Jesus was getting at, and there was a wave of muttering, a small epidemic of headshaking. Jesus swept his arm out over the congregation. I realized, at that moment, why he had not gone anywhere near religion on the campaign trail: everything he said on the subject, every word he uttered, was going to make someone uncomfortable, or worse. And when you make people uncomfortable, they do not usually vote for you.

"Maybe *you* would be today's equivalent of those who are called 'The Jews,' in the Gospel of John," he went on, as if the point needed further clarification.

"Heresy!" someone screamed, when this sentence had sunk in.

Jesus held up his hands, calm as ever. My heart was beating hard by then, and both Dukey and Enrica were looking at me with expressions that seemed to say, "Are you nuts? Get him out of here!" But I did not feel I could interrupt the sermon at that point. And I did not want to.

Jesus went on calmly, a bit more loudly: "Part of the crowd, it says in the Bible, was thinking, 'He is a good man.' In fact, a bit later in the text, when the temple guards are sent to arrest him, they come back empty-handed, saying, 'No one has ever talked like this before.' And Nicodemus, in a famous passage, stands up for Jesus's right to speak. So, you see, as painful as it might be for us to admit this, we could draw a parallel to our situation today. If—"

"You are not God!" A woman screamed. "You are not the Risen Christ!"

Jesus looked at her patiently. "I might not be," he said slowly. "I might not be. But my question to you is this: would you know him if he came into your midst? If he came into your midst and did not look the way you expected him to look, and did not speak as you expected him to speak, would you know him?"

"Blasphemy!" a few more people shouted.

"Sinner!"

"Anti-Christ!"

One or two lunatics in the back began chanting, "Crucify him! Crucify him!"

Jesus held up one hand. "Later still, in that same chapter, John writes that many in the crowd were saying, 'When the Messiah comes, can he be expected to perform more signs than this man?'"

There was widespread yelling now, throughout the church. Reverend Pitchens made no attempt to quiet his flock. Sitting in his high-backed chair, legs crossed, he shifted his weight from one hip to the other and kept his chin cupped in one hand, as if he were giving serious consideration to what Jesus was saying.

"I'll leave you with this," Jesus went on, trying to speak above what had now become a tumult of accusations, threats, and curses, "and it is something I will say only once in this campaign, and only here: I was sent by him who has the right to send, and him you do not know."

A two-count after Jesus uttered those amazing words, I saw Pitchens make a small upward movement with his right hand. It was the type of movement you'd make to someone, indicating that you wanted them to stand. Immediately the crowd was on its feet, and people were shouting, screaming, and flinging their pointed fingers in Jesus's direction. "Blasphemer! Sinner! Cast him out!" And so on.

I rushed across the open front aisle, Dukey and Enrica and three Massachusetts motorcyclists a step behind me. I grabbed my brother first, and then Zelda and my mom and dad and pushed them hard up the carpeted steps that led onto the stage. Members of the congregation were crowding forward. The noise was absolutely deafening. Pitchens was still sitting there. Jesus had not moved either. Once on the stage, our small and highly unprofessional security force managed to get Jesus away from the pulpit and as far as the side door before we were surrounded and stopped. People were swinging at us, not punches so much as accusatory forward swings of the hand and arm. And the faces, the faces were awful to behold, contorted in rage, ugly with hatred, men and women and even a few children yelling as loud as they could, the adults reaching out over our shoulders to take hold of Jesus's clothes and hair. He squinted, winced, did not raise his hands to defend himself. But Dukey and his pals had had enough. They started swinging. And these were not the looping right hooks of a TV sitcom, these were short, vicious pistonlike blows, aimed at the men closest to them. Enrica was flinging hard kicks at the loudest of the women, not hurting them so much as knocking them over sideways like bowling pins. She wielded her feet with an astounding accuracy. I saw — it was one in a series of quick glimpses between pushing people away — that my father had taken his boxing stance and was about to hurt someone who did not realize he was about to be hurt. That goofy old guy with the gray hair and big eyebrows? What's he doing standing like that? And then, *bang!* There was blood sprouting from the face nearest him, and people falling over in all directions, tripping, leaping, and more screaming, and if the police hadn't violated their agreement and come pouring into the church at that moment, God knows where it would have ended. Someone would have been killed, certainly. All it took was a few swings of the nightsticks, and we saw an opening and popped out through the side door, and pushed ourselves, and were pushed, in a mad scramble, to the doors of the limousines.

Somehow we got out of there, everyone accounted for. Stab and Zelda and my mother were weeping. My father had a broken right hand, and a bad cut over his left eye, to which my mother was attending through her tears. My arms and legs were shaking, and I was having flashbacks to my only previous adult violent encounter, the famous mugging in the parking lot. Jesus's tie was torn down from his neck, his shirt collar ripped wide, the sewn shoulders of his suit jacket opened at the seams. He was grimacing in pain; several blows had landed right where the bullet had cut him, and broken open a couple of the stitches.

"The bastards, the bastards," Wales kept muttering, as he blotted my brother's bloody face with a monogrammed handkerchief.

Enrica, who had crowded in with us and was squeezing herself against the armrest to avoid sitting on Jesus's lap, gave me a "See, what did I tell you" look.

We were all breathing hard. The cars were back on Interstate 94 at this point, sirens all around, and it took us the whole ride back to the airport before we were able to make coherent sentences, to ask each other who was hurt and how badly. Things quieted down for a moment, and then Stab burst into tears again, and I started swearing, and my mother shushed me, and Zelda looked traumatized and was squeezing my hand hard, and when we got to the airport gates my father did the strangest thing: he took hold of Jesus's hand with his good hand, lifted it to his lips, and kissed his fingers. It was the only thing like that I ever saw him do.

✷✷✷ THIRTY-FIVE ✷✷✷

Out of that whole awful hour, what reached and remained on television screens across the country was only this: the image of Jesus being chased into the limousine. A certain channel—it shall remain anonymous here, but it has the same name as an animal known for its slyness—made it a point, in newscast after newscast, to linger on the furious faces of the parishioners who had spilled out into the churchyard. Viewers heard the words "Blasphemy!" and "Heresy!" over and over again. This was followed by a brief interview with the Reverend Pitchens, whose famous line was to go down in the annals of spiritual egotism: "The members of my church," he said, "have an instinct for false witnessing."

It was not exactly fair and balanced coverage. And what Linneament calls "the drive-by media" did not do much better. Lost in the fuss, for instance, was the story (which came out only a week and a half later and only in a minor way) of a woman named Annabelle Rundegren who had been driven all the way from Williston, North Dakota, by her daughter, Helga. Annabelle was blind, and had told her daughter that she wanted to hear Jesus in person. She managed to get into the church, and sat with her daughter in a pew in the back. As soon as Jesus started to speak, her sight returned. She cried out, naturally, who wouldn't (that was the first noise I'd heard, before things got crazy), and the people around her had figured her for a Jesus campaign plant, a phony, and quickly ushered her out of the building. She'd been so traumatized, first by the miracle and then by the nastiness of the others in the pew, that she'd told her daughter not to say a word to anybody about it, and she'd holed up in her house in Williston for nine days, secretly ecstatic. Finally, when she saw the kind of press we were getting, she went to her local newspaper and told them what had happened. But her story seemed suspect to the more sophisticated news outlets, and you would have had to scour the back sections of a few national papers to find the half paragraph they gave her.

Still, we survived the ambush, physically and otherwise. When I tried to talk with Jesus about it on the plane—where we were tending to our wounds and drinking hard liquor—he waved me away. "Forward, forward," was all he said. And then, "Get my mother on the phone, she'll be worried when she hears about it."

BRUISED AND SCRATCHED, wearing newly purchased clothes in some cases, we kept to our upper Midwest schedule, which was to culminate in a photo-op of Jesus greeting his mother at the source of the Mississippi River in northern Minnesota. The mad scene at the Church of Christ in God never repeated itself, nothing even close. But—and this was so strange to me—after that awful day the polls did start to waver. At first, Alowich and Maplewith wisely avoided direct comment on the debacle, choosing instead to highlight the point that Jesus was refusing to debate them. They did utilize the unfortunate church appearance in their ads, after a few days, but what they really hammered away at was the debate issue. Combined with Jesus's fast rush for the limo door, the refusal made him look, to some eyes at least, less brave than he had looked in the rodeo ring. Justin Dreaf took advantage of this opening to roll out a new advertisement, played repeatedly in the key battleground states (unlike Jesus, he *did* care about the electoral college) in which scenes of Jesus hurrying toward the limo were combined with a voice-over saying, "Is this the person we want to lead us in a time of war?"

And Colonel Alowich struck a similar note, putting together a spot that showed Jesus outside the church, and Alowich in his military uniform with his TV-star wife at his side. "Some run," the voice in the ad stated, "and some stand and fight. Alowich, for president."

This stuff had its intended effect, I'm sorry to report. At least to the extent that the poll numbers slipped back to where Maplewith and Jesus and Alowich were all in the high twenties or low thirties, with a few un-decideds. Strangely enough, Jesus, who had been upset at having only an eight-point lead, now seemed content to be locked in a statistical tie. For those next few days he did nothing but shower us with compliments and encouragement as we braved the cold and windy upper Midwest on his behalf. I was beginning to think he was playing some kind of game with us—and with the American voters: everything he did seemed designed to break us out of our usual expectations, our assumptions. It could be very, very frustrating.

TV stations and newspapers loved the fact that things were tighten-ing up as we went into the final month (though, as Wales reminded us, races almost always tightened up in the last weeks of a campaign), and they loved the fact that virtually the whole Jesus team was going to be appearing on one show or another on TV and radio. Zelda was working way too hard. On one morning, after we'd had a private hour together and a room-service breakfast, there were seventy-three messages on her cell phone when she turned it back on. Eighteen of them were from the Linneament people, asking if she was sure they couldn't get the candidate himself on Hurry's show, even as a call-in, rather than just the parents of one of his chief advisors. "Mr. and Mrs. Thomas are chief advisors themselves," Zelda fibbed. And then she added the clinching line: "And they're huge fans of Hurry."

★★★ THIRTY-SIX ★★★

It may sound at times as if I disdain the many-headed beast we call the American media. I apologize. As a former television personality, I know all too well how easy it is to make newspaper, TV, and radio reporters into punching bags, to portray them only as the kind of people who will come up to you after your best friend has been killed by a mugger, stick a microphone in your face, and ask how you feel. It's easy to criticize the big media companies, too, because they have been known to spend twenty percent of their broadcast time on a teen movie starlet's drug problem when there are hungry kids in East Kentucky or roving bands of rapists in Somalia.

Probably nowhere is this penchant for heartlessness, this tendency to highlight the fluff and ignore the substance, more obvious than during a presidential campaign. But, in fairness to the reporters on the beat and the owners of news outlets, it has to be said that the campaigns go on so long now that the people who cover them are like refugees on a sixteen-month walk, searching the roadsides and forests for any scrap of nourishment, any small dirty puddle they might drink from. And I also have to admit that, during our famous campaign, there were some substantive investigations and analyses, not only of the candidates, but of the problems America had to wrestle with in those days. The *Jim Wearer News Hour,* for example, was decently good at giving these issues in-depth coverage. Wearer could have dressed better, in my estimation, and they could have done with more video, more life, but at least they were good enough to spare their viewers an endless recounting of the tribulations of celebrity marriages, the criminal adventures of NFL stars, the sorrow of the parents of kidnapped girls, and the daily shifting of the polls.

On the opposite side of the political spectrum, Harry "Hurry" Linneament had his moments, too. Like an angry bulldog who goes around chewing on every piece of furniture in the house, even Hurry (in a more extreme case, on rare occasions, even Shawn "Not So" Mannily) would occasionally get his teeth into an issue that wasn't purely a thinly veiled partisan infomercial. Linneament would shake it and growl over it and run around the house with it, and you'd come home to find, I don't know, pieces of your television remote scattered on the carpet. But at least some of the time he took on the big issues, though he and his carefully screened callers ("I'm *such* a huge fan, Hurry!") could seem, to my critical ear, totally lacking in compassion for those less fortunate. Whereas you'd turn on America Free Radio and Wendy Shriller would be cackling about Colonel Alowich's penny loafers, or helping to spread a rumor that Margie Maplewith had run up a big bill at the Victoria's Secret store in the Mall of Idaho. Essential things like that.

But here I am again, waxing sarcastic. What it comes from, probably, is my own frustrated ambition. I'm willing to admit that I am envious. Throughout my adult life, all I'd wanted was to be nightly anchor on a big station. Boston. Atlanta. New York. To bring Big News into the homes of millions of people.

So consider this an apology for taking easy jabs at the creature we depend on to tell us how the rest of humanity is behaving. Consider it a prelude to my report on the third from the last week of the campaign, the week in which Jesus's people took to the airwaves — and got slaughtered.

Here's the play-by-play:

1) Batting first: Dukey McIntyre on the *Lenny Queen Show*.

Whatever you think of Queen, he's been doing what he does for a long time, and he's a pro. Like Linneament, he wasn't pleased at being thrown a crumb instead of the frosted cake, but he took what he could get. The Jesus-for-president story was the kind of thing that comes along once in the lifetime of a talk show host, so they ended up making a big fuss, in advance, announcing that Queen had landed *an exclusive interview* with Jesus's deputy chief of security and the CEO of Scorched Earth Protective Services, Ronald McIntyre.

Despite this hype, it took Queen himself about half a second to size Dukey up. Loose cannon that he was, Dukey went on the show wearing a camouflage T-shirt under a black leather jacket — the ultimate in tough-guy apparel, as far as he was concerned. For the first twenty minutes, Queen fed him a series of softballs right over the middle of the plate, "So, Mr. McIntyre, tell us, what are the special challenges involved in protecting a candidate like Mr. Christ?"

And Dukey bunted every one of them right into the dugout. "Well, Mr. Queen, the special challenges is that you have your scum everywhere, your loose screws, you know? My boys and I, well, let's just say we're not hesitated about using what has to be used?" As he concluded his sentences on the interrogative upturn, the serious grown-up face he'd affected during the first part of his answer would suddenly desert him. Dukey would look up at his famous host from under his rust-colored eyebrows like a second-grader waiting to hear what his dad thought of the two boards he'd nailed together down cellar.

A few minutes from the end of the interview, Queen hitched up his suspenders and made the mistake — at least I thought it was a mistake — of resurrecting the homosexuality issue. He did it in a roundabout, gentle way, alluding to the attacks Justin Dreaf had financed, ads featuring an open closet door behind our man, perhaps the glint of an earring. Dukey had street smarts, if nothing else, and he saw right through this question. "Listen," he said, and he could not keep himself from jabbing a finger at Queen across the table where they sat. You could see Lenny's big rectangular head jerk back two inches, the glasses slide even further down his nose. "Listen, this is the most BS thing ever, I'm tellin ya, okay? The next person, I'm tellin ya, who starts calling our man a fa—, who starts calling him a homo, deals with me. Get it?"

Queen got it. His producer and technicians got it, too. The camera left Dukey's face and never returned. For the last two minutes of the show a visibly shaken Lenny Queen rambled on about "the unusual situation we have here, a first in American politics, of protecting a candidate, already the target of an assassin's bullet, who claims to be Jesus Christ. Folks, we've seen nothing like it."

He limped to the end of the interview without mentioning Dukey's name again, and made a phone call to Zelda the second it was over. He let her know that he wasn't happy, he'd felt threatened, and that he'd give the campaign none, zero, zilch in the way of coverage the rest of the way in.

One out, nobody on.

2) BATTING SECOND: My parents on the *Harry Linneament Radio Show*, coast to coast.

Linneament, who didn't often have guests in his studio with him, led off by saying this to my father: "Mr. Thomas, my understanding is that you are a member of the Hebrew faith, and that—"

"I'm a Jew," my father interrupted him.

"Fine, a Jew, if you will. Tell me, how is it that a Jew comes to be working on the campaign of a man named Jesus Christ?"

"I've been straightforward about it from the start," my dad said. "Ask anybody. To me, this guy is the best guy for the job, that's all. In this country we're not supposed to pay so much attention to what color somebody is, what religion he is. To me, this guy is a rabbi, a teacher, and he's smart as a whip. Gutsy, too. Exactly what we need in the White House for a change."

"So the religious differences don't bother you? The fact that your people consider Jesus to have been merely—"

"He's a great rabbi," my father said. "I stick by that."

"And, Mrs. Thomas, tell us, how is it, exactly, that you came to serve as a key advisor on this campaign? You have a degree in political science, I understand?"

"I'm a mother," my mother said. "I don't have degrees in anything. My son got involved. Like any good mother, when he asked for my help, I went forward with my arms wide open. I'm a Catholic, by the way, and I raised my children in that faith."

"But it's preposterous, isn't it? I mean, with all due respect to you two—you seem like friendly, intelligent, good people . . . and they're big fans of mine, besides, folks, so I guess the intelligent part is obvious, heh, heh. . . . But, number one, how could you really believe that this man is *the* Jesus Christ? Number two, that he's come back to earth. Number three that he's come back to earth to run for president of the United States, of all things!"

"It's a matter of faith," my mother said. "You're the one who's always talking about God and the Bible. Well, put your money where your mouth is."

"I'd like to say I don't believe he is God," my father had to put in. "For the record."

"But, and forgive me, ma'am, I direct this question to you: In a time of grave crisis, you are asking us to trust our lives to someone who seems to have almost no past, who certainly has no political experience that we can find a record of. The country is unraveling from within, and being threatened with destruction from without . . . and you are asking us to elect a young, unmarried, unknown?"

"It's a matter of faith," my mother repeated, using the tactic she had used with my father for forty-two years. It had always worked with him, and she saw no reason why it wouldn't work with Hurry Linneament. She would simply say the same thing over and over until she wore him down. "Plus," she added, "unmarried isn't such a bad thing. A lot of marriages don't work out these days. Plus, it's a matter of faith."

"But faith in *what?*" Hurry blustered. His rich voice was going squeaky. Plus, he'd been married five times.

"Faith in God," my mother said.

"Or in a good man," my dad put in. "A teacher."

Things went along this way for much of the hour, a stalemate, it seemed to me. I was lying in bed listening on the hotel radio, eyes closed, right hand wrapped tightly around my lucky hole-in-one golf ball. Linneament would shoot an arrow; it would bounce off my mother's shield. Another arrow, a bounce off dad's hard surface. I wasn't displeased. But then the show was opened up to callers, and one after the next we got things like this: "I'm a good Catholic, Mrs. Thomas," Jane from Maryland said. "A *real* Catholic. I think you should take note of the fact that the cardinals have not acknowledged this so-called Jesus. You never mention that. If the cardinals and bishops don't say he's God, how can he be God?"

And Robert from upstate New York: "Hi, Hurry, I've been a fan of yours since you started, way back when. I thank God every day that we have a voice of truth in this troubled land, but I have to say that I'm surprised you'd have these liberal screwballs on your show."

And Eddie from Wyoming: "We don't suffer fools gladly out here, Hurry, as you know. In the next election, I'm thinking of claiming to be Buddha or something, and I'm running for Senate. Can I give you a Web site where your listeners can send donations?"

Hurry gave this comment a big belly laugh. By the end of the show, according to my dad, my mother was in tears; my father felt personally insulted, tricked even. "I would have punched him in the mouth with my good hand, if I thought it wouldn't have hurt the campaign," he said to me.

For days afterward, Harry Linneament got a lot of mileage out of repeating the words "on faith," in mocking tones, whenever the subject of the Divinity Party, climate change, dark-skinned people living in poverty, or the *New York Times* came up.

Two outs.

3) BATTING THIRD: Mother of God.

Roger Popopoffolous, I have to say, treated Anna Songsparrow with a good deal of respect. With the exception of Anne Canter (sitting in for Corker Lobbits, who I thought was the prettiest mature woman on television and who'd switched over from public radio years before because the money was better and she was no fool), Roger and his colleagues asked her straightforward, substantive questions—about her ideas on universal health coverage, inner city crime, the drug problem, the state of the public education system, terrorism, Native American living

conditions—and she gave answers that were long on sincerity if a bit
short on detail, often making reference to the way things had been done
in Navajo society many generations ago. The third or fourth time she
mentioned her grandfather, the famous wise man and chief, Ms. Canter
(who'd written a nasty best seller, and who cultivated a reputation for
meanness) could no longer take it. In fact, every time Songsparrow mentioned tribal values, Canter swung her long blonde hair this way or that,
rolled her eyes, and winced painfully, as if someone in the room had
opened the door of a refrigerator in which an uncovered dish of baba
ghanoush had been rotting for weeks. At last, she could not remain silent,
"Ms. Endish—or perhaps we should call you Mrs. Christ?"

Anna looked at her a moment, and then said, "We Navajos trace our
lineage through the mother."

"Ms. Endish then, I'm going to say something to you I haven't said
to anyone in twenty years of reporting. And in those years, I have been
in the company of some unsavory characters. I think you are a phony. A
fake. I think your son is a fake. And I think this charade has gone on long
enough. My feeling is, Roger, that, come Election Day, the American
people are going to realize they've been taken in, and they are not going
to entrust the fate of their country, their family, and their children, to the
hands of a charlatan."

"You're welcome to your opinion," Anna said evenly.

"That's it?" Canter snarled. "That's your reply? I'm welcome to my
opinion?"

"I wonder if we could talk about the issues," Songsparrow said quietly,
"instead of starting fights with each other."

Popopoffolous tried to say something, but Canter was flustered and
upset, and she liked starting fights: "This *is* the issue, I would argue. The
central issue is the authenticity and experience of your son, your running
mate, whatever we should call him. Excuse me, but we're not talking
here about a race for reservation dogcatcher, for chief of the casino. We're
talking leader of the free world."

It was a big slip, even for Anne Canter. So big that Popopoffolous reached out and put a hand on her forearm, something no one had ever seen him do. Canter reacted to that in something like the way the president of Germany had reacted to a former American president's impromptu neck massage.

The camera went to Anna Songsparrow, who was not blinking. "I would suggest," she said steadily. "I would suggest, and with more respect than you've shown, that a tribal chief embodies many qualities that would be invaluable in a president. Foremost among them is the responsibility of protecting his people—not only physically but spiritually . . . to use a word you will perhaps dislike. He is additionally responsible for fostering a spirit of unity among what can be diverse personalities. Of seeing to it that the aged are respected and cared for. That the earth is respected and cared for. That some sense of history, of the value of tradition and ritual, is passed on to the younger generations. My grandfather, for instance, had the experience of being surrounded by a hostile force that wanted nothing more than his people's extermination. Clearly, in these times, that kind of experience and those qualities are not only desirable in a president, they are essential. My son understands this, not only as someone who is part Navajo, but as a man of mixed heritage, in a nation of mixed heritage, and as someone who decided to run for this office, not for personal gain, nor for egotistical reasons, but as a gesture of ultimate self-sacrifice."

The table of talkers sat in stunned silence, partly at what Anna Songsparrow had just said, and partly at the way she had said it, without a tremor of recrimination, calmly, surely. All Anne Canter could do was press her lips together in derision, look away, and brush her long blonde hair out of her eyes with two fingers. There were a few awkward seconds of silence, something no TV or radio host likes. At last, Popopoffolous broke in and said, "George, a final word?"

Tapping his pencil on the desk, George Bill hesitated, then shocked his host, his guest, me, and I suspect, about forty million American conservatives by ending the program with this remark: "I'm going to do something I've never done either, Anne. I'm going to quote John the

Baptist: In the Gospel of John, chapter 1, he is reputed to have said this: 'I confess I did not recognize him. . . . Now I have seen for myself. . . . This is God's chosen one.'"

Songsparrow triples to right.

4) BATTING CLEANUP: Patterson Wales on the *Bulf Spritzer Hour*.

I think Bulf is a decent guy, but he can never quite convince the viewer that he isn't ecstatic about being in the limelight. People probably said the same thing about me, and no doubt with good reason. Like me, Spritzer is a professional, and in Wales, at least, he had someone who wasn't going to jab a finger at his chest, someone who, if he couldn't swim very well, at least understood that the political waters are deep and filled with sharks.

"What's the real story here?" Spritzer started off, bluntly.

"The real story," Wales replied, "is that the American people are seeing the candidate of their dreams. A guy who's smart. Guy who's compassionate. Guy who's unfettered by special interests. A man whose campaign has been financed by people who believe he can save America. The real story is you have a unifier on your hands. People are so used to fighting that some of them don't know what to do with that."

"Fair enough. That's spin, that's what we'd expect you to say."

"It's the—"

"But isn't it true that we would prefer to have the same qualities in a candidate with a less . . . inflammatory . . . name, and one with more governing experience?"

"Sure," Wales admitted, "because that's what we're used to. That's the best we think we can do when it comes to political figures. But he is who he is. He's not going to change his name or what he believes. He's not made that way."

"But is he claiming to be God?"

"Ask him."

"I would, if I could get him on the show."

"Well, other people have asked him."

"And what does he say? This, it seems to me, is the central issue of his campaign, is it not?"

"The central issue of his campaign is unity, kindness, compassion — not for some people but for all people."

"Three issues there," Spritzer noted. "And you didn't answer the question."

"Which was?"

"Which was, Mr. Wales, is he God or not?"

"He calls himself the Son of Man."

"A classic cop-out. Is he God or not? The nation wants an answer."

"I think *you* want the answer, Bulf."

Wales said this with a smile, but when the camera turned to Spritzer's face you could see the hairs of his beard jumping, he was so pissed. "God or not?" he repeated, with an edge in his voice that could have sliced through a block of New Hampshire granite.

"President or not is what I'm interested in," Wales said.

"God or not?"

Bulf has been taking lessons from my mother, I thought.

Wales had started to perspire. Spritzer had him pinned in a corner and was not going to let him out. "I'd say God, yes," Wales admitted after a moment.

"Thank you," Spritzer said. "At last. So there we have it. God is running for president. Or a man who calls himself God, who believes he's God, who claims to be God. What is the average thinking person going to do with that, I ask you."

"Vote for him," Wales said, and, in the hotel room, I leapt to my feet and applauded.

Spritzer smiled, but not in a friendly way. "According to the latest polls — let's put them up here on the screen, shall we? — what we're seeing is the opposite, a rapid slippage of support for the candidate who calls himself God." On the screen, Spritzer showed a chart with three lines on it. The purple line representing support for Jesus was headed south. Bulf had a pointer in one hand. "After peaking a few weeks ago, as you can see on this chart," he stabbed the top of the purple line with the pointer, "the number of those who say they plan to vote for Jesus has gone from almost forty percent to near thirty. Meanwhile, the other two candidates have picked up the slack. Care to offer an explanation?"

"The attack ads work, unfortunately," was the best Wales could come up with, and though he tried to affect confidence, the camera showed the sweat on his forehead, and showed him making a nervous movement with one hand, as if he had been reaching up to smooth his eyebrows but then thought better of it. For the rest of the show he did his best, but Spritzer kept stabbing and stabbing, showing one chart after the next: female voters with children, male voters with incomes over eighty thousand dollars, Democrats, Republicans, Independents—all of them losing faith, or interest, in Jesus for president, which undercut every good thing Wales tried to say. In the end, the impression that remained was of a locomotive that had been speeding along then been shunted onto a dead-end track.

Out number three, I thought, though Wales had at least gotten in some good swings.

IT WAS NOT a great week. After this series of interviews, some polls showed us slipping into third place, behind the surging Alowich. In short, we had finally been exposed in all our rampant unprofessionalism. There is a reason, I guess, why they have old pros running big campaigns. It's hard, nasty, exhausting work, not for amateurs like us. We'd managed to get away with it for a few months, largely on the strength of our candidate's performances, his strategic brilliance, his name. But during that one week of big media appearances (made bigger, I guess, by the fact that the campaign, and the candidate, had done so few of them), it came crashing down around us. With the possible exception of Anna Songsparrow, we looked like what we were: a bunch of city people trying to cross the Everglades on foot in the dark, no insect repellent, no flashlight, no compass.

It would be a tremendous understatement, then, to assert that we had a lot riding on Jesus's *Meet the Media* appearance, and though a gloomy

mood had fallen over the group—larger now, since Anna Songsparrow
had rejoined us—we still had our long ball hitter coming to the plate,
and we tried to cheer each other up as best we could.

5) BATTING FIFTH: Jesus on *Meet the Media.* I was so nervous
I went to a bar by myself to watch it.

If one were to judge, solely on his physical appearance, whether or not
the Jesus we knew was God, then there is no question in my mind that
viewers of the Bobby Biggs show would have given him an enthusiastic
thumbs-up. On the day before the show (the press covered this shopping
spree), Jesus went out and bought a gorgeous black Armani suit and other
clothes, tossing money around Manhattan like a rap star. Shined shoes,
off-white shirt open at the collar, the Armani, the great haircut, the
cheekbones, the smile. If Jesus didn't look like God when he sat down
opposite Bobby Biggs, nobody did.

Biggs had a reputation for fairness, and he did his part by devoting the
first two-thirds of his show to substance, giving Jesus every opportunity
to rebut the charges that he was lightweight on the issues of the day.
Jesus went into some detail about his past, giving the names of the places
in India, Tibet, and Nepal where he'd studied yoga and meditation, the
famous spiritual teachers he'd known. Watching it on the TV in a bar
near Akron, Ohio, my personal feeling was that Joe Sixpack and Ellen
Soccermom cared nothing about some New Delhian yoga master, or the
persecuted saints of Ladakh. But Jesus acted as if they *should* care, and,
with that and a few facts about his other activities (he had, it turned out,
served in the Peace Corps in Guatemala for a year, before deciding to
make his eastern pilgrimage; not foreign policy experience, but at least it
was *something*), he did sound more forthcoming than he had been earlier
in the campaign.

As far as actual proposals went, he offered a couple of new ones, specially aimed at critics who said he was long on compassion and ideal-
ism but short on budgetary common sense. He reminded viewers about
the Feltonov Group's Green Investment Initiative, and Pavel Feltonov's
endorsement. He said those plans had the potential to pump billions in

tax revenue into the economy while at the same time adding hundreds of thousands of new manufacturing jobs—and he trotted out the numbers to back that up. There was no reason, he insisted, why our tariffs on foreign imports should not match those placed on our goods in other countries, dollar for dollar—his campaign was about fairness, if nothing else. And then he surprised us all, Biggs included, by saying, "I'd also like to note that each of my opponents, over the course of this campaign, has come up with excellent suggestions. Marjorie's ideas about protecting our children, the colonel's education proposals—those are the programs of first-class minds, and ones I would be eager to implement within the first hundred days of my administration."

Biggs listened respectfully, probing once, twice, as was his style, then going to the next question. As the program went on, he moved gradually away from policy issues and into more personal territory: "Our understanding is that you are a proponent of nonviolence, and I know that I and many Americans admire that. We admired it in Gandhi. We admired it in Dr. Martin Luther King. We admire it in the Dalai Lama, who, we should mention, came out yesterday and gave you his enthusiastic endorsement, something he has never done before."

"A great holy man," Jesus said. "I wish he was eligible to vote."

Biggs gave an indulgent smile. "But, at the same time, pacifism makes most Americans uneasy. They wonder what you would do about the terrorist threat; if there is any situation in which you would use force; if you'd try to stop weapons production or disarm the military."

Jesus paused for a moment in thought. I could feel voters all over the country leaning toward their sets. One of those voters was perched precariously on a stool a short distance down the bar from me. "Nuke the bastards," he yelled. "Let God sort 'em out!"

The bartender threatened to cut him off.

Jesus offered a more measured answer: "Morally, it is an extremely difficult question," he said, "and one that people of conscience have wrestled with from the beginning of time." I was afraid, for a moment, that he was going to try to squeak by with a politician's nonanswer. But that wasn't his style. "As I have said before, while it is tempting to believe—especially for those of us with safe, comfortable lives — that there are no truly evil people in the world, that is a moral dereliction of duty. There are evil people."

"Bet your sweet brown arse there are," the drunk yelled.

"The threat to America is very real, excruciatingly real. You cannot talk to these people. You cannot reason with them. They harbor such hatred in their hearts that they see kindness as weakness."

"Yes," Biggs cut in, "but my question was about your response. Would you use force or not?"

"I am coming around to that," Jesus said. "You will notice two things about my campaign, Bob, by the way: first, I never criticize my fellow candidates; second, I never avoid a question. My answer is that, yes, I would use force in certain circumstances, though I would use it only after every — and I mean every — other reasonable possibility had been exhausted. Earlier in the campaign, when I said that I thought the proper response to the terrorist threat was a police action — by which I meant police and special forces — I received a lot of criticism. But I stand by that remark, as long as we do not face a nation-state with a standing army. Our job is to protect ourselves, not convert people from violence to peacefulness by trying to kill as many of them as we can. Forget the moral aspects, let's talk practicalities. Armed invasion simply does not work in the long run and there is no — zero — historical record of its working in the modern era in circumstances similar to those we now face. In the case of Hitler, Mussolini, and Hirohito, who had standing armies that numbered in the millions of soldiers and who were determined to conquer the world, killing many of them was unavoidable and necessary — though wiser leaders might — *might*, I emphasize — have avoided or minimized the conflict had they acted differently in the years leading up to the war. We are not dealing with Hitler or Hirohito or Mussolini here, but with a relatively small number of hateful, dangerous souls. Would I direct members of the armed forces to kill those souls if it meant preventing the deaths of innocent people? Yes, I would. We are not all capable of allowing ourselves to be crucified. Certainly we should not consider it a holy deed to stand by and watch our children be hurt or killed.

"But there is so much room for subtlety, even in this issue, Bob. The idea of enlightening societies, of ending dictatorships, is a good, noble, even a sacred idea. But you do not accomplish that by invasion, by assassination, by force. Violence is not only morally wrong, it simply does not work, or it works for only a short time. You create peace by peaceful example. Defend ourselves, of course, yes, it is the first responsibility of a president. But take the beam out of your own eye before you try to remove the mote from the other's. Make us a shining moral example to the world. Good things will then follow."

On that note, Biggs went to commercial break. Only five minutes were left in the show, and I was feeling that we might have a chance again. Jesus's long, thoughtful, direct answer had silenced even my friend down the bar, and I thought it might have brought us back into the game, changed the minds of some of his doubters—though others would always view him as hopelessly naive.

When the commercials finished, Biggs, rocking forward as he often did, offered this: "I would be remiss if I did not explore one other issue with you. I won't ask if you are God, I won't do that. But I will ask this: *if* you are God, if you are not only Jesus Christ in name, but *the* Jesus Christ of biblical history, the man some people believe is the son of God, and others believe was at the very least a wise teacher, *if* you are that person, that creature, whatever word you want to use, and you have decided to come back into the human realm, and *if* you are elected president, will you act in that office simply as a human being, no doubt a wise, capable human being, or will you—this is difficult to phrase properly—will you have recourse to extraordinary powers in discharging your presidential duties?"

It was a question, of course, that had been on the minds of everyone in the country since Jesus's name had first been spoken on the stage in Banfield Plaza in West Zenith. Until now no one, no media figure at least, had had the courage to ask it to Jesus directly.

Jesus flashed him the tremendous smile. "I will use the office to do good, Bob. That, after all, is the whole point of my coming back to earth, and the whole point of coming back, not as a teacher this time, but as a politician, if you will. I will do good. I promise the American people that. My whole point and purpose here is not to perform miracles. Had I wanted to, I could have done nothing but miracles from day one, and perhaps my poll numbers would be better." They both chuckled at this. "My purpose is to demonstrate to human men and women that you do not have to settle for what you have settled for to this point in your spiritual and political history. Wars, greed, corruption, nastiness of all kinds — America does not have to settle for this, and each of you, as individuals, does not have to settle for this. We can aim our sights higher. If elected president, I will not just talk about such things, I will demonstrate them in every aspect of my leadership. Exactly as I have tried to do in this campaign."

Biggs seemed relieved. He leaned forward again in what was almost a gesture of reverence, almost a bow, and thanked Jesus for coming on the show. Jesus thanked him in return. Biggs mentioned an upcoming guest. A commercial for an investment firm came on. My fellow American at the end of the bar said, "The guy's all right."

The bartender nodded.

And we were back in the game.

✷✷✷ THIRTY-SEVEN ✷✷✷

With only fifteen days remaining before voters went to the polls, the other two candidates participated in a televised debate, the last in a series of three. Jesus had not been invited to the first, which took place before he announced he was running. He might have been included in the second, if we'd pushed for it, but we were too focused then on getting his name on the ballot in all fifty states and in struggling to get our logistical act, such as it was, together. By the third debate he was such an important player in the whole drama that not inviting him would have undermined the debate's legitimacy. So the League of Women Voters contacted Wales and extended a formal invitation. Wales and Zel and I went into a meeting with Jesus and told him about it. And it took him all of three seconds to decide not to participate. He stuck to the decision, too, even as the numbers slipped and the pressure mounted during our bad media week. I was surprised at that. I worried, as did Wales and Zelda, that his refusal to participate would be seen as cowardly and un-American, motivated by nothing more than fear of getting into it with his opponents face-to-face.

To some extent, that is what happened. Especially after the good performance on Biggs's show, a performance that kicked us back into the lead in at least one poll, Maplewith and Alowich started hitting us hard on the debate issue. Alowich, who had dropped back again into third place, but not by a very large margin, resurrected the run vs. fight ad. Maplewith attacked Jesus at every stop, using surrogates for the really dirty punches. And it seemed like every call-in radio show had people questioning Jesus's backbone, wondering if he really cared about winning, or if it was only a game for him, speculating on what it was he must be afraid of, some big dark secret—underworld connections, one commentator suggested—and so on.

The League of Women Voters and CNN both knew it would be a better debate with Jesus on the stage, so they kept extending the deadline, giving us more and more time to say a final yes or no. They extended it right up to forty-eight hours beforehand. Jesus declined.

"I refuse to be another clown in the 'gotcha' circus," he said, when we had our final meeting on the subject, in yet another hotel suite, this one in central Ohio. We'd been getting huge crowds there; the poll numbers were improving slightly; Jesus said he saw no reason to mess with success.

"They're going to do a number on you without you there to defend yourself," Wales suggested, looking down at his notes. I knew my boss well enough to see the strain in his face. He'd been working night and day for the past four and a half months. The ambush publicity and the errors of the previous week had put a large dent in the optimism he'd shown on the beach in California.

"Let them do what they do," Jesus told him. "We didn't send my mother to the vice presidential debate, and both Clarence and Maileah essentially ignored her."

"With all due respect," Wales went on, still not raising his eyes, "she's not you. Alowich's run vs. fight ad is getting traction in the South and West. Some broadcasts have started showing the video clip from the Montana church all over again."

"We did nothing wrong at the Montana church."

"I know that. But they took a fourteen-second clip out of it. Clip makes us look like we're running away from something."

"We were."

"And now they're going to say we're running away from the debate."

Jesus considered this point for a moment, fiddling with the band of the expensive watch he sometimes wore (I noticed that the hands never

moved). In these situations, I had the feeling that he was only pretending to give our suggestions thought. His mind was already made up, it
seemed to me, and he was just being polite about it, making us think we
actually had a say in what he did. For example, since the assassination
attempt, I'd been after him constantly about choosing venues that were
easier to secure—indoors, where we could get people to pass through
metal detectors, and where we didn't have to worry about rifle-wielding
lunatics on rooftops. He pretended to give this some consideration, then
told me he hated metal detectors and liked to be outdoors whenever he
could. Basically, then, he was offering himself up, event after event, to
any nut who happened to hate him enough to kill him. It kept me awake
at night, I can tell you.

"Annie Ciappellino has endorsed us, hasn't she?" Jesus asked, as if he'd
just thought of it.

Annie Ciappellino was a Jersey girl who'd won the silver medal in the
marathon in the previous Olympic games. It was a huge upset. Predicted
to finish no better than twentieth, she'd nosed out the Russian favorite in
the stadium lap and come within twenty-five feet of catching the Kenyan
winner. Her dad, who had coached her from the time she was in grade
school, had died of a heart attack three days earlier, having flown halfway
across the world to see his daughter run. It was a sad, wonderful story,
made more wonderful by the fact that Annie was a sweet black-haired
beauty who donated to children's charities a third of her substantial earn-
ings from commercial endorsements. On a tour to promote her latest
running shoe, she'd accidentally crossed paths with Anna Songsparrow
somewhere in the Deep South, listened to her talk, liked what she heard,
and had come out publicly for Jesus the next day.

"Get her on the phone, would you? I have an idea."

Jesus's idea was that he'd take his opponents' charge that he was *running* away, and use it to his advantage. He and Annie Ciappellino would
"run" from her home in Cape May, New Jersey, to West Zenith, Massachusetts, a distance of 361 miles. "Run" in quotes, because they wouldn't
actually run the whole distance, but would run between five and ten
miles each day for the last ten days of the campaign, side-by-side, along

city streets and country roads, and then, after stopping someplace for showers and changes of clothes, they'd go another twenty or thirty miles by bus, making brief stops along the route.

Annie C. agreed without hesitation, and this odd end to our supremely odd campaign was announced on the day before the big debate.

I ask you: which do you think was a more interesting item on the nightly news, that Maplewith and Alowich were going into their third debate, preparing to say bad things about each other, or that Jesus would be running up the eastern seaboard with a beautiful Olympic silver medalist who gave a lot of money to sick kids?

The next evening, while all of us but Jesus watched on a TV in the back room of a fried chicken restaurant in Altoona, Pennsylvania, Senator Marjorie Maplewith and Colonel Dennis Alowich both used a great deal of their air time attacking the candidate who had chosen not to show up. There was some substance to their attacks. Senator Maplewith hammered away at what she saw as the ludicrous idea that we could fight the "Islamo-Nazis," as she called them, without using ground troops in large numbers. She cited the comments of two respected generals to back this up. Attacking from the other side, Colonel Alowich, the inventor of GreenBiscuit, called Jesus's stance on making environmentalism the new engine of the American economy "the pipe dream of someone with no real-world business experience." For the first half hour, I thought Anne Canter's prediction (that, as we drew closer to the actual election, voters would turn away from Jesus in droves) might be correct. Alowich and Maplewith had honed their styles over the long campaign, found their voices, and they lobbed grenades at the missing candidate—and occasionally at each other—like infantry corporals who'd seen service in four wars.

The problem was that, after the first half hour of the debate, and the first few effective explosions, they kept doing the same thing. The moderator, Lance Panderson, a charisma-loaded network anchor who had pioneered the gray-haired-and-proud look, kept pressing them for specific answers to specific questions, and they kept using the questions as a jumping off point for their next anti-Jesus tirade. At the forty-five minute mark, Zelda said, in an excited voice, "They're both blowing it!" And by the one-hour mark, we had started to cheer loudly every time they mentioned Jesus's name—which was about every thirty seconds. With a few minutes remaining, Alowich seemed to understand, suddenly, what was happening, and he inserted vaguely complimentary language into his closing statement, saying that Jesus had run a strong campaign ("for a first-timer") and was obviously a good man ("though perhaps not quite as good as he claims to be"), but Maplewith kept battering and battering. She was trying, Esmeralda suggested, to counter the antiwoman voters by showing how tough she was, that she could give it out with the best of the big boys. But Stab summed up what a lot of viewers came away with when he said, "She's *mean!*"

Not at any point in the campaign was I happier than when that debate ended. We all felt we'd been given a new lease on life, and we celebrated with a couple of nice bottles of wine back at the hotel. Jesus returned from what he said was a three-mile jog in the dark ("so I'll have half a hope of being able to stay with Annie C."), and we greeted him with a chorus of happy analysis, all talking at once, giving different versions with the same conclusion: the other two had screwed up big-time.

The seesaw polls bore this out. To the shock of TV's smartest pundits, Anne Canter included, not only were voters not turning away from Jesus in the last leg of the campaign, they were clearly turning back toward him. We had worried—all three camps had worried—that, in a three-way race, no one would emerge with a majority of electoral votes. And as the new numbers came out, that seemed to be our main problem. On the day that Jesus and Annie C. met at Cape May and had a photo-op there in their tracksuits and wool hats in the forty-degree late October chill, the *Christian Science Monitor* poll had it this way:

JESUS CHRIST (Divinity Party)	35%
MARJORIE MAPLEWITH (Republican Party)	33%
DENNIS ALOWICH (Democratic Party)	27%
UNDECIDED/OTHER	5%

✳ ✳ ✳ THIRTY-EIGHT ✳ ✳ ✳

The "Run for the White House," as Wales christened it, was both a brilliant idea and a security chief's worst nightmare. Even with the help of local and state police, even with another dozen Harley Davidson aficionados that Dukey had summoned from the western New England chapter of the Panthers (and who had volunteered to work for Jesus without pay), even with the enthusiasm that greeted us at every stop and seemed to multiply with each mile, the fact was that our candidate—who'd already had one narrow escape from death—made a perfect target for any lunatic who decided God wanted him or her to sneak onto the top floor of an abandoned building in Tom's River or Rahway and try out his new .30-06. Every afternoon I scouted out the next day's running route in the company of a couple of uniformed cops. Every night I sat down with the Simmeltons and tried to assess which of the several threats we'd received in the past twenty-four hours posed real danger. I was up before the sun every morning—not easy for me—making sure we had thorough protection at the point where the day's run would commence, that the bus had been checked and rechecked for explosives, and that the next hotel was as secure as we could make it.

Zelda kept the same hours, trying to handle all the press requests. She printed up and distributed position papers, arranged for credentials, secured rally permits, deflected requests for TV interviews. Everybody was working sixteen-hour days: Mom helping Zelda with local promo, supervising the caterers, and watching the two youngsters part-time; Dad mapping out the best travel routes, arranging for separate housing for the bikers (who had adopted him, strangely enough, as their wise elder, and who preferred seedy motels where they could drink and swear and break things without calling so much attention to themselves), and printing up a daily schedule; Stab handing out the glossy leaflets on which had been printed a half-dozen key points of Jesus's platform, several big endorsements, and a couple of inspirational quotes; the Simmeltons helping with Web site problems; Dukey acting as Annie Ciappellino's personal bodyguard (which made Ada—who helped Zel with press errands—jealous); Enrica Dominique providing both runners with daily therapeutic massages; Wales keeping tabs on the national picture, the polls, and reports from hundreds of local Jesus for America chapters. He also monitored the other candidates' advertisements and the schedule of Anna Songsparrow, who'd gone to the three northern New England states with Esmeralda for a final swing through an area we had probably not paid enough attention to.

The stress level was enormous. I think the only thing that kept us going, really, was the legions of smiling, screaming, applauding, praying, fainting, ordinary New Jerseyans who lined the route. They held up homemade signs saying things like: WE BELIEVE! and PRESIDENT CHRIST FOREVER! They covered whole sections of roadway with flower petals or palm fronds. They tossed rosaries at Jesus to bless or sang hymns as he passed. They held out photos for Annie C. to autograph. Between worrying about Jesus's physical well-being and dreaming about what life would be like if we actually made it to the White House, there were whole days when I ate almost nothing between my six a.m. coffee and dinner.

With a week to go and the polls holding steady, Annie and Jesus could be found running side-by-side up Broadway in Manhattan (what a permit nightmare that was!). We had a large rally in Harlem, where local storefront preachers came out in force, and the Harlem Globetrotters put on a brief show to warm up the crowd; another enormous rally in a Spanish-speaking section of the Bronx; another, the following afternoon, in Westport, Connecticut, where the entire staff spent the night at a mansion owned by Walter W. Estabrooke, the real-estate developer and casino owner, who claimed he'd been a lifelong atheist before seeing Jesus on *Meet the Media* and being converted.

Converted to what? was the question no one ever seemed to ask. In my rare quiet moments I puzzled over the fact that, with the exception of the one fateful sermon in Montana, Jesus had stayed clear of churches, mosques, temples, chapels, crucifixes, men in dark robes, and the language associated with such things. He told Wales he thought organized religion had done many wonderful things in individual cases, but that it was too often divisive, creating an us-against-them mentality that was the polar opposite of what he was trying to accomplish. (This did not stop the ACLU from filing suit against the campaign, claiming it blurred the constitutional distinction between church and state. For a day or two it worried us, but the suit ended up before a judge named Winston Washington, a friend of the Simmeltons, in the Sixth District of New York, who threw it out as frivolous.)

After his day of running and stumping, Jesus would come back to the hotel, or wherever it was we were staying that night, go over strategy with Wales, hang out with Stab for a few minutes, call his mother, and then basically lock himself in his room. He rarely ate dinner. Unless it was something extremely urgent, he told us not to bother him, he'd see us at breakfast, he needed some downtime. We had learned, by then, to accept this; with the possible exception of my brother, no one took it personally.

We had it timed so that we'd arrive in West Zenith on the Sunday before Election Day. Somehow, remarkably, we kept to that schedule, even as the crowds thickened through central and northern Connecticut, and the press corps expanded before our eyes. The polls continued to be favorable, though in the final week the undecideds appeared to be swinging ominously into the Maplewith camp, and Colonel Alowich was leaking votes in that direction as well. Wales told me in private what all the news broadcasts were mentioning: that while Jesus held a lead narrowly outside the margin of error, that lead did not translate well into the electoral college. There were, it seemed, swaths of the country where, for whatever reason—a barrage of negative ads, contrary influential religious figures, historically powerful Democratic or Republican machines, a lack of attention on our part—Jesus's appeal had been muted. Michigan, Illinois (which we had been counting on), and Ohio were too close to call; Arkansas and neighboring Oklahoma were leaning Alowich's way, along with his home state of Washington and traditionally Democratic states like Maryland, Delaware, Hawaii, and Rhode Island. Florida was unpredictable. Texas, with its heap of electoral votes, would be a fight between Maplewith and Jesus. We appeared to be safe only in California, perhaps New York, New Jersey, and Pennsylvania.

During one of the rare conversations Zelda and I managed to have that week, she said, "I don't think I could handle another election in which a candidate wins the popular vote but doesn't get elected. I don't think the country could handle that." And the political shows spent a lot of time on the same subject, speculating, predicting, waxing confident in their opinions despite what most people said was the strangest and most volatile configuration of states in recent electoral history.

So we arrived at the West Zenith Hilton (part of which we'd booked for Jesus, our staff, and key supporters from around the country, and which would host the traditional Election Night rally/party/acceptance or concession speech) physically exhausted, hopeful, worried, enthralled at our success, and floating on a small raft out in the middle of what felt like a huge, dark, roiling sea of uncertainty.

At which point, Jesus disappeared.

THIRTY-NINE

We pulled up to the Hilton at eleven o'clock on Sunday night, but even at that hour, a mob of well-wishers filled the circular driveway out front. Jesus wanted to say a few encouraging words to them before going inside. This brief speech was the usual just-before-the-vote mixture of gratitude, optimism, and encouragement ("On Tuesday, let us start the long process of turning this nation in the direction it must go!"), except that it ended on a strange note. I was standing a few feet away from him. He was wearing only a light sweater and jeans against the November chill, no gloves, no hat, no scarf, and he was delivering the lines with his usual vitality and responding to the wild cheers with his usual sunbeam smile. At the end, though, instead of summing up with a bland comment like, "Let's all get some rest now. We have one more day of hard work in front of us," he said, "And now I shall disappear," and ducked through the glass front doors with lines of West Zenith police officers to either side and his crew of faithful associates following close behind.

And now I shall disappear.

I noticed the remark, of course. I felt a twinge of anxiety, but Jesus said he would like to have a last, quick meeting with us in his suite, so I did not dwell on the "disappear" part.

The meeting was short. He gave a couple of suggestions for the last day, and told us that on Election Eve, as a gesture of thanks for our work, he would be taking us out to the Taj Mahal, an Indian restaurant in Wells River.

"What's this, the Last Supper?" my father joked, another of his funny remarks that did not quite clear the humor bar for everyone in the room. The next day, Monday, after Jesus did, in fact, disappear, my mother would accuse my father of having offended him and demand he apologize, even though there was no one to apologize to at that moment. My father told her she had no sense of humor, and they got into it again the way they'd been getting into it for forty-three years.

Hearing them take verbal jabs at each other upset Stab, though, as was often the case, he could not articulate the cause of his feelings and so just spluttered, waved his arms, and shouted "No! No! No more!" Stab's anger upset Zelda. Seeing her upset made me angry, so I yelled at Dukey, who went to the window and sulked. Ada shot me a dirty look. Their miracle son, Dukey Junior, walked over and kicked me in the shin. Amelia Simmelton lectured him about how nothing worthwhile was ever achieved by violence. Dukey told Amelia not to talk to his kid in that tone of voice. Norman Simmelton told Dukey not to talk to *his* kid in *that* tone of voice. It was a nice moment all around, and our candidate had gone missing, besides.

But I've gotten ahead of myself. Let me back up. It was nine o'clock on Monday morning, the day after our triumphant return to West Zenith, less than twenty-four hours before the polls opened. We were down in the hotel breakfast room having toaster waffles and ready-mixed hot chocolate, and Jesus not only didn't join us, but we realized he had not spoken to anyone that morning, despite the fact that a last big press conference was scheduled for the hotel's main meeting room at ten a.m. After a while, Zelda told me she had an intuition that something was wrong. The first thing we did was call upstairs to Jesus's room. No answer. The second thing we did was send Dukey up. Dukey knocked. No response. He badgered a housekeeper into opening the door. No one inside. No note. The bed had not been slept in. Dukey came downstairs to the breakfast room with his report—he and Enrica were sure there had been foul play—and started blustering at me that I hadn't been careful enough, an assessment of my work which I did not appreciate, coming, as it did, from my subordinate. Zelda was wrapping her hair around her fingers as if she wanted to pull it out.

So we argued and fretted for a while over the remains of our breakfast. We made phone calls to the rooms of various regional chair people—in some cases rousing them from sleep after a late night of partying. No Jesus. We contacted our downtown headquarters. No sign of him. With some reluctance, and after a small argument, Wales made me call the police and tell them we had a missing person on our hands.

After that, we went upstairs to the suite (the West Zenith equivalent of a presidential suite; none of us slept there; we'd gotten it for our meetings, for watching returns on the last night) and waited for him to appear. When ten o'clock arrived and Jesus did not, Zelda was left to take the elevator down to the main meeting room, stand at the podium, and tell two hundred and fifty reporters and photographers from all over the world that our candidate was not available. "Why isn't he available?" they wanted to know, sensibly enough. She was tempted to lie, she told me later, to cite physical exhaustion from all the running. But in the heat of the moment she told the truth: Jesus had disappeared, we were looking for him, the police were looking for him, we hoped to be able to reschedule the conference for three p.m. that afternoon. In the meantime, she said, Anna Songsparrow would be happy to answer questions.

The press was, at that moment, about as interested in what Anna Songsparrow had to say as they were in the final score of that day's cricket match between the Bombay Buddhas and the Islamabad Ironmen. they had a new hot subject. Fox ran it across their screen more often than their terror alert: BREAKING STORY. JESUS DISAPPEARS ON EVE OF PRESIDENTIAL VOTE. NOT SEEN OR HEARD FROM IN TWELVE HOURS. STAFF FRANTIC. LOCAL, STATE, AND FBI OFFICERS ON THE CASE. PERSON OF INTEREST SOUGHT.

There was no person of interest, of course. I was the point man with the law enforcement people, and would have been the first to know. But Jesus was gone.

Depressed, my faith wobbling like a kid on his first two-wheeler, with no security arrangements to take care of because there was no candidate to protect, I listened to Chief Bastatutta tell me about the search he'd organized, listened to the Secret Service honcho, Richard Diamond, lecture me about never allowing a candidate to refuse protection. I gave Angelina Monahan, the FBI agent in charge, a list of everyplace I could think of that Jesus might have gone in West Zenith and the surrounding area. When that was finished I held Zelda in an embrace for a few seconds and then slipped away to a local bar.

It was a lousy thing to do, I admit that. Cowardly, even. I should have stayed with the rest of the gang, with my mother and dad and Stab and Zelda. As security chief, I should have been there to have face-to-face meetings with the various law enforcement officials who were all fighting with each other about which one had jurisdiction in the case of a disappearing Jesus. But I was absolutely sure there was no foul play involved, and I admit that made me angry at Jesus, I felt we deserved better treatment from him after our months of work. I felt my new, solid house of faith tipping sideways, and I suppose I was ashamed of that and didn't want anyone to see, so I pretended to be going outside to talk to the police and I sneaked away.

I was tempted to head back to my condo, but instead I grabbed a cab to the Wee Drop Inn, a gloomy pub near the Connecticut River. I knew the patrons might recognize me in the unlikely event they were still sober at that hour (noon), but I also knew them to be the type of people who had enough of their own troubles to have adopted what I thought of as the Code of Nonintrusion. I was right. They left me alone. I sat on a stool, nursed a dark ale, chewed stale peanuts, watching Fox on one TV and CNN on another. I kept my phone on the bar where I could see it. Pundits of every stripe had been rushed before the cameras from their corner offices and penthouse suites, and to a man and a woman they said that this latest bit of unpredictability (assuming it wasn't foul play) could be devastating to what had seemed, until then, a fairly safe lead, in the popular vote at least.

With thinly disguised triumph bouncing and jumping in her voice, Anne Canter noted that "if there's one thing the American people don't like it is a lack of dependability."

Bulf Spritzer called the turn of events "worrisome in a handful of different ways," and added, "The drama doesn't get any higher than this!"

The Alowich and Maplewith campaigns issued statements saying they sent their best wishes to the family and hoped for a happy outcome to the mystery—while privately spreading the word that it was just this kind of behavior they'd expected from the outset. You had to be in the public eye for years in order to earn the trust of American people. And Jesus hadn't done that. And now his followers were getting their just deserts.

I kept crunching peanuts and waiting for my cell phone to ring. It did not, unless you count the periodic reports from Dukey, trying to make up for his insubordinate outburst, who informed me, several times, that he and his buddies were "doing shakedowns all over the city, man." He assumed I was at the hotel, and I said nothing to make him think otherwise. I drank moderately but steadily. I spoke to no one. I tried to keep my faith from leaking out entirely, but the more I thought about what Jesus had done, the angrier I became. The angrier I became, the harder it was to believe he was God, or holy, or even someone worthy of our massive efforts. The more I doubted his worthiness, the guiltier I felt. And the guiltier I felt, the less motivation I had to head back to the hotel. It was, in other words, the classic profile of a sinner.

Finally, at two o'clock, when I couldn't bear the news reports any longer, I got up off my bar stool and made myself hail a cab. I thought I saw my ex-mother-in-law near the hotel's front entrance (it might have been what psychologists call a TMM, traumatic memory mirage), so I walked around and used my card key in the back door, and then had to trudge up twelve flights of stairs because work was being done on one of the elevators and the other elevator was very slow. At the suite, with the exception of Anna Songsparrow, the whole gang was sitting around in various postures of devastation. Anna had wandered off somewhere to pray. No one seemed to have noticed I was gone, though after Zelda kissed me she sniffed, squinted her eyes, and said, "Beer?"

Dukey saved me from answering. I flipped open the phone and heard, "Nothin', man, nothin'. Somebody grabbed him, I'm tellin' ya."

"I don't think so. I think he went off by himself."

"For what?" Dukey yelled.

"To pray or something. You know how he is."

"No way. Not today, man. He ain't _that_ crazy."

"Just keep trying. Look in the places you'd least expect him to be. Check Parsifal's. Check the Wee Drop Inn."

"Good idea, Boss," he said, and I hung up. It was hours before he called again.

The "command center," as we'd named the suite in better moments, had the feel of a visitation room in a funeral home where someone too young is lying in the casket and friends are standing around in small groups wondering why. When she wasn't on the phone with press people, Zelda could be found standing at the window with teary eyes. Amelia Simmelton would go up and put an arm around her, and try to convince her, with a nine-year-old's wise certainty, that everything Jesus did, he did for good reason. Stab kept looking at me as if I had the explanation for all this sorrow and was purposely keeping it from him. My mother had decided the best thing to do was make escarole soup, and she had taken my dad out shopping for ingredients, and they were in the kitchen now, locked in one of their postfight silences, chopping garlic and opening cans of white beans. We paced, we drank bad beer, we nibbled at sandwiches and brownies the hotel management sent up, and some of us cried and some of us swore and some of us did both, but no one could bear to turn on the television.

"Do we go up to the Mahal without him or what?" Wales asked, and the room was split. More arguments, more minor-league recriminations. A phone call from the FBI agent, saying there was a report that Jesus had been seen in a church on the south side. They were checking it out.

At three o'clock, Zelda had to go down and face the press again, and she was still there when the call came in on my cell phone at fifteen minutes before five.

"Russ, Chief Bastatutta. We found him."

"Alive?"

"Yup."

"Okay?"

"Yup."

With the phone still to my ear, I gave the room the thumbs-up. "I have never heard finer words, Chief. Where?"

"Hunter Town."

"Huh?"

"Been here all day apparently, playing touch football in the mud with some kids. We have him in a car. We'll get him back to the hotel. Gotta tell you, though, somehow the word leaked out. A few press types were there at the end, just before it got dark. Turn on your TV, you'll see."

Someone pushed a button on the remote, and the second the picture came on, there was our candidate, covered from teeth to shoelaces in mud, his arms around four or five black kids dressed in dark hooded sweatshirts. One of them was tossing a football up and down in his hands.

"We've been Willie Hortoned," Wales said, in a tone of voice you might have heard from a guy who'd been told he had to have four root canals on his birthday. I saw Norm Simmelton cringe. "We've Willie Hortoned ourselves."

"Nah, listen," I told him. "I spent some time in Hunter over the years. I even think I recognize one of those kids. They're good kids, most of them."

"Right. You know they're good kids. I know they're good kids. Question is, do Suzy and Mitch Hazlegood in Whistlestop, Missouri, know they're good kids? Don't think so."

"Will it ever stop," Nadine Simmelton moaned.

Hunter Town was a sort of poorer Fultonville, a section of the city that white cabdrivers would not take a fare to. Even the Jamaican and Ethiopian cabdrivers would often refuse to go there. ZIZ reporters asked for police escorts when they were assigned a Hunter Town story.

"I don't understand," I said. I was on the couch next to Wales at that point. Zelda had come around behind and put her hands on my shoulders. "I mean, I know he cares about the poor, and wants to make a symbolic statement about that and wants the country to finally get beyond racial problems, but why didn't he go to Hunter Town and have a rally or something? Why blow off the press? Why not tell any of us where he was going? It's like he has a death wish or something . . . You know what I mean."

Wales was trying to unwrap a cigar, but his hands weren't working right. He stared at the television screen without saying another word.

We watched ZIZ show the pictures over and over again of Jesus with his football pals. Jesus smiling, waving, and, for the benefit of the TV cameras, tossing one last perfect spiral before climbing into a squad car. Noelle Prendergast, who'd been promoted to roving correspondent when I quit, was on the scene, "Reporting live from Hunter Town, for the Wizard, WZIZ News at five." She looked frightened and was holding the microphone too far up into her face, but otherwise seemed to be doing a competent job.

When the police escorted Jesus to the suite, Stab hugged him with more gusto than usual. My mother convinced him to have a bowl of soup. He stood at the counter in the kitchen, mud caked on his shirt, running shoes, and sweat pants, looking utterly unconcerned about the fact that he'd stood up two hundred plus reporters, twice, that the pundits were predicting a wholesale abandonment by the fickle swing voters in key states, and that he'd caused us so much worry.

Jesus was polite enough to finish the soup and to compliment my mother on it. He told us plans were still on for the Indian meal in Wells River and that he was going to his room to shower and change. I couldn't take it anymore, couldn't hold my anger in. I followed him down the corridor and when he turned to close his door he saw me. He smiled, motioned me in, shut the door behind me, and stood there with mud in his hair. "Let me guess," he said, "you are upset."

"I would like a momentary exemption," I said, trying to keep my voice calm.

"From what?"

"From you being, you know . . . God or whatever you are. I'd like to be able to say what I want to say without fear of punishment."

He laughed.

"I'm serious. I want an exemption."

"You can always tell me what's on your mind, you know that, Russ."

"This isn't always," I said stupidly. And then it spilled out of me: "You made us all miserable today. It was rude, it was inconsiderate, it was ungrateful, after all the work we've done. And most important, it was a completely stupid thing to do from a strategic standpoint—you kept hundreds of press people waiting not once, but twice, and they don't like that kind of thing. You might have blown the whole election with one day of touch football."

He had not moved. The expression on his face was pleasant, attentive, respectful, even friendly. He seemed to be waiting for more.

"That's all I wanted to say."

He kept looking at me.

"No offense intended. No disrespect. But I think it was a lousy thing to do, a crazy thing, and I couldn't just go up to the dinner tonight and pretend everything was hunky-dory. I'm not like that."

"I know you're not," he said. "That is why you're here, because you're not like that. That is why I chose you. When it comes time to tell my story, I don't want someone who is going to prettify it. I am not interested in being the Jesus of someone's syrupy imagination."

"All right," I said, but I was confused.

He held me in his gaze until I was uncomfortable, and then he said, "And I know about your doubts."

I was suddenly interested in the color of the hotel walls.

"Look at me," he said.

It was exceedingly difficult to move my eyes back to him. "I'm sorry," I said. "For the doubts."

"I am used to it, believe me. If it makes you feel any better, I can tell you this: it is as impossible for you to conceive of the reality of the God realm as it is for you to imagine yourself breathing underwater, or flying with your arms. Later, when you have passed out of this body, the full power of the presence of God will be made manifest to you, and then there will be no possibility of doubt."

"That scares me, for some reason."

"For good reason. It is an awesome experience for everyone, and terrifying for a person who has lived a life filled with violence or hatred or greed. For someone who has lived a life of kindness and generosity, however, it is vastly different. In that moment when such people first feel God's presence they are protected from fear by the understanding that they have God's goodness in themselves. Clear?"

"Not exactly, no."

"The eye God sees you with is the eye with which you see God."

"That's funny. I remember that from Sunday school. It always confused me."

He gave me the frown of impatience I'd seen from him so many times. "Feeling the godliness in yourself in God's presence can be compared to certain moments of unity on earth. The best moments of lovemaking, friendship, family togetherness—those instances when you felt yourself linked to another soul. Ring a bell?"

"A faint bell," I said.

Jesus smiled at me then. The smile was like warm bathwater being poured over you. "That feeling is an inkling of what you feel in the presence of God if your conscience is relatively clean. Doubt is banished. Self-hatred is banished. You become aware of your true divine identity. To make a crude comparison: the child understands the parent's love, at the same time that the child understands the parent's need for him or her, the way the parent's life has been expanded by the child's existence. It is the purest form of reciprocation."

"All right," I said. "Thanks."

"Still angry?"

"A little bit, yeah. Only because of all the work we put in. Only because we want so badly for you to actually get elected and start—"

"Only because you think you know better," he said, calmly.

"All right. Sorry again. I just—"

"Go take a shower. They are preparing a special meal for us at the Taj Mahal. Let's not keep them waiting."

So I went back down the hotel hallway with a cold current of confusion running underneath everything. *Only because you think you know better.* Like the scent of an evil spirit, the dregs of my anger and doubt followed me into my room. I could hear the shower running and thought of what I would say to Zelda when she came out, how I would tell her I'd let Jesus have it on behalf of all of us, that he hadn't apologized, that I was wondering if he even cared about winning.

And then I went and stood at the window and came to my senses.

Darkness had fallen over West Zenith, and I could see the streetlights forming straight lines across the neighborhoods, and offices still lit up in the buildings downtown. Life seemed so massive to me then, so complicated, so many thousands of souls working out an interconnected puzzle. Next to that, even a presidential election was small-time.

Only because you think you know better.

My cell phone buzzed in my pocket and then started ringing and when I said hello I was profoundly sorry to hear the voice of Randy Zillins. "Help out an old pal. Give me the inside story on what happened today."

"Randy Zillins," I said, "the guy who only calls when he needs something."

"Yeah, well, listen, I got a story to file. Can you give me something? You know, on today? Inside info? And no more of that Bible crap either. Can you?"

"Sure. What happened today was a lesson in humility."

"Aw, Christ," Zillins said.

"Listen," I said, because I had truly had it with him at that point. Looking back now, I can see that I was experiencing the opposite of what Jesus had told me moments before: instead of being with God and sensing the goodness in myself, I was talking with Randy Zillins and sensing the darkness in myself, the doubt, the pettiness, the insistence on knowing better. "I don't want you calling me anymore, okay? It's the night before the election, I have nine million things to do, including protecting the guy you think is a phony, and who is staying in a hotel that anybody can walk into off the street. So please, go find your inside info someplace else, okay?"

I waited a second before hanging up. I could hear R.Z. breathing on the other end of the line, insulted, hurt, shocked—who knows exactly what he was feeling? As I was about to apologize, or at least soften my remarks, he slammed the line closed.

✯✯✯ FORTY ✯✯✯

The thing I will always remember about our last supper is the feeling of warmth that emanated from Jesus. We'd seen sparks of it during the campaign. With all the travel and the public appearances, though, and the incredible strain of getting up there day after day to say basically the same thing over and over again, he'd been aloof at times. Not cold, but distant.

At the Taj Mahal—as if to make up for his day of absence—he was fully present, and the only word you can use to describe the way he treated us is *love*. Everyone at the table felt it. He smiled radiantly at us, he touched the people sitting closest to him, he cracked jokes with my brother, and generally made everyone feel he had a special place for them in his heart. Near the end of what turned out to be a very good meal, he presented each of us with a twenty karat gold pin with THE JESUS CAMPAIGN inscribed on it. Not counting Anna Songsparrow, fourteen people had been invited to the dinner, so there were fourteen of these pins, made by a Manhattan jeweler. (Now, after what happened, and after enough time has passed to give people a perspective on the magnitude of what happened, these pins, I have been told, are worth in excess of a hundred thousand dollars each. None of them, to date, has been sold.)

Jesus walked around the table handing them out. He stopped to give each of us a warm embrace and to say words of thanks for our particular contribution. Standing beside my chair with one hand on my shoulder, he said, "I want to thank Russ for his sass, his reverent irreverence, and for knocking me over in Jocko Padsen's shed."

I said, "You're welcome," and he laughed and seemed genuinely pleased.

When he was finished with this ceremony, he told us to remain seated. As if on some invisible signal, the door to our private room opened and two waiters came in. One was carrying a silver bowl filled with water; the other was carrying a bar of soap and a towel. Jesus knelt in front of my mother, who happened to be sitting next to me. Before she could do anything to stop him, he was taking off her shoes and washing her feet, tenderly soaping her misshapen toes, then rinsing them and carefully drying them with the towel. She allowed this to go on for one foot before she broke apart. Over the course of almost forty years I had seen my mother cry, of course—at her own mother's funeral, during times when my father did something to frustrate her, or I did something to disappoint her (the day I told her I was getting divorced leaps to mind as a memorably weepy occasion). But I had never seen anything remotely like the sorrow that began pouring out of her as Jesus moved on to her second foot. My father was sitting on the other side of her, and even though they had not been getting along well for the past few days, he could not bear to see her like that—her cheeks shaking and soaked, her hands fluttering across her thighs like wounded birds, her lips working convulsively. Dad leaned over and put his large hand on both her small ones and kept saying, "Mudgie, what? He doesn't mean anything bad by it, honey. Mudgie, honey, stop, please."

I was saying something along the same lines. Stab had started to cry as well. Jesus kept doing what he was doing, with a gentleness you don't often encounter in a big man.

"Ma, what?" I said, pretty weakly I guess, because I was as puzzled and upset as the rest of us. In the circles in which I traveled, you didn't often see a man washing a woman's feet in a public place. "It's something he wants to do. It's his way of saying thanks."

She was shaking her head at me, hard.

"Ma, it's all right," I repeated.

"No it isn't, Russ," she answered, but the words didn't come out straight like that; they came out in bursts of sound from underneath the wave of tears and sorrow: *"No . . . it is . . . no it isn't. . . . No, Russ, it isn't!* Arnie, it isn't. It's from the Bible. This is what he did in the Bible right at the very end. Now he's going to say he's going away to a place where we can't follow!" Her voice lifted and broke on the last syllable.

It was like talking about someone who wasn't in the room. Jesus was so focused—head down, hands working—that he seemed almost to be *inside* my mother's feet. But when she spoke those words, I noticed a peculiar twist of the muscles at the corners of his mouth, and when I saw that reaction I felt like the door had been thrown open and a gust of ten-below-zero air had blown onto the back of my neck. I got down on one knee so that my face was at the same level as Jesus's. I took a risk and put a hand on his shoulder, and I said, "Is she right?"

For a few seconds he ignored me. He concentrated on the second foot, washing between the toes, then rinsing and drying them. With that same exquisite gentleness he squeezed her foot in both hands and set it down on the carpet. Another wave of sobbing spilled out of my mom. "Is she right?" I repeated. "Was what you did today some weird way of preparing us?"

Jesus slowly turned his head toward me, and in his eyes I could see something I had not seen there before. It was as if they opened into a series of deep brown worlds, one standing behind the next, each larger and wider and more complicated than the one before it. The special feeling of friendship I'd had with him in the desert, and in his hotel room that afternoon—it was there all over again, except this time magnified by a factor of ten, as if he was seeing through me and through me and through me, reading the pages of my future and my past, seeing everything and bathing it in understanding, forgiveness, and love. He was the Jesus I'd grown up imagining, except he didn't care as much about my sins as that Jesus did.

"I am expecting the best of you," he said quietly, and while this "you" clearly meant all of us, the word just about knocked me over.

I shivered, I couldn't control it. I needed five or six seconds to recover. I said, "You didn't come all this way to leave us again, did you?"

His face was as still as the sky on a winter night, full of this massive, sparkling openness. Dark and light at once. He said, "It is not something you can understand."

"Try me."

"I have to fulfill the prophecy."

"To hell with the prophecy. There *is* no prophecy this time. Nothing's written down, nothing's set in stone."

Stab was hugging him from the other side now, also on his knees. My mother seemed like she was going to faint. I was aware of Zelda leaning down toward him, and the others at the table crowding around. Ada Montpelier was bubbling over nearby, and Dukey was trying, in his own way, to comfort her. "It's nothin', it's okay, he's all right."

"Everything is fine as it is," Jesus said. "Everything plays out as it should."

"But are you going?"

Jesus paused and drew in a slow breath. "Don't be foolish," he said.

At that moment I could feel . . . this sounds weird, but I could feel him coming back into the room. It was as if, after he'd started washing my mom's feet, he had expanded in three dimensions, turned himself into something larger than his body, something gigantic, something loving and terrifying at the same time. Much later I would remember the part of the Last Supper where he was reported to have said, "This is my body, and this is my blood," and it gave that passage new meaning for me, as if his disciples were on the slow side, mentally, and full of fear, and he was trying to convey to them the idea that a being as great as the Jesus-spirit could not be encapsulated in a human body. I believe now that he was preparing those disciples, trying to get them to focus on something other than the physical dimension.

"So you're not going anywhere?"

"Don't be foolish," he repeated. "Where could I go?"

"See, he's all right," Dukey said with a laugh, as if trying to convince himself.

Stab stood up and started doing an awkward dance around the room. He bounced on one foot and then bounced on the other foot, like some kind of Native American warrior celebrating peace. They were happy sounds coming out of my brother's mouth, but underneath the happy sounds I could tell he was afraid his world was going to fall apart.

"All right then," I said, trying for a lighter tone and half succeeding. "It was nice what you did. I appreciate it. My mom appreciates it. But you scared us."

"Resist fear," Jesus said. "Fear is always in the future. Cut through it. Resist it."

Wales piped up, "Now that we know you're going to be around, tell us one thing. Are we going to win?"

"Without question," Jesus said, and we cheered loudly. But there was a false note to that moment. I have gone back over it a hundred times. I remember that Zelda and I let our eyes meet for a second and then had to look away from each other. Norm Simmelton started to speak and abruptly stopped. I believe that, deep down, we all knew something, we sensed something. When Jesus washed my mother's feet, I don't think he was expecting the best of us, I think he was expecting too much of us—he was assuming we had learned, by the parable of his presence in a political campaign, that we were supposed to figure things out for ourselves. That we were on our own in a certain way. That we had some power and control over our spiritual fate, a power we did not know we possessed. That we might even have a little godliness in us.

People got up off the floor. My mother put her shoes on. The waiters carried away the water bowl and soap and towel, and came back with tea and rice pudding, and we took our places again and acted like we were an ordinary campaign staff on the eve of an election, nothing more than that.

"Your missing the last press conference hurt us today," Zelda had the courage to say.

Jesus gave her the look he had been giving me when we were kneeling beside each other on the floor. I saw it register on her beautiful face—the fear, and then something covering over the fear. I wondered if he were preparing each of us in a different way—Zelda and me with this mysterious signal, my mother with the foot washing.

"I know," he said. "Awkward for you, wasn't it."

"Very much."

I thought Jesus might apologize—something I'd never heard him do. Instead he reached across the corner of the table and took hold of her wrist. She put her hand over his. I was not jealous in the slightest. "You know," he said, "they don't let presidents play touch football in the mud. I knew it would be my last chance for anything like that, and if I had told you in advance, what would everyone have said?"

"No freakin' way we would've let you go," Dukey yelled. I noticed that, since he'd seen Jesus washing my mother's feet, he'd been touching Ada almost continuously. This was rare for him. Though I don't think he was mean to her, there was almost no public tenderness between them, not in touch or words, and not much either between Dukey and his son. It would have been too much of a risk for him, doing that and letting people see. It would have been the psychological equivalent of walking around without his flak jacket on. Now, suddenly, he had an arm around Ada and was massaging her shoulder with the fingers of one hand. She looked like she was being fondled by an alien. So maybe Jesus had sent them a message, too.

"Exactly," Jesus told him. "You would have tried to stop me."

"At least you should have let some of the guys go down there with you. Safety's sake."

Jesus smiled at him, indulgently, I thought.

The Simmeltons wanted to pick up the tab, but Jesus wouldn't let them. He produced a roll of bills from his pants pocket and pushed it into the hands of the host, who bowed to him as he went out the front door.

In the limousine convoy on the way home, we were sitting in our usual positions, Zelda and I across from Jesus and Stab. I could feel Jesus looking at me, but I kept my eyes turned away. I was trying to figure out what had happened, what he had actually told us, if he had promised us anything, if my intuition was on target or way off. I tried to catch Zelda's eye, but she was talking to a reporter on the phone, trying to smooth over her candidate's earlier no-show.

There was a dark stretch of highway, the exit ramp, and then I watched the bleak city of West Zenith roll into view, the storefronts with sheets of metal covering their windows, the shadowy alleys, the street people huddled in blankets in doorways, the idling cars and young men avoiding the light. I thought about what Jesus had said to me once: earth was the dimension of pain. I thought about Wales, on the beach in San Diego, saying we had to learn to say yes to everything.

When we pulled up to the hotel, Zelda stepped out, and then Stab. For a moment Jesus and I were left alone in the backseat. I motioned for him to go first, and I was able then to meet his eyes. He looked at me, looked into me again, put his hand on my knee and said one word.

"Courage."

VERY LATE THAT NIGHT, when we felt we'd done everything we could to prepare for voting day, Zelda and I lay beside each other beneath the sheets of the hotel bed, warm skin against warm skin. Neither of us could sleep. Neither of us had said a word about what had happened that evening in the Taj Mahal. As if to avoid talking about it, we'd sat up in our room watching TV until almost two a.m. The pundits were predicting that, despite his election eve antics, Jesus was still favored to win the popular vote, perhaps by as much as five percent, but the electoral college was absolutely uncertain. Alowich was probably out of it, but Maplewith might have the edge over Jesus, depending on how things played out in half a dozen key states.

"You can't sleep either, right?" Zelda asked quietly in the darkness.

"Not even close."

"You know what I wish, Russ?"

"What?"

"I wish we were able to not worry. I wish we could have the attitude that, no matter what happens tomorrow, we've been privileged to do this, to be around him, to meet the people we've met in the last few months. I'd like it if we could just be grateful for that, whether we win or lose or . . . no matter what. Before he came into our lives we were doing pretty well . . . I was happy, you were happy . . . but I feel like a whole other dimension of ourselves has been opened up now. Look at how much he's given us, each one of us. And what did we do to deserve it? Nothing, really."

For a moment or two I lay there without speaking. I could hear the elevator doors closing in the hallway, the faint sound of a siren in the street below. I could feel the warmth of Zelda's leg against my skin.

"Do you ever wonder," I asked her, "why he came to us? I mean, look at it: me, my mom, my dad, Dukey McIntyre, for God's sake. We're not exactly the twelve apostles and Mary Magdalene. Jesus coming to West Zenith, to be with a pack of jokers like us! Don't you ever wonder?"

"He had to pick someplace. He had to choose some people."

"I know, but it's not like we're particularly holy or smart or that we've done some great work in our lives."

"Your dad was brave in the war. He and your mom raised Stab with a lot of love. You went through what you went through with Esther and you didn't turn permanently bitter. The Simmeltons grew up in the New York equivalent of Hunter Town, and somehow worked themselves out of that, and they've given away millions to good causes."

"Right. And you were raised in foster homes and have spent your life since then helping people, and you put up with a guy like me. I know. But—"

"We've all lived good lives," she said quietly. "We've all been heroic, in an ordinary kind of way."

"Still . . . look at Wales, I mean. The guy watches football on Sundays with a glass of vodka in his hand. He goes fishing on summer weekends. He's not exactly, you know, John the Baptist—"

"Maybe Jesus doesn't want us to see people that way. Think about it. On the last day of his campaign he went and played football with those boys, and had his picture taken with them. Most people look at boys like that and without even knowing them think: gang members, criminals, people you wouldn't want to meet in a dark alley. Most people look at your brother and immediately turn away, or they see him as an idiot who can't be quiet when he should be, who has no real understanding of life. With Stab, at least, you see beyond the surfaces and so do I. Maybe Jesus is trying to show us he does that with everybody, looks past the exterior to something perfect inside. Maybe that's what he's trying to teach us, and if he's president. . . ."

Zelda stopped abruptly.

"I can only do that with very little kids," I said, in a joking tone, because with the way she'd stopped after the words "*if he's president,*" something cold had blown into the room again. "Babies, little kids. After they get to be about two, I start to see what's wrong with them. Even with somebody I love, even with you—no offense—I can see that perfect part about one minute out of every hundred. I see it in myself about one day out of every two years, and as I get older I see it less and less. Today, when he disappeared, I sneaked down to the Wee Drop Inn for two hours and sat there drinking and watching TV, and I was so mad I stopped believing there was even anything good in him, never mind that he might be, you know, that he might be—"

"Sent from God," she said.

"Exactly."

After a while, Zelda turned onto her side and rested her cheek against my shoulder. "When I had my practice I often used to wonder what it was that made everybody hate themselves so much. Or not hate themselves maybe but have such a low opinion of themselves, as if there was a perfect standard they'd been told they were supposed to live up to, bodywise, brainwise, as parents, as lovers, as children. Sometimes I thought we had it upside down: we believed we had to be good so that we could love ourselves, instead of naturally loving ourselves and then naturally doing good because we loved ourselves."

"You lost me," I said.

"Every once in a while on this trip I'd see somebody—a waitress or a driver or someone in the crowd—remember the man who sold us those flowers in Chico?—and there would be an expression on their face. . . . It was as if, when they looked at Jesus they were seeing themselves, as if he were the manifestation of how they felt about themselves, deep inside. I think they've come to a place where they are perfectly at peace with their humanness.

"My mother says that, when she comes out of confession on Saturday afternoon, she feels holy. Is that what you mean?"

"I bet there is no way on earth your mother can be unkind to anyone or do anything hurtful while she is in that state of mind. She believes her sins are forgiven, really believes it, so she can forgive everyone else."

"Even my dad . . . for a few hours."

"I think Jesus has been trying to teach us something about that during this whole thing—the talks, the tricks he played, the courage, the calm, the warmth, the insistence on kindness, the turning our assumptions upside down. Disappearing today. Even that foot washing at dinner tonight. It's all been one big lesson."

I thought about that for a minute, feeling her skin against mine, and then the darkness and coldness beyond that. I thought about my father insisting on using the word *rabbi* or *teacher,* instead of *God.* And then I thought of the last thing Jesus had said to me before he got out of the limo. The foreboding that had been at the back of my mind circled around and around and then pushed itself out into the air: "He's going to be killed, isn't he," I said.

"I think so."

"And we're going to have to deal with that, and deal with the country we have, without him."

"Yes." Zelda reached her face up and kissed me, and we were silent after that for a long time, and eventually we fell asleep that way, holding on.

★ ★ ★ FORTY-ONE ★ ★ ★

The TV networks have this cute thing they do on Election Day. They get information from their own exit polls, people stationed at key precincts who ask certain questions of voters after the deed is done. To the networks' credit, while the polls are still open, they hold themselves back from making projections based on this information. Once the polls close within a particular time zone or an individual state, the fun begins. When that happens, it sounds something like this: "ABC news is now able to project that Mickey Mouse will carry the state of Florida. So Florida, with its twenty-seven electoral votes, goes into the Mouse column." And so on.

What's interesting to me as a journalist is what they do before these projections can be made. Inevitably, they trot out some second-tier reporter, and give her a four-minute segment during which she can talk about the answers voters have given at the polling place. These answers can't be anything as direct as who they actually voted for—it's too early for that to be allowed on air—so they fall into the category of shocking conclusions like: "We found that voters who describe themselves as 'very religious' generally placed 'values issues' above foreign policy strength." Or, "Our research has demonstrated that women aged twenty-five to forty, living in the suburbs, with between one and three children, whose husbands earn more than a hundred thousand dollars a year, who prefer to buy cars made by American companies, and who favor pantsuits when they go to the office, these women said, overwhelmingly, that environmental issues have gotten too much play in this election cycle."

In order to guess who is doing well and who isn't, you have to be able to read the code, get between the lines of this stuff. You have to know which parties are considered stronger on national defense or environmental issues in any given election cycle; which candidates said what about gun control, birth control, mind control. If you listen carefully, say, around six p.m., you can start to get an idea what the actual returns will look like.

As a former media insider, I am usually pretty good at reading this code. However, this time around there was a big wrinkle: precincts that, in the past, had been statistically predictable, had now been rendered statistically insignificant by the new candidate. There had never before been a holy man in the race. If you judged by what Jesus had said during the campaign, you'd have a hard time locking him into either camp. He'd accomplished the seemingly impossible: he'd made half the electorate into swing voters.

So, though we sat (or, in my case, paced) around the twelfth-floor hotel suite most of the day, watching the news channels, and though we had supporters calling us from various parts of the country telling us what their own exit polling was telling them (that turnout was particularly high, for one thing), and giving us suggestive information here and there, as the afternoon and then the evening wore on, we were as confused and concerned as everyone else. A lot of pizza was consumed on the twelfth floor that day. A lot of doughnuts. A lot of chicken wings, spare ribs, and so-so sushi. A lot of coffee and Busch Lite and Coke. Between waiting for the results and worrying about the previous night's conversation with Zelda, I felt like I was sitting on the edge of a twelve-story razor blade, getting fatter by the second. A breeze would come from this direction and I'd almost fall over one way. A breeze from the other direction half an hour later, and I'd be holding tight to keep from falling off the other way. The longer I sat there, the deeper it cut.

We all handled this unbearable tension in our own fashion. Every hour or so my father went out and sprinted the length of the corridor ("You're going to have a heart attack, Arnie!" my mother yelled each time), returning to the room red-faced and sweating, cradling the small cast on his broken hand, and heading for the beer cooler. When she wasn't yelling at him, my mom was praying the rosary. Stab got very loud—so loud that we sent him down to the lobby to pay for every new food delivery. Dukey walked around and around outside the hotel with a pistol in a holster under his vest, no gloves on—though it was not far above freezing that day in Massachusetts—no hat, a few biker pals taking turns keeping him company. Norman Simmelton read sections from F. Scott Fitzgerald's *Tender Is the Night* to his wife, who had put herself in charge of Web watching on her laptop. Dukey Junior watched Barney videos over and over on a small TV we had set up in a corner of the main room. Amelia acted more or less as babysitter. Ada Montpelier restarted the Barney DVDs, warmed the pizza, poured the coffee, and from time to time would stand at the window to see if she could catch a glimpse of her restless mate. Enrica took up a position in the hall. When I went to check on her I saw that she was trying to kick out the light fixture on the ceiling and coming alarmingly close. Wales took notes, chewed two cigars in half, and covered pages of paper with various combinations of states that would carry us over the 270 electoral vote mark. Esmeralda was glued to the TV set, leaning forward, elbows on knees, relaying everything that had even the smallest significance. "Huge turnout in Utah!" she'd announce, and somebody in the room would grunt or let out a syllable of surprise or a Bronx cheer. "Maplewith's husband is standing on a corner in Boise giving out free Bibles!"

Zelda used the other phone line to massage the press, telling them how optimistic we were, and that Jesus was huddled in his room with Anna Songsparrow, working on his speech.

This last part was not technically true. Jesus was huddled in his room with Anna Songsparrow, yes, but the few times I went in there I found them playing board games. "Mom, which of the following was a popular Frankie Valli song in the 1960s?"

From time to time, haunted by the previous night's conversation, I would take the single working elevator down to the main ballroom where a few of our lazier supporters were standing around drinking free booze, their signs and placards leaning in a corner. I'd check the entrances, talk with the policemen stationed there, then go out into the lobby and confer with Chief Bastatutta, who'd arrived at the hotel at breakfasttime and had not left. "I hope you voted first, Ace," I said to him.

"Bet your ass, I voted. How many candidates like this are we ever gonna get?"

"So you're convinced he's God, huh?"

He gave me both barrels, his interrogator's gaze. "I don't need him to be God," he said. "A guy who says what he says, who thinks like he thinks—that's enough for me."

Not enough for me, I found myself thinking, but I did not say it.

I need to confess something here: I have weird and unpleasant thoughts. When I am under stress, those thoughts come more often and with more power. Almost like I am out wandering in the desert and some devilish part of my own mind is tempting me to jump into the pickup truck with these thoughts and ride off into some upside down paradise where the beer is cold and I make all the rules. "Not enough for me" was a perfect example. Now what did that mean? And why did it pop into my head under the gaze of Chief B., a strong, uncomplicated guy who made up his mind about something and never wavered?

By six o'clock, an hour before polls closed in some of the eastern states, we started to hear, from a variety of sources, that Alowich was out of it. The race was between Maplewith and us. Not shocking news, but a confirmation of the trends we'd been seeing over the past week. It was going to be closer than expected, our sources told us.

"Even the popular vote will be close?" I asked Zel.

She nodded somberly.

"Not good."

Although the network had not been kind to us during the campaign, Esmeralda kept switching back to Fox news. They somehow got the results a few minutes ahead of everybody else, and she said she liked their graphics better, though my personal feeling was that she must have had shares in the company. Brett V. Ruhm was their chief election correspondent, and he had two experts with him: Cham Grinwealthy, the former Speaker of the House, whose Contract on America had been nearly forgotten by then so he was considering a run for the White House himself in the next election cycle; and Billy Betbette, author, former cabinet member, and moral leader. They were excellent examples, I thought, of how much chutzpah a person needed in order to have a successful career at the highest levels of American politics. Really, one of the essential qualities — and not many people talk about this — was a complete lack of shame. You had to be able to cheat on your wife with a younger woman, in the White House no less, and then appear on TV with a big smile on your face. You had to be caught with a dominatrix during the Democratic National Convention, then switch parties, become an analyst, and make biased predictions that never came true. You had to skip out on military service and then send other people into combat. Not only did you have to steal and cheat and lie — anyone could do that — but you had to steal and cheat and lie and have every person in the world hear about it and still be able to appear in public and speak as confidently as if you had the word of God bubbling out of your heart.

Grinwealthy, a moral paragon, had left his first wife on her deathbed, skipping out with his new woman. Betbette, moral paragon *numero dos*, had a gambling problem — which had not stopped him from writing stern books about old-fashioned morality, and not kept him from campaigning with Maplewith in Nevada. As payment for their sins, there they were, front and center on a big news network on Election Night, passing on to the electorate their wisdom . . . and their off-the-mark predictions.

"Pretty clear that, with the possible exception of New Hampshire, Colonel Alowich is going to take Democrat country, meaning New England," Betbette said shortly before the network announced, at 8:12, that Maine, with its four electoral votes, would go for the Republican, Marjorie Maplewith. This made me tremendously nervous and upset, and not because I felt embarrassed for Betbette. Maine was a state we had hoped to win. Seeing it fall into Maplewith's column so early in the night set off another run of bad thoughts, an interior monologue to the effect that Wales had blown it by taking northern New England for granted. Jesus had never even made an appearance there, and we'd sent Anna Songsparrow only at the last minute, and only on a limited tour. I kept this opinion to myself, of course.

Later, after Grinwealthy said he now thought Alowich wouldn't win a single New England state, we learned that the colonel seemed to have held onto Rhode Island and was making a strong showing, along with Jesus, in Massachusetts.

Watching these erudite analysts would have been amusing—they erred so spectacularly and with such straight faces—except that a cloud of doom was descending over our exhausted team. None of us said anything, but I would place a bet that we were all thinking the same thing: we'd already lost Maine and Rhode Island, two states we hoped to win; what did that say about the rest of the blessed night?

It got worse: Maplewith was soon projected to take New Hampshire by a comfortable margin. Connecticut was up for grabs.

All that work, all that sacrifice; the exultation of watching people standing three deep in front of the Simi Valley Feng Shui Academy, or along Arthur Avenue in the Bronx, hoping to catch a glimpse of Jesus; the terrible feeling of the hissing, jeering crowd in the church in Montana; all those ups and downs, all those gorgeous golf days spent sitting over coffee and doughnuts with police captains; the big balloon of hope . . . and now we could feel it slipping out of our hands and floating into space. We kept our eyes fixed on the TV screen, but it was with a sense of dread.

The next announcement did little to brighten the mood: A few minutes after Brett Ruhm speculated that Alowich might be back in the race after all, and would probably make a stronger than expected showing in the South, thanks to his military background, Maplewith took Virginia and North Carolina. And then, ten minutes later, South Carolina, too.

"God help us," my mother moaned. "God help us."

Grinwealthy said, "What we're starting to see here is what my colleague Anne Canter predicted a couple weeks ago: in the solitude of the voting booth, Americans are vigorously rejecting the whole Divinity Party show."

And so, naturally, not ten minutes later, Maryland and New Jersey went into our column. Wales got out a fresh cigar and clamped his lips around it.

Delaware went to Alowich. Florida was too close to call.

The phone rang; no one answered it. We were paralyzed. None of us wanted to lift the receiver and hear someone on the other end say, "We're getting early results from the Midwest. It's over. We're finished."

"We have to answer the phones, people," Wales complained, but he made no more move to do so than anyone else. After the fifth ring, the phone went silent.

When Betbette spoke the following line, Fox's coverage got to be too much even for Esmeralda: "Once we see New York go for Alowich, which I'm starting to think it will, the Jesus campaign, so-called, will have to fold up its tent and slink back into the wilderness where it came from." Ezzie switched to NBC, just as they were putting New York in the Jesus column. A huge cheer went up . . . until they said Ohio was leaning to Maplewith.

"We're still in it," I remember Wales saying at about that point. "Don't lose faith, people."

And, though it didn't feel like we were still in it, he was right. The long and the short of it was, by the time we got to zero hour in the Midwest, the tallies looked like this:

Alowich—Rhode Island, Delaware, West Virginia = 12 electoral votes.

Maplewith—Maine, New Hampshire, Connecticut, Virginia, North Carolina, South Carolina, Georgia, Ohio, Kentucky, Mississippi, Alabama = 109 electoral votes.

Jesus—New York, Massachusetts, Maryland, New Jersey, Vermont, Pennsylvania = 92 electoral votes.

At that point in the evening, thanks to big margins in New York, New Jersey, and Pennsylvania, we had 42 percent of the popular vote, Maplewith 37 percent and Alowich 21 percent, but we all knew how little that meant. The only thing the popular vote demonstrated was who the American people most wanted to be president.

"It's going to come down to Florida," Wales said ominously. But even that seemed optimistic to me. I felt like the hope of victory was leaking out of me through both shoes. I was beginning to find myself wishing we would at least keep it close, that the final results wouldn't represent a wholesale rejection of everything Jesus stood for.

"Popopoffolous is predicting the same thing," Nadine said, from her place in front of her laptop. "Florida, Florida, Florida. George Bill thinks Alowich could be the new Nader. He could take enough support from us in Palm Beach County to throw the election to Maplewith."

"Who is the secretary of state there now?" her husband inquired.

"Not one of our people."

"How do you think the Supreme Court would vote if it goes to a re-count and there's a challenge?"

"Let me answer this way," Nadine said. "Two of the justices go elk hunting in Saskatchewan with Aldridge Maplewith."

Zelda alternated between answering the phone (we would never learn where the one unanswered call came from) and walking over to stand with me. She'd put a hand on my arm, and I'd stop pacing for a time. "We're still in it," she'd say. Or, "A lot of states still haven't reported." Or, "I just spoke with him; he's not worried." And I'd nod and pretend to agree, but, as I read it at least, the television code was saying: Maplewith, Maplewith, Maplewith.

At ten past nine, as the full weight of despair was pressing down on me and I wanted nothing so much as to walk out of the hotel and pound the streets of West Zenith until it was over, Jesus emerged from the back room. He had showered and changed into cowboy boots, new jeans, and a long-sleeved orange T-shirt with JETHRO TULL printed on the front. He had a spring in his step.

"Where's Anna?" my mother asked, just to have something to say to him.

"Praying," Jesus told her. "She has a lot of work ahead of her. We were choosing jobs for all of you in the new administration. You're going to like what we've decided."

This bit of absurd optimism was met with a resounding silence. Even Stab couldn't raise his spirit enough to ask what Jesus supposedly had in store for him. Our candidate was standing there with his hands on his hips and a smile in his eyes, as happy as if we were watching the second quarter of the NBA Playoffs, and he'd been held up in traffic and had just breezed in, grabbed a plate of buffalo wings and a Corona, and was about to sit down and watch his team extend their lead.

Esmeralda gave him an update, saving the worst for last: Florida was still too close to call; and Illinois, which all our victory combinations had taken for granted, was also looking like a toss-up.

Jesus shrugged, put his arm around Stab, who'd gotten up to grab more doughnuts, and motioned me over with his free hand. "The brothers grim," he said, when he was encircling both of us. "Arnie, how did you and Mudgie produce these two jokers?"

"Just lucky, I guess," Dad told him grimly.

"Security stuff all set?" Jesus asked me, releasing us and reaching for a stick of celery. I almost had the feeling he was making fun of me for worrying so much, making fun of all of us for caring so much. Another ugly whisper of doubt floated around me then. Maybe Anne Canter had been right: it was a game to him, a quick stopover on planet earth to reassure himself that nothing had changed, that we'd never learn our spiritual lessons. The voters had sensed that. In the end, after flirting with the idea of electing a sacred creature as president, they'd seen the absurdity of it, realized they didn't deserve it, decided there must be two Jesuses and this one didn't matter, and voted their pocketbook.

Trying not to let that line of thinking show in my voice, I told him that the hotel was as tight as we could make it, given the fact that the public had access to the lobby, the meeting rooms, and the lower floors. "We've sealed off the top two floors, this one and the eleventh," I remember telling him. And I remember, even now, the odd twist of a smile on his face when I said it. "There is a floor above us, no rooms, just machinery—elevator engines, one of which is not working, air-conditioning and heating units, ductwork. Dukey's boys and the local police have been instructed to let only workmen with passes get up there, using the stairs. The hotel people have reprogrammed the elevator so it goes only as far as the tenth floor, but they can change that for us when the time comes, if we call down. Until then, if any of us wants to use the elevator, we'll have to walk down two flights and take it from the tenth. Chief Bastatutta is in the lobby, keeping an eye on people there. The state police and the Secret Service are ready in case you become the president-elect."

"In case?" he said, lifting his eyebrows at me. He chomped on the celery, chewed and chewed, never breaking eye contact. "You're the best security guy in the business," he told me. "Don't ever doubt that, no matter what happens."

But I doubted it, of course, and I did not care for the implications of the "no matter what happens" remark. It had occurred to me at some point during the previous hour that the bubble of confidence in which I'd lived before joining the campaign had been slowly deflating, not just since the results started coming in, but for the past several months. When Jesus had first called me, I'd been sure of my job, my popularity, my place in the world, my future in television. Now I wasn't sure of anything, least of all that I was the best security guy in the business. As the minutes ticked down, I sneaked glances at Jesus, trying to see past his happy expression, looking for another hint about what might happen, and when. But he was playing poker with us that night, holding his cards close and betting the farm. He knew the future, of course he did, and it is astounding to me, in retrospect, that he seemed so happy and so at ease in those hours.

"I'll stay out here and watch with my good friends for a while," he announced, and we took up positions facing the screen. Out of respect, we gave him the remote. He flipped from channel to channel—ABC, CBS, NBC, CNN, Fox, PBS—sometimes getting up to grab another celery stick or a doughnut, or ducking his head into the back room to have a moment with his mother. One by one, returns started to trickle in from the Midwest. And announcement by announcement, I felt a creature of hope come to life in me again.

Minnesota, Michigan, and Wisconsin, states that had been in the Democratic column in recent elections, all seemed to be going for the Divinity Party this time around. "The margins are small," Wales noted, as we watched the numbers appear on the screen. "But the electoral college doesn't care about margins."

North and South Dakota, two places you'd expect to go Republican, were next to fall into our column, the margins more comfortable. Kansas and Nebraska also went for Jesus by a percentage point or two.

Zelda had come over and was squeezing my hand. The pundits on every channel kept puzzling over this turn of events, shaking their heads, saying that nothing like this had been seen for as long as anyone could remember. "Nebraska not going Republican in a presidential election," Slam Davidson marveled, "when is the last time that happened?"

"There will be some questions about vote fraud, I can assure you," Betbette was saying with his usual confidence, when we stopped over briefly at Fox. Anne Canter had joined the big two now, and her ebullient early mood was sliding into the swamp. She seemed personally offended. She swung her hair to the side, she frowned. Before Jesus switched channels, I heard her say, "A lot of the rural precincts have not been counted yet, and rural voters tend to—"

Jim Wearer kept his face expressionless, neutral, objective. He let the analysts from both sides have their say, and after ten minutes of watching, you weren't sure if there was a good and a bad in the world anymore, a right and a wrong, a winner and a loser.

Bulf Spritzer was strutting excitedly back and forth across the stage, holding a clipboard in his hands, calling for underlings to put this or that chart up on the screen, and practically shouting, "High drama!" News was being made, big news, and big news gave him a tremble.

But, despite the run of good reports, it was too early to open the champagne. Senator Maplewith was easily winning Texas, with its huge load of thirty-four electoral votes. Neither Jesus nor Anna Songsparrow had set foot in the Lone Star State during the campaign, even though he'd supposedly been born there, and again I thought Wales's inexperience had been at work. He was a news producer, a *local* news producer, and Jesus had picked him to run a national presidential campaign. It was a cosmic joke.

The hyenas of doubt had smelled the fear in me, and come to feast.

I spent five minutes calling around to my security people—the stair landings, the elevator, the lobby, the perimeter of the hotel, everything locked up tight. Someone from the management called to ask about releasing the elevator lock. "Absolutely not," I said, maybe with too much force. "He won't be coming down for another hour at least. If we need to move earlier than that, we'll use the stairs." I hung up and turned my attention back to the TV.

In Indiana, Maplewith enjoyed a comfortable lead. She was piling up the big and medium-sized states, while we tacked on Montana (three) and New Mexico (five), and kept fielding phone calls from associates in Florida and Illinois, hoping for good news and getting none.

But, then, as Palm Beach County started to be tallied, we nudged ahead by a single percentage point in the Sunshine State. We pulled even in Illinois. The room had grown louder. Stab was standing up, watching not the TV set, but my mother and father's faces. My dad was pounding his cast rhythmically into his left palm and saying what he liked to say at the dog track when his greyhound was making a move on the far turn, "Come on, come on now. One time!"

With things still very much uncertain, we came to the West Coast, where Alowich was expected to take Oregon and Washington, and we were almost guaranteed California. As more numbers were posted, more precincts tallied, our lead in Florida wobbled, disappeared, reappeared.

"Maplewith," Jim Wearer told us, "is now two points ahead in Illinois."

Nevada was also up for grabs. "We lose Florida, Illinois, and Nevada," Wales said, checking and rechecking his math, "and we end with 269. Even with California."

"One short," I heard myself say.

"The site I'm looking at says Cook County is going for us," Nadine put in excitedly.

The phone rang. Zelda answered it. She put her hand over the receiver and looked across the room at me. "Illinois!" she mouthed, with her eyes opened wide in excitement. I would not let myself believe her.

At quarter after eleven, Jesus stood up and walked over to stand beside me near the end of the couch.

"The difference between you and me," I said, glancing at his face, "is that if you win you're at peace, and if you lose you're at peace."

"My whole point in coming to earth," he said, "is to demonstrate that there is no difference — ultimately — between you and me." I assumed he was joking. We were both watching the TV screen. After a second or so I turned and I was looking at him with such an expression of puzzlement that he laughed. "Muse on it when I am gone."

"Where are you going?"

"Downstairs to give my acceptance speech."

At that moment, almost as soon as those words were out of his mouth, twenty-six minutes after eleven, eastern time, ABC news was the first to announce that their projections gave the state of Illinois to Jesus Christ. An enormous, deafening cheer went up in the room. Forget Florida, forget Nevada, with Illinois in our column, as long as California didn't disappoint, we would come in at 290. "We're in," I said in a voice so full of astonishment that Zelda sent a beautiful smile my way. She was getting phone calls telling her the same thing. Norman Simmelton urged caution. My mother passed the beads through her fingers faster and faster. My dad came around behind me and gave me a deep tissue shoulder massage with his good hand. But Jesus stood there calmly sipping apple juice, as alert as an owl on a tree branch at dusk.

As long as California didn't disappoint.

At 11:40 Jesus suggested we switch to CBS—of which ZIZ was an affiliate—and after we'd been watching for fifteen minutes or so, in a state of intense excitement that I can compare to no other feeling I've ever had, CBS's chief election correspondent Mortimer Redds (an early idol of mine), spoke these famous words: "Based on hard returns and exit polling from the state of California, CBS news is now prepared to declare. . . ." He paused for two seconds and checked the latest information coming in on his earpiece, "is prepared to declare that Jesus Christ has been elected president of the United States."

There was a roar in that room to burst your eardrums. We jumped and we hugged and we kissed and we wept, we surrounded Jesus and touched him anywhere we could—shoulders, elbow, face, hair, fingers. Anna Songsparrow came out of the back room with tears on her cheeks. She and her son had a long embrace, and then the phones were ringing off the hook. It was not long before Colonel Alowich called and conceded. Jesus was exceedingly gracious. It took Maplewith another hour—she was hoping for a turnaround from rural counties in Illinois, and did not get it. Jesus was gracious again. "Marjorie, listen," I heard him say, "I want you to consider something. I said the same thing to Dennis, I want you both to consider serving in my cabinet. No, no. For the good of the country. I want you to sleep on it."

And then Secret Service types were coming through the door and telling me they were officially taking over security for the president-elect; we had no choice in the matter this time. I should order my men to "stand down" as the head guy, Richard Diamond, put it.

I felt the bottom of my stomach fall away. On the one hand, I had gotten used to protecting Jesus from harm; it was my work, my identity, and I was sorry to let that go. On the other hand, I had been weighed down by a premonition for so long by then that I thought I'd end up dying of anxiety before I saw whether Jesus had been playing another trick on us with his hints, or whether he'd drop dead, dematerialize, or be killed by another nutcase. I did not want to leave the jubilant feeling in the room, and I did not relish the idea of going downstairs and telling Dukey and his guys that we were off the case, that their moment in the spotlight was over. At the same time, I felt this immeasurable relief, knowing that Jesus's safety was now in the hands of professionals. In my excitement, in the mix of feelings of the moment, I neglected to call the hotel and tell them to release the one working elevator.

I stayed in the suite for another few minutes to enjoy the celebration. Walesy was popping open expensive champagne the Simmeltons had bought, and everyone was getting a taste. Stab was jumping up and down, yelling. My father had tears in his eyes and was hugging my mother. I peeled Zelda away from the phone long enough for a prolonged kiss; we got a round of applause for it.

"He's going to make me under secretary for Health and Human Services," she whispered into my ear, and I squeezed her extra hard in congratulations and told her she'd be perfect for the job.

Enrica came in and howled like a wolf. Norman, Nadine, and Amelia had a family hug. I made sure Richard Diamond had been introduced all around, and then I said I was going downstairs on a last errand. As I was about to turn away, I caught Jesus's eye. For a moment I thought he was going to come over and tell me what post he had in mind for me: chief spokesperson, advisor for ecumenical relations, head of the FCC. But he only winked and gave a quick, almost sad smile. It was the last time I would see him alive, but I did not know that then. I nodded at him, paused for a final look at the happy scene in the room, and went out.

I walked down the hallway to the elevator, and while I was waiting there, I remembered about the lock, and called down to the front desk. It was pandemonium in the lobby, the night manager said; it was going to take another ten minutes to change the elevator setting so it came up to the twelfth floor. "Fine," I said, "they'll be celebrating for another ten minutes at least. Just don't forget to switch it."

This, again, is difficult for me to admit, but as I turned and walked toward the stairwell, showed my pass, and trotted down the two flights, I felt another wash of bad thought come over me, a twinge of anger or envy or doubt. It makes no sense, I realize that. I had no good reason to be anything but happy and proud at that point—we had won, after all, and against enormous odds—but I felt as though a demon was whispering in my ear. I tried to ignore it. I kept telling myself that Jesus was going to lift the country up, that things would change. I kept telling myself that I would be part of that change, that he had a job in mind for me, something prestigious, essential even, but that he was waiting to surprise me. As a kind of distraction, I told myself that my country, my great country, had elected someone so special that nothing would ever be the way it had been. Inside all of us, there had been this secret hope that one day we would have a leader who actually understood our problems, someone who was not ambitious, and not conniving, and not divisive, and not partisan, and not out to help his friends line their pockets, whose good intentions were not corrupted by foolish philosophies or personal weakness. Down deep inside us a dream had been hiding, and now the dream had risen into the light. Soon it would turn into our national reality. I tried to take the focus off myself that way, but it didn't work.

A bad Muzak version of "Hotel California" was playing in the one functioning elevator. It seemed to take a long time to descend ten floors. In the marble-tiled lobby—wall to wall with people at that point—I caught sight of Randy Zillins. I could see that he was trying to work his way over to me, but I forced myself through the bodies in the other direction and went out a side door. God knows what would have happened if he'd been able to say a word to me then, if I'd apologized for being curt with him on the phone, or even just taken the time to listen to him rant about something. He might have felt important, for once in his life. He might have ended up changing his mind and allowing Jesus to have his hour of glory and his four or eight years of hard work. Or he might have turned on me instead. God knows. You can drive yourself crazy looking back over the past and thinking you could have been five percent kinder and changed the course of history. You can drive yourself crazy like that.

Chief Bastattuta was standing in the cold entranceway between two sets of doors. He shook my hand and said, "Good job, kid." I told him I was no longer on Jesus's official security detail and that I had to go find Dukey and his pals and give them the news. Already, all over the place, you could see big-shouldered guys with dark suits on and wires in their ears.

"Don't let your guard down, I don't care what they say," Bastatutta told me. I remember having the funny thought that maybe I'd try to fix him up with Enrica Dominique.

I went outside into the cold and the dark, ducked away from the press types near the entrance, and found Dukey in the shadows at the back of the hotel. He was smoking a joint. I came upon him by surprise, and he flung it away as if it had burned his fingers. "Hey, dude," I said. "We won. They just announced it. We're in."

He wrapped me in a bear hug, and when he released me I told him the Secret Service had taken over from us, as of twenty minutes ago. He sulked and smirked. "Can we do crowd control, at least, or something?"

"Sure, just don't get in the way of the big guys in the dark jackets."

"Like they scare me," he said.

I was about to turn away from him when something took hold of me and kept me standing there. Looking back at that moment, I wonder if the sight of Randy Zillins had infected me, sent my mind twirling in a bad direction; if envy and doubt are contagious in that way, even across a crowded lobby. In any case, the fact is that at moment a stream of demon-thought pushed its way out through my mouth in seven puffs of gray vapor. "Duke," I said, and then I paused and I could have changed my mind, but I didn't. "I have a question for you."

"Yeah?"

"I've always wondered, you know. I mean, the story we did about Dukey Junior falling and everything. I mean, that was a long way to fall." He was watching me intently. I kept on. "I'm glad he's all right, of course. Great kid. But I've always wondered, was that really the way it played out, with Jesus coming by and touching him, and so on?"

Dukey stared at me, the celebratory smile fading from his face. Five seconds. Ten seconds. Arms held out away from his body, short rust-colored hair standing up straight, eyebrows pinched down, ears and nose red from the cold, whiff of marijuana about him. "Wow," he said at last, and it was as if he had hit me in the jaw. "After everything you seen, man, everything we done . . . you ask a question like that?"

"I didn't mean anything by it. Just curious, you know, it's hard to—"

"What good does it do to be smart, man, if you have to ask a question like that?"

"No good," I said, just to get away from him then, to get away from myself. "I'd be better off being stupid."

"Right."

I remember turning away and walking back around the corner of the hotel, in the dark, trying not to worry about what I had done. An innocent question, I told myself. The skepticism of a born journalist. But such a surge of shame was filling me then that it was all I could do not to run the rest of the way to the front door and sprint up the eleven flights of steps. I wanted to look into Jesus's face at that moment. I wanted to see something better than me.

I was at the back of the hotel by then, out of sight of Dukey and the press corps. My cell phone rang. I took it out of my pocket, saw Zelda's name on the caller ID, and flipped it open. "Hi, beautiful," I said into the phone.

"He's on his way down," she said. "I was calling to see if you're ready."

The fact is, when Zelda spoke those words, I felt a presence behind me. I whirled around, thinking it might be a Secret Service agent, or Dukey come to give me a hard time, or a crazy person trying to sneak into the hotel, but no one was there in the darkness.

"And to say I love you," Zelda added.

"See you in a second. Love you, too."

As soon as I closed the phone I heard sirens—not exactly a startling and unusual sound in the West Zenith of those days, but it cut into me like a blade between the ribs, and I started to run like a crazy man. I sprinted down the cold grass strip that separated the wall of the hotel from the parking lot, turned the corner, and saw, at the front of the building, a crowd of supporters there, the press, and others who had sneaked past the barricades. I felt a momentary wash of relief . . . and then the first ambulance and the first police car came screeching up in the circular drive, and then it was as if a signal had been given to the crowd, some word had been spoken that raced from body to body. I felt sudden, aimless panic. It wasn't like the time in Seattle when Alton Smith had taken his two shots. Then there had been something real, the sounds, the bullets, the blood. This was only news, only words, but what monumental words they were. "Jesus has been shot," people were saying. "He's been shot."

I pushed hard through the crowd, toward the door, and then I was inside the lobby, and the sirens were piling one on top of the other outside, and people were shoving and yelling and wild rumors were flying around beneath the chandelier. There was a period of pure confusion, ambulance attendants and police trying to push through to the elevator. I remember some of the police hurrying toward the stairwell, and I remember that I felt paralyzed, as if in a nightmare, unable to get through the crowd, and then, when I turned and tried for the stairs, unable to move at all. After what seemed like many minutes, the door of one elevator opened. Four men hurried out and tried to run through the crowded lobby. They were moving awkwardly, and I realized they were holding a stretcher between them. One of the men was Richard Diamond. I called to him, but of course he could not hear me. Over the tops of the heads in front of me, I could see the expression on his face; it was not something you would ever want to see on the face of a human being, a contorted combination of agony and failed duty; he knew he was holding history in his hands, and history was bleeding to death. He was screaming for people to move out of the way, but those in front of me were doing the opposite: pushing toward the stretcher, yelling, "It's Jesus! It's Jesus!"

I could not get any closer, I saw the stretcher go out the door, I caught a glimpse of dark hair. The bodies were pressed so tight around me that I could not get my hand into my pocket to take out my phone. I was still trying as hard as I could to move past the people in front of me. With my left hand, I was raising my photo ID above my head in the direction of the policemen, who were forming a line in front of us and trying to herd us to one side of the lobby. No one paid the slightest attention to it. The same elevator opened again. Another stretcher. Four more men carrying it, a woman running with them. This time I was close enough to recognize the face of the person on the stretcher—my father. There was a wide patch of blood on his shirt, near his right shoulder, and the woman, an EMT maybe, was pressing a towel or a balled-up shirt against it. I pushed as if I were trying to push down the whole building, and took four steps forward and then popped through the last person between me and the policeman. I waved my ID frantically and made it past the policeman to the side of the stretcher.

"Pa!"

He turned his head an inch. His eyes were open, the muscles around them squeezed tight in pain.

"Pa!"

"Shot him," was the only thing he said. His voice was small, and then the stretcher was hurried past me and I tried to follow close behind it, got through the front door, tried to force my way into the ambulance with him. "That's my father!" I was screaming. "I'm on the staff! I'm on Jesus's staff! I'm Russ Thomas! It's my dad!"

But it was no go. The ambulance doors closed. It pushed out through the crowd, slowly at first, and then sped off toward Springfield Hospital, the siren blending with a dozen other sirens. The scene in front of the hotel was a madhouse of ambulances and squad cars and faces and policemen running this way and that way and people screaming and crying. I remember one image from out of that chaos: a woman about my mother's age was sitting in the cold grit at the edge of the driveway with her knees spread out wide and her face in her hands.

I felt somebody grab the collar of my leather jacket from behind. I spun around, thinking it was a cop trying to get me out of there. It was.

Bastatutta did not say a word. He was practically dragging me beside him, holding the collar of my jacket with one hand and shoving people aside with the other. He pushed his way up to the nearest police car and shoved me against the passenger door. "Get him to the hospital," he barked at the officer standing nearest the car. "GO! NOW!"

Thirty seconds of nudging the front fenders through the crowd, and then we were screaming at seventy miles an hour through the heart of the city. The radio was squawking, the sergeant listening intently and saying, over and over, "I don't know no more than you know." My cell phone rang. I had forgotten it. I yanked it out of my pocket and flipped it open and heard Zelda weeping, and in one sentence asking me where I was, if I was hurt, who was hurt and how badly, telling me she was still up in the room, she'd stayed behind to call me and to get something she thought Jesus had forgotten. As she was heading out the door and into the corridor, she was met by Secret Service agents. They pushed her back in. My father and mother and Stab and the others had gone with Jesus, and Stab, where was Stab? They wouldn't let her out of the room! There were conflicting stories on the TV. "Your mother is here, but where is Stab!"

"I don't know! I'm in a police car," I shouted three times before she stopped yelling long enough to listen. "Going to the hospital. Jesus is shot. I saw them carry him out. Pa is shot. He was talking, he's alive. I'll have Bastatutta send someone to get you. All of you. Are you there? Zel! Zelda!"

The line had gone quiet as death. I tried calling her again, twice more, and got only a no-service message, and then we were at the hospital, and the policeman was calling Bastatutta on his radio, and I was sprinting toward the emergency room doors through an army of blue uniforms. I remember the fluorescent lights of the waiting area, and one fist-sized splash of blood on the linoleum. I made it past one or two officers who tried to stop me and as far as the door of the treatment rooms, where a stocky young orderly with a beard blocked the way.

"I'm on Jesus's staff," I said very loudly and with as much authority as I could manage. I was waving my ID. I was spraying words at him. I was trying to push past him and he was holding me tight by the shoulders. "My father's in there. I'm on the staff! Let me by!"

"I know who you are. No one goes by."

"My dad was shot."

"No one goes in."

"Chief Bastatutta said—"

"The chief is not in charge here."

He turned me roughly and pointed toward a side treatment room, and I argued with him for another few minutes and then gave up and went through the door he had pointed to. In that sterile room, instead of sitting, I got on my knees. I was breathing as if I had just sprinted a lap around the city. I didn't care who saw me—the doctor, the policeman, the nurses—I got on my knees. I could hear them working on Jesus, or my father, I couldn't tell who, a few yards away, through a doorway, behind a curtain, a female doctor barking orders for this and that to be done. The sound of her voice, the tone of it, the professional calm over a layer of suppressed terror—it was like listening to the one thing you would never in your life want to listen to. I squeezed my eyes shut and squeezed my hands together in front of my chest and whispered, "I'm sorry, I'm sorry, I'm sorry," without thinking about what I was sorry for. A kind of communal guilt had wrapped itself around me, guilt by association with the human race. Guilt by association with my thoughts. After a while, I heard Zelda's voice, and then my mother's voice, and then Stab's, and I stood up and went to them, and we held each other in a circular embrace. I told them I had no news, about anybody, about anything. I told them we should pray, which, in the days before Jesus, would not have been like me at all.

✯ ✯ ✯ FORTY-TWO ✯ ✯ ✯

Almost everyone in the world knows the historical details of what happened that night, but I have some personal information that was never
in the newspapers and on TV. As Jesus stepped out of the hotel suite,
his mother, my dad, Wales, Ezzie, Stab, and Enrica were beside him,
a cadre of Secret Service agents in front and behind. Ada Montpelier
and my mom had stayed in the suite to watch the children. Zelda had
started out of the room with Jesus, and then decided she should go back
for a notebook in which were written names of people he might want to
thank. On her way back into the suite she decided to call me and give
me a heads-up. "Hold the elevator for me," she yelled over her shoulder.
Mom changed her mind and waited to go downstairs with Zelda.

It would come to light that, simmering in his jealousy, Randy Zillins
had used his investigative skills and local connections to find out certain
security details having to do with the hotel: that one elevator had been
programmed to prevent it from going above the tenth floor, that the other
was broken, that only workmen with passes could get to the thirteenth
floor, where the machinery was. There are conspiracy theorists who believe more than one person was involved, that the elevator malfunction
itself was part of the killer's plan, but none of the evidence unearthed
by the Leahy Commission supports that, and I believe it would be giving Randy Zillins too much credit. He was not much different from the
overweight middle-aged man I'd imagined when talking to Wales on
the beach. He was a thirty-eight-year-old reporter with an insecurity

complex the size of Jupiter. He was a little man, not so much physically as psychologically, and he was tormented, in a society obsessed with celebrity, by his own stunted ambitions.

While we had been on the road with the campaign, Zillins had written a series of articles about Jesus, all of them soaked in cynicism. I read through them, much later, when I was able to bear it. They had titles like, "False Gods, False Witnesses," and "The True Sinner."

In any case, near midnight, when Jesus and his entourage came down the hallway, the one working elevator had not yet been reprogrammed to go up to the twelfth floor. (Conspiracy theorists see this as part of the plan, too, but I know better: I simply forgot to call the manager when I should have, and then in the confusion the manager simply forgot to give the order when she should have.) When it did not appear on the twelfth floor after a minute and a half, the Secret Service people became suspicious and steered Jesus toward the nearest stairway. They cleared the stairwell, of course, but by luck, fate, local connections, or some hidden criminal genius, Randy Zillins had secured a workman's pass, and was hiding one floor above. He heard the door open, heard voices, guessed the moment that Jesus would be moving from the corridor below onto the landing. He moved out from his hiding place, descended two steps, and fired two quick shots down between the flights. It was a fluke that he hit his target. He had made, it would turn out, only a few dozen visits to the shooting range in East Zenith; he was no expert. He would have had a clear look at Jesus for only a fraction of a second, and even then, a clear look at only a piece of his torso. I believe now that some divine plan was at work, though that is something I do not say to many people. The first bullet missed and went zinging around the concrete stairwell. The second pierced Jesus's body at a sharp downward angle, entering two inches above his right lung, exiting through his lower back. My father, combat veteran that he was, reacted instantly and sprinted up the stairs toward the assailant. Richard Diamond's second in command, a man named Elliot Welner, was half a step behind him. Zillins fired a wild shot as he turned and tried to run, and that bullet tore through my father's right shoulder. Welner then fired three shots, one of which hit

Zillins directly behind his heart, killing him instantly. After that there was a frantic race to stanch the bleeding of the two victims, find out why the elevator was stalled, and carry Jesus and my dad down to the ambulances.

They managed to get Jesus to the hospital while he was still alive, but he'd lost so much blood that it was impossible to save him. For forty minutes the doctors tried. And for that time we waited in a nearby room, praying and crying. Word came to us quickly that my father's wounds were not life-threatening; it was the one comfort of that hideous night.

It was strange, the way our vigil ended. This part, of course, was never reported in the press: about a minute before we received word that the doctors could not save Jesus, my brother Stab suddenly stopped sobbing—which he had been doing nonstop—and looked at me. I had looked into Stab's face several million times in the years I'd known him. There had always been a sort of covering across his close-spaced, droopy eyes and rounded mouth, a dimness—that's the only way I can describe it—as if his brain were cloaked in fog. But, for that minute or so, a change came across him. He sat there with a look of surprise on his face. I believe that, for better or worse, he was seeing the world around him as the rest of us do. And shortly after that, Dr. Wendy Weston, the head surgeon at Springfield Hospital, came into the waiting room and told us Jesus was gone.

Our grief then was beyond personal, as my guilt had been. It was a universal grieving—for the loss of Jesus, but also for us, our country, humankind. Zelda told me later she thought it was grief that grew out of the fact that we live in a world where evil can triumph so easily over good.

I stayed there a long time. My father had lost a lot of blood and would eventually require two shoulder surgeries, and would never regain full use of his right arm, but his life was not in danger. We were allowed in to see him, though he was still sedated and spoke to us only later in the night.

Before that, dividing us into two groups, the doctors let us into the room where Jesus's body lay. Zelda and I and Wales and Ezzie and Anna Songsparrow were in the first group. From the shoulders down Jesus was covered in a sheet. His face was unnaturally pale, the eyes closed, the hair tousled and wet. It was as if no light was in that room, no air.

"Rise," I said beneath my breath, in a trembling voice that no one could hear. I felt emptied out and bitter, and I could not stop looking at him. "If you're going to rise, rise now. Don't wait. Don't make us wait. Please. Rise."

He did not stir. Zelda was squeezing my hand and weeping loudly. We moved half a step back so that Anna Songsparrow could go up close and have a private moment. I watched her lean down and press her forehead against her son's forehead, and I heard her mumbling words—a prayer or incantation in a language I did not understand. She went on for a long time, and after a while her body started to shake, and Zelda and Ezzie went up and held her, and Wales and I moved closer, too, though we did not look at each other and could not speak.

⋆ ⋆ ⋆ FORTY-THREE ⋆ ⋆ ⋆

In the small hours of that morning, after Zelda had stood up in front of
the press corps and told them everything she knew, and after my mother
and Stab had insisted on staying the night in my father's hospital room
(even though he was awake by then and telling them not to), and after
Dukey and Enrica and I had accompanied the body down to the morgue,
I called Chief Bastatutta and asked him to post a second special detail (in
addition to the disgraced Secret Service cadre) to make sure no one tampered with the body, and after Anna Songsparrow and Wales and Ezzie
and the Simmeltons had gone back to the hotel to pray or to drink or to
field the endless phone calls, I wandered away again. I cannot explain
why. When she was done with the press, Zel asked me to take her back
to her apartment, which I did. And then she asked me to stay with her,
which I did not do, not right away at least. "I'll come back," I said.

"Where are you going?"

"I don't know. Walking. I just need . . . I don't know what I need. I
won't go far. I'll come back. I need an hour."

After the trauma of that day, a lot of other women would have made a
fuss and insisted I stay. And a lot of other men would not have left. But
Zel and I are both different in that respect, and it is a difference that has
persisted in our married life, and we both see it as a strength, a way of
letting the other person move in his or her own orbit, while holding on
to the gravitational attachment we feel for each other.

In any case, I went out walking. It was past three a.m. by that point, the darkest part of a dark night. I did not set out with any conscious destination in mind, just turned right on the sidewalk in front of the building and kept going, past the row of redone Victorians, and then across the bridge and into Fultonville. Maybe I was subconsciously heading for the scene of the first miracle, I don't know. I walked in a cold daze. I remember that a few lights were on in the windows of the buildings I passed, a few cars and cabs in the street. Under ordinary circumstances, at that hour of the night, I wouldn't have been caught dead strolling through Fultonville without a police escort, or at least the accompaniment of a camera crew. But you had the sense that even the muggers and dealers and gang bangers were taking a break (in fact, as statistics would later show, there was a seventy percent drop in violent crime, nationwide, in the twenty-four hours after Jesus's death).

Still, it was an eerie place, a neighborhood haunted by the memories of awful news stories, and it was almost as if those stories lived on in the brick faces of the buildings, in the littered vacant lots and school playgrounds, in the molecules of the fire hydrants, telephone poles, and rusting chain-link fences.

After a while, tired and cold, I came to a place called Liberty Park, a nasty three or four hundred square yards of urban foliage and trash, a place frequented by street people who could find no safer spot to lay down their cardboard boxes. I had done a dozen stories from Liberty Park, none of them happy. It was only blocks from the place where Dukey Junior had been brought back to life. I was very cold by then. I should have turned around and headed back to Zelda's apartment, but I was in a peculiar mood, a mood that went beyond sadness. It was more than missing Jesus, more than sorrow that he would never inhabit the White House, more than anger at the violent fool who had shot him. I had sunk into a spiritual depression, you could call it. A feeling that, in this realm at least, good would never triumph, hope was nothing more than a waste of energy, and my own personal demons would always haunt me.

I sat on one of the wooden slat benches in the half darkness, and I looked out across the empty park.

And now I come to another part of the story you won't find in the history books. I will tell it the way it happened, which is what I was asked to do.

I was sitting on the bench in Liberty Park when I saw a shadowy figure come walking through the same entrance I had used. I felt a stirring of fear, of course—in that neighborhood, at that hour. And yet, I was in such a strange mood that I almost didn't care, one way or the other, if somebody tried to hurt me. I could see that it was a man. On the tall side, dressed in dark clothes. He was shuffling along in a street person's gait, moving vaguely in my direction. When he passed beneath the dim streetlight I caught a glimpse of his face. I stood up. He shuffled over to me. I made a move to get down on my knees, but he took hold of my right arm and held me upright. "I do not want that from you," he said. "Let's sit."

We sat side-by-side, but I turned so I could look at him. The clothes were dirty and old and there was mud on his shoes, but it was the same face, eyes shining in the darkness, a hint of impatience around the mouth. There was no evidence of blood anywhere; he did not seem to be in pain; he had a human consistency, if that's the right word, and was nothing like a walking ghost. I could feel my body trembling, the smallest of vibrations, as if grief were strumming a funeral song in my cells.

"I'm sorry," was the first thing I said, and even my voice was shaking. "Sorry for me. For the guy who did it. For all of us."

"I don't want that from you, my friend," he said. "You are the high priest of reverent irreverence, don't go disappointing me now. Where is the sass? Where is the Russ Thomas I knew and loved?"

"Crushed," I said. "All the wiseass remarks have been squeezed out of me."

"Why?"

"Why? Because I liked having you around. It changed things, inside me and inside all of us. For a while there I thought we'd have a future that was . . . I don't know, three cuts above the ordinary human pig trough. I thought I might even turn out to be the Russ Thomas of my imagination or something."

"You don't think our campaign made any difference? As far as the country is concerned? And as far as you are concerned, personally?"

"Not as much as it could have if you'd stayed around," I told him. I was going to say something else then, that I would miss him, miss his presence, that I felt I had a million more things to learn from him. But a spark of anger burst through me and what came out instead was: "And what upsets me the most is I know you did it on purpose. When you disappeared that day and played football in Hunter Town, people thought maybe something bad had happened to you. But I didn't. I knew it was part of your plan. And this is exactly the same. People are going to say this terrible guy did this terrible thing to you, which is true, but you let it happen and that's the salt in the wound."

For a while he didn't say anything. I turned my face forward, into the park, and pushed my hands deeper into my jacket pockets. I felt like I was risking my soul, talking to him like that, but I couldn't seem to stop myself.

"Let me ask you something," he said. "The last time I came to earth, did it make any difference?"

"Sure. Of course. Not so many people talked about turning the other cheek and giving to the poor before you showed up. Pretty much the whole world marks the years starting with the time you were born. You have religions named after you. Your face is everywhere. Your name. All those paintings and sculptures and books. . . . They don't do that for just anybody."

"I let them kill me that time, too," he said. "And not everyone who heard about me believed. And the revolution I started did not really change the balance of power. It did not rid the world of evil. Instead of uniting people, I ended up causing a rift that has persisted until now, a rift that has caused countless deaths. My closest friends, people like you and Zelda and Wales and Stab and Ezzie and the rest of you, they were upset at me for leaving, as you are. They had doubts while I was alive, as you did."

"And you left a lasting positive impression on the planet anyway," I said.

"Precisely."

"Fine, so that could happen again this time. But why not finish what you started? Stay around. Lead the country for eight years. Show the world a new way of doing things — kinder, smarter, more farsighted, more tolerant, more compassionate. What's wrong with that plan?"

"In the realm of human understanding, nothing."

"The realm of human understanding is the only realm most of us have access to," I said.

"Right. And that is the whole problem. I was trying to show you how to go past that."

"How?" I asked him bitterly. "By giving us a glimpse of a better way of being, a taste of paradise, and then — "

I stopped right there, midsentence. Without turning to look, I had the sense that he was smiling at me. I thought my way back to the beginning, to what would have been if Hay-Zeus had not wandered by when Dukey Junior had taken his three-story fall; to what would have been if Amelia Simmelton had suffocated slowly up there on the third floor of Mercy Hospital. Both sets of parents — rich and poor, couth and uncouth, people who made a great contribution to the well-being of others and people who did a little cocaine on the fire escape to relax — they would have had a glimpse of the purity and innocence of their kids, maybe a glimpse of the love they themselves were capable of giving to those kids; they would have had three years or ten years of that paradise . . . and then it would have been brutally snatched away from them. I'd reported on so many stories like that I'd lost count — the sweet high school kid killed in a car crash on prom night; the little heroes of the pediatric cancer ward; the nineteen-year-olds shipped home in flag-covered caskets from the Endless War. Way down below the cool journalistic detachment, I'd asked myself why a thousand times. Asked myself why, and asked myself what I'd do if it ever happened to a child of mine. You'd want to die. For days, months, years, you'd want nothing more than to be allowed to die. You'd feel bitterness and anguish like nothing the rest of the world could ever know. And then . . . you'd either live in that bitterness, in that death-wish, in that pain for the rest of your days . . . or you'd somehow get past it and keep getting past it and come to some sort of impossible truce with it, as if you had one eye on some other dimension, some other explanation, as if you were stoking a small fire of hope that there was someplace finer than this cauldron of pain.

"I'm sorry to have to say this," I told Jesus, when I had thought it through, "but it's a crappy system. Nobody should have pain like that, I don't care what paradise it points them toward. If I was setting up the world, I'd set it up so nobody dies, nobody suffers. No rape, no cancer, no kids hit by cars, no Alzheimer's, no war. That would be my idea of loving my created ones. Sorry if that sounds arrogant or something, but that's what I'd do. And I'd be willing to bet that almost everybody else you ask would feel the same way."

I turned to look at him then. He was staring out into the park, expression unreadable. I thought for a while that he'd gone into one of his trances, and wasn't going to say anything else; or that he was about to disappear back into whatever realm it was that he'd slipped out of. But after a stretch of time he put his hand on my shoulder—and it was a real hand, not the hand of a ghost or a spirit. I felt that electric current go through me again, a song of love to push away the dirge my cells had been chanting. He said, "Everything happens the way it is supposed to happen. Everything that happens moves you eventually toward good, toward peace, toward the kind of peace and love you cannot possibly imagine. Everything."

"That is a very, very, very hard thing to make yourself believe," I said. "Some of the things that happen are so awful, it's impossible to say yes to them."

"I understand that," Jesus said, and then he went silent for another long time. "You have to somehow cultivate the humility to trust that I understand that, and that your perceptions about what is ultimately best for you are . . . clouded."

"How do you uncloud them, is what I want to know."

"I have given you a hundred lessons in that over the past few months. Go back over everything, your memories, your notes. . . . You will begin to see the path you can travel to that unclouding. . . . Begin with the questioning of your assumptions." As if it were one more lesson, he brought a flask out of his pocket and took a sip. "Which reminds me," he said, passing the flask to me. "I never told you what job I had in store for you, postelection."

"Kind of doesn't matter now, does it?" I took a sip—good red wine that tasted like pure acid in my mouth—and handed it back to him.

"Anna will serve as president for four years, and then she'll refuse to run for reelection, mostly because she won't want to endure the vicious attacks the two parties will throw at her. During those years, she will need all of you. Are you interested, or do you want to go back into the news business?"

"I'm interested, of course. After this, the news business would seem like getting paid to roll around in goat dung."

He almost smiled. "Your job," he said, "my journalist friend, is to bring the news into people's lives, to write this down the way it happened. All of it. The good, the bad, the confusing. Do not paint yourself and the rest of your colleagues as something you are not. And do not change my words or my behavior by so much as a single comma. Will you do that?"

"Of course," I said.

"We are finished then, for the time being." He kept his hand on my shoulder while he stood, and such a current of love was flowing into me that I could not describe it without resorting to drug or sexual imagery, and even then it would be too weak. I felt loved in a way no human being could possibly love me. I felt that I was about to start weeping. The nice hard crust of protection I'd built up around myself over the years was crumbling into bits of bad jokes and pretend straightforwardness. I managed to put my hand on his for a second or two, and to keep the sobs from pouring out. "Don't get up," he said, and I realize now, writing this, that it was the first thing he ever said to me—when we'd met in Pete's Cafe in Wells River, in what seems like another lifetime. He squeezed my hand warmly. "Wait until I'm out of sight and then go back to Zelda. She is still awake. She's worried."

I made myself nod. I thought I saw the tiniest of twitches at the corner of his lips, as if he were sad about something. I thought he might wink, or offer one last word, or even start to cry himself. But he did not. I tried to say something more, but I could not.

When Jesus turned and shuffled off toward the entrance of the park, I felt an actual, physical pain in the middle of my chest, as if someone had shot me there, too. My breath started coming in big heaves, and it was suddenly a lot of work to do what I'd done naturally for almost forty years, just get the air into me and push it out again. I felt a pressure behind the bones of my cheeks and forehead, and then the grief was spilling out of me, unstoppable as the river of thought, and my face was soaked and hot, and there was a drip-drip-drip-drip on the top of my right hand. I wept like a boy. I watched him go, a dark watery figure slowly blending with the blackness beyond the park lights. I could see his legs, the soles of his shoes, one last flash of the bare skin of one hand, and then nothing.

"Come back," I said in his direction, but I said it quietly, just with my broken-up breath, just once. And then I could no longer see him.

Acknowledgments

So many people had a hand in the making of this book — or have been supportive of me in my writing life — that it is impossible to acknowledge them all. I would like to express my gratitude to my fine editor Chuck Adams, and everyone at Algonquin, especially Ina Stern, Brunson Hoole, Robert Jones, Michael Taeckens, Courtney Wilson, Christina Gates, Anne Winslow, Craig Popelars, and Elisabeth Scharlatt.

Special thanks to everyone at Marly Rusoff & Associates Literary Agency, especially Marly Rusoff, Michael Radulescu, and Julie Mosow.

I'd like to thank Lynn Pleshette for her efforts on my behalf in Hollywood; and, for their generosity of spirit and helpful conversations about the creative life, my gratitude to Peter Grudin, Michael Miller, Craig Nova, Dean Crawford, John Recco, Sterling Watson, and Les Standiford.

My most heartfelt thanks go to my wife, Amanda, and our daughters, Alexandra and Juliana, for their unfailing love and encouragement.